A MOTHER'S WORDS

"Mama, I'm sorry," Susanna said. "I didn't mean to tear into you. I didn't mean to upset you, you know I didn't."

"But you did," Julie said. "So much!" She stood up. "You're all so young, and already so cynical. Why? Has life so disappointed you? What have I done that I shouldn't have done? Could it be, could it possibly be that the three of you, my wonderful, beautiful daughters," she paused to sigh, and to look back at some spot near the ceiling, "are just a bit *spoiled*? Thinking Daddy and I would never stop being Mama and Daddy? That the magic power of our parenthood would always make life right for you? Is it true spoiled children turn into adults who are spoiled children?"

Karen pointed her shoe at Julie, was about to speak, but Julie cut her off. "Taras is waiting for me, girls," she said, and, without meeting anyone's eyes, she smoothed her skirt and walked down the steps and through the hall, heading for the front door. There she turned and looked at her daughters, who were clustered together on the stairs. "And girls, could you possibly be a bit worried that I might live a life that doesn't revolve only around you? And is it conceivable, could you possibly be, just a tiny bit *jealous* of your mother?"

BOOK YOUR PLACE ON OUR WEBSITE AND MAKE THE READING CONNECTION!

We've created a customized website just for our very special readers, where you can get the inside scoop on everything that's going on with Zebra, Pinnacle and Kensington books.

When you come online, you'll have the exciting opportunity to:

- View covers of upcoming books
- Read sample chapters
- Learn about our future publishing schedule (listed by publication month *and author*)
- Find out when your favorite authors will be visiting a city near you
- Search for and order backlist books from our online catalog
- Check out author bios and background information
- Send e-mail to your favorite authors
- Meet the Kensington staff online
- Join us in weekly chats with authors, readers and other guests
- Get writing guidelines
- AND MUCH MORE!

**Visit our website at
http://www.kensingtonbooks.com**

SECOND CHANCES

MARLENE FANTA SHYER

KENSINGTON BOOKS
KENSINGTON PUBLISHING CORP.

http://www.kensingtonbooks.com

CHAPTER ONE

She watched her husband's mouth pucker up, not for a kiss.

They were standing in the foyer of their daughter's Bedford Hills house and Julie lowered her voice so no one would hear. Two or three guests were still lingering in the living room, where the girls huddled around the debris of empty coffee cups and unwrapped gifts. "Come on, Gilbert. Give me the car keys, please."

This was the way he looked before an argument, lips out, expression all business. Later she would remember making a mental note to resew a button that was coming loose on his raincoat and taking a tissue out of her purse to wipe the lipstick—from his daughters' kisses—from his cheek. He took her arm and guided her across the lawn, its cover of wet leaves shining with the reflection of the lights from the living room windows. The October air hung between them, dark and wet as a cave. It had rained before and was about to again. "Please, dear," she said, when they neared the car, "be sensible."

"Watch your step, it's very slick," he said.

She stopped in her tracks, gearing up.

"All right! I'm not setting foot into the car until you hand me the keys, Gilbert."

"You had a couple too, dear." Julie saw her husband's teeth flash a pugnacious white.

"A few sips! You know what alcohol does to me. You think I want a forty-eight-hour headache?" She looked daggers at him as he opened the driver's-side door. "Remember that time at the DiLorenzos', you backed into the hydrant getting out of the driveway? I said, 'Let me drive', you said, 'After two drinks?' Next day we're at the body shop with a fifteen hundred dollar estimate. Refills, Gilbert, the devil is in the *refills.*"

Gilbert had a two-drink rule he'd broken tonight.

She picked up her pocketbook, the gift her husband had given her last August for her fifty-third birthday. It was from Crouch & Fitzgerald, made of the softest Argentinian leather, dyed burgundy. At tonight's party, everyone had admired it.

Now, feeling tired, she tossed it onto the fender. He stood glaring at her over the hood. How many television public service announcement warnings had she and Gilbert watched together about drinking and driving? She glared back.

"Don't be so damn stubborn, the roads are very slippery!" she snapped. Then, she said other things. She called him a child, denounced him as spoiled, obstinate, foolhardy.

That did it: Gilbert slammed shut the driver's door. "I'm warning you, Julie, one scratch, it's a brand new car, you've driven it all of two times, one dent, you're never going to hear the end of it!" He slapped the keys on top of Julie's burgundy pocketbook and threw up his hands as if she'd pulled out a revolver. She grabbed them before he could change his mind, and marched to the driver's side of the car.

* * *

There was a light rain, but hardly any traffic on
684 South. Julie put on her glasses, turned on the
car radio, which defaulted to Gilbert's bluegrass station and twanged out a chorus of *This Ain't No Thinkin'
Thing,* before she switched it to WQXR. A weather
report, more rain tomorrow, a colder spell coming
at the beginning of next week. Gilbert had adjusted
the seat to the reclining position and was stretched
out, eyes closed, looking as if he were waiting to be
tucked under a blanket. The car still had the new car
smell and an illuminated spaceship dashboard, most
of it incomprehensible to Julie. This E420 had side-
impact airbags and a high predicted reliability rating
in *Consumer Guide,* precision handling, all the bells
and whistles, the car salesman had said, as he'd patted
the car's hindquarters. The car was reassuring and
solid, a quiet ride, like being swept along the highway
by wind, instead of Hi-test pumped into a German
motor. Julie relaxed, moved to the center lane from
the right. She tried conversation, but Gilbert closed
his eyes, wouldn't speak. A few minutes later, he
began to snore.

She was annoyed. He'd be over his mad tomorrow,
but she was in the mood to talk now. In her eyes,
their youngest daughter's engagement party had
turned out to be less than a complete success. The
caterer, well, all that baba ganoush and those chewy
stuffed sun-dried tomatoes, not nearly enough
shrimp, and then that tacky sheet cake! Everybody
thought it amusing he'd spelled Gaby's name Gabby,
but at those prices? Julie would have liked a second
opinion, preferably Gilbert's. And then, why did
Susanna, the second, always look so intense? Like
someone scrutinizing the obituaries for names of old
enemies? Was it her thick eyebrows? The contact
lenses? If only Julie could get a genie to pop out of

a bottle, she would wish that her children smiled more and got along better. Three daughters, their agenda a spiky graph of loyalty, affection and rivalry, confused Julie, the do-no-wrong baby sister of a much older brother, Dickie, now dead, poor soul.

Not that Susanna and Karen hadn't generously given their sister the party, written out the invitations *by hand,* rented the coat rack so guests wouldn't have to throw their coats on the beds upstairs. But as a mother, and because Julie had a particularly sensitive nature, she tended to pick up the undercurrents and feel unfairly tossed about by them. The girls so often put her in the middle. Each one so different: Gilbert privately tagged them The Beautiful, The Brilliant, The Baby. Julie saw the Baby as a locked vault, the Brilliant as too fervent, and the Beautiful as Glass Half Full—no matter what. Telling tales on each other right and left, and always ending with the same question, "But, Mama, don't you think she was *wrong?*" To which there was never a utilitarian answer.

Julie stifled a yawn. The clock on the dashboard read 11:50. Important to stay alert. At this time of night, with so little traffic, the trucks whizzed by, left and right, with a breaking-the-sound-barrier noise. She and Gilbert should have left the party earlier. It had not been Julie's idea to have an engagement party in the first place. There would probably be at least one or two bridal showers and then the wedding, and really now, how many gifts could one expect friends to dig in for? She'd told the girls what she thought, but was overruled. Gaby would be thirty in three weeks and hey, they said, after all those frogs she'd had to kiss, finally landing Wally deserved a celebration, didn't it?

Now the rain was really coming down. Julie adjusted the windshield wipers and eased up on the gas pedal. She'd tried to get Gilbert to leave right after the gifts were opened, but he kept going on and on with Gaby's fiancé, Wally. They'd go at it in the kitchen doorway like old chums at a school reunion, as if Gilbert were really interested in cork, as if Wally wouldn't rest until he'd heard the latest on what was happening in Gilbert's electric timing device factory. "They're bonding," Gaby whispered to her mother, "and all they really have in common is the *Wall Street Journal*. Isn't it lovely?"

That was the best thing about Gilbert: If his relationship with his sons-in-law, present and future, was iffy, he was always cordial. To Julie he once said, "One's too German, the other's too old." "I like him best," he whispered in her ear about Wally just tonight, but he never let his opinions of his daughters' choices seep past Julie's ear.

When she turned onto 287, Gilbert stirred and mumbled, the fingers of his left hand moving, falling away from their sleeping grip on the shoulder belt over his heart and landing on the gear shift. Julie moved it gently back, reminded of every overseas flight they'd ever made together. It's all it ever took: he closed his eyes after the meal service and went into peaceful dreamland on the spot, while she, wide awake, read his issues of *Time* and *Newsweek* and chatted with the flight attendants.

She thought now of their vacation trips, when she and Gilbert breathed life into their affection for each other, when they refreshed the currents that had passed peacefully and uneventfully between them throughout their marriage. Lust returned sometimes—and sometimes not—on these trips, and occasionally great surges of boredom, but most of their vacations were like the flaming desserts at the end of a meal, rewards for staying in a marriage that had become for both as necessary and mundane as vegeta-

bles and bread. For Julie and Gilbert, daily life con-
sisted of peace, sex on Sunday nights, an occasional
crescendo of transitory anger, and occasionally, a
sweet, burning love.

Julie remembered once—was it five years ago?—
when Gilbert had had food poisoning in Juan-Les-
Pins after a lunch buffet of salads that had been in
the sun too long, how desperate she'd been to see
him shaking under his blanket, his face the color of
the seashells she'd picked up on the beach. He'd
spent half the night vomiting and his fever was high;
she was afraid Gilbert might actually die of eating
cold *moules* before help arrived. She'd run back and
forth from the bathroom to his bed, putting cool
compresses on his feverish head and waiting for the
hotel doctor to save him. She remembered now how
sweet his recovery was, when they sat together on the
little balcony outside their room, holding hands and
looking out at the sea, two people still in love a lifetime
after they'd first met.

Now, Julie felt another yawn coming. And no wonder, with the havoc at the resale shop, one of the
women surely stealing, another out with a sudden
miscarriage, and her most reliable volunteer in Bermuda. Julie had stood behind the counter selling
binoculars and sequined evening bags, sweaters and
teapots, sorting contributions, answering the telephone and trying to reach young mothers who had
put their names on her volunteer list and then made
themselves unavailable. Three times this week she'd
given away baby snowsuits to women whose sad eyes
told her their pockets were empty. She'd pulled out
her own wallet and paid the cash register. Once she'd
spotted a shoplifter and had simply let her go. People
who had to steal children's used sweaters did not
need more trouble, she'd told Gilbert. "You got a

Campfire marshmallow where your heart should be,"
he always told her.

What a week it had been, eight hours a day on
her feet, then coming home to walk two miles with
Gilbert, doctor's orders. At his last checkup, Dr. Joe
Goetz, friend and physician, had berated Gilbert, the
gym dropout, for his sedentary lifestyle. Squash, his
old sport, was now too strenuous for his rotator cuff,
and he'd never developed an interest in golf, like
Ruthie DiLorenzo's husband. "Forty you're not, but
you're not ready to fall off your perch," Joe Goetz
had told him, the day they got their flu shots two
weeks ago. He told Gilbert he had the organs of a
thirty-year-old, and although his father, the cigarette-
smoker had died young, there was no reason Gilbert
couldn't live to blow out a hundred candles. A comfort to think she'd have him till they fell off their
perches together.

Every evening, Julie and Gilbert marched around
the Scarsdale high school track together, eight revolu-
tions, or, walked their suburban streets, those familiar, leafy-treed avenues that had hardly changed in
the twenty-eight years they'd lived at 66 Morris Lane.
This past week there were also the phone calls of
congratulations from friends far and wide who'd spotted Gaby's engagement announcement in the *Journal
News*, and would offer best wishes and catch up for
an hour at a clip. Then, since Gilbert preferred dinner
at home during the week, Julie would have to broil
fish and toss salads, and even though she left the
dishes in the sink for Mariadora to clean up when
she came in the morning, somehow she never got to
bed before midnight.

Sleep deprivation was catching up to her now. The
motion of the car was making her drowsy, and she
opened the driver's side window just enough to allow
in a little cool air. Just enough was too much; the
rain spattered in on her wrist and hair. She pushed

the window Close button fast and glanced at the dashboard trying to find the fan and air conditioning controls, but didn't dare take her eyes off the road. Now was not the time to read the glowing digital displays to the left and right of the steering wheel, not the time to try to decipher the numerals and knobs and little mystery icons. She thought back to her own first car, a cheap and comfy Ford Falcon, red as the Elizabeth Taylor roses she'd begun growing in her garden. So simple, so easy, so non-digital. But then, everything was so uncomplicated before the children, in the low-tech good old days. Julie always remembered herself as the image in the women's locker room at the club, in that flowered bikini Gilbert had bought for her at Bonwit Teller. All that tanned skin, the high taut breasts, the stomach almost concave, doing stripteases for her husband while he watched from bed, and all she could think of in those days were the two or three practically invisible varicose veins on the back of her calves, the almost nonexistent horizontal lines across her forehead. *I wasn't so bad looking, was I, Gil?*

Since then, and she had admitted this only to a very few, she'd had her eyelids and the beginning of the bags under them surgically corrected, and just a month ago, had undergone laser treatments to remove every unsightly thread of color accumulated over the years from her ankles to her thighs. Next summer she might take up golf, would buy shorts to play in, or at least, a mid-thigh golf skirt. Everyone was always telling her that she looked nowhere near her age. It was Harold's double-process hair color, chestnut amber 61, Teri, the personal trainer, the alpha hydroxy, the sunscreen. "You're a knockout! You don't look like *anyone's* mother," one of Gaby's friends had said just tonight, not two hours ago. Not that looks were all important, but vanity, after all, had its firm place in the richest county in America.

Somehow, this was both the penalty and the privilege of affluent society, and sometimes Julie secretly envied her middle-American counterparts, living in subdivisions, happy with their mama-plump bodies and graying hair. They seemed more placid and content, had discovered the elusive secret of Inner Peace, often missing in Scarsdale. Women and looking one's age were incompatible here; the gyms, the Diet Center, the plastic surgeons, the cosmetically oriented dermatologists had among their best customers the pretty, never-to-be-olds who lived here. The look in Gilbert's eyes when they were getting ready to go out to dinner or to a party was important to Julie. Like her neighbors, she'd keep up the fight against nature as long as she could. "You'll be the prettiest one in the room," he'd say. Tonight he told her she'd better be careful, or she'd outshine the girls.

He woke suddenly. The water might have splashed his face too. "What time 'zit?" he muttered. Before she could answer, he'd fallen back to sleep. She must remember to ask him if he'd taken his Pravachol today, and his multivitamin. She had to remind him constantly, and push him into eating a healthful breakfast. That was another thing: if she didn't get up, he'd try to leave the house without his bowl of Special K and the banana she managed to slice into it. Or an umbrella if the weather report was rain. Worldly, successful and smart, Gilbert was a bad-boy child in so many ways. The part of him that had never matured since Dickie, her brother and his roommate at Washington University, had brought him home that fateful Christmas weekend, resisted the idea of wholesome nutrition, imagined he really was immortal, was impressed by silly things like fireworks displays. He took cornball bluegrass lyrics seriously. She'd given up pushing opera and broccoli and pulling him into her idea of Perfect Gilbert long, long ago.

Dvorak's *Slavonic Dances* poured out of the sound system as Harriet turned off route 287 and headed down the Hutch. Then, a bit of news: Medical crises in Iraq, the possibility of germ warfare, fund-raising corruption, the sins of the president. Everything seemed light years away from the protected boundaries of Scarsdale. A Schumann piece now: *Traumerei.* Relief. A familiar theme, familiar territory. And, the rain had stopped. How nice; it had been a long day, but they'd be home in no time. Their heads would hit their down-filled pillows in twenty, twenty-five minutes. She felt as if she could sleep indefinitely. Now, again, the same news, same weather report and Tchaikowsky as Harriet turned off the Hutch and onto Weaver Street, an empty slick ribbon of dark cement ahead and behind her. The entire village of Scarsdale was asleep and no wonder—she yawned again—it was already tomorrow. As for tonight, despite the caterer and the minor sisterly foment, it had actually tallied up to a good evening. Their last daughter engaged, three down and none to go, as Gilbert kept saying, made Julie feel honeycombed, if not with absolute happiness, at least with sweet contentment. She leaned back, relaxed, and fought her eyelids, which felt weighted down and kept trying to pull themselves very obstinately down over her eyes.

She never did manage to remember the rest of the trip, the right and left turns, the two or three stoplights. Stamped in her memory was the explosive burst as the airbag deployed and the crack of her eyeglass lenses as they shattered on her nose. Then, she remembered turning to Gilbert, who was lying next to her, eyes neither open nor quite closed, seemingly unscathed, except—Julie couldn't immediately understand this—his head turned at an oblique angle, as if he'd stretched his neck as far as it would go and then spun around sharply to see if someone was following him. And, the smell. Her first thought was, Oh God, the car. She'd hit something; he'd kill her. "Gilbert?" He didn't answer. Oh, the odor! She tried to open the car door but her arm seemed to be flopping uselessly, groping at the buttons and handles at her side. Terrible damage, she'd never hear the end of it. For a moment, or was it many moments, her eyes closed. She shut herself down. Lightheaded, she waited for the dizziness to pass. She slowly became aware that now there were people to the left and to the right, splintered images of faces peering at her from everywhere through what was left of the windshield. So embarrassing that Gilbert had lost control of his bowels, poor thing. Someone got the door open, or did she finally manage it? She was led out and sat down on a lawn next to a rock engraved with a house number. The front of the car, crumpled around a tree trunk, no longer had a shape, but looked like a Whitney Museum sculpture of aluminum foil and cellophane. The back looked showroom new. Julie, never given to hot flashes, felt a dank heat steam her body and swamp up into her cheeks and forehead. Red lights, sirens, police, commotion, faces left and right, spectral noses and open mouths, never seen before. She heard the sound of voices; something ghastly had happened—was she awake or not?—she felt the wet lawn soaking her, right through her brand new St. John wool-knit suit skirt, her underpants, the clammy nylon of her shredded pantyhose. Had she left the car? When? "Gilbert! Where's my husband?" Again, "My husband?" Her own voice cracked, sounding like a digital recording. She prayed someone would clean him up, that Gilbert wouldn't make a scene in front of all these people, but then, where was he? She had to try once more, no answers were coming, until finally, a baby-faced policeman, maybe Hispanic, maybe Italian, certainly younger than any of her children said, "Can you tell me your name?" Yes, of course, she could. "Could you spell it for me, ma'am?" She tried and tried, but no, she couldn't get the letters in the right order. She put up her hand to shield her eyes from the beam of a flashlight and a pain ran in both directions from her right elbow.

The policeman leaned over her and spoke loudly as if she were deaf or demented, or both. "It's all right, we got him breathing again. Don't try to get up, ma'am. We're taking you both to emergency," he said.

CHAPTER TWO

What Susanna had not expected was seeing her father's bare feet, the wrinkled soles and pasty toes sticking up as if they were already dead and not worth the bother of covering. The rest of him was a dummy the color of winter rain, his mouth taped closed to hold the O_2 tubing forced into it, bent arms wrapped with cuffs that held the plastic snakes hanging from IV poles and hooked into his veins. He was surrounded by the blink of monitors left and right and in her mind's eye she saw her father's fragile neck bone split in two beneath his chin, just where, growing up, she'd watched him run his electric razor up and back a thousand times.

Next to her, Mama, a zombie in a knit suit, no longer bore any resemblance to the smiling mother who had carried a gift-wrapped Cuisinart into her house just a few hours ago. She was a marionette, all knees and elbows, about to corrugate. Dieter was behind her, ready to catch her if she went down, and Gaby was on her other side, Mama's pocketbook under her arm, tears rolling out of her eyes like oil out of a medicine dropper.

Wally's hand was on Gaby's shoulder, his eyes on her face. He'd actually taken out a handkerchief and was trying to mop her cheeks, his devotion written all over him in letters everyone could read. Gaby's fiancé was handsome as a head-shot except for one tiny bald spot, an "up and comer"—Daddy's own words—big on hugs and kisses and endless conversations about profit margins, new product lines and expanding markets. The son of a humble Portuguese builder Wally said died of "everywhere cancer" the year before he met Gaby, Wally was a good catch. He'd taken out loans and managed an MBA going nights to NYU, then started his own business. He talked cork a lot and was bound to be as successful as Daddy. So Gaby often said.

Born a lucky third, with size six hips and obedient thick dark hair, required a certain humbleness, or gratitude, missing in Gaby. Unlike her sisters, she was a small package very much like her mother, and carried herself with the assurance of a child used to being the focus of love and attention of two doting parents and two protective siblings. She had become a devotee of looking organic, as if she'd been born in the country in fresh air, very far away from Scarsdale. Her Birkenstocks and bland wardrobe were her subtle way of making everyone else feel overdressed, her way of saying, I am so good I don't need embellishing. From the time she was a tot, she always seemed in control, and kept things to herself. She loved secrets.

Susanna watched her hovering over Daddy. "I don't believe it, I can't process it, I just wiped icing off his chin two hours ago!" Gaby said, in her volume-controlled voice. Her small shoulders, covered with a nothing-colored J. Crew sweater set, hunched over the gurney. "He was telling me he wanted to go to

Italian conversation class so he and Mama could speak
to the Sicilians when they go in the spring . . ."

"You got it wrong, they're going to Siena, not Sicily,
isn't that right, Mama?" Karen spoke in a liquid and
wavery voice, totally uncharacteristic of her. She was
still in her dripping raincoat, her husband Elliot, his
eyeglasses steamed, right behind her. She had been
the last sister to arrive. Her husband, Elliot, wiped
rain from his brow with the colored handkerchief
that matched the ascot tucked under his beard. Karen
had been his student at the School of Visual Arts,
where she had learned Digital Art and he had taught
Hand Book Binding. It was his second career; he was
a pharmacist by profession, had owned a few drugstores
eventually bought out by Duane Reade.

Theirs was a romance Mama and Daddy did their
best initially to discourage; Susanna knew Daddy was
quietly averse to a potential son-in-law who was of his
own generation, wore a gray ponytail tied back with
a leather thong, and the thought of whose possibly
fathering a child incurred in him an acid stomach.
Also, Karen was his firstborn, with amber loopy curls
that cascaded down her back and an imperfect nose—
Daddy's nose, too long, too sharp—that just suited
her. She was tall as a runway model but somehow,
Susanna thought she never really understood the
power of her own looks. Elliot Granit was sweet, but,
well, what was she doing with a man old enough for
prostate problems and splotches of freckles on the
backs of his hands? Elliot has depth, she kept saying,
but no one quite understood what that meant, though
everyone suspected it meant money. Daddy was generous, had spoiled his family, but one thing was clear: he
expected his daughters to cut loose from his portfolio
and create their own.

As far as money went, Elliot did have pots. He now
spent his time not having to work for it by covering
books with leather, watching CNBC and whistling old

songs; what, Susanna had asked herself, was sex like with Elliot? And, what did they find to talk about?

Seeing Karen leaning over the gurney, whispering, "Daddy, can you hear me, Daddy? I love you!" Susanna was overcome. She remembered her father fiddling with the hands of a wooden clock in her room the year she started kindergarten. The face of the clock was a cat, the hands paws. "This is three o' clock. This is half past three. Quarter to four. See?" She thought of the clock, his fingers spinning the hours and minutes. "Bravo!" he'd said when she got anything right. "Bravissimo"—wonderful! made the "bravo" that much sweeter. She'd meant to have BRAVO BRAVISSIMO engraved on a pewter paper-weight when he was awarded the Electrical Industry Man of the Year, but never did. Too late. She would try to tell him she was sorry, but not now, when his nose was twitching and a corner of his mouth was spewing foam. Later. If there was a later.

Now, Susanna's eyes darted around the waiting room. It was a roomful of resin figures, set up for an exhibition. At any moment something ghastly might happen here, down that tiled corridor, behind the curtain where the nurses were "stabilizing the patient," her most wonderful, irreplaceable and dar-ling Daddy. He'd been talking to Dieter not an hour and a half ago, animated and alive, a conversation about the new car. Maybe Daddy didn't exactly love Dieter. These were complicated Jewish-German issues even though Daddy always said he himself was invisi-bly Jewish—"Deeds, not creeds!"—but they had their man-to-man subjects, could go on forever about German cars, reunification, beer and the Airlift. In fact, Dieter was certainly secretly envious of the new E420, had wanted a Mercedes for himself. What Ger-man didn't? Just touching the leather upholstery brought a spark to his eyes.

Now Dieter jumped up, reached into his pocket for

change. "You sure you don't vant a soda, somet'ing?" Susanna wanted only release from terror, and relief from the radiating pelvic pressure she felt now. No wonder they called it The Curse; the curse was you couldn't lie down under a quilt of eiderdown with a heating pad on your stomach and have someone give you a cup of chamomile for two or three days a month. The curse was also that you weren't pregnant, again. As agreed. Dieter already had a grown child, had lost another to meningitis. That was enough parenthood for him. Susanna understood a deal was a deal and didn't want children anyhow. At any rate, that's what she'd told Dieter then, when passion was driving spikes into her reason, but she wasn't sure now. It turned out there could be days like this, Daddy laughing with a glass of Piper-Heidsieck in his hand one minute, and a pasty near-corpse the next. With no child coming from her now or ever to ease the loss, to replace a life with a life, one had to reconsider.

Dieter was fidgety, fingers drumming, offering a sip of his soda, looking at his Junghaus watch, a gift from his daughter. When there were two other watches in his top drawer among his socks that he could have worn—one a gift from *her*—pulled some irrational strings in Susanna. For the moment, she and Dieter, married three years, were still in the marital block-building stage. They were getting past the joys of being single and learning the ropes of adjusting to someone in the same bedroom, bathroom and kitchen, the someone from a totally different world. She herself was working on being tolerant of a man who had to have cucumber salad and pork sausages for dinner twice a week, who refused to sleep on anything but white linen, whose eyes glowed like hot coals if she was a minute late for anything. And if anything could get Susanna's cramps to intensify, it was the thought of Liesel, who lived in faraway Potsdam and should have been insignificant as a drop of dew on the rose of Dieter's and her married life. Yet, a week didn't go by that Liesel's phantom presence didn't kick into the marital equation. Why did he have to talk about his nineteen-year-old daughter as if she were a canonized saint? And why did he refuse to become a citizen of the United States? His reason, that he owed German citizenship to the memory of his father, made no sense whatsoever. It had to do not with his father, but with Liesel. Her pictures, taken on a ski slope in Lech, in front of a Christmas tree—Dieter always pointed out the real candles, which he considered vastly superior to American electric tree lights—and on a bench at a bus stop, were all over the house.

"I think I go make a phone call," he suddenly said, looking left and right for a telephone.

Now, with poor Daddy on that gurney and their lives about to plummet into the abyss of mourning?

"Who are you calling?" As if she didn't know.

"I thought I'd call home."

Home. He called it *Home.* She often corrected him: *"This* is your home." This time she let it pass.

"Must you call now?"

"I wanted Liesel to know what's happened here."

"It's six in the morning there."

He looked at his watch. "Seven."

"You're upsetting me, Dieter."

"Listen, darling, I just call, five minutes I'm back."

"Can't she wait until we get more news?"

He looked at Susanna, then shook his head. "What heaven sends, ve must endure," he sighed. This sounded like a translation of one of his German proverbs, but Susanna used to be more impressed with Dieter's pedantic side than she was now. He caught the look on her face and puckered his mouth, throwing her an air kiss. "Okay, darling. I call later."

A fluorescent light above them flickered; it seemed a warning. At that moment, an Indian doctor, followed by a small Asian with a stethoscope sticking out of his breast pocket, bore down on them. The Asian was wearing running shoes; they squeaked their way toward them across the vinyl tiles. He must be another physician, someone in charge, the best man here, a man with a wall full of diplomas, his face shining with knowledge and determination. Out of the pocket of his white coat, along with the stethoscope, many pens were sticking up, ready for action.

Susanna, her cramps radiating, held Dieter's arm, nodded with the others when he was introduced. Dr. Lau. His voice had the mesmerizing lilt of a medical savior. "Let's move into the Emergency Holding area," he intoned. "It's quieter." He was clearly in charge of detaining Death, maybe keeping it off the premises entirely.

The family shuffled together behind him, winding up clustered and terrified in the corridor they'd walked through earlier. Dieter and Wally held Harriet, each taking an elbow. Her eyes had started to blink in a sort of defensive Morse Code, and she looked as if she were having trouble breathing.

With his forefinger Dr. Lau carefully pushed his half-eyes back against the bridge of his nose. "We've examined the X rays, Dr. Soomthornsawad and I, and we are in accord as to the extent and nature of the patient's injuries." He took a breath and waited, a role model of patience, while a nurse pushed an IV pole between them. "Mr. Gilbert," he began, and second-checked his chart. Behind his glasses, his eyes raced horizontally, then, peered over them. "No. It's Mr. Kessler—yes. Mr. Kessler has had his spinal column crushed by dislocated vertebrae. Furthermore, there is a fracture of the hyoid bone and irreparable damage to the thyroid cartilage. His heart, lungs, and vital organs were not initially affected, however—" the doctor, looking as if he delivered death sentences on a regular basis, hesitated, lifting his shoulders and putting his hand on his stethoscope, where it rested over his breast bone. We're doing our best, his face said.

"There are four blood vessels that lead to the head. If they are crushed in an accident, blood does not reach the brain. The medulla oblongata, which is located in this area," two fingers circled his ear and moved to the back of his head, "and is the source of respiration, circulation, and many other bodily functions." The doctor cleared his throat, and looked for a moment into a space beyond Julie's head, "We've done a nuclear cerebral blood flow study and there is such a low level of electrical activity, well, at this moment, the patient is already being kept alive by mechanical means. The brain damage is irreversible. It happened instantaneously. We are sorry to have to—"

Despite a voice flat enough to sound as if he were reciting menu specials, Susanna detected in the doctor's demeanor some hint of feeling and compassion. After a hesitation, he added, "He is not in pain."

Mama pursed her lips, her eyes blinking like speeded up film. "He's an amazingly strong man. A powerful man. Only fifty-nine years old!"

Fleetingly, Susanna remembered Mama's wistful smile when she'd said, "I can't believe your father wants no party. Just a night with me at the Four Seasons Hotel." Mama had wanted to celebrate his sixty years with a bash and invite all his 178 employees.

"As a result," Dr. Lau said, reverting to coolly doing his job, "I'm afraid there is no possibility . . . of meaningful improvement or recovery."

"When Dr. Goetz gets back we'll have a conference, all of us." Mama hurtled on as if she hadn't heard. "We have a call in to him now. His service is trying to reach him, but hasn't been able to get through. He's at a film festival in Montreal. I happened to remember he told us he and his wife were going.

Their son made an independent film about—I believe it was Jehovah's Witnesses."

"Mama!" Gaby reached for her mother's hand but she winced in pain and jerked it away. Her elbow hurt but she refused to go for an X ray.

"He—my husband—wanted to drive. Oh, Gilbert, darling. Oh, God forgive me," she said, her fist flying to her mouth. Her eyes wet, she looked at Dieter, then glared at the doctors. "He's not going to die. Certainly not. You can bet on that! He is going to live. We are going to Sardinia together in May." Harriet's knees gave way. If Dieter and Wally hadn't been holding her, she would have folded her body right onto the vinyl tile. "We were planning on leaving on Mother's Day," she said, "and, no offense, but I'm not, no, I have no intention of canceling our trip."

CHAPTER THREE

Julie climbed the three Indian slate tile steps that led to the jetted bathtub full of steaming water. She was moving automatically now, dropping her towel on the padded chaise next to the tub, testing the water with her toes, sinking slowly into its depths. Eight feet above her head was a trio of skylights, through which she could see the Scarsdale sky at dusk, and the yellowing leaves of the elm that had once held a garden swing for the girls.

It was not Julie's first bath of the day. Behind the locked door, far away from the telephone in what *House & Garden* had called "Possibly the most beautiful bathroom in Westchester County," she now tried finding solace in the soapy, scented depths of her tub, oblivious to the cable radio music piped in through the speakers the architect had hidden in the pitched roof rafters.

She soaped her legs without actually seeing them and although Gilbert had shaved with an electric Norelco as far back as she could remember, she imagined going into his bathroom and finding an old straight razor in one of the cabinets, saw herself slashing her ankles, then her wrists, watching the bathtub water turn tomato red . . . Who would discover her in a tub of blood here? The girls were due to arrive in short order, would come upstairs to find her, force open the door and—*what am I even thinking?*

Karen had recommended Elliot's Swedish psychiatrist friend, who had suggested during their first session that Julie put a rubber band around her wrist. Whenever the guilt and anguish became intolerable, she was to snap that elastic as a sort of aversion therapy that might help stop the lacerating thoughts. Finger stabbing the air, he warned her severely: Children of suicides were four times as likely to take their own lives. He prescribed Zoloft, which made her anxious, then Paxil, which upset her stomach. Julie promised she wouldn't jump or overdose or sit in the garage inhaling carbon monoxide. It was as if she were doing the doctor a personal favor.

She heard the telephone. The machine would pick up, or Mariadora would. "How is he?" someone would ask, the question on everyone's lips these last two weeks. "The same," she'd say. "No change." And no one would know how to go on. Tilda Novak, Gilbert's administrative assistant, always loyal, ever addled, called every day. "May I come see him?" These days Tilda, her hair dyed the color of a cantaloupe, would fill the air singing praises to her daughters and grandchildren and rattle on about her neighborhood in Jackson Heights going to the dogs. Julie didn't want poor Tilda anywhere near the hospital.

Grandchildren! *Gilbert, I'm willing you to beat the odds and live to see grandchildren!*

There was a knock.

"Missuz Kessler? That was Gaby on the phone. Going to be a little late. A client came in last minute."

"Thank you, Mariadora." Whatever would she do

without her housekeeper, a bit of an anachronism in
modern Scarsdale, where Polish and Hispanic day-
workers and cleaning services had replaced the uni-
formed black family retainers of the last generation?
But heaven had sent Mariadora from Honduras seventeen years ago. Closemouthed and mysterious, Mariadora wore talismans around her neck and New
Balance sneakers on her feet. Gray-threaded black
hair parted in the middle and disciplined with combs
and clips, she herself had lost her husband (was it a
flood? A hurricane?) twenty-five years ago. Now, gold
wedding ring in place, she was frozen into widowhood
and spent weekends in an EMS van in Mount Vernon,
saving lives in his memory. Mariadora had enough
sensitivity not to ask questions, made Julie a mocha
every afternoon and managed to make Gilbert's *Wall
Street Journal* disappear every morning. Julie had not
been able to get herself to stop delivery of Gilbert's
paper.

"I'll be going now, all right?" through the door.

"Fine."

"Missuz Kessler. You want me to wait on you till
you come on outta there?"

"No, it's all right."

"You sure now?"

"I'll see you tomorrow, Mariadora. Thank you."

Everybody being so thoughtful, so sweet. Friends,
neighbors, some no more than nodding acquain-
tances, Milt Gladstone, Gil's acting CFO, who had
actually cried on the telephone, other business col-
leagues, the women at the resale shop, it seemed as
if there were hordes stopping by and leaving bakery
goods, roasted chickens, baked hams, others sending
flower arrangements to Gilbert, who couldn't see or
smell them.

*　*　*

"When I saw Daddy this afternoon, and I read him the card from Ruthie and Lou DiLorenzo, I swear I saw his eyelids flicker," she told Susanna and Dieter, who were the first to arrive. Julie's eyes were red and felt grainy from weeping, but they were dry. The tears—delayed for two days—had hit like a squall, and Julie had wandered from room to room with a box of Kleenex in one hand and a crumpled tissue in the other. Now she was all cried out. "That night, oh, God, if I hadn't insisted—" she began, and stopped. Their faces showed how tired they were of hearing it.

"It vas the circumstances, Mama Julie, and you shouldn't blame yourself." Dieter drummed his fingers on the table. Of her sons-in-law, Dieter was the best dressed, best groomed, most formal. Julie would not originally have picked him for any of her daughters anymore than she would Elliot, but now, like it or not, Julie's affection for Dieter had crept up on her. She forgave him his slicked back flamenco-dancer's dark hair and his jumpiness, his foreign-ness, considered him polite and thoughtful. His pretty daughter Liesel had even sent Gilbert get-well wishes. The note was in misspelled English, but English nevertheless. "It's very kind of her," Julie had told him. "Kindness breaks no bones," he replied. "An old German proverb," he added.

As soon as Karen and Elliot stepped into the kitchen carrying bags filled with lo mein, spring rolls, vegetable dumplings, cartons and cartons of shrimp and chicken and rice they could not possibly finish in one sitting, Julie went into action, an automaton pulling dishes and napkins, glasses and cups out of the cupboards. The twinge in her elbow was almost nonexistent now, but the absence of pain was worse than the pain; she'd gotten off too easily. If every bone in her body had been broken, *good*, any punishment would make her feel better.

Karen and Elliot set the brown bags on the counter. The most affectionate of her three daughters, Karen put her arms around Julie and wiped her eyes with the back of her hand as she pulled away. Her husband sat in Gilbert's place now, wearing a paisley ascot under his beard, his hands folded tight on his yellow place mat. Julie thought for a moment of asking Elliot to move to another chair, but changed her mind. Forever somber, he hadn't spoken a word except a greeting since he and Karen had walked in. One never knew what damage the simple request might do to his recondite artist's soul.

They waited, drinking tea, hunched over the table in Julie's kitchen, like her bathroom, an architectural transfiguration. It was all hand-painted Mexican tile, terra cotta and country pine, with a custom molded cement vegetable sink and a wall of shelves for the salt and pepper shakers Gilbert and Julie had collected on their travels over the years. The floor-to-ceiling Palladian windows buckled out, seeming to bring the outside—the large patio, the dark garden and the ghosts of many summer night barbecues—right in. The white sun umbrellas had been moved into the garage but the topiaries stood in a military row under their burlap winter covers. The skeletal winter remains of the canvas awning hovered over clay pots of marigolds, the replacements for Julie's summer roses, lit by the last diffusion of daylight.

"I don't know why you feel the need to work such terribly long hours," Karen said to Gaby as she and Wally walked in, half an hour later.

Let them please, please, not bicker now!

But Gaby replied amicably. "I'm Atlas. Holding up the job." She was wearing her dark hair straight to the jaw and sometimes looked Eurasian. Wally helped her out of her ancient tweed jacket and hung it on the back of her chair. His profile was classic, more Greek than Portuguese, like a face stamped on a medallion. "I tell her every day," he said, sitting next to her, putting a proprietary arm across the back of her chair. Gaby patted his hand and went on like an amiable talk show hostess as if it were just another Sunday night at Mama's.

They began piling food on each other's plates, hopping up to find more napkins, mineral water, ice cubes, complimenting each other's clothes and haircuts. They praised the food and the bottles of Great Wall Karen had found in the Sub-Zero. No one mentioned Gilbert. Julie managed to eat some shrimp, a few snow peas, a little brown rice. Under the lights from the fruitwood eighteenth-century chandelier Julie's architect had found in a shop in New Hope, her daughters and their partners were being uncommonly interactive, sweet to her and each other. The kitchen glowed with bonhomie.

Until the table was cleared and the fortune cookies cracked open. They read the fortunes aloud, as always, between bites of cookie, sips of tea and tastes of quartered orange. It was Susanna reading Julie's that turned them silent. It was as if a shot had been fired, a dead bird crashed into their midst: "Let your heart lead your mind." *Let Your Heart Lead Your Mind* was the name of one of Gilbert's favorite bluegrass songs.

As Julie flashed back to all the times she'd made fun of this particular corny number— *"Gil, the Smoking Armadillos? Are you serious? How can you listen to this?"*— a reflex reprise of tears caught her by surprise. Gaby leaned over to touch her shoulder and looking ready to cry herself, said, "Mama? For heaven's sake, please—don't!" and Susanna jumped up out of her chair. "I shouldn't have done that. Why did I have to read what was written on that stupid little piece of paper?''

What did people without good children do in times of crisis? Ruthie DiLorenzo had lost her only child in a boating accident on Long Island Sound and it took two days for the Coast Guard to find his body. Ruthie's misfortune now refreshed itself in all its horror in Julie's mind. She, at least, had this circle of family steadfastly surrounding her. Her darling children, alive and well, were here to love and protect her.

"You couldn't have known, it was just a coincidence, the name of Daddy's favorite song!"

Gaby said, "That was not his favorite, *Blue Moon of Kentucky* was his favorite."

"You're both wrong. It was *The City Put the Country Back in Me!* He always sang it in the car, aren't I right, Mama?"

Julie put her hands to her ears. She wanted to run out of the kitchen, up to her bedroom, close the door and never come out.

"I'm sorry, Mama, sorry! Didn't mean to!" It was a chorus, three voices.

Elliot cleared his throat and everyone turned silent. Over his ascot, under his clipped beard, his Adam's apple activated. "We really came here tonight with a special purpose. We came to talk to you, dear, not to argue about Gilbert's favorite songs." His voice, cleared or not, often sounded laryngitic.

Julie sat erect in her chair and stared at him. She tried to imagine a young Elliot, a schoolboy Elliot, a toddler Elliot. He leaned forward, reminding her of her old elementary school principal, also born old, whose obituary she'd read just this year. "Darling, Gilbert really isn't alive anymore."

"He is, he is very much alive. I told you, didn't I

tell you how just this afternoon, his eyelids—'' Her voice went into a tailspin as the girls sneaked glances at each other, then lowered their eyes to the table.

Karen, possibly tacitly elected to fire the first shot, shook her head. ''I know it's an awful decision to make, Mama, but the truth is, God already made the decision for you.''

''God, you're talking God? Don't talk God to me now! Consider his résumé!'' To the very secular Kesslers, God was a respected abstraction and about as relevant to their lives under normal circumstances as George Washington.

I'm going to quit taking the Paxil, too.

''I mean, Mama, Daddy can't feel anything, hear anything, taste anything. He's gone. It's just his body there.''

''Dr. Goetz came back from Canada, sat right in this house and told you, 'Low level of electrical activity. Hopeless', he said. He's virtually gone, Mama.'' That from Susanna.

Elliot reached across the table to pat her hand. Julie instinctively pulled hers away. ''Give it some thought, darling. It's time, dear.''

They were all in cahoots, had discussed it, bunched up into a cohesive, adversarial group to conspire against her.

''And the expense!'' somebody said it; one of the girls, but Julie, looking into her cup of green tea, wasn't sure which one.

''Expense?'' Julie, her eyes blinking ferociously, scrutinized their faces, one by one. ''It's Daddy's life we're talking about here!'' She pulled the wide red rubber band out as far as she could and snapped it hard against her wrist. And did it again. And again. And again, each time wincing prodigiously and biting her lip when it stung her skin.

"Mama, what are you doing?" Gaby's eyes bulged with horror. "What is that you're *doing!*"

"It's my decision!" Julie pulled the napkin off her lap and threw it on the table. She'd killed Gilbert once. She couldn't, *wouldn't*, do it twice. "I'm not pulling the plug on your father! I am telling you, I will not!"

CHAPTER FOUR

The minister sat in front of a heavily curtained window, giving his study a January atmosphere, despite a November spell of Indian summer heat. The office smelled of fresh paint, and in fact, a small painter's ladder leaned against one paneled wall, under a picture of pigeons flying over rooftops. He offered Wally and Gaby a drink from the pitcher of ice water on his desk and then poured a glass for himself. Between sips, and after some somber remarks about vehicular tragedies, he made small talk with a vengeance, sensing, no doubt, the electric tension typical of most prenuptial counseling sessions.

On this Friday, he would discuss items from the Prepare-Enrich Inventory, and its function was to reveal, well, psychological fitness and tenuity. Gaby was struck with the minister's resemblance to a bartender at the Sticky Fly, the downtown pub where she'd met Wally. The bartender, Gus, had the same round-as-a-ball face and friendly pink complexion, the same ask-me-anything demeanor. Gus had introduced her to Wally, and here he was in another incarnation, trying to make the bond legitimate.

Gaby had been living in a cramped Alphabet City apartment with two aspiring actresses and one aspiring songwriter, and spent time getting away from the reading of sides and the sound of the guitar by stopping in at the Sticky Fly, more a seedy getaway than the neighborhood Cheers. One night, there was Wally, having a beer while waiting for the Copy Center down the block to finish copying a marketing report he'd worked on after hours. Wally's longing glances in her direction, Gus's introduction, and one long conversation later, they were "freeze-dried together," according to Wally's recounting to Mama at their engagement party the very night of the accident.

There had been the business of romance, hadn't there? There was the going to sleep and waking up thinking about him, the long glances and furtive knee-feels under tablecloths, little notes and gifts, midnight phone calls, an exciting first sexual encounter in his room when his roommate was out doing laundry. There were all these first-rush memories, but lately, like those hydrangeas she'd once hung upside down in the bathroom to dry, hoping to preserve them for all time, they'd lost their juice and color.

The minister asked his questions, looking from one to the other, his expression warm, hopeful. Money, for example: Who would be the main breadwinner? Who should control the checkbook, make the investments?

Wally and Gaby looked at each other and simultaneously said, "Both." A smile from the minister. His denomination was Congregationalist with a liberal twist, a man of the cloth with a fellowship here, a few miles above Ossining, acceptable to both bride and groom. Okay with Mama too, who'd never been keen on Rabbi Waller, prominent in Scarsdale, but who she said talked too loud and said too little. This minister was not wearing a clerical collar and looked in his sports shirt as if he didn't own one. Wally had in fact met this ecumenical servant of God playing tennis.

More money talk: How much would they save and what would they be saving for? And charities? What would they contribute and to whom?

Some to wheelchair tennis, he suggested. Wally coached the disabled weekends. She mentioned The World Wildlife Fund and her alma mater, Northwestern. They would save for a house, Wally said. Gaby nodded heartily; she thought about Morris Lane, the house in which she'd grown up, her blue and white bedroom with her old stuffed wallaby sitting on her white coverlet, her poetic tree-shaded/snow-covered street, the pretty terrace and garden, in which she would now be married.

The interrogation continued. Social life? Gaby thought back to the panorama of family celebrations: birthday cakes stuck with Roman candles, the long dining room table covered with glass and silver, and Mama's Elizabeth Taylor roses with the white stripes Mama could never breed out, the pewter chargers Daddy always said were ridiculous, and Daddy, at the head of the table. *Always*.

Certainly there were a few tiffs, some problems, competition, flare-ups, but not the major dysfunction one read about every day. Gaby had volunteered at a soup kitchen in White Plains, dished rice and chicken onto the plastic plates held out by local indigents. She'd seen the clientele at Second Chance. She was neither smug nor insensitive; her eyes were social-consciously wide open. Growing up with dinner on the table every night at seven, Mama and Daddy together and always in synch, her upbringing had been predictability and security every step of the way. Except for teenage bumps, it had been a life in clover, she was well aware. She thought of the town she'd grown up in as a plump and protective parent in itself, a twenty-five mile distance from the hard edge of the city, twenty five *thousand* miles it could have been. She'd felt privileged and blessed.

So it went, through questions about in-laws, religion and the number of children they'd agreed to have, if any. "Three," she said, and Wally added, "or more." When it came to questions about sex, she thought *Here it comes*—folded her hands on her knees and sat straighter in her chair. Now certainly they'd upset the marital inventory applecart. "Let's get to the core of marriage stability," the minister began, and, somewhat tentatively, inquired if there were any sexual problems.

On Wally's part, there was absolutely no hesitation. "Sex is high-test," he said, without the slightest embarrassment. His wide smile was directed at the minister, at Gaby, at the world at large. "Couldn't be better," he said, eyebrows raised, head nodding, a glance at Gaby for confirmation.

The minister returned the smile with a wan one of his own, then turned to the bride-to-be.

She did not dare to hesitate, for even a moment, or he'd read it all in even one second of silence.

She imagined a Velcro sleeve on her upper arm, monitoring her heart rate, pictured the needle vacillating on a lie detector machine. "Fine," she said, voice soft, feeling as if she would like to plead a headache and head for the door.

Secretly, perhaps subconsciously, she was hoping the minister would pick up his ballpoint pen and mark their questionnaire with a black X here and there, or just jump up from his chair and announce that here was the sticking point, the trip-up. Incompatible here and here and here!

Instead, a warm, all-encompassing benevolence. "The smell of paint—I have to apologize," is what he said, and simultaneously, the telephone in Gaby's

purse rang. She had buried it under the miscellane-
ous clutter at the bottom of one of the large Coach
satchels she carried winter and summer, wrapped a
scarf around it, and still, the persistent faint ring
could be heard.

She scrambled out of her chair, the leather momentarily sticking to the back of her thighs. "If you'll
excuse me a moment . . ." She headed out of the
office. "I'll take this in the hall," and added, "my
boss is working today" in answer to Wally's questioning look. The minister half-rose out of his chair,
a gentleman of the old school. "Of course. Be careful
of the fresh paint."

Gaby stepped into the hall, and looking furtively
left and right, determined that although it might look
deserted, the church office hall might have ears. She
walked quickly past two closed office doors, a bulletin
board and a window that looked out over the church
parking lot, made her careful way past a folded drop-
cloth and some paint cans, to finally find the door
marked "Women."

The telephone had stopped ringing, but Gaby knew
he'd try again.

Sure enough. "Where are you?" he wanted to
know.

"In the third stall of the ladies room at the Central
Community Church in Ossining."

"No."

"Yes."

"What the hell are you doing there? Writing on
the walls?"

"Not feeling ding ho," she said.

"What?"

"Premarital counseling."

Stretch let out a rumble of a laugh. "Never go
to bed angry? Don't give fifty percent, give ninety
percent?"

"I can't talk now, Stretch."

"I'm in the office. Come down. I'll wait for you.
I'll bring in some sushi and fake champagne. We'll
picnic. I've turned on the air conditioner, believe it
or not."

"It's—" Gaby looked at her watch, "past two. I
don't think."

"I can't get through until Monday without seeing
your birthmark."

Before she snapped shut the telephone, he'd told
her that his wife's mother had come for the weekend.
It gave him a bit of freedom, freedom to daydream
about what life would have been like if it hadn't
turned out the way it had turned out. Mitzi's doc had
increased her Prozac to eighty milligrams and there
was less crying now, he said.

Gaby leaned her head on the wall of the toilet
booth. *Less crying*.

"You've never said anything before about Mitzi
crying."

"Did I have to?" he'd asked, and changed the subject. He told her he'd seen a woman who looked just
like her on the commuter train. "I thought it was
you. When I realized it wasn't, I still tried to sit next
to her," he said. "I'm going crazy. Delusional. Believe
it or not, I went to two meetings today. One up in
Nyack before I went to work, then one down here.
Yes, I did that, I did. It adds up to twenty four steps
just today, if you want to do the math. And tomorrow
I'm going to mass and I'm going to light a few extra
candles."

The minister rose again as Gaby reentered. "A bill-
ing problem," she said. She'd taken a few extra minutes in the bathroom, time to compose herself. *My
voice will give everything away!* "My boss thinks I'm
indispensable." The three smiled agreeably at each
other and the minister rubbed the palms of his hands

on his desk. "Perhaps it would be wise to cut the session short," he suggested, looking from one to the other. These renovations were taking much longer than he'd expected. The odor must really be bothering them on such an unusually warm fall day. He got up and shook hands, said he'd enjoyed meeting Gaby, who would make a radiant bride, and assured them that they were off to a healthy and positive start. If they needed to, they could come in again, but in his estimation, another counseling session, since there were so few meaningful disagreements, would be superfluous.

For a split second she was tempted to blurt it all out, but instead, they shook hands. "A pleasure to meet you, such an open-and-shut couple," all smiles, and the minister walked them to the door; he was certainly, he said, looking forward to the Big Day.

CHAPTER FIVE

"What happened yesterday was this," Stretch was saying. He was six feet four, a former hockey star, a graduate of Notre Dame, an alcoholic, now addicted to AA. When he spoke, Gaby heard in his words the resonant voice of a college professor at commencement, a combination of authority and sincerity. She also heard what she didn't want to hear: guilt and melancholy. Nine years older than Gaby, still without a gray hair, he already seemed part of an older, life-battered generation. "Life threw me a dirty puck," he'd said once, as they were sitting on his suede couch, whiskey-colored, in the small room behind the conference room with the one-way mirror.

There, during working hours, Gaby interviewed potential consumers of products and services that made the world of commerce spin. There they would sit at a conference table, six, eight, ten or more souls chosen at random from their 18-34, 35-49, 50+ married/divorced/widowed, database slots, to answer questions, fill out questionnaires, eat deli sandwiches, drink coffee and give opinions of this and that toothpaste, bank or spa. From these, clients would extrapolate whether to use a more minty flavor, lure new depositors with toasters, mention loofa rubs in their advertisements. Gaby was always nervously aware that behind the mirror, Stretch, and sometimes a client, was watching, listening and recording, as she prodded her groups:

"—And how many times last month would you say you used moist towelettes?" She also knew that over the last four years, since she had joined the company, the client list had grown by sixty-seven percent and the staff had enlarged from zero to six. She thought of herself as a background person, quiet, sensitive to nuances in people's faces and voices, a good listener and slowly gaining in Stretch's professional esteem.

Now he was handing Gaby a mug printed with the company logo: Global Market Research. It was filled with French Vanilla flavored coffee, his favorite. Gaby took a sip, looking over the rim at him. The office was officially closed today, the day after Thanksgiving.

When Stretch spoke, she could see his Adam's apple move as if it had a little life of its own. Whenever he spoke about his wife, there were hesitations and pauses, throat clearings.

"Her mother flew in from Arizona. She's always after us to move to Scottsdale, she has a place there, so there's always tension, but she brought in the cooked Butterball, her sister came in with some cranberry thing, I did carrots. I cut my finger slicing them." He held out his thumb to show Gaby the Band-Aid. "My mother came over and set the table, then her mother put her in a dress and I tied a scarf around her neck—"

"A scarf?" Gaby interrupted, trying to picture it all, the dining room, maybe a lace tablecloth, the children, small faces just like his.

"Mitzi always wants a colored scarf around her neck. She says it makes her face less—oh, I don't know why." His wife's name was Madeleine, but everyone called her Mitzi. He'd said it once, at the beginning, that she'd once loved sailing and rappelling. Gaby saw it all, the bright silk to offset the pallor, the circle of devotion at a family table in a frame house in Nyack. All the things Mitzi had once loved to do, historical footnotes.

"We lit a few candles. The kids were great—made paper turkeys in school and pasted them on the windows—look, we got through it." Stretch leaned over and ran his fingers along Gaby's cheek. She pulled his hand away, held his Band-Aided thumb in her palm for a moment, examining it.

"Can she—eat without help?" she asked.

"I cut her meat and she picks it up and gets it to her mouth . . . mostly. The kids help."

Gaby got up and walked over to Stretch's desk. It often struck her that having given up the real thing, he'd chosen a color scheme nostalgically alcoholic: champagne-colored walls, Merlot tweed carpet, wood the color of brandy for his desk and bookshelves. His wife's picture in its green leather frame—bottle-green, to stretch a point—stood there, next to the computer. It had been taken—when? When she was still able to wear a halter top and lean against the fender of someone's RV and look young and cool with sunglasses on top of her head. Judging by the ages of the boy and girl, it must have been five years ago, when she was not in a wheelchair, could still put one healthy arm around each child's shoulder and cut her own turkey at Thanksgiving.

He sipped from his mug. Stretch held a coffee mug or a bottle of water in his hand; the protective talisman beverage was always there, around the clock.

She remembered the first time she'd met Stretch, the day he'd hired her. All shaggy eyebrows and chin, she'd hardly thought of him as a man but simply as a big redhead in a blah gray suit, huge freckled hands spread across her résumé on his desk, a generic boss. She was a few years out of Northwestern, and ready to stop "working" in employee benefits, monitoring phones and answering consumer queries at Daddy's electrical supply company. Daddy, her darling, poor Daddy, had treated her in the workplace as he'd always treated her at home—"like a princess with training wheels" Mama always said, never to be taken seriously, his baby everywhere and always.

"You didn't ask about *our* Thanksgiving."

"You've only been here fifteen minutes. I've been waiting for you since noon."

"As you know, Wally didn't go to work today."

"So you made him blueberry pancakes, and then what?"

"Stretch—there are times you make me crazy." Actually, Wally had gone off early to take his mother, who was no longer able to drive, to the dentist, before meeting Gaby at the minister's.

"You're standing twelve feet away from me and if you want to know what makes *me* crazy, that's what does. My eyes get blurry just from looking at your *accoutrements*. The pearls in your earlobes and the buttons on your blouse. Even your belt buckle gives me a hard-on."

Gaby wanted to hear it, every word, how thoughts of her disrupted his dreams and his dinners, how her name slipped out of his mouth at inadvertent times, how wild-jealous he was of Wally. Then again, it was useless and absolutely tragic, because he was decent and a Catholic. Sometimes she tried to determine which came first, the decent, or the dogma? What Gaby knew was Mitzi's MS would keep him rooted in the house in Nyack with her as long as whatever it was kept fertilizing his conscience. Which of course was the most admirable thing about Stretch and the thing she hated most about him.

She talked fast, to get past the image of Stretch at

home, tying a scarf around his sick wife's neck. Now there was not one, there were two hells on earth, one here on Twenty-First Street and one in Daddy's room at the White Plains Hospital. She felt she was being punished, by whom she didn't know, for what, she did.

"Mama insisted she would make the turkey and she made Brussels sprouts knowing we all hate them, because she said Daddy loves them. Daddy is lying in a coma miles away and she has to make Brussels sprouts, besides which, they always gave him gas."

She could talk to Stretch. When it came to pain, he plugged in fast. He again nodded a heartfelt sympathy nod and let a sacred moment of silence pass, which was exactly what and all she needed from him. It was the influence of his Friends of Bill W, what else? The meetings were held at the Brotherhood Synagogue two blocks from the office, and he never missed a day.

"Mama's lost eight pounds. Mariadora makes tapioca pudding and pea soup and ties colored ribbons to Mama's bedposts to ward off bad spirits or summon good ones, I'm not sure, but still Mama won't eat."

"Every bite I took, Gaby. You were there. I tell you, it's like I'm living two simultaneous lives, it's like a constant double exposure. Did you hear what I said, Gaby?"

Gaby walked to the closet that held office supplies, a coffee machine, small microwave and an Amish quilt, that she now took down from a top shelf. The first time they'd made love, it was a week and a day after the accident. She had been fighting off for months what was in her, is how she thought of it. It was like a virus—an attack of the libido. After the car crash, her immune system just went down. With it, her honor and integrity. When she looked in the mirror, she thought her mouth had completely changed. It looked bloodless, thin and pitiless, with new little crosshatch lines at the corners.

The first time it happened on the suede couch, but the couch was short and Stretch was all elbows and knees awkwardly trying to find space for his bones without crushing her, and the stain they left on the back of the left cushion—despite her later diligently rubbing it with suede cleaner and a foam rubber sponge—never did completely come out. Every time she was in this room her eyes went to The Spot.

Now Stretch got up and took the quilt out of her hands and put one arm around her—if it had been just a bit longer, it could have wrapped entirely around her. His hands alone were as big as her feet, a Gulliver's touch, making her feel even smaller. They stood for a moment locked mouth to mouth, hardly breathing, and then parted to move away the little glass coffee table and spread the quilt tidily in the middle of the floor. Wavering, she thought, all it takes is one kiss and my conscience falls on its sword every time, but the hesitation was only that. She took off her engagement ring so it wouldn't scratch when she touched him and began to unbutton her blouse, hurrying as if a timer was set to go off. Stretch went to the office door to make certain it was locked, then, tending to be orderly and systematic, turned up the thermostat by five degrees and turned on the telephone answering machine. When he pulled closed the blinds she unhooked her slacks, leaving the brassiere and the panties to him to carefully and as always, slowly, languidly, to remove.

When the phone rang it was when they were already naked and bathed in sweat.

"Oh shit. Let the machine take it," Stretch groaned.

Gaby thought of her father; every time the phone rang she thought This Could Be It. They waited for the machine to pick up. "Gaby? Hey, Hon, where are you? Thought you'd be there by now."

"It's Wally." Gaby sat up. "I know who it is," Stretch said, closing his eyes, then squinting them open to look at his watch. "I'd better," she said, getting up, thinking again, *This is the last time.*

When she crossed the room, she felt awkward. There was that asterisk birthmark on her right hip and her small breasts that still jiggled with every step. She was accustomed to holding a robe or a towel around her naked self out of habit and modesty, but on the other hand, she did not altogether mind sensing Stretch's eyes burning under half-closed lids, the sandy lashes almost meeting as they pretended not to follow her. He had told her time and again how much he liked her body. "Your buns, especially. Like a pair of honeydews. The birthmark, too. It's shaped like a little morel. Did you know that? It's like your personal logo. Oh, I love it."

"How's it going?" Wally said he was chewing on a piece of raw broccoli, about the only thing in the refrigerator since he'd finished the turkey slice leftovers Mama had given them to take home. Also, he couldn't find the church key to open the last bottle of Sam Adams. Did she know where it could be?

"Is that why you called?" Gaby was aware of Stretch's nonchalantly industrious eavesdropping.

"No, I called to tell you I'm heading up to Stamford. Shingo wants me to go up and help him coach tonight. I'll be home before ten, though. Okeydokey?" Shingo was Wally's close friend, written up in *Tennis World* a few months ago—a cover story calling him the Pied Piper of the Disabled—for teaching paraplegics how to hit power strokes and rush the net. Shingo had recruited Wally, who was now Assistant Pied Piper.

He told her to please buy a quart of Turkey Hill

ice cream, chocolate, and some paper towels; they were out.

She told him he'd used the bottle opener to pry open his can of shoe polish yesterday, to look for it in the bedroom. Wally owned footwear that took up a special shoe cabinet and half the floor of her clothes closet, most of it tennis sneakers.

She ordinarily might have called him dear, or just, Wall. "I won't be too late," she said, and realized she'd overheard Stretch say those same domestic-talk words to his wife any painful number of times. "Love you," Wally said before he hung up.

"I don't get it," Stretch said as soon as she'd put down the receiver. "You don't play tennis, you're a quiet, private person, you have a soul. Wally is—"

"My fiancé."

"He's a good-time Charlie, a jock. Well, isn't he? He's got to be surrounded by people all the time, selling this or that, hitting a ball, sort of a centrifugal force of sports and commercial activity, isn't that right?"

She wouldn't answer when he hit a nerve.

"Sometimes, I have a primal need to talk about Wally. Name one thing you and he have in common. One."

"Sixty Minutes."

Stretch gave her a look of disdain.

"And vegetarian chili, very hot." *Replication and Fisher-Price! You have yours and I want mine. That's the sine qua non, the bottom line.*

Being crazy about him did not stop her from wanting to make him bleed. "Listen, Stretch. We set the date. The Sunday after Labor Day. It's a *fait accompli.*"

"Ha. Would Wally understand French?" She became especially testy when he put Wally down.

"A hundred and fifty guests. You own a tuxedo?

You're invited.'' Gaby lay down next to him on the Amish quilt. For a few moments they lay shoulder to shoulder staring at nothing on the ceiling. For the moment, thoughts of Daddy, a skeletal question mark under a sheet lying helpless and alone, went. Gaby touched the corners of her mouth to see if she could feel the little lines she'd seen in the mirror this morning.

"It's gonna rain if I have anything to say about it.'' Stretch turned on his side, kissed her hair above her ear, then moved his hands and mouth and body back to where they had been before the telephone rang.

CHAPTER SIX

Susanna sat in the den, her feet up, an unread *New York Times* folded in her lap, staring at the precautionary bucket of water half obscured by the Christmas tree's lower branches. They'd had to move a lamp and end table to make room for the seven-foot tree, which Dieter had decorated with more little white candles than anyone wanted to count. The tree and the room looked cheerfully ready for the holiday, while upstairs, Dieter was packing to leave for Potsdam.

Susanna felt anger churning, but confronting Dieter was dangerous. From their first kiss, the night after they'd met at the travel agency where she was booking corporate tours and he was the agent for the Kaiser-Gelb hotel chain, she'd been steamrollered. Dressed in dove gray, with meticulously shined shoes, a crisp, snow-white shirt, hair slicked back from an aristocratic forehead, he was ambassadorial, urbane. He spoke three languages, had been to fifty-eight countries. He showed her videotapes he'd made of Potsdam and the house he'd grown up in in Berlin—

stone, substantial, grand—and she immediately lost interest in the professorial Russian interpreter she was seeing, took up trying to like Wagner and Mozart and began renting Fassbinder movies and reading up on King Friedrich the Great (none of which—except Mozart—actually interested *him*).

If his father flew with the Luftwaffe, it was never discussed. The one time Susanna asked, she was told that Papa was not so much patriotic as obedient: he was told what to do and did it. Following that discussion, Dieter went to the window and opened it, as if even the fumes from the question had to be eliminated. And the look on his face? She had not forgotten it. It sealed off the subject permanently.

Dieter liked Susanna enough, called her *Meine Liebe* when they were in bed, told her her cucumber salad was by far better than his mother's, compared her legs to Dietrich's and brought her tea when she was having cramps, but in their relationship there was always a But. It was unspoken, but Dieter was the love of Susanna's life, and his daughter Liesel was the love of his.

Part of it was her own insecurity. Susanna wore it like a coat with a missing button. At five years old she could multiply and divide, define words like "migrate" and "erode" and recite Pope couplets, but it didn't seem enough. More recently, she had taken a course in the Genealogy of the Russian Nobility and gotten one of only two A's in her class of forty, then had, to Mama and Daddy's horror, dropped out of the Ph.D. program in Russian Studies at Columbia a month after meeting Dieter. Because Daddy had designated her the family sage, fair was fair, she did not feel she could also be allotted beauty. When she looked in the mirror, she saw not her bright blue eyes, so much like Mama's, but her contacts, and above them colorless eyebrows that always needed plucking. She'd tried going blonde last year, but as

Mama had said, "Not everyone is meant to sing arias, not everyone is meant to be blonde, darling." Maybe if she would stop looking like the ordinary Bedford matron she was and turn herself into a flamboyant package of sexual fire, Dieter could never leave, especially now. If she had his child, for sure and definitely, he would not leave at all, let alone take off a week and a half before Christmas.

It was outrageous that he was flying to Germany tomorrow, and wouldn't return until Christmas Day. Especially with things so critical with Mama and Daddy. Just last week, Susanna had practically had to drag her mother out of the house to go to the Westchester Mall for some Christmas shopping. Her parents had always had a tree and a beautiful Christmas dinner—Daddy always said Christmas was about as religious as Flag Day—but now Mama was not interested in celebrating or cooking or buying her daughters the usual gold charms to add to their charm bracelets. She was interested only in buying gifts for the nurses on Daddy's floor. Daddy had to be turned and bathed and his nails trimmed; his corpse body had to be rolled this way and that on and off his mattress while sheets were changed over his foam rubber bubble mattress; a barber came to shave him and to snip away a few threads of gray hair. Watching the barber at work was an experience Susanna wished she didn't happen to be on hand to see, Daddy's lifeless head being turned right and left, the scissors taking off little wisps that floated to the floor like thistledown.

Dieter would fly back Christmas Day, jet-lagged and full of stories about how well Liesel's job was going and how they all sang *Tannenbaum,* ate goose and drank Erdbeersaft at a party in the Babelsberg Castle.

She'd gone with him last year, bringing a suitcase of gifts for Liesel, who had gained twenty pounds working at the Grüner Garten Restaurant, didn't fit into the TSE cashmere sweater, and whose hands were one or two sizes too big for the deerskin gloves from Saks. She did wax enthusiastic over the little fourteen karat Statue of Liberty on its gold chain but never put it on, just kept right on wearing her old gold and pearl cross between her newly expanded pair of German breasts.

Liesel had just started her English conversation class, and Susanna's German, improving day by day, was still no match for the locals'; the jokes and gossip were beyond her, and she could see how tedious Dieter found translating every German idiom and one-liner, and how between the *Guten Abend* and *Auf Wiedersehen,* she and Liesel did not have two words to rub together. As far as Liesel's mother Lotte went, it was all too *gemütlich* at a family get-together where in fact, Susanna felt more like the former wife than Lotte, when Lotte and Dieter dived into a backlog of reminiscence. With tears in their eyes, they talked about their deceased child, then chatted about relatives and events as foreign as the atmosphere in the Bierstube in which they gathered. Once or twice they threw back their heads and laughed together like new lovers instead of old divorcés. Lotte, friendlier and even rounder than her daughter, went so far as to copy some recipes of Dieter's favorite dishes for Susanna, but playing the American-style good sport intensified Susanna's cramps. She counted the days, then the hours, when they'd be back in their Lufthansa seats heading home.

Now, finishing her cup of chamomile, Susanna decided she was calm enough to go upstairs and discuss her feelings without histrionics. In their bedroom, Dieter was in his plaid bathrobe, his hair slicked back, looking freshly shaved, showered and ready to be photographed, which is the way Dieter always managed to look. He was watching CNN and simultaneously moving from the highboy to their bed, where his open suitcase was swallowing his socks and shirts. His Christmas gift to Liesel, a laptop, was wrapped in red and green striped foil, ready to go.

"I was going to vait to pack until tomorrow," Dieter said, as Susanna walked into the room, "but you know I don't like to put things off to the last minute."

She knew very well he didn't procrastinate or forget things. He was never late, always polite, always moving; it was in his cliché Teutonic genes.

"I am going to miss you so much this week," Susanna began. It was supposed to be the last sentence of her speech, not the first, but out it came, sounding cloying and sappy.

"I'll call you, Su. I try to call you every day."

"Liesel will love the computer."

"We vill E-mail. It makes sense."

"Listen, Dieter, I wonder if you could try to come back a few days early." Susanna hated the wimpette she sometimes became with him, but there she was, her voice tiptoeing as if she were talking to a policeman who'd just caught her going through a red light.

"You know the problem."

What Dieter called a problem was not a problem. Liesel's holiday work schedule did not allow a great deal of time to spend with her papa. Which is why Dieter had to allot extra time so that he could fit himself into *her* schedule. To him, seeing his daughter at Christmas was as mandatory a tradition as creating a fire hazard with two zillion candles on a Scotch pine.

"You call it a problem?" Susanna's own sparks ignited. "I call what's going on *here* a problem." That was more like it. *Yes.* She was stepping up to being firm. Standing up to him.

" 'Nothing is new with your father, Susanna."

"Every day it's something new. Mama spent six

hundred dollars on gifts for his nurses yesterday. She's resorting to bribery to get him extra attention. That's new.''

"What has that to do vith my going to Potsdam?'' Dieter was taking wooden shoe trees out of a pair of shoes and simultaneously glancing at CNN Sports. No pause, no letup.

Susanna was eyeing the shoe trees, imagining them as cudgel-like weapons. "I want you to stay home!'' It burst out, almost against her will.

"Schatzi, please. Ten days. It's not so long.''

Susanna sank into the one chair in the room and tried to pull herself together. She'd messed up. What could she say now? What magic words or sexual acts could keep him at home? Dieter came over and took her hands in his, lifted her chin and looked into her eyes. "PMS?'' he asked tenderly. Then he gingerly removed the raincoat he'd draped over the back of the chair, on which Susanna had inadvertently leaned, and carefully shook out whatever wrinkles she may have incurred. Susanna, distraught, leaped out of the chair and grabbed a shoe tree off the bed. She swung it over her head like a mace, considered hurling it at Dieter— but no, she could never cause Dieter pain and injury. She considered pitching it through the window, smashing it against the wall or the highboy. But she'd just furnished this room, had the walls carefully painted that marvelous buttercream color, the highboy was a hundred twenty years old. The window panes? Damage? Forget it. She dropped the shoe tree to the floor, where it landed on the carpet with a heavy and impotent thud.

Dieter, the raincoat held high in his hand, stared at her as if she'd gone mad.

"Don't you get it? I want.'' She hesitated at the precipice, gulped in air. "I want—''

"What?''

You know goddamn well what I want! A little Dieter is what I want!

"What?"

"I vant to get pregnant!" Susanna belted it out, a Leontyne Price in her own kitchen. "A baby, *ein Kind,* I vant a baby!" It would never do to make fun of his accent, which he couldn't help at all. It wasn't meant to be sung this way. A wholesome dialogue is all she'd intended. A sweet, reasonable nonmusical request is how she'd planned it, an affectionate après sex chat, while the afterglow was still glowing, and Dieter was spun out and mellow.

Dieter's face got pink in certain spots and white in others. Susanna ran out of the room, into the hall, down the stairs and into the kitchen. She poured herself a glass of water, took a sip, then threw the water back into the sink, where some of it splashed back at her. She dried her face with a paper towel, then opened the refrigerator, saw a hunk of Braunschweiger—she hated liverwurst—and slammed it shut. It was not PMS, this time it was not cramps, it was life, spraying cold water in her face.

She ran out of the kitchen to the hall, went to the coat closet, pulled on her heavy boots and put on her overcoat. Standing at the foot of the stairs, she raised her voice so loud her throat hurt. *Damn him and his Nazi father!* "I'm going out!" she yodeled, and she grabbed her purse and ran out the door.

Mama was sitting in her bed, watching a movie about lost Arctic whalers. She was wearing a faded, pindotted bathrobe Susanna didn't immediately recognize. Susanna sat at the foot of the bed and pretended for a minute or two to be interested in the action on the ice-crusher boat on the screen.

Her mother's tastes in television ordinarily ran to PBS, the three tenors, old movies and sometimes, the Food Channel. Now she turned her face—very reluctantly, it seemed—toward Susanna. "I'm not really watching, dear."

Susanna got up, turned off the set and said, "What did you do today, Mama?"

"Not too much, dear."

"You saw Daddy."

"Not today. I might be getting a cold. Too risky. I don't want him to catch it."

"So, did you go out?"

"No, dear."

"You stayed home?"

"In bed. I stayed in bed, dear."

Susanna, in all her growing up years, had seen Mama take to her bed only twice—once for a few days after Gaby got strep and her mother caught it, and again when she had food poisoning after eating mystery seafood at the DiLorenzos'.

She noticed for the first time the bluish veins in her forehead and the quarter inch of virgin gray growing out of her scalp. For her mother, monthly touch-ups were as necessary to a civilized life as knives and forks; had she completely stopped looking into the mirror?

"Mama. Dieter and I had a fight."

"Oh, I'm sorry to hear that, dear. A fight?"

"Yes. Well, I caused it. He's going away tomorrow. It's outrageous of him to go away now."

"Hmmm. Poor Susanna." Susanna wanted the old, motherlike Mama back, some showing of concern, some light of emotion, a touch of empathy.

"Mama. I told him I wanted to get pregnant."

A blank, questioning look.

"He didn't say anything. He looked shocked, though. He doesn't want any more children."

"Yes, dear. But we knew that. You told me that long ago." Her mother looked unconcerned. Absent. *Bored.*

Susanna felt as she had during one of those falling dreams, when she'd hurtle down steps and never quite land anywhere. She got up and went obediently to the thermostat. *No one to catch me, no one!*

Now she spotted something else, some disturbing new thing, some un-mother thing. "Where did that robe you're wearing come from?" she heard herself ask. The old robe had kicked in. It wasn't Mama's.

"It's Daddy's old one, from Paul Stuart. Don't you remember when I gave it to him, before that trip we took to the Côte d'Azur?" Mama had the disconnected look of someone who just awoke, or is about to fall into slumber.

Susanna stood still, her hand on the thermostat.

"You have a closet full of robes. Why are you wearing Daddy's?"

"It was Mariadora's idea. It's silly, I know, but I guess I just feel better wearing Daddy's robe than my own. That's all there is to it." She tugged the collar of the robe a bit closer together, bunching it up against her collarbone, as if to illustrate proprietorship.

Worse and worse, is how things were going. Wearing Daddy's robe was *sick.*

And then, her eyes blinking fast, her mother, not the one who'd held her in her lap and comforted her after a bad dream, not the one who drove eight hours to Maine when Susanna broke her collarbone at camp, this new Stepford model, said, "When I wear this, he's with me. I can hear his voice. He's saying, 'I'm still here and Spring is right around the corner, just wait, darling, just wait.' "

Susanna sank into the old blue chaise near the window; it's where Mama had read to her when she was three and four and five, and where now, she wanted to curl up, forget about her crushed and finished father, her mother's demons, and concentrate on being the happy, cosseted little girl turning the pages of *Are You My Mother?* her favorite and beloved picture book. Where was that book now? Where was that mother now? As gone as dust, as gone as the day before yesterday.

"Mama, I'll make you a cup of mocha. Would you like that?"

"That would be nice, dear," this new, partial, partially present, distant mother, replied, in her washed-out, washed-up voice. "Thank you, darling. That would be nice."

CHAPTER SEVEN

The weather had turned mild, the streets muddy.
Spring.

The word "baby" had not been mentioned to Dieter or to her mother again, but seemed to Susanna
a hovering thing like a fireworks. It could at any time
explode into fiery bits and rain down on her marriage
with a devastating bang. On the other hand, since
he'd come back two days before Christmas, the sex
with Dieter had been very good and very hot. It was
Mama that was preoccupying Susanna, Mama, the
subject of the conversations she had with her sisters
day in and day out and the reason for this unusual
lunch on this Wednesday at one o'clock.

Susanna checked her watch as she pulled her car
into the parking lot, packed full today, requiring her
to drive around it four times before finding a space.
She'd wanted her sisters in on this, but Gaby was
working, and Karen had canceled at the last minute
because Elliot was having a tooth extracted and
needed her.

* * *

As she expected, Ruthie DiLorenzo was already inside, waiting for her at a table next to a mirror, a club soda with lime—her signature drink since becoming a nutritionist—in front of her.

Susanna plopped breathlessly down opposite her and began with apologies. Ruthie DiLorenzo was no kin, but had been "Aunt," since Susanna could remember. Her only child had drowned on the Sunday Susanna had tried her first joint in a then-boyfriend's basement laundry room. Little Guy had been an almost-cousin, a quiet, expressionless child never seen without a soccer, basket or any other sort of ball in his hands. Ruthie and Mama had been "hand in glove" ever since they'd been neighbors in the old New Rochelle neighborhood where Mama and Daddy had bought their first house and where she and Karen had been born. The DiLorenzos still lived in the same Cape Cod, which they'd perked up with black shutters and a yellow door and then messed up by adding aluminum siding and a wing that looked like a toolshed.

Ruthie DiLorenzo, born in a row house near the Bronx Zoo, hesitated before speaking in her modulated finishing-school voice, and except for the auburn rinse that gave what used to be graying hair a calf's liver glow, might pass for a Bouvier. She was wearing a suit of a color that was sort of a charcoal green with a ruffly collar of white, practically eclipsing a huge cameo pin, a jewelry gift from her husband, Lou. Ever since the death of their son, he marked even the smallest occasion with a gift box from a local jeweler, and once, on their twenty-fifth anniversary, had presented her with a diamond love-and-kisses bracelet from David Webb she never took off. And why not? Mama had always said Ruthie had a good heart, which meant, Susanna supposed, that it pumped kindness and unselfishness through her veins and that she deserved whatever gems in life, real or metaphorical, came her way.

Susanna hoped that Mama was right. Certainly, since poor Ruthie had lost Guy, she'd have a greater understanding of the suffocating bunker of others' tragedies. The problem was that although Ruthie had a heart, she sometimes seemed to hide it behind a personal mortared wall.

After Guy's death she'd gone back to school, but nutritionist's degree or no, was still unemployed. The few jobs open to a woman of her age were either low-paying or in Philadelphia, she said, but somehow, Susanna suspected, Aunt Ruth hadn't tried too hard. Lou had a very successful stone and gravel business and Lou and the Scarsdale golf club were her career. They'd just come back from their new condo in Boca, from which they'd called Mama every week begging her to visit.

"I was so glad when you called me," Ruthie said after asking about Gaby, Karen and the "travel biz," looking at Susanna through tinted ovals and showing her wonderful row of teeth. They seemed a testimonial to excellent nutrition and practically flashed between her lips like plaster of Paris dental impressions. She had shown Susanna the photos of the new place, the views of palms and surf, the lobby too.

Susanna felt guilty about ordering a drink, when with Aunt Ruth, all alcoholic beverages and most foods seemed to break some codes of well-being.

Today she ordered Scotch on the rocks and the hell with it.

Ruthie didn't flinch. She reached across the table and held Susanna's wrist, where it rested near her knife and spoon. Her own wrist sparkled with X's and O's. "You know you're still a baby to me." She recounted The Day You Were Born story Susanna had heard many times, which was also the day Ruthie's long-awaited wall-to-wall was delivered in the wrong color. "I was thrilled you were finally in this world, but will I ever forget that swamp-green rug! Of course your Mom and I were such babies ourselves!"

Seeing Susanna's face, Ruthie tried to lighten things up. "Let's have a good lunch. It's what Mother would want us to do." This was Ruthie's warm side, although "Mother" was a term never used for Mama and neither was "Mom." "Mama" was a soft but solid appellation buttressed with tradition and respect, old-fashioned as it was, the one and only perfect name for Mama incarnate.

Ruthie looked at the menu. "Their tandoori lobster and chicken Kashmiri are wonderful. We'll be fine if we stay away from their vegetable fritters. They *fry* them."

Now there was a great deal of meandering conversation about the chicken Kashmiri, white rice versus brown and Susanna's last year's family trip to Delhi and Bombay, where Mama and Daddy had one day planned to go. Susanna took a piece of the pancakey *Nan* and began tearing it delicately into bite-size pieces, sending as much of a beam of a smile as she could muster across the table. "So, Aunt Ruth, we've been desperately waiting for you to come back from Florida. Since before Christmas, things had gone from worse to worse with Mama."

Aunt Ruth touched her napkin delicately to the corners of her mouth. It was a dainty gesture so much like her that Susanna thought she might actually remember witnessing this Aunt Ruth movement from her high chair.

Ruthie put down the napkin and scrunched it under her palm, then took a breath. "You know what both your parents have meant to Lou and me." Interrupted very briefly by the waiter taking their order, a few pauses and many sighs, she chronicled a friendship that had spanned thirty-odd years, overlapped the terms of six presidents, a war, desegregation, an impeachment and the death of her child. As an epilogue: "You may not know this, Susanna, but your father saved Lou's life."

Susanna had in fact heard the abridged version of her father's valorous act: Responding to Ruthie's hysterical midnight call, he had burst into the DiLorenzos' house and wrested a revolver out of Lou's hands at the risk of his own life. "To this day I don't know where he got it. When I first saw Lou with the gun in his hand, I thought it was a cigarette lighter." Aunt Ruth tried for a smile, but it vanished before she finished the sentence. "It was two weeks after we buried Guy." The gun did not go off, but fell harmlessly into the dog's dish on the DiLorenzos' kitchen floor. Lou ultimately spent three months at the Bloomingdale Psychiatric Hospital not far from this very restaurant in White Plains. Not only was Gilbert Kessler a savior, but also a constant visitor, who helped Ruthie find Lou's old Tommy Dorsey records—Ruthie mentioned these three times—so he could tape his friend's favorite pieces to bring to the patient's hospital room.

"Of course, you probably never knew any of this. No one did—we kept it quiet, don't ask me how— for the better part of a year. If it weren't for your parents . . . well, dear, a day didn't go by that I didn't lean on one or the other. I don't have to preach to the choir, do I? Let's just say your father is noble, a *prince.*"

Susanna wanted to correct Ruthie but swallowed the words. *Was* noble, *was* a prince.

"A hero, pure and simple," Ruthie said now, lowering her voice, which was low enough as it was. "Your dad—well, he didn't deserve to be punished any more than Guy did, did he?"

Susanna was rattled to see, through the misting in her own eyes, the possibility of moisture behind the tinted lenses across the table. She had not intended to meet with Aunt Ruth in order to spill tears together at this Indian restaurant. She had a mission, which, if she were Dieter, would have been accomplished a half hour ago.

"Aunt Ruth, I really came to get you to help us do something about Mama."

Ruthie was using the napkin to dab at the corners of her eyes and next to her, so was her mirror image. Simultaneously, Susanna glimpsed her own reflection in the mirror. Haggard, anyone would say. Her beige hair more limp than usual.

"You're her closest friend, so, well, you know what's been going on."

"Oh, yes. And I'm so worried about her, don't think I'm not! And I've been praying. On my knees, darling."

"Aunt Ruth, she's breathing guilt, drinking it, sleeping with it. It's become her new deity, her *religion!* She's hardly eating, can't seem to—doesn't seem to want to—get her feet back into life. And you know, Aunt Ruth, how forgiving a woman she is, but when it comes to forgiving herself—" Susanna curled her hand around her Scotch glass. "She's lost so much weight she looks like she's—she's wearing someone else's clothes. And, half the time, she's wearing Daddy's. It's so scary to see!" Susanna thought it was politic not to mention Mama's disinterest in her own problems. "And have you seen the rubber band? Every time anyone suggests going somewhere, doing something, it's snap, snap, snap. Aunt Ruth, it's been six months!"

At some point the waiter had dished food out of steaming braziers, brought another loaf of *Nan*, refilled Ruthie's club soda and poured another Scotch for Susanna. Now Susanna sipped from her

glass but couldn't get herself to register the taste of
anything. "Delicious," Aunt Ruth said at one point,
but Susanna might have been munching kelp. She
went on describing the efforts she'd made with both
her sisters, to get her mother back into the thrift
shop, the hairdresser, the business of life.

"And Mama won't give up the idea that some day
Daddy will simply open his eyes, give her a kiss and
sing the *Tennessee Waltz.*"

"Oh, Susanna, dear, I don't think she thinks that
at all."

"Well, look what's happening! Daddy's down to
eighty-nine pounds! He gets turned every two hours
around the clock so he doesn't erupt in God-knows-
what sort of skin lesions, he's got these tubes getting
stuff in and tubes pulling stuff out—" Aunt Ruth
interrupted with a shhhh; Susanna stopped talking,
not realizing she'd raised her voice enough to attract
glances left and right. She leaned forward, lowering
her voice. "And, you know what else? He signed an
organ donor card years ago, so almost every day someone points out that some of his organs could be used
to save lives. I told Mama, 'It's a way for Daddy to
live on,' but still Mama won't budge. Listen, Aunt
Ruth, Karen and Gaby wanted to come but couldn't
be here, but I'm speaking for all three of us, and
we're pleading, *pleading,* for your help. You've got to
convince Mama to let Daddy go. Seeing him every
day like he is is killing her!"

Ruthie's eyes got so small they looked suddenly
Asian behind her glasses. "You want me to talk Mom
into letting your father die." Her mouth curled right
around the word "die," elongating it as if it didn't
want to let go.

"It's not *Mom.* It's *Mama,* Aunt Ruth."

To Susanna, Ruthie seemed almost leisurely in her
reaction, taking a new interest in the Bengali hang-
ings on the walls, her eyes circling the restaurant,

avoiding Susanna's. She examined the tablecloth and the spoon she kept turning in her hand. Had the woman never seen a spoon before?

Turning and turning her coffee spoon, Ruthie retreated into the private place in which she was hiding her good heart. If she'd stepped into the Cape Cod in which she lived and gently closed its yellow door, it couldn't have been more clear. "Don't you see, darling? It's like this: We're all just like fish in the sea, surrounded by a net. When our time is up, the net gets pulled up and that's it, we die. So, it's just not up to us. It's not up to *me*. It's up to The Fisherman," she said, and her eyes left the walls to catch the waiter's. "Could we have the check, please?" she asked him sweetly. Turning back to Susanna, she touched the cameo at her neck. "It was the same with Guy. It was his time. That was it. Do you see what I'm saying, dear?" and then she put out her hand to stop Susanna reaching into her purse. "No, no, darling. It's my treat today. Please. I insist."

When they were putting on their coats, Ruthie looked at her watch. "Lou is at home waiting for me, darling. I better run."

Susanna thought for a moment of throwing herself against the door, blocking Ruthie's exit. Instead, she politely thanked Ruthie for lunch, and allowed her to give her cheek a farewell peck. Pulling away, Susanna reached into her purse for a tissue.

Ruthie was pulling on a pair of gloves, then stopped. She stood watching Susanna extricating the Kleenex from its little packet, blowing her nose.

"Wait a minute," she said, and in concert, she stretched her mouth over her perfect teeth. She put a gloved hand on Susanna's sleeve. Getting a closer look, Susanna noted that there were gaps between the lower incisors; the teeth weren't perfect after all.

"Something just occurred to me, right up here."
With her gloved finger, Aunt Ruth pointed to her
temple. "There is one thing your mother and I always
said we both wanted to do. Funny how it just came
back to me out of the blue! I don't know why I didn't
think of it long ago. It's a little crazy, but—Susanna,
where are you parked?"

"In the lot around the corner."

"I'm parked in the other direction. Do you have
time to walk me to my car so we can talk about it?
You know Lou. He worries so if I'm a minute late."

CHAPTER EIGHT

Gaby was the first to arrive at 66 Morris Lane. Pulling into the circular driveway, she sat behind the steering wheel alone for a few minutes. Scarsdale in May after a rainy April was all opaline light and polychromatic landscaping: not only Mama's roses, but azaleas in riotous pink, new tulips in color-wheel pastels and hydrangeas in yellow were shooting the works around neighbors' stucco, brick or clapboard houses; trees and shrubs in every imaginable green shaded streets that curved left, then right, showing off Mercedes, Audis, SUVs in gravel driveways between lawns that looked like chartreuse wall-to-wall. The neighborhood had stayed comfortingly the same for as long as Gaby could remember, despite a new fence here, an expansion there, now an occasional piece of abstract lawn sculpture in stone or steel. Home.

Gaby wanted to hear the rest of the James Taylor song that was coming from her car radio. It reminded her of the time not long after she'd met Wally and long before Stretch, when they'd found a place in Stamford, somewhere near the water, a dump really, where there was live music. The music was running through their veins with the alcohol and they had sex in the car—her sisters would throw up if she told them—and it was the best sex she'd ever had with him. *Fire and Rain* was coming out of the radio then too. Wally let out a Holy God so loud she was afraid the police would come and find them, bottomless in the back seat of his old Honda with those sheepskin seat covers he reversed in summer, the goofus cork Statue of Liberty dangling from the rearview mirror.

Now, here she was and without Wally, who was visiting his mother in Norwalk. Gaby had dutifully called her future mother-in-law to wish her a happy Mother's Day, to ask if the azalea plant had been delivered, and gotten the usual quirky rundown of the things that were leaking, creaking or falling apart in her apartment. You had to feel sorry for her, alone with her photos, bronzed baby shoes, and her collection of bottled sand from every Florida beach she'd ever visited. Luckily she had good neighbors, and she had Wally.

Three weeks ago, as Gaby had picked out a wedding dress at Kleinfeld's, she was not thinking of her fiancé. Instead, she pictured Stretch arriving at her wedding in the white Chevy Blazer, the same car that had taken them to the Mayflower Inn, that paradise in Connecticut, for a stolen overnight the week before. She had kept the memory of the four-poster, the Frette robe, the amenity body lotion he'd applied to her everywhere and the kisses under the Weeping Atlas Blue Cedar, but there the image stopped. Her boss at her wedding in Scarsdale was a movie dream sequence, and if her sisters and Mama knew he was her lover too, the sky would fall.

Gaby had thought of going to a hypnotist to rid herself of Stretch, thought of taking off for Paris, or moving to Seattle, where her college roommate had settled. In the end though, she did nothing except make four visits to a psychologist, who told her what she already knew. Stretch made her feel as if she was more than she was, the way Daddy had.

Her thirtieth birthday had just passed and she could practically feel the eggs in her womb desiccating; fifteen childbearing years were already behind her. She had spent her childhood years dressing Luffy, the family cat, in baby clothes and even now never failed to stop at little faces peering out of buntings and strollers, pictured babies lined up in her womb just waiting to be born. If Susanna hadn't talked her out of it—"You'll get tired of wiping noses and buttoning snowsuits"—she would have become a kindergarten teacher and taken her Master's at the Bank Street School instead of going to Chicago for postgrad courses in market research. Now heaven had sent her a temporal imperative, Wally.

Their small co-op apartment on the sixth floor of an old building on Garth Road in Scarsdale, Daddy's gift to them even before the engagement had been formally announced, had a pair of vis-à-vis blonde leather couches Karen had found at some furniture warehouse in Long Island City, and there they sat most nights, facing the set and each other, taking turns with the remote control, but when Wally watched Monday night basketball, Saturday golf, and almost daily reruns of old tennis matches, Gaby went into the bedroom to read. Even if hers wasn't going to be like the matching bookends marriage of her parents, she and Wally surely had more in common than Susanna and Dieter, and were certainly better matched than Karen and Elliot.

Their car pulled up next, with Elliot sitting in the passenger seat. Karen was dressed in a geometric print jacket over a black dress that swooped over her body, and glass beads, each bead a different shape; Gaby would never be caught dead in these costumes her sister pulled together, but Karen lit up every room she'd ever walked into. The fates had provided Gaby with a Picasso of an older sister who had skipped from pen and ink illustration to acrylic to multimedia in a few easy leaps, and was now doing digital art at home. Not only did Karen sit at her computer and effortlessly create beautiful paperback book jackets, but she looked pretty much like the touched-up models on the covers herself. For her, life was all effortless magic. Gaby pushed aside a bit of envy and her sister's cascade of hair to kiss her cheek and tell her she looked snazzy, as always.

Elliot was in a conformist jacket, pants and normal-guy tie. He'd cut off the ponytail. Was something going on? Perhaps it was in honor of his mother, long deceased, and sure enough, he planned to make a visit to the cemetery in Hartsdale later in the day. Elliot had no available family—both parents gone, a sister he wouldn't speak to and a younger brother in a home for the mentally challenged in Florida—but Karen always called him a "real family man," whatever that meant. It seemed to Gaby her creative self had given birth to a bigger-than-Elliot person, like a still life she'd infused with extra light and better colors. In the gospel according to Karen, Elliot was perfect.

Now, getting out of the car, he talked about the traffic jam on the Saw Mill, the reservation he'd made at a restaurant famous for duck breast and the book by Elisabeth Kübler-Ross he'd personally leather bound and was giving Mama today. Gaby thought that a book on death and dying did not seem like a feel-good present, but said nothing.

"Where's Dieter?" she asked her sister when Susanna appeared without him. Susanna, with her

résumé of top grades and academic awards, her portfolio of letters of praise and laudatory recommenda-
tions, had made her intellectual mark all through
school; it was as if her sisters had siphoned off the
best genes. All her adult years Gaby had had to be
the little actress, chin up, pretend a confidence she
didn't feel.

"Kaiser-Gelb is opening a new hotel." Susanna
shrugged, and it was obvious he was on the road
again and she didn't want to get into it. Susanna,
who looked a bit tired herself and should never have
worn that pants outfit—why *lilac?*—reached into her
purse and pulled out the card she'd bought Mama,
with the gift certificate tucked inside. They stood in
the driveway and took turns signing it with Susanna's
Mont Blanc, Dieter's Christmas present to his wife.
Susanna had never forgiven her husband for giving
his daughter a laptop and her a pen at Christmas,
had actually offered it to Gaby, smiling wickedly and
saying, "You can do German crossword puzzles with
it. It automatically umlauts."

Mama's looks were an improvement. Aunt Ruth
had taken her to Harold yesterday, and he'd touched
up her roots and given her a shorter version of one
of his swooping do's, and the new girl had given Mama
a "therapeutic manicure," creaming and rubbing her
hands while surf tapes played. So here was Mama at
the door, the spiffed up version in an unfamiliar suit
of pale rose plaid that almost camouflaged its being
too big. She had on sparkling faceted gold earrings,
cheeks touched with blush and bright lipstick, and
while she wasn't the old Mama, nowhere near, she
looked presentable, if not pretty.

Mama sat square in the center of her taupe velvet
couch in the den and smiled at the leather-bound
book, and at them. It was a smile that Gaby recognized

as full of obligation, not heart. She said that yesterday
Daddy had made a funny sound she'd never heard
him make before, almost as if he was trying to speak.
Everyone fell silent and then Karen got up from her
chair to sit next to Mama on the couch. She put her
arm around her shoulders and wished her a happy
Mother's Day.

"Shouldn't we give Mama her present now?" To
Gaby the gift seemed like a rope thrown to someone
at the bottom of a well. She imagined the old Mama
revived, fussing with her hair, her table settings, her
roses, *laughing* again.

Mama put on her glasses, smiled at the Hallmark
card (a kitten telling a cat, "Sorry about the stretch
marks, Mom") and began reading the parchment
gift certificate, which was decorated with a gilt border
and a pair of dancers in black silhouette.

"You're not serious." She looked from one to the
other and back to the gift certificate.

"Yes. Aunt Ruth took me to lunch and she spilled
the beans!"

"What beans?"

"Well, Mama, didn't you tell her that you always
wanted to learn the tango?"

Mama shook her head, took off her glasses, and
placed the gift certificate on the coffee table. "How
much did you crazy kids pay for this?"

Karen was standing next to Elliot now, and took
his hand, as if for support. "It's a gift you can't return.
You've got to call and make an appointment."

"An appointment! And when I learn how to do the
tango," Mama said, looking at Karen and shaking
her head, "who do you suppose I will be doing it
with? Your father barely knows how to fox-trot, let
alone do the—"

Mama, get real! Gaby wanted to run over, grab Mama
by the shoulders and shake her. Daddy would never

get up out of bed again; why couldn't she, why *wouldn't* she, get that through her head?

"So that's it," Susanna said, pulling on the jacket she'd tossed on a chair, "It's all settled. You'll call the number on the certificate tomorrow, Mama. Speak to a woman there named Heather; she's very sweet and she's waiting to hear from you. Now, happy Mother's Day, Mrs. Kessler, and let's all go eat duck breast, or whatever."

CHAPTER NINE

Julie had already procrastinated, postponed, then canceled the first appointment, and now, struggled to overcome the desire to cancel the second. The girls had tried so hard to please her and instead, created this Everest of obligation, and here she finally was, parking her car at an expired meter across the street from the dreary building on whose second floor the place was located, feeling one inch away from desperation. What would Gilbert say if he could see her now, climbing these seedy wooden steps to go ahead with life, to dance without him?

She had spent an hour with him this afternoon, kissing a cheek that was so hollow it looked as if every tooth had been pulled out of his head. She had whispered in his ear, "I'm only going through with it for them. They'd be crushed if I didn't," and waited for a sound or a sigh of response, but all she heard was the quiet, unrelenting, perverse *sssss* of the machinery to which he was attached.

Heather was a young woman with a boy cut and a tattoo of a Star of David on one upper arm and a crucifix on the other. In her mind's eye Harriet pictured Heather with dark waves of hair to her shoulders, a big improvement for a pretty receptionist who now looked ready for a uniform and guerrilla warfare.

"Nice to meet you at last," she said warmly, when Julie unfolded the gift certificate and put it in her hand. They had had so many appointment rescheduling conversations on the telephone they already felt acquainted. Heather pointed to a fake-leather settee in the reception area. Taras, her instructor, was through with his last lesson and would be out in just a minute.

"Terrence?" Julie asked.

"Taras," Heather corrected. "Rhymes with Paris."

"What kind of a name is Taras?" Julie wanted to know, but Heather had taken a telephone call and was flipping the pages of her appointment book; commerce could obviously not be postponed. Julie went to the settee to wait and thought for a moment of simply jumping ship, dashing for the door. Taras was a name that did not inspire positive vibes, and for that matter, neither did the dowdy New Rochelle Fred Astaire Dance Studio.

Why she had expected a Hispanic instructor she couldn't say, but Taras was a surprise. He reminded Julie of the young man who used to deliver her dry cleaning, who always looked very crisp, as if he himself had just stepped out of a cellophane bag. They both had a very straight nose and short upper lip that reminded Julie of the fishermen she and Gil had watched pulling in their nets in Crete when they did their Greek Isle trip four years ago. His fishermanlike dark hair looked both unruly and just-combed wet. It must be some sort of gel that made it look forever damp. Julie knew the girls would roll their eyes, but

Julie, in a snap decision, decided she liked the sheen. It gave Taras a professional tango look.

She expected, also, an accent, the flavor of a foreigner, maybe a satin shirt and shiny black trousers, but Taras was certainly American, born and bred, judging by his chinos and first English sentence. "Mrs. Kessler? Hello. My name is Taras, I'll be your instructor." and then, "Would you come with me?" He led the way into the ballroom. Self-confident through and through. Nothing like the dry-cleaning delivery man, who called her ma'am in every sentence and couldn't look her in the eye. This Taras was obviously a take-charge person, a dance studio kingpin with big shoulders and—she just noticed—half of his right index finger missing. She immediately thought of Gilbert's grandfather, dead forty or fifty years, a photo in a family album, who'd had his three fingers bitten off when he poked them into a zebra's cage at the zoo. This missing finger of Taras's immediately aroused in Julie a great sympathy and some curiosity.

It so distracted her, that minutes went by in the ballroom before she actually looked around. A small high school gym is what the place looked like, the walls mirrored floor to ceiling, the floor polished to a basketball court shine. In one corner, an elaborate system of stereo equipment, in another corner a plastic ficus, and in-between, a couple wrapping up what looked like a first fox-trot lesson. The woman, Julie noted, was an even older student than she. White hair and gold slippers, and a wide I'm-having-fun smile, as the instructor walked her to the door to the last chords of *Satin Doll*.

"Is this the first dance lesson you've ever had, Mrs. Kessler?" Taras was facing her on the dance floor, a politely interested look on a face that Julie sensed was hiding deep-as-the-ocean boredom. Here was a young man who would probably rather be skydiving, sleeping, or driving to Atlantic City, a closet clock-watcher filled all day with suppressed yawns for the necessity of cashing in his weekly paycheck. Julie felt sorry for him, looking into the face of a fifty-three-year-old woman, probably one of dozens of suburban matron customers he'd already led through steps and spins and swirls this week.

She told him it was her first class ever, except that of course her brother Dickie had taught her the jitter-bug and box step back when she was in junior high. Dickie would have quite a laugh to see her now.

That was fine with Taras. Not by word or deed did he let on that he wanted to be elsewhere, or that he wished she were twenty and about to learn the tango topless. He put her left hand on his beige-on-beige striped cotton sleeve and showed her where it must always rest. Never on the shoulder, never. Just below, on the upper arm, where she would sense him lead-ing. His right arm circled her back. He must always lead, he explained, that was the big part of this lesson: learning to follow, not only an instructor, but what-ever future partners she would encounter.

"I wish you hadn't said that," Julie responded.

Taras's eyes widened. They were the same very green as Karen's. Kiwi, the girls called it.

Now she would have to talk about it, having defi-nitely decided not to. They were still face to face, her hand on his sleeve, his right hand, the one with half a finger, on her back. "Well, my husband, Gilbert, he's in the hospital. He's very, very—" she stopped. Very what? She couldn't finish. It sometimes came over her like this, a temporary shutdown.

"Oh, he's sick. I'm sorry," Taras said.

"An accident."

Taras's very dark eyebrows went up. "An accident?"

He was probably one of those rubbernecks who stalled traffic on the highways just to glimpse shat-tered fenders and spilled blood. "I'm actually here to get it off my mind," she said pointedly, trying for a softening smile. *Be kind!* Taras instantly dropped the subject, obviously adept at human relations, possibly due to job training. "The best therapy."

He moved on into what Julie presumed was the Fred Astaire Dance Studio's boilerplate patter. "All dancing is simply walking to a beat. If you can walk, you can dance," his voice scrolled. Wondering if she'd worn the right shoes, worried she'd never remember a thing he was about to teach her, wishing the lesson were already over, she kept an I'm-listening look cooperatively fixed on her face. Although, Dickie had always said she was smooth on the dance floor. *Smooth,* his word.

"Every American dance begins the same way. The man takes a step forward with his left foot, and the lady takes one back with her right. Will you remember that?"

She would remember that.

He was serious as a mortician, following what must be instructor outlines for student-teacher basics, strict studio protocol. He lifted her right hand with his left and took a formal vis-à-vis position, looking over her shoulder. "Okay, it's easy. It's just slow, slow, slow, quick, quick. Slow, slow, slow, quick-quick." She repeated the words as he said them. He held her hand firmly and began walking her through it; "slow, slow, slow," she recited to herself. They walked it out maybe three more times, maybe four.

"Very good. I'm going to go turn on the stereo, and we'll try it to music." Taras left her standing alone in the middle of the polished floor. She watched him walk across the room, then glanced at her image in the wall-to-wall wall-to-ceiling mirror. To her own eye she looked like a statuette in navy blue, so blah, colorless, insignificant—a lifeless doll without her husband. She felt like a nobody, an inanimate object, simulating life. She hated this pants suit, it was baggy and shapeless, the color drab; why had she ever bought it? Never her color, navy blue.

She would take it to Second Chance or better yet, give it to Mariadora first thing tomorrow to send back to Honduras. Gilbert had never known that whenever Julie gave Mariadora clothes, she always tucked cash into the pockets. She'd seen photographs of the Honduran homestead; Mariadora's mother was back there, suffering with rheumatoid arthritis, trying to keep a corrugated tin roof over her head.

More than once Julie had thought about fate's flip of the coin. While she and her family lived in Scarsdale with a cornucopia of privileges that included the Garden of Eden bathroom upstairs, the living room Steinway baby grand no one seemed to play anymore downstairs, the global selection of edibles in her refrigerator and the attentions of a gardener who weekly clipped the topiaries and checked her bumper-to-bumper roses outside, Mariadora's mother often couldn't afford medical attention or new shoes.

In the early morning hours, when she was sleepless, Julie tried to manage her guilt and sorrow, sort out its logic, consider and reject one ridiculous premise of cause and effect after another. Sometimes she imagined that cruel punishments were a payback for smugness, excess, and other crimes of the rich.

One day she might get up the nerve, sell everything and move out of Scarsdale. Go to an island somewhere, where life was simpler. And then again, told herself that this is where she belonged and this is where she'd stay. In her home, near her daughters.

The *Yo soy el Tango* burst out of the stereo, sounding as if it were coming from the ceiling, walls and everywhere, and in a moment, Taras was back, positioning her firmly, his hand authoritatively on her back.

"Okay, Mrs. K, let's dance," he said, giving her a standard issue smile. One front tooth slightly overlapped the other, the very same imperfection for which Gaby had worn braces for two years. On closer examination, he was not really at all like the dry-cleaning delivery man. He was stockier and taller and had the self-assurance of a senator. If someone came up to him and stuck a microphone in his face, she imagined he could come up with something slick to say on the spot. It was as if he had the equanimity she had recently lost. He half closed his eyes, waited for the proper beat to begin. "Let's wait for the music," he said. Then he opened his eyes and genuflected, his signal to her to begin, slid his polished black shoe confidently forward. Julie put her right foot back, and mentally recited the *slow-slow-slow* mantra, trying to feel the music with her feet.

Gilbert and she had seen a stone-deaf man dancing the rumba on a cruise around the tip of South America, and now Julie remembered seeing him move in perfect rhythm. It was said he could feel the vibrations of the music on the floor under his feet. She herself felt that resonance now. As they danced, she caught glimpses of herself with Taras as he slid forward and she stepped back, a navy blue marionette, held in the beige-on-beige striped arms of a tall, thirtyish dance instructor who might rather be windsurfing or channel surfing or in bed with his sweetheart.

Thirty minutes since she'd walked into the ballroom, just half an hour, and here she was, actually dancing the tango. Well, walking it through, anyway. "Don't look down at your feet. Don't look down," Taras reminded her now and again. She thought of it as a metaphor, she would try never to look down. *Forgive me, Gil.*

"You're doing swell, Mrs. K," Taras said, and she felt that maybe he meant it; maybe she really did have grace, a knack for learning new steps. On the other hand, *don't be so gullible!* Taras probably said exactly the same thing to every student. So far, she had not tripped, not misstepped once, so maybe she was indeed doing "swell." In any case, she would quote him to the girls; they'd be so pleased.

When the lesson was finished Taras walked her to the door. "Do you mind if I ask you something?" he said, touching her sleeve.

If he intended to ask about the accident, she would simply refuse to answer, maybe pretend she hadn't heard. In the last six months, she'd become used to fending off questions she didn't want to answer.

"Is there any reason why you're wearing a rubber band around your wrist?" He looped his finger under it and looked at her with a perfectly ingenuous smile. He obviously thought she'd slipped it on for some unknown reason and absentmindedly forgotten it there.

It caught her off guard. *He's certainly observant.* "Oh, for heaven's sakes," she said. Only the girls had commented, Karen most recently. "How long are you going to walk around looking like an office temp, Mama?" Julie touched it with her finger, hesitated, thinking it over for a moment, not knowing exactly what to say without using the word "psychiatrist". Without, God forbid, opening up about Gilbert. Trying to sound offhand and casual, she gave him a bit of a throwaway smile. "I've been, um, preoccupied, a little harried," she said.

"A little Harry?" Taras parlayed it into a playful bit of comic relief. "You've been a Little Harry? Now you're a bigger Harry?"

He made her smile, had a certain innate knack for breaking ice, connecting with the clientele by parceling out a bit of humor. This aptitude must stand him in very good stead around here. "I'm going to call you Harry from now on, okay?'' he said. ''I think it's friendlier than Mrs. Kessler, don't you?''

''Definitely friendlier, yes.'' Julie, letting out a little embarrassed laugh, took the rubber band off her wrist and looked for a wastebasket. Not seeing one, she handed the elastic to him. ''You can throw it away for me, Taras. Would you?'' She was thinking, *I'll get another one if I need it,* as she went to Heather's desk to make an appointment for her next lesson. *Harry.* That's cute, she thought, as Heather put her name down in the book for next week.

CHAPTER TEN

Dieter was hacking and sneezing upstairs in the master bedroom and had been for almost a week. His bronchial viral infection had kept him home and in bed, coming on the heels of yet another "mini"-transatlantic hop and today, although he was feeling better and had decided on a short walk around the neighborhood, had turned quiet and uncharacteristically sedentary. Whenever they were in the same room, Susanna felt the static crackling between them.

Mama was on her way over. She had a freezer full of Ruthie DiLorenzo's nutritional offerings, and some of Mariadora's mystery food and was bringing them to Dieter. It was Sunday. Mama hadn't been here to the house since That Night, and it had been her idea to drive up to Bedford today. That was, in Susanna's estimation, a Homeric step forward, although she and Gaby had just yesterday had a major difference of opinion on that. Gaby as much as told Susanna off:

"Mama is still sitting around in Daddy's robes, looking ten years older than she did last summer. She hasn't gone back to Second Chance, and when I was over at the house last week, she was up in the attic, going through old boxes of photographs, inhaling all that dust, with tearstains on both her cheeks."

Susanna wanted to slam down the telephone on her little know-it-all princess sister. Here Gaby was, about to be married to an absolute peach, and who would guess it? She was moody as hell half the time and more than ever negative about everything. Not only that, Susanna might call her on a Wednesday night, never get a return call until Friday. "So what have you been up to?" Susanna could ask in a casual, non-probing way and get nothing but zigzags for answers. One would think Little Miss Mystery was stealing jewels or dealing in crack.

By the time Mama arrived, Dieter was back in bed. Susanna hustled Mama out to the patio and sat her at the tempered glass table Dieter had dragged out of the garage on the first warm day last week. Mama immediately noticed the azaleas just coming into bloom along the driveway, and offered Susanna some rose cuttings with an apology: "I can never seem to hybridize the white streaks out of these Elizabeth Taylors!" and Susanna was heartened; no question about it, her mother was back in touch, and, if she was coming around, it was without a doubt thanks to Fred Astaire. She asked her mother about her lessons first thing. "I'm enjoying every step," Mama said, sounding actually lighthearted, and added that she'd brought along a "little show and tell." Susanna would always remember her mother this way, a shopping bag in each hand, pulling small gifts, food items or clipped copies of *Vanity Fair* or *Travel & Leisure* out of Saks or Neiman Marcus shopping bags.

She had made a salmon soufflé that couldn't wait,

so after putting Ruthie DiLorenzo's perishables into
the refrigerator, Susanna brought a pitcher of raspberry iced tea out to the patio, and that cole slaw
with red peppers her mother always liked. In the
refrigerator, she had the real whipped cream ready
to sweeten the strawberries she'd picked up fresh at
the market this morning; a special lunch, anyone but
Dieter would say. In four years of marriage she had
not been able to change his eating habits any more
than she'd been able to turn him into an American
citizen.

It was still a bit cool out here, but if they went
inside, Dieter might overhear what she had to say, or
worse, want to join them. Susanna put Mama's chair
with its back to the sun so she wouldn't get cold
and want to move inside, then watched her mother
surreptitiously as she began eating. Mama was not
just picking at her salad, but actually scooping it up
with her fork, eating *heartily*. She had pinked up her
cheeks again but this time, blush or no, her complexion had a naturally summer glow. Gaby was wrong;
Mama looked as fit and healthy as she had last spring,
very perky in what looked like a new black-and-white
polka dot blouse and matching scarf. And, she
inquired about Dieter, was he still running a temperature, could he be talked into eating some of Ruthie's
eggplant and mushroom rollatini?

Susanna leaned forward and lowered her voice.
"I'm so angry at him, Mama." She put down her fork
and plunged in, full steam ahead: The way he jumped
whenever the phone rang. If she answered it, there
would be Liesel's voice, "Is my *Vater* there?" and not
another word, not even a 'how are you?' from the girl.
"Does she think I'm a bloody *switchboard* operator?"
Susanna asked, her voice rising. And the goddamn
stubborn way Dieter refused to talk about her own

maternal needs. Just yesterday, she broached the subject, right after she'd made him a Schnitzel à la Holstein, with a fried egg on top, the way his ex-wife had explained he liked it, and then tried to engage him in a conversation about his sperm and her egg. Sat on the side of their bed, fixed his pillows, while sick as he was, he cleaned his plate. " 'I'm almost thirty-three years old,' I said to him," Susanna told her mother, " 'and if not now, when? Soon my eggs will be using walkers!' "

Mama put out a sympathetic hand, touching Susanna's arm.

"And you want to know his response? He said, 'I'm getting old. Now I vant to *be* the baby, not *have* one.' " Susanna, over the last few years, had honed her mimicking skills.

"I feel incomplete. Look at this house. All those empty rooms. We should be parents. We're healthy. We can afford it. We're both damn good breadwinners."

Her mother smiled her own, wonderful, familiar smile.

"Antiques, professional landscaping, two Audis in the garage, four acres in Bedford? Cakewinners, I'd say."

"Right. And I deserve motherhood."

Mama's smile went. "You never wanted babies. You wanted travel. You agreed no children. Is it a baby you want or is it actually a ball and chain on Dieter, disguised by a diaper?" Mama had not moved from her chair but it was as if she had stood up, put a hand on her hip and wagged a finger at Susanna.

"Dieter is how old? Forty-eight? You know how old your father was when you were born?"

Was it too much to ask that her father would not creep into today's conversation? Just the weight of his name threw her mother's judgments completely out of whack. She'd married at eighteen herself, gotten pregnant on her wedding night and despite the mores of those Golden Oldie days, and the fact that Mama had not much more formal education than some college humanities courses fitted in between travel, babies and Second Chance, Susanna had always considered her mother perspicacious and filled with some sort of rare, innate wisdom. She had wished to get all her mess with Dieter out on the table, pull some sagacious words from Mama's mouth about what to do to fix her life, and now Daddy was in the equation again, the living-dead intruder into all of Kessler family life. "What does this have to do with *Daddy?*" she snapped.

Mama looked down at her plate, waved away an invisible bug with her hand, which Susanna saw as looking shaky. It was the left hand, the one with the wedding band, and what Karen called "The Hopeless Diamond." Daddy had bought Mama a huge one for their twenty-fifth wedding anniversary but it stayed mostly in the bank vault. The engagement ring with the tiny stone was the one she still wore. It had taken Daddy's last penny, back when he was still a poor postgrad with a degree in accounting, working as a gofer in his father's electric timer business. Mama always said the karats were less but the sparkle was more, and the ring represented for Susanna the essence of her mother's platinum values. The sight of it now upset her further; her mother was cool, unsympathetic, unmotherly, and didn't she understand a person could change?

"Don't you want *grandchildren?*" she exploded, and Mama's lip trembled. "Oh, I'm sorry. I'm so sorry, Mama!" Susanna's own salmon soufflé lunch was spoiled. Her mother's downcast eyes, the sun throwing shadows that made hollows in her cheeks, unnerved her. She jumped up, began clearing her own place, her half-eaten lunch. Mama put down her fork and stopped eating too, and there was a silence, one of those bleak spaces where one's mind races in its vacuum trying to come up with something—anything—to fill it. "Well, tell me about Fred Astaire," Susanna finally blurted. "Does he come back from the dead every Thursday night?"

Mama stopped watching the birds. "I brought documentary proof of my appreciation," she said, and began bustling through her shopping bags, pulling out an old issue of the *New Yorker* that described the murder of a chef in one of the hotels in the Kaiser-Gelb hotel chain and would interest Dieter, two packages of glycerine soap of the many people kept bringing her for Gilbert, a box of Russell Stover chocolate-covered cherries from the women at Second Chance and the photo Heather, the receptionist, had taken of her dancing with Taras in the Fred Astaire Studio ballroom. She'd had three copies made, one for each of her daughters, and had put each into small seashell frames she'd picked up on sale right there in New Rochelle in one of the stores on Main Street.

"Well, look at him!" Susanna said, raising her eyebrows. "Whoopee, Mama! Better looking than Fred himself!"

"He looks like the dry-cleaning man, I forget his name, the one who used to pick up for Ambassador Cleaning, doesn't he?"

"You mean Gerard? Not in the least! Gerard was a *dork!* This man is a *hunk*. What's his name?"

"Taras."

"Taras?" Susanna said. "Did you say Taras?"

"Isn't that a strange name? He had to spell it for me."

"It's a Russian name. After *Taras Bulba,* I bet. I

read it in the original. Oh, God, all the trouble I had with Gogol and the Cyrillic alphabet, and now look. I've forgotten everything I learned. I do remember Taras Bulba, though. He was a famous Cossack.''

"Taras's roots may be Russian, but he used to live in Louisiana. That's all I know about him. We don't really talk. We just dance.''

"Then how did you find out where he was from?''

"Last time I told him I thought he behaved like a real southern gentleman, the way he treats me, I mean, helping me on with my jacket, and walking me to the door, so very polite in every way, and he said, 'Bingo! I used to live in Baton Rouge, Louisiana.' It was cute, the way he said 'Louisiana', like I wouldn't know where Baton Rouge was. And that's all I know. That and half his right index finger is missing. And last week, I came a few minutes early and he was eating coconut jellybeans. Remember, how I always tried to find coconut jellybeans at that candy place in the mall?''

"Oh, my God, Mama,'' Susanna said, squinting another look at the photo. "He's named after a Cossack and you both like coconut jellybeans? Be careful you don't fall in love with him!'' Susanna wanted to take it back, but Mama had taken it as the little joke it was intended to be and even managed a little smile, saying, "It's not a big risk,'' as she rummaged through her shopping bag again. "So! Last but not least! Do you remember this, dear?'' she asked, and pulled out Susanna's old wooden cat clock with the hour and minute paws. "I thought I'd given it away long ago, but I found it in the attic last week. Do you want it, or should I just take it to Second Chance?''

As soon as her mother left, Susanna brought the clock up to show Dieter. He was sitting up in bed, half asleep, the TV off, the remote control still in his hand. "Dieter, are you awake?''

"Yes."

"How are you feeling?"

"Better."

"Mama found this old wooden clock in her attic. My father taught me to tell time with it."

Dieter took the clock and examined it.

"I had a big cardboard clock in my room ven I was a child. It was a ship's wheel, but of course there was no A.M., no P.M. It was just one to twenty-four hours, the European vay. Better logic, I think." He handed the clock back to Susanna, pushed his white linen feather pillows up and shifted himself higher in bed.

Susanna didn't think it was better logic—watches only had room for twelve numerals, after all—but she didn't want to argue about this, or, right now, about anything. "I'm going to hang it in the empty room next to the new bathroom and possibly some-day, who knows? Maybe you'll agree that that room will become a nursery."

Dieter half closed his eyes. "Please, not again, not now, Schatz," he said, with a long-suffering bronchitic sigh. It started him coughing again.

Susanna left the room and stood holding the clock, looking at its faded whiskers and kitty paws, her head leaning against the blue and white feather wallpaper of the upstairs hall. "Oh, fuck you in two languages, Dieter," she said under her breath, and a few minutes later, when his coughing had died down, she marched through the bedroom into their adjacent bathroom, opened the medicine cabinet and reached for the pink plastic disk on the first shelf.

Dieter had turned on the TV and was immersed in Monty Hall pitching denture cream on CNN.

She hesitated, holding the pillbox in her hand, then put it back into the cabinet. A moment later, when she heard Dieter turn the TV off with the remote control and pick up the telephone next to the bed, she retrieved it. With her heart pounding, she lifted the lid of the toilet, threw in what was left of her supply of birth control pills, flushed, and watched the swirl of the water as they disappeared into the waste pipe with it.

CHAPTER ELEVEN

Taras put the Julio Iglesias disk in place and held out his arms. Julie put her left hand on the spot right below his shoulder, slid her right hand into his left palm. She'd mastered Steps One through Five, remembered to place herself correctly for the side, the closed and the promenade positions, knew enough not to move her shoulders and remembered—most of the time—not to look down. Taras had told her at the end of the third session that she was doing eighty percent better than his other students. She allowed herself to soak up the modest praise, but suspected it as being a bit of a sales pitch. Her gift lessons were due to expire, and of course it was part of his job to try to get her to take out her credit card, sign up to learn everything from the allemande to the waltz, wasn't it?

Even so, today Julie felt that in Taras's arms, she was light as Styrofoam and barely skimming the floor. This time she had worn a deep blue skirt that billowed a bit, and shiny patent leather shoes with high heels. The fabric of her skirt—it had a random pattern of

green leaves and white and yellow buds—fluttered
and swooped around her knees, and the heels of
her shoes clicked against the polished wooden floor.
Catching glimpses of herself in the mirrors left and
right, she saw herself, her skirt swinging, dancing a
smooth, fully actualized, totally accomplished Latin-
American Tango. And, in only four sessions! She
would thank the girls again for a gift that turned out
to be a tourniquet, a prison break and deliverance
all in one. She felt as if she had always known how
to do this Slow, Slow, Slow Quick-Quick step, that if
she were pulled out of a deep sleep, she'd jump to
the floor and move as well as any Latin-American
dance virtuoso. Of course, she had to concentrate,
miss no steps, be alert for sudden turns and twists,
and keep looking not into Taras's eyes, as one would
imagine, but over his right shoulder, into space. Dancing with Taras seemed as basic as dreaming.

He had a wardrobe of stripes, it seemed. This week's
had a crisp white collar and fresh white cuffs, the
body stripes in variegated colors, reminding her of
the awnings over the dining terrace at the Scarsdale
Country Club. Taras carried about him a *GQ* look,
unnatural for a dance teacher who one would think
might be somewhat perspired or crumpled so late in
the working day. She wanted to ask if he changed
clothes between clients, but it seemed too personal
a question. She was not about to scrape a friendship
out of business rapport.

When they danced, all of life flew out of her head.
When they moved across the floor together, even
Gilbert, to whom she'd brought the old photos she'd
dug out of the attic last week, was excised from her
thoughts. He had not reacted to any of the snapshots,
even the one taken by their breakfast waiter on the
little balcony outside their room at Devon de Mer in

Juan-les-Pins. His eyes, fluttering open ever so slightly, might or might not have actually sent the images into the pathways to his brain. Julie had no one left to ask if there was that possibility; only Mariadora listened. "The mister is still there," she said, confirming Julie's deepest wish and obstinate suspicion. "The dear mon hasn't left us yet, Missuz." Now, the steady arms of Taras around her, the steps and the music, had become Julie's anesthesia.

"I'd recommend you to anyone as a teacher," she told him quite spontaneously, as they walked off the floor together. When he allowed them to show, which wasn't that often, she caught a glimpse of his overlapping teeth. "Did you know?" he answered, "that one of your eyes is bluer than the other?" A comment that could have slid out flirtatiously, was delivered as a statement of fact. Taras might have been announcing a change in the price of postage stamps.

On the other hand, this was the most personal remark he'd made in the four weeks she'd been dancing with him.

"One is darker," he said. "The left one."

Eyes of Blue. Julie remembered sitting in a friend's garage listening to Gilbert's little band practice. The boys' repertoire was limited, but they could play, *Five Foot Two, Eyes of Blue,* and almost never hit a sour note. And she remembered the trumpet at Gilbert's lips, his cheeks puffed out, the way his shoe tapped the cement floor in rhythm, and then, the wink he sent her that meant, "I'm playing for you."

"No one ever mentioned that to me before," Julie said to Taras.

He offered her a stick of gum.

"I don't chew gum," she said, and thanked him anyway.

"Next time you're near a mirror, check it out. The right one's much lighter. No kidding."

* * *

It was Heather's birthday, and on a table in the small, cluttered reception area, there was a white birthday cake covered with blue roses, green leaves and 'Happy birthday Heather' in chocolate script, with two candles, one shaped like a two and one a three, already burned down and blown out, standing in the center. A bottle of white wine stood uncorked in a cooler, next to stacks of paper plates and plastic wine glasses, and doing the honors with a cake knife was Heather's look-alike sister. There was also a boyfriend and some assorted drop-ins, a couple Julie recognized as other Fred Astaire clients, all of whom were digging into their cake with plastic forks, and discussing the recent tornado in Texas.

"I'll cut you a piece," Taras said, taking Julie by the elbow, and leading her toward the little crowd.

Julie had no intention of staying for Heather's birthday party, but she didn't want to seem standoffish, and by the time she had reached for her pocketbook, stashed behind a shoji screen next to Heather's desk, Taras was handing her a piece of cake on a paper plate, a napkin and fork.

"I got you a piece with a flower, 'Harry'," he said, and put up his thumb. "It's who you know."

He walked her to the small three-seater green couch against the wall, took off some magazines someone had thrown on its cushions, and told her to "buckle your seat belt" and wait while he brought her a glass of wine. *All right, I'll stay,* and looking down at the piece of cake on her plate, Julie commanded herself to enjoy it or at least pretend to. She raised her fork and wished Heather a happy birthday and admired the cubic zirconia tennis bracelet she came over to show her, a gift from her boyfriend, the one with the T-shirt that had the Nike logo in front and the 'Just Did It' in back. Harriet told her the cake was wonderful, and Taras came back with the wine and his own piece of cake and sat down next to her. She asked if he didn't have another student coming in? He looked at his watch. "In forty-five minutes, if she's on time. Gives us time to party, Harry. You really don't mind if I call you Harry?"

Julie figured not forty-five, but seven or eight minutes, the length of time it would take her to finish both cake and wine and maneuver out, without looking rude or snobbish. She told him her brother Dickie had a friend named Harry, who looked just like Gary Cooper. She didn't think Taras knew who Gary Cooper was. She sneaked a look at her watch.

"So, how is your husband?" Taras inquired after telling her that growing up he'd had a mutt named Harry that lived to be twenty and understood forty different commands.

It was a question Julie had to answer what seemed like a thousand times a week. At the bank, the dentist, the post office, in person or on the telephone, the polite, obligatory question to which there was no answer, Julie now had a new rote reply: "Best as could be expected." Taras raised his plastic glass of wine. "What's his name?"

"My husband's?"

"Yes."

"Gilbert."

"To Gilbert," Taras said, and touched her plastic glass with his. She tried not to be caught looking at the half-finger.

"To Gilbert," she said, and she sipped the $6 Pinot Grigio without actually tasting it. She pushed out of her mind what he'd say if he saw her sitting here drinking it, pictured his lips turning disdainfully down at the corners. *Don't be a snob, Gil; they're nice people.* She let a moment pass, then asked Taras if he was of Russian descent, and had he been named after Taras Bulba? She repeated what she remembered of what Susanna had told her. Gogol, a hero, a literary classic, and wasn't there an opera by the same name?

"So what do you know? You're the first person I've ever met who heard of Taras Bulba, but actually I was named after a poet, Taras Shevchenko. But how'd you know all this anyway?" Taras had stopped eating and was holding his glass near his lifted eyebrows.

"My daughter. She was a student of Russian in graduate school." Julie had always secretly loved dropping that tidbit into her conversation. Simultaneously tried to keep it from sounding like the obvious mother-boasting that it was. But then, falling in love had wedged between their daughter and a Ph.D. It took Julie and Gilbert a time to forgive Dieter. "Unfortunately, she left school."

Taras had stopped drinking and seemed, for the moment, to look impressed. His cheeks had turned rosy. It was the wine and the room temperature, too high. The air-conditioning in the studio was iffy.

"My parents were Ukrainian," he volunteered after a moment, as if he had to think it over. "I'm White Russian. All my life I was stuck with this name, which is real big in Russia, when I really wanted to be called Tom, like my father. And my last name was Dobre. When the kids weren't making fun of my first name, they were making fun of my last name, calling me Doberman. As soon as I turned twenty-one, I translated my name into English. Dobre means good, so now I'm Taras Goodman."

"I like your name, you know, I really do," Julie said, and she polished off the wine. Julie's usual preference was Sancerre or maybe a good Chardonnay, but this was smooth going down, not bad for something out of a plastic cup.

Taras wanted to pour her another, but she refused, perhaps too vehemently. "I have to drive home, don't forget." Her face felt severe, tight, as if she'd just scrubbed it.

Since the accident, she'd had to regain her confidence behind the wheel. The drive to Susanna's in Bedford in her reliable Volvo had taken much push and determination.

"So, Harry, what happened to Gilbert?" Taras leaned toward her, a bit too intimately, she thought. *The wine, definitely.* "It was vehicular, huh?"

Julie blinked a few times in surprise, reining in her desire to jump up and run down the rickety steps and never come back. Did Mr. Dancing Stripes think she was about to answer any personal questions? And, how could he possibly know about her accident?

"Did someone tell you that?"

Taras got the look of apology around his mouth. "Heather? I guess it was her. She mentioned it last week."

But, of course. When the girls had ordered Julie's lessons, they tipped the receptionist off, no doubt about it. Not that it was a big secret, having been written up in the *Scarsdale Inquirer,* the *Journal News* and two city tabloids. But, that was six months ago.

Taras put his hand around the cuff of her blouse and looked penitently into her eyes. "So it's a barbed wire subject, Harry?"

She softened; he was sorry, *he means no harm,* but Julie couldn't scramble up a change of subject. A cement chunk of embarrassed silence passed between them. "So, what do you do when you're not dancing?" she finally thought to ask. She sensed she'd made it clear as the plastic glass in her hand she wouldn't talk about Gilbert, ever.

"I take care of my son. I got sole custody, Harry," he said.

Julie felt her lips curve reflexively into a smile. Gilbert had once said that paternity softened everyone's edges. Then he'd said that after having three daughters himself, he'd even lost his edges.

Julie thought paternity added maturity. And didn't

sole custody say it all? She looked at Taras more closely. "You must be a good father," she said.

"I got no choice, Harry. Those were the steps *I* had to learn." He stopped, gazed at some empty place in the distance. "And, you know how kids can introduce you to God one minute and convince you there's a devil the next."

When she thought about her lesson on the way home, it was the look on his his face when Taras said, "I take care of my son." He was so young himself, so businesslike, but just for a blink, the guard went down and he looked age-old and, somehow, well, *stung*.

CHAPTER TWELVE

On the way up to Shippan Point in Stamford, Mama was wearing a flowered sundress, nice straw hat and sunglasses. She was looking at her watch, doing that a lot lately, and for no reason, since she obviously didn't really give a damn what time it was. On the other hand, Gaby was thrilled not only to discern that Mama had been to the hairdresser and was back to smelling one hundred percent Carolina Herrera, but to see the rubber band gone from her wrist. It had taken the dance instructor to throw it into a trash can. Gaby had gotten the little framed photograph of them dancing together and he definitely was not hard to look at. A well-made dude, as Karen once said about Wally. In the photo, Mama was *smiling big*.

"It's not just the ordinary tango," Mama said, continuing a conversation dropped two exits back. "Taras is also showing me advanced steps." Her mother's feet were actually tapping on the cork mats on the floor of the car. "It's almost like a little box step. One two three. Fourfive. Then we part, I circle him, very theatrical. One two three. Fourfive. I'll show you one day."

"You're really enjoying yourself there, aren't you, Mama?"

Her mother's voice took on an edge of something that sounded like guilt. "Well, you know your father played the trumpet all through school. That's how he met your uncle Dickie; they were in a little college band together in St. Louis. Dickie was the drummer."

Gaby knew the trumpet story backward and forward and her mind defaulted to Stretch. At the wedding, would he ask her to dance? Even with his wife sitting there in her wheelchair? For one manic moment, she was tempted to pour out her heart to her mother.

"The speed limit is fifty here, isn't it dear?" Mama asked, luckily breaking the circuit. If her mother found out about her affair, she'd really unfurl! Gaby slowed down.

"So your father was always in a band, playing for everyone else. That's why he never really learned any steps. And that's why he didn't even like to get up on a dance floor."

"He danced at Susanna's wedding. And at Karen's."

"Just for the video, dear. And not the tango. Certainly never the tango." Mama's voice practically dropped back into her throat, and Gaby wished she hadn't said anything about her sisters' weddings. It was like underlining the fact that her father wouldn't be dancing at her own, if he was alive at all. In childish moments, Gaby had wished on a first star, then on a lucky penny, had even thrown two nickels into the reflecting pool at the mall, each time saying, *Let him go, please, one way or another, in painless peace*, and here he was, still alive, looking more and more like a photograph in the Holocaust Museum. And the wedding was breathing down her neck, less than three months away.

* * *

Shingo greeted them in the parking lot. He always reminded Gaby of a movie black hat, with those diabolical arched eyebrows that went into a V over his black olive eyes. He was from Guam and when wearing tennis whites, as he was now, his skin looked even darker, the color of coffee ice cream, his expression even more malevolent. It was always a surprise to see how affable and polite he actually was, a good example of nature's miscasting. He took Mama's hand and helped her out of the car, told her she wouldn't need her hat, the matches were to be in the air-conditioned inside courts. Mama took to him immediately.

Coming up behind him was The Girlfriend, also in whites. Suntanned skin, streaky blonde hair, perfect little-knob knees, the look of outdoor health and a cigarette between two fingers of her right hand. *Like Shingo, a big, fat paradox.*

He introduced her. "Benita Raffle."

Benita Raffle! How would one get through life with a name like Benita Raffle?

"I've just started tennis. Shingo is giving me lessons," Benita was one of those militantly friendly people ready to unlatch the locker of her personal life and immediately toss out its contents. Originally from Connecticut, now a resident of Chelsea, New York, not happy in her apartment because of the smells from the Chinese restaurant below, studying to be a psychologist.

A psychologist?

As they walked to the courts, Benita poured out more: trying to kick the nicotine habit, new sneakers hurting the backs of her feet, Shingo just bought a 1941 poster of the Davis Cup, an original, from the gallery in which she worked part time. She hoped they'd start a collection together.

Mama looked bemused by Benita.

She talks a lot, Gaby thought.

Shingo, barely getting a word in, led the way to their seats, in the very first row, right behind the referee. Special aerodynamic wheelchairs, the balls could bounce twice, some students were quite seriously disabled. *Fantasmo dudes,* he called them and when Benita finally took a talk break, on he went, trying to prepare them for the sight of the players.

Mama was very involved, that was the good thing, asking questions, leaning forward in her seat and taking off her dark glasses to peer at the court.

"Where's Wally?" she wanted to know.

He was giving last minute instructions to the ball boys. He'd be here in five, Shingo assured her. "I'm crazy about Wally," Benita said. She'd gone to school with him, elementary and high, lived right down the street growing up, but hadn't been in touch until they'd run into each other at a tennis shop in Stamford.

The court surface had to be held to exceedingly high standards. "Smooth and level matters," Shingo said. "Level and smooth!" Wheelchairs had to maneuver across the court and the balls' bounce had to be true.

Gaby swept aside Benita's verbosity as best she could and focused on the game. These were men's doubles and the scene on the courts was riveting. How come she'd never seen this on TV? Some men were spastic, or missing limbs. One hit the ball by holding the racquet with his left arm, his one remaining limb. Another player seemed to be missing the entire lower half of his *body*. With whatever body parts were available, they swung and they hit. The balls flew back and forth across the net with power and hurtling speed. She herself could never get a ball to fly that fast! Mama was sitting forward in her seat, her eyebrows raised in awe. When Wally finally came to sit with them, he put his arm around her shoulders. "Are you enjoying? You ding ho, Julie?"

Wally had picked up Shingo's street talk; so had everyone else.

"Still holding, Mama?"

"Still holding."

"Me too," Gaby said. As the games proceeded, the images took on a new meaning. Snapped right into focus. She felt like smiling, but this was a serious competition and what would Mama make of an idiot smile on her face coming out of nowhere?

It was a vision Gaby had, a spin of her imagination, a psychological snap of the fingers. She clasped together her hands, holding herself down. *A new slant!*

These wheelchair-bound human beings were not only not helpless, they were high-energy people competing in a challenging sport. Neither defenseless nor forlorn, they were living full nondependent lives. *So! People who are confined to wheelchairs are not all necessarily out of commission!* It was simply a matter of will and determination, push and ambition, the evidence right here, not twelve feet away. They were going at it like crazy on the tennis court, athletic testimony to resolution winning over physical fragility. A smile did creep slowly into Gaby's heart and onto her face; she couldn't help or stop it. She saw Stretch's wife in a motorized wheelchair, zinging along the streets of Nyack, then hoisting herself into her specially equipped car. Mitzi was going into a beauty parlor to have her hair done, and later, would wheel herself into a restaurant or a movie theater. She herself might even take up a racquet sport.

Gaby's mood lifted. The wife would surely someday hardly need him, a man who after all, no longer loved her. Had recently removed her picture from his office. Which said *so much.*

A player without an arm aced in a serve.

"Mama, aren't they absolutely wonderful?" she asked.

"You mean the players?" Mama answered.

"Of course? What else would I mean?"

"Well, I was actually just thinking of my dance classes. Weren't we talking about them on the way up? They're wonderful too. But yes, these players, they are an inspiration. Absolutely."

CHAPTER THIRTEEN

Julie sat in her bath, her head resting on a small inflatable pillow Mariadora had found for her in a store in Brooklyn, listening to Chopin's *Revolutionary Etude*. Maybe she'd buy a tape of Iglesias's, the one on which he sang, *Adios, Pampa Mia*. It kept going through her head, seemed to be swimming up there in its own fluid. Tomorrow, on the way to the hospital, she'd stop in White Plains, at Sam Goody on Main Street. Poor Gilbert; she'd missed going to see him yesterday. She'd been overcome by an inexplicable inertia, maybe just a matter of psychic exhaustion. The wheelchair tennis tournament, intending to be inspirational and uplifting, wasn't. All through it, Julie was thinking if Gilbert ever did recover, he might wind up not only in a wheelchair, but forever a member of "the halt, the lame, the blind," diapered and drooling. Then, there was that endless trip home, Wally falling asleep in the back seat, and Gaby without four words to say until they were practically at the Scarsdale exit.

Nine weeks away from her wedding day, and not

even a glimmer of anticipatory cheer. "I know you've got Daddy on your mind, but dear, try hard not to let it overshadow your prenups," Julie had tried brightly when they were stuck in a snake of traffic near Port Chester. Gaby was tapping her fingers impatiently on the steering wheel. "I wasn't even thinking about Daddy," she said, turning to her mother. Her face, today looking so much like her own baby picture, sealed off. "Then, dear, for Wally's sake, try for a bit of *joie de vie,*" Julie whispered. She didn't want to wake Wally, didn't want him to hear this. Gaby shrugged, turning herself off like she'd pushed a personal mute button. Then, another exit later, "You know those photographs in women's magazines that go with cake recipes? No matter how hard I try, Mama, it's N.G. I've never gotten any cake recipe to wind up looking just like the pictures."

"Whatever made you think of that, dear? We were talking about your wedding, not Martha Stewart."

Gaby lowered her voice to a sputtering whisper. "Because—because he talks about cork all the time, Mama."

"Darling, you know what they do to make that food look good in the magazine? They use shaving cream, shoe polish, shellac and God knows what else."

"He wears a cork *visor,* Mama."

"Was that cork? I didn't notice."

"We eat from cork place mats, he wants to install a stiffo cork floor, he brought me a pair of cork *earrings* and a cork *bracelet.* For Christ's sake."

"Sshh. It's pre-wedding jitters, dear, that's all."

Gaby was silent again.

"Wally is a good, good man, dear."

"I know, Mama. I know," Gaby said. "But I want you to know it's not going to be ding ho like the whipped cream in a photograph."

Altar panic, Harriet thought, thinking back to her own. Only because she was too young, a baby, had never seen another city, never set foot on an airplane, never written a check, hadn't had real sex yet, was terrified, knowing her new nightie was folded in her honeymoon suitcase, waiting not to be worn. The fear had nothing to do with Gilbert. Gilbert was four-square, a good man, would always be there when she needed him, the type of man Bessie Smith sang was hard to find.

Now Julie held a hand mirror to her face and examined her eyes, not for the first time. All the times she herself had fussed over her lashes with a mascara wand, she'd never noticed that the left iris was more intense in color, well, not as blue as a Manet lake but almost, and in a certain light, her right eye was certainly more pallid, a sky reflecting the lake, and all these years no one, not Gilbert, not her girls, had seen it. Amazing that it had taken her dance instructor, this casual acquaintance, to notice.

Perhaps 'casual acquaintance' no longer applied to Taras, who week before last had shown her photographs he'd taken of his son Thomas, and, in a lowered voice, told her a secret. The boy had been caught stealing a month ago, not for the first time. On this occasion, a twenty dollar bill from the woman who lived in the basement apartment. What had turned this eleven-year-old, former exemplary child, into a thief? A boy who Taras, forgoing all Ukrainian possibilities, was named after one of his heroes, Thomas Jefferson? So, against the odds, here was Thomas Jefferson Goodman, a little perpetrator. Despite his one hundred percent American regular-guy name. Despite the fact that no one had ever made fun of him and that he had a name he should have been busy living up to.

As a mother with grown children, did Julie have any thoughts? What made kids go awry? His expres-

sion was so tormented that she felt as if she should
reach out and put her hand to touch his face, as
she would comfort a child. Instead, she pulled back,
pressed herself against the green leatherette of the
couch in the waiting room where they were sitting
side by side, and tried to think of some sage and
comforting words. None of her girls, to her knowledge, had ever committed a felony. Yet, their cumula-
tive teenage sins could add up to a mountain of
emotional misdemeanors: the marijuana cigarettes,
the sex play in the basement playroom—Gaby's boyfriend caught once with his underwear down to his
ankles—the school cuts, the ripping, shocking defi-
ance, the reptilian language picked up on the Easy
Streets of Scarsdale or the velvet halls of its high
school. All three, even Susanna, had brawled and
sputtered their way through adolescence. She and
Gilbert had barely survived it. But, stealing, no, never.
"Make him give the money back." "Oh, I did. Sure,
first thing." "Take him to the beach or some nice
place, talk to him. Talk to him day and night." Julie
kept wondering, *Where's the boy's mother?* but Taras
seemed query-proof. Asking him anything would
almost be like pushing herself over some mortared
boundary. But, *Where's the mother?*

As she spoke, Taras looked down at the floor, then
up at the ceiling. "My head is full of useless stuff
like the liberation of Kiev in 1648 and the Ukrainian
famine of '32 that brought my father's family here.
Then the American stuff. I got started with that helping the kid with his history homework. Everything
about Thomas Jefferson. The other presidents, too.
Tell me what year you were born, I'll tell you who
was president, who was vice president and what they
ate for breakfast. So what? I know shit about being a
father. Pardon my French."

His beeper suddenly went off, startling them both.
She'd never even noticed it, latched to his belt. It was

a smaller model than the one Joe Goetz used, less obtrusive. "Be right back." Taras shot up, and as he ran to the telephone, music suddenly burst from the studio. Three young couples practicing the fox-trot to *Close to You.* Julie watched them shuffling their box steps across the dance floor, all smiles and happiness, their jerky movements reminding Julie of a marionette show. She was that young too, once. She was all smiles and happiness once, too.

She watched Taras as he spoke on the telephone. His back was to her, but she could read his back, the way his shoulders were moving up, then down and up again.

"My landlady," he said, when he came back. "Thomas was trying to light a cigarette, Harry. At least it was only nicotine. Got a pack from somewhere, that's part one. Smoking in the bathroom, that's part two. Matches and fire, that's part three." He was looking not at her but at the floor, as if he were watching something crawl across it. "As I said, I know squat about parenting."

His expression reminded her of the focus of a lifeguard spotting trouble in the breakers. She imagined him leaving here, going home, maybe to a frame house with three or four floors, divided into apartments. The boy would be punished in one of its rooms. How? A slap across the face, as in days of old, when a slap was not only permitted but *de rigueur*, an absolute must, a rite of passage? (Although Gil never raised a hand, not once, not that it wouldn't have been justified, not that he didn't threaten!)

"What will you say to him?"

"What should I?"

"Let him have it."

"Yeah."

"Maybe you better tell him you love him first. And then again, last."

Taras brushed some invisible piece of lint off the

knee of his chino pants. Then he scratched the spot between his eyebrows and turned to Julie. "You know something? You'd make a good Seeing Eye dog, Harry, you honest to God would."

"Don't lay a hand on him, Taras."

"Hey. You know me better than that. Or, should I say, I hope one day you will."

The dance lesson was like a bright asterisk in Julie's week. The little time between her lesson and his next appointment became part of the asterisk, a little point in its star. While they danced, Taras was all instructional business: "Closed position now," or "Outside partner, Harry, let's try that again," or, "Okay, rock step," or, "Very good, Harry, but wait for the beat, don't look down, take a larger step back," but afterward, when they walked together into the waiting room, and while she sipped water from a paper cup from the cooler, he came to sit beside her to wait for his next appointment. She told him this and that about her daughters—mostly about the times they were small, rather than the complexities of their lives in the here and now. Julie never spoke of Gilbert.

On Thursday of last week, when his next student arrived half an hour early and Taras got up to lead her into the ballroom, Julie felt as if she wanted to call him back, ask him something—but what?—just to keep him with her a few extra minutes. She went to get her jacket, feeling an unexpected letdown, but suddenly, he was next to her, helping her put it on. Julie was so startled, she nearly jumped.

"I thought—could you wait until this lesson is over so we could talk for a few minutes? It's just a half hour?" Taras's face was now a lifeguard's again, dead serious, primed and ready to dive into the coldest water if necessary. "It's the latest development. Thomas."

But she couldn't. Ruthie and Lou DiLorenzo were coming by to take her to Pinocchio in Eastchester. They were back from a Bermuda cruise with stories to tell and snapshots to show and would be picking Julie up at eight-thirty. As it was, she hardly had time to get home, freshen up.

"Next time, then," Taras said, showing no change of expression, just a quick view of his front overlapping teeth. He practically zoomed away, rushed off to the plump young woman waiting for him in the ballroom, but then, turned for a moment in the doorway. Julie felt a visceral tangle: He looked so young, Gilbert would certainly have referred to him as a "kid," as he did all his employees and just about anyone under fifty. But Taras was no kid. The wet-dry hair must have been thicker at the temples five years ago. And no question about it, his eyes, so much like Karen's, had grown old faster than his college-boy cheeks and full, florescent lips. "Have a nice dinner, Harry," he said. On the way out, Julie asked herself, how could *Have a nice dinner, Harry,* a most ordinary of mundane farewells, have such vigor, such dash?

On the way to Pinocchio, Lou and Ruthie argued about Bill Cosby. Was it him in the shop in Hamilton buying Wedgwood plates or just someone who looked like him? They argued about the Bermuda photographs: Lou had forgotten to bring them. Finally they had words about the suntan oil Ruthie had packed into Lou's luggage that had leaked on Lou's sports jacket. Julie sat quietly in the back seat, *Adios Pampa Mia* flowing through her head, hardly listening.

When they got to the restaurant, the argument switched gears. Ruthie wanted Lou to order the broccoli rabe and skip the scampi del giorno, and tried unsuccessfully to snatch away from him the butter the waiter had set down on the table. As he slathered a slice of bread with it, she said, "If you don't care about yourself, Louis, think of me. Do you think I want to be a widow before I even hit menopause?" and then her mouth snapped closed and she looked at Julie, her glossed lips in a guilty pucker, and Lou glanced at Ruthie and under his breath he said, "Oh, boy," and all the while, Julie had really been trying to remember what *Corte* meant, and worrying about whether she'd forgotten how to make the turn in the outside partner step. Her toes tapped surreptitiously under the table.

CHAPTER FOURTEEN

Julie was near tears when they embraced and hugged her and told her she was brave and must be going through hell, but had never looked better. She had decided to return because they'd called her last week, said they really needed her right before the shop closed for summer. Every item in the place was marked down to half-price so business was brisk. Could she lend a hand?

It was like a celebration. The "girls" at Second Chance had baked cookies and made a sign that read, WELCOME BACK JULIE. Cindi had lost twenty pounds, Doris had finally sold her house, Estelle, usually sullen, was all smiles; her breast tissue biopsy had just come back negative. A sad-eyed "Bobo" Newkirk, whose husband was back in rehab, had brought thermos jugs of her special iced tea and a cooler full of ice cubes—in each of which a strawberry was embedded.

When the store closed at five, they insisted she take home the umpteen uneaten cookies and the hand-lettered sign to show Gilbert. How was Gil doing, they asked, their faces concerned. Any improvement?

Holding his own. Julie was thankful for these kind women, her friends. Well, not quite friends. When they handed her the cookies all tightly wrapped in aluminum foil, none of them seemed close enough to admit to it, that to her great shame, her first thought had been to bring the goodies to the dance studio and share them with Taras. But there was no lesson tonight; her class had been canceled. Heather had called this morning to tell Julie that the air-conditioning was on the fritz. The studio would have to close until it was fixed—early tomorrow, she hoped.

The first day at the shop—Julie thought of it as her first day back in her old life—she found exhausting. Perhaps the canceled dance lesson was a blessing. She was taking two a week now, and thinking about a third. Julie told herself it was only because Terri was pregnant and unable to return for her floor mat workouts. Certainly no one could expect her to march around the Scarsdale High School track without Gilbert? He himself surely would want her to exercise; she could practically hear his voice telling her to reduce her stress, stay fit and to turn herself into Terpsichore, if that's what it took.

When she got back to the house, Julie went through the stack of mail that Mariadora had piled on the table in the front hall, and the note she left in perfect spelling, reminding her that she needed to pick up some Glass Plus and a new mop on her next trip to the supermarket. Julie sat in the kitchen, her mail and a cup of mocha in front of her, and her eye fell on a letter in her daughter Susanna's handwriting, sent from the travel agency at which she worked.

For a few minutes, she sat looking at the envelope, turning it over in her hands. She carried it with her to the sink, into which she deposited her empty mocha cup, feeling wary, tired. What *now?* Reluctantly, she tore open the envelope and out fluttered a check, wrapped in a note: "I'm so sorry to have to remind you of this. I love you, Mama. Susanna." It was the refund of Gilbert's deposit for their trip to Sardinia.

Julie put her head down on her arms on the table and pictured Costa Smeralda, the picture of the Cala DiVolpe Hotel, under a turquoise no-cloud sky, a flashback from the travel brochure she and Gilbert had pored over together. Then she thought about the tedium of her life, the repetitive purchases of cleaning materials and coffee filters, the constant replenishing of the tools of civilization, and her return to the nightly rituals of flossing teeth, alpha hydroxy treatments and cream on her elbows. Why and what for? Her life seemed tonight like a sunless landscape she couldn't endure.

When the telephone rang she had one foot on the step leading upstairs to her bath and the book by Elisabeth Kübler-Ross Elliot had given her. She was trying to read it more than reading it; most evenings the words marched across its pages like sluggish ants.

"Hi, Harry." It was Taras, calling to tell her the air conditioner had been fixed, was humming along fine. Had she made other plans tonight or could she come at the usual time? Julie sat fixed on the lowest step, revived, rapt. She had never heard his voice on the telephone. He sounded like a newscaster her mother had listened to on the radio every night when she was growing up. His voice would come out of the yellow plastic box in the kitchen, in this exact husky-man's croon. "It's cool as vanilla ice cream down here, Harry, so 'you can use me to the limit.' You know who said that?' Julie, eyes on the roses Mariadora had cut from the garden and put in a vase on the foyer table, told him she'd guess Thomas Jefferson. "Way off. Way, way off. It was Teddy Roosevelt. 'I am as strong as a bull moose and you can use me to the limit!' He said that when he was charging up San Juan Hill during the Spanish-American War." Taras laughed, now sounding animated, a new telephone version of himself, with an edge of authority. "You can use me to the limit, Harry. I'll be waiting for you."

Taras's familiar-unfamiliar telephone voice rang in her ear as she rose from the stairs and went to the table to inhale the perfume of the bouquet, where they now glowed in duplicate. Tonight the roses seemed luminous and poetic, a mixture of Casablancas, her favorite Elizabeth Taylors and a few hybrid teas. She must remember to thank Mariadora for being so thoughtful. Sardinia evaporated as she touched the silky petals.

Julie hurried upstairs to run her bath and to check her closet, to see if Mariadora had also found time to iron her white linen blouse with the embroidered collar. Her eye caught the colored ribbons she'd tied to the bedposts. They represented hope that the "Mister would sleep soon again in his own bed." Sweet, Mariadora's persevering and obstinate loyalty to Gilbert. Julie would take them off sooner or later, but it could wait. So could the book. Everything would, while she ran back downstairs and went to the CD player to put on her newest disk, *Adios Pampa Mia*, and turned the switch that would transmit it to the speakers in the ceiling of her bathroom. She could soak it in, she thought, pleased and mellow, while she soaked.

"No stripes tonight. I'm totally surprised," she told him, sounding a bit like she used to, so very long ago—playful and coquettish—as he led her onto the dance floor in his solid gray shirt with its very crisp white collar. He admired her linen blouse and told her his mother had had one like it; in fact he thought he had a photograph of her taken in that very blouse on the doorstep of her house. She asked about his

mother; it slipped out: "Where is she now?" His face
fixed in an unreadable expression, he told her she
was "Gone." Julie, asking no further questions, put
her hand on Taras's sleeve. It was time to dance.

The steps were becoming, as she would describe
the experience to her daughters, second nature.
There was no more reason to count or to think, when
she was in Taras's arms. The music, her feet, her
muscles took over, perhaps even her *soul*, as she
became Ginger and Margot and Twyla and Julie Kessler, born to dance. They could laugh all they wanted
at her clichés, but she was in a different sphere when
Taras moved her across this humble, polished gym
floor in New Rochelle. No wine or champagne high
could compare to this sense of being weightless and
very, very young, of obliterating yesterday and tomorrow, and feeling that every turn and heady spin was
life's only reality. "Okay, rock step, slow, slow, that's
it." It was dreamlike and smooth, the way she was
skimming the floor, a vital wisp of gossamer in her
white linen blouse and long pleated skirt.

If she had been unable to concentrate on a book
on death and dying, she'd absorbed every word of
the history of the dance Ruthie had found in an old
copy of *Entertainment Weekly*. There was more that she
wouldn't share with her daughters, something written
about the tango long before she herself bought the
silver shoes she was wearing now. It had to do with
its intensity and power, violence and sadness. And it
had to do with sex.

It had stirred life in Julie as she danced. She
couldn't have put a name to the feelings that washed
over her as she moved, letting the dance take her
over. If as Taras had said, the tango belonged to
the night, if it belonged to passion and dreams and
mourning, it also throbbed with lust. The heart that

pumped blood through Julie when she moved with him, pumped heat through her as well, kicked up in her the long-lost charge, the surge and the rush. In this unexceptional rectangle of a bourgeois salon, a space lacking swaying palms or perfume, moon or bright stars, a place designed not for romance but for matter-of-fact commerce, she began to be overcome by a devastating, ravishing, radiant, and sublime longing.

Which, step by step and turn by turn, slowly transferred itself to her partner Taras, surnamed Goodman.

He walked her off the floor, watched her take a tissue from her purse and pat her damp forehead and the space between her nose and lip. Inside, she was all tumult, fighting off a tremor in her knees. "I know I'm a mess," she said, sitting on the couch, sounding to her own ear adolescent and foolish. She felt a twinge in her back, and sat up, very straight. She remembered when she'd put her back out lifting a suitcase three years ago. Agony for two weeks, floor exercises for six.

"Bluer. The left eye definitely is," Taras said, looking, no, gazing at her; it couldn't be her imagination. Had he also noted the small crinkles beginning in the skin of her neck? It was not all in her head, crinkles or no, he was, yes, *admiring her.* "Harry, my star student."

She held her hands tight in her lap. It was only the spell of the dance, she thought, its sultry moves, its heat and its tension. With its history of belonging to prostitutes in the *enramadas*—Argentinian whorehouses—its music of loneliness, sadness and desire, its intricate steps, with legs entwined, hips communicating, the whole smooth and erotic package, it could set the dead—or even Julie—on fire.

They exchanged a look. Her eyes to his, his to hers. Now, cooled off, cooled down, she was embarrassed.

Fifty-three years old and stars in her eyes? What was she even thinking? She could hear Gilbert's voice in her ear: "He's a *kid*, for God's sake!" and sat up straighter, gave Taras a very down-to-earth smile. "You were going to tell me something about Thomas," she said.

CHAPTER FIFTEEN

"He found a dog. Looks like part retriever."

"You're letting him keep it?" Julie was sipping water from her paper cup, her eyes on Taras's face.

He looked somber and distracted next to her on the green Naugahyde couch. She pictured herself putting down her cup, leaning over and putting both arms around him in a maternal squeeze, but crossed her legs and took another sip of water instead.

"If he promises never to steal again." Taras had found in a shoe box under the bed in his son's room what looked like two more stolen twenties, from where Thomas wouldn't tell. Animated, shifting in his chair, Taras described to Julie his confrontations with his son, the long talks she'd recommended, his fear that the next misdemeanor could lead to the juvenile courts, and his own deficiencies as a father. He said he didn't know how people managed with three and four kids when he was having such a time with only one; did she know that President John Tyler had had fifteen? He talked about the dog, named Ridgeway after the street on which she was found, went on about how glad he was they'd fixed the air conditioner in time for their lesson. He hoped he wasn't making her uncomfortable, going on about his personal life—"You don't mind my bending your ear, Harry?"—but he found her easy to talk to. Very, very easy, like on old, kind friend. She had a nice way about her, he said, something "cushy." You could open a thousand doors and never find it until one day, you did.

Sipping from her paper cup, her gaze alternating between his eyes, hair, and a wrinkle in his collar, Julie told Taras that no, no, he wasn't making her uncomfortable and that he could talk to her all night if he cared to. She started to say that she enjoyed listening to him, that she looked forward to this time with him, that the hospital seemed far away when they were dancing, but didn't. As it was, her own eyes were probably giving everything away. She crumpled up her paper cup and as he took it out of her hand to throw it into the wastepaper basket—a sweet gesture!—he caught her glancing at his finger. "You're wondering, right, Harry?"

She nodded, feeling she should pull something out of the air to say, but what? She imagined a bar brawl, a box cutter, lost blood, an ambulance stretcher. A wax museum image, no matter what.

"Hungry alligator," he said, baring his teeth. When he caught the look on her face, he said he was only pulling her leg. "It's a long story. Another time, Mrs. Kessler."

Another time might mean at a more intimate moment. Or, it might mean never. She was after all, only one of Taras's many students. For all she knew, he had the same *post hoc* chats with a half dozen other women. A bit of a line, maybe. *I should be a bit suspicious at my age.* Julie had, in fact, just seen his next student come into the studio and take off her raincoat. She was young, short and stocky, had to reach to hang it on the coat rack near the door. "I think I better be going," Julie said, getting up.

Taras called over to the student. "Sheila, it's raining outside?"

"Where else would it be raining?" Sheila threw Taras a flirtatious beam of a smile as she shook out her umbrella. She was a longtime student, he had told Julie, came all the way up from the Bronx twice a week. She probably knew everything there was to know about Taras. No doubt about it, with women coming in droves, one every hour, then the group lessons, well, it was very unlikely Julie had any kind of an exclusive.

Julie looked down at her new Italian leather silver shoes, bought in the Saks shoe department for a hefty price, worn a very few times, only to this dance class. They were strappy, shiny Barbie shoes, with delicate heels, higher than Julie usually wore. Heather began to search for a pair of plastic bags to cover them so Julie could walk to the car in the rain. Downpour, Heather kept saying, having just been out to catch a smoke. So far, the search had uncovered only one Baggie, punctured by the plastic forks inside. Julie decided on the spur, sank back into the couch and began unfastening the straps that held them around her ankles. "I'm going to leave my shoes here."

"Mrs. Kessler, you're not going out in your bare feet?" Heather looked up from her desk where she was still opening and closing drawers, rummaging.

"I don't want to ruin these—" Julie pointed to her shoes. *If you knew what I paid.*

Taras stood for a moment watching her fiddle with the ankle straps. "You can't walk out there barefoot. Where's your car?" He stood over her, legs apart, looking taller and broader than he actually was.

"Across the street."

"Right across?"

"Almost."

"Leave them on."

"Leave the shoes on?"

"I'll carry you," he said, no hesitation.

Julie's one shoe stopped midair in her hand. She thought he was joking. "Under which arm?"

"Put the shoe back on. Don't give me a hard time, Harry." Taras's voice took on a deep, patriarchal, thunder-rumble.

"You could put your back out, Taras, as I did a couple of years ago."

"Put the shoe back on."

"Hey, Godzilla!" Sheila was standing with her hands on her hips. "Never mind your back. You going to ruin *your* dancing shoes?"

Taras began rolling up the cuffs of his pants. "I got twenty pairs."

"You're crazy," Heather said, yawning.

When Taras smiled, all his features, his eyebrows and lashes, seemed to engage. He told Sheila he'd be back in a minute, and asked Julie if she was insured for breakage.

Heather waved an envelope at Julie. She'd let her hair grow a bit and had begun to look less butch and more gamine. "He must really like you, Mrs. Kessler. Taras doesn't usually carry his students through the streets." She stuck out her tongue and licked a flap. "I can't even get him to go pick up a pizza."

For one short moment they stood together in the doorway of the building, looking out at the downpour. "You can't," Julie said. There was no sky, no sidewalk, no street. Just rushing, gushing, moving, swishing water. " 'You must do the thing you think you cannot do.' Now, who said that?" Taras asked. They were in the doorway, shoulder to shoulder, looking out. The smell was heady, the ozone of a greenhouse.

"I'll try Jefferson again."

"Wrong! Another Roosevelt."

"Franklin."

"Eleanor!"

"How do you know all this, Taras? I read her autobiography and all I remember is her picture on the cover."

"I may be trying to tell you I'm more than a pair of dancing feet, Harry."

More than a pair of dancing feet. Taras was unexpectedly turning her rainy day into the sort of day she would describe as a surprise package. This not-so-little absurd adventure was something she would definitely tell Ruthie and the girls. A dance lesson perk, she would call it, skipping what she had to admit to herself was an underpinning of scintillation.

"Okay. You ready?" Putting one arm under her knees and one under her arm, Taras hoisted her off the sidewalk, pretending it was easy, holding back the groan she imagined was lodged not too far down in his throat. He was not a wrestler, not what you'd describe as strapping. And, she'd been steadily putting back the weight she'd lost after the accident. So, it was not quite a facile sweep, not the effortless, heroic way firemen scoop children out of burning buildings, no Rhett-Scarlett swoop. She put an arm around Taras's neck, and grabbing on to his shoulder, tried to keep the pocketbook in her other hand from slipping out of her grasp. "Eeeezy does it," he said, but she was no child; her weight was knocking the breath out of him. The rain was coming down from the sky like a spritzing full throttle out of a shower nozzle. *He must be regretting this!* Julie was watching his shiny black shoes sloshing through the water that swirled along the cement. His shirt was pasted to his shoulders and the rain running down his temples and cheeks made it look as if his face were melting. It was a messy, dripping sixty seconds that Julie would later re-create in her imagination, investing it with theater and poetry.

He was showing off for her.

"Which one is your car?" he asked, breathless. The water was gushing along the curb the way it did from a garden hose. She felt his shoulder under her hand, the power of his arm under her thighs. A strand of wet hair was falling into his eye and she wanted to reach up and push it back. The air smelled of country rain and so did he. If she had a handkerchief, Julie would mop Taras's forehead and cheeks, pat him dry under his chin, behind his ears, everywhere. She wanted to tell him that no man in her life had ever lifted her or even asked to, that she'd never met anyone who would willingly carry her across a city street through puddles and a formidable downpour, just to save her from ruining her shoes or walking barefoot.

For the few short minutes that she was being held safely aloft, bumping along in the rain in the arms of a young man who hardly knew her but wanted to caveman-protect her, she felt herself leave the present, grow light as a magician's scarf, and transmogrify into a delicious and pampered young girl. The rain flattened her hair, soaked her linen blouse and drizzled along her cheeks. Tickling her nose, it dripped onto her mouth in cool, tasteless drops. Holding tight to Taras, she closed her eyes for a moment, saw herself as a maiden in a myth, being carried through an evening storm far away from these asphalt streets and darkened shops. For the length of a half-minute, reality, Gilbert, the smell of the hospital corridor, everything was gone; it was all opera.

She pointed out her car, which had been through the car wash this morning. Although she always parked here in this very spot, tonight a curling, soaked parking ticket had been stuck under its windshield wiper. Reality cut in; the rain stopped sounding like music. "What did I do wrong?" she asked, looking at the ticket.

Taras set her down, carefully, solicitously, on the driver's side, standing in the downpour as if it didn't exist. As she fumbled through her purse for her car keys, as the rain continued to drench them, he put his hand on the shoulder of her sopping linen blouse. Later she would see the fabric had turned transparent enough to reveal the outlines of her old, pink, Lily of France brassiere. "So far, I haven't been able to find even one thing," Taras said.

There was a moment when something—maybe it was some debris from the street, a dribble of rain, or a fleck of green blown from a tree—stung Julie's eyes, and she squeezed closed her lids. "Give God a minute to turn the page," she used to tell the girls when they were small and in a hurry to get somewhere, or impatient for dessert. Now, she pictured a bearded God turning a large white page in a big book, and felt herself moved forward, propelled in the direction of folly and danger, all this against her will. It was all picture book make-believe, the way she'd described God and the saints as being in charge to her daughters so many years ago. Here she was back in this reverie, allowing what was about to happen to happen. Later she would ask herself if Taras had kissed her or she'd kissed him; it was a question of science, physics, motion, his mouth moving toward hers or hers toward his, either way, a page decisively turned.

It was sweet, it was soft, it was shocking. She was being kissed by a dance instructor from the Fred Astaire Dance Studios, *My God, on the street!* and she was letting it go on, actively living it, feeling his breath while hers stopped, her eyes closed, her mouth welded to his in the singe of a man-woman, knock-you-dead, go-to-ruin, hot-lips open-mouth kiss.

And now, headlights approached; a car was coming. They flew apart and Julie tore herself free, clapped both hands over her mouth and felt as if her skin could send off sparks of shame.

He said he was sorry. And a moment later, he said, No, he had to take that back. He was not sorry at all. He felt knocked for a loop, he said.

"Listen," Julie said, trying to regain her composure, frozen at her car door as he pushed a wet strand of hair out of her eyes. Her silver shoes were soaked, despite everything. "It never happened. Please."

His arms dropped to his sides. "Okay. Rewind and erase." He waited in the rain as she put her key in the ignition and maneuvered the car out of its parking space and then, looking at her through his wet lashes, said, "Oh, what the hell, you know damn well it's the one thing you can't do. You can't rewrite history, Mrs. Kessler."

CHAPTER SIXTEEN

When Tilda Novak turned up at the hospital the following day, the parking violation provided some much-needed topic of conversation. "I parked about eight inches away from the curb and they actually gave me a ticket," Julie said, pretending to be nettled about the New Rochelle traffic police when in fact she was more exasperated at finding Tilda sitting near the foot of Gilbert's bed.

She had been dodging calls and requests for months from Tilda—and just about everyone else—to visit Gilbert. It certainly wouldn't help her husband, to hear Tilda go on and on about the executive disorder at Gilbert's electric timing device plant. "If I weren't there at eight every morning, keeping my eye on every file and interoffice memo, I don't know where we'd be," she now sighed. Gilbert had long since put in place a marketing team, an efficient young accountant and trustworthy Milt Gladstone, to allow himself time for long weekends and longer vacations. The bookkeeper called Julie every week to see if the check had arrived and to sigh about Gilbert,

and Milt, a Francophile and the C.O.O., was on the
phone at least twice a week. Business was flat, but no
"inquietudes," and, *"je rappellerai plus tard"*—I'll call
again—and he did. Milt had the decency not to
intrude by coming to gawk at Gilbert, as Tilda was
doing now.

Julie tried to humor Tilda, twenty-six loyal years
with the firm and addicted to Bufferin for job-related
headaches. "It's lucky he has you," Julie told the
woman, as the sun streamed in on her orange hair
through the hospital windows, making it look as if it
had caught fire. An enormous Godiva box was sitting
on the window sill, where the same sun would soon
turn the truffles into mush.

She was overstaying this visit, which should never
have been made in the first place, and giving Gilbert
mordant looks through her trendy gold-and-black
eyeglass frames.

Julie pulled up her sleeve and pointedly looked at
her watch. She wanted to be alone with Gilbert. *It
didn't mean anything, it was just a kiss, Gil!*

Tilda, in her athlete's warm-up suit despite August
heat, her feet in tricolored sneakers, crossed her
ankles daintily, indicating no plans to depart in the
immediate future. "We all feel so sorry for you, dear,"
she said.

If Tilda had seen her dancing last night, glimpsed
her being carried through the rain by her handsome
dance instructor, kissed like some twenty-year-old
after a prom, she'd take it back in a hurry.

Tilda let her chin point to the head of the bed,
where the pallid Gilbert lay entwined by plastic, looking particularly bloodless and practically blue in the
brilliant light. "I thought at first I'd walked into the
wrong room. Our poor Gilbert is unrecognizable,
darling. *A shadow.*"

Julie, who had been sitting in the only lounge chair,

felt a twinge in her back. She moved up, straightening her spine and squaring her shoulders.

"Sometimes, when you love someone who is suffering, you have to be a cheerleader for death." Behind the lenses of her glasses, Tilda's eyes closed in an Amen.

"Well, I'm a cheerleader for life." Julie tried to hold on to a stainless steel smile, just as a nurse, Dolly, one of her favorites, appeared in the doorway, holding a catheter, and breaking up the party. Julie felt like running over to kiss her.

But in the hall, outside Gilbert's room, Tilda lingered, and politeness, like a hand on her shoulder, padlocked Julie against the corridor wall. "I wouldn't tell you what to do, Julie," Tilda took her sleeve, practically pinning Julie against a wheelchair left empty in the hall, "but hanging on could be considered selfish, by those who see Gilbert, the poor, suffering soul, as nothing but a victim of your guilt."

With her lips pursed, and her eyelids crinkling behind her lenses, she reached into her pocket, pulled out a roll of Lifesavers and offered Julie one, while Julie stood transfixed, staring at her with her mouth open. "Hospitals always have the same disinfectant and old-time laundry smell, don't they," Tilda sighed. And added, "I think mints help."

Julie pushed the Lifesavers—and Tilda's hand— away. She considered saying, "Gilbert is not suffering! And if he'd heard your comment, you'd be out of a job tomorrow," but instead, imagining a confrontation, the scattering of the ashes of this sad sack's self-respect, she simply extricated her sleeve and walked toward the elevator.

"Let me take you to the coffee shop and buy you a cup of coffee," Tilda offered, in a voice that sounded like two alcoholics' voices spliced together. Not that Tilda was ever involved with alcohol. Bufferin, Tylenol and Advil were her Scotch and vodka.

"Seeing Gilbert like that! I'll never get over it!"

Feeling a rush of compassion, Julie saw the woman as bottled-up and defenseless, probably going home to pace the floor of her small cage of an apartment in Queens. "I know how upsetting," she managed, and agreed to go to the coffee shop. "Just for a few minutes, a very quick cold drink." Tilda threw Julie a beam, looking as if she'd just been upgraded to first class.

"You know when I came to work at Kessco? I was twenty-nine years old. My mother came and took care of my girls, so I could go to work, that's how long I'm with the company." Equilibrium apparently fully restored, Tilda was now back to sounding like a power tool. They'd been seated at the counter and presented with a pair of iced lemon teas and a bowl of pink and blue artificial sweetener envelopes. Tilda had also ordered a blueberry muffin. Julie tried to concentrate on what she was saying, but had caught sight of a man at the cash register wearing Taras's stripes. That's how she was destined, possibly forever, to categorize vertically striped cotton shirts. She wished she were in her car on her way to the studio right this minute. She was dancing four nights a week now and had left an umbrella and an extra pair of shoes at the studio. "Almost a second home, Mrs. K?" Heather had re-marked.

Julie, watching Tilda crumble the blueberry muffin and pucker her mouth around the straw, sat quietly through interminable tales of loyalty, devotion, the firm's early history and memorials to long-departed personnel. Finally, she interrupted. "What you said in Gilbert's room today upset me terribly, Tilda." *I should have told her off an hour ago.*

"I loved that man like a brother, Julie. And I think," a long exhale, "I think you ought to let him be where

he belongs"—now came an endless, scratchy sigh—
"with the angels." Now it was clear how Tilda spent
her free time. Touched by talk shows. "Because you
think he doesn't feel? Well, if you want to know, I
think he feels *plenty!*"

Julie squeezed her cold glass of tea with both hands.
"What you think, Tilda," she said, her voice disciplined, steady but two degrees from hysterical, "is
irrelevant!"

Tilda gasped. A waitress at the end of the counter
looked their way.

"The way you talk to me, after all what I did for
Kessco, and for him. My God, the times I worked late,
with no overtime pay, mind you, and no complaining,
came in with headaches that would send anybody else
to the emergency room, and the way"—Tilda gulped
in a fresh supply of air—"the way I always stuck up
for him!"

"Stuck up for Gilbert?"

"Exactly!"

"Why would you have to stick up for my husband?"
Julie's voice went from pianissimo to forte. The waitress, and now a customer, sandwich in hand, had
turned to watch whatever drama might be unfolding.

"It's between him and God and me what happened
at Kessco!" Tilda rasped, and she slammed down the
napkin with which she had been blotting her mouth.

Julie felt out of breath, as if she'd run a mile uphill.
"Let's get the check," she said, and waved at the
waitress.

Tilda switched into a diplomatic gear. "It's nothing
I wanted to bring up," she said, using the napkin to
draw moist rainbows along the edge of the counter.
Half a blueberry muffin lay untouched on her plate.

"Then don't," Julie snapped. She looked at her
watch; she could be safe in her own bathtub in half
an hour. Or maybe, she'd do a bit of work in the
garden first; she'd certainly been neglecting her roses

lately. She'd sprinkle Epsom salts on the flower beds
and do a bit of pruning.

"Some bad stuff went down a few years ago," Tilda
continued, looking at Julie out of the corner of her
eye.

Julie conjured up improbable, impossible tableaus
in fantasy colors. "Bad stuff" could mean anything.
Gilbert, her pure, honorable ramrod of an American
citizen and darling of a husband, was not capable of
stepping into any sort of workplace sludge. More
likely, it was crazy Tilda, prevaricating to punish her,
to step out of her little phone booth and become
Superwoman.

"It was talk, just talk, not a word true," Tilda said,
as the waitress presented a check and Julie, after a
bit of a tug of war, won it.

"What talk?"

"There was a Mexican computer programmer,
Lina, she lived on Roosevelt Island, had to come by
tram. Ever meet her? She saved the company twenty-
five thousand dollars, found a mistake the accountant—remember Barry Gelb?—made. Gilbert sent
her a bouquet of flowers every week for a year. Believe
it or not, Barry transposed two numbers. This was
when he was already getting on, may he rest in peace.
Lina discovered it, Gilbert was so grateful, so why not
a little reward? Then he bought her a membership
at the Y because she had a weak heart and was supposed to swim for exercise. That's all he ever did,
and you should have heard the comments! Those
women in the office, they were so jealous they started
the rumor that he was sleeping with her, keeping her,
and whenever she came into the place wearing a
new blouse or a bracelet or something, they went off
chirping like a bunch of birds on a telephone wire.

"I told them they were way off base, and I told him,
too, but all he did was laugh."

Julie now pictured Tilda in her apartment, no little

cage, but probably the most beautiful penthouse in
Jackson Heights, enjoying her dinner and painkillers,
and a wicked last laugh, having greatly annoyed her.

"I remember the whole episode, Tilda," she said,
feeling higher and mightier than she had all day. *Stick
up for Gilbert indeed!* "And not that he wouldn't have
appreciated it, but you really didn't have to defend
him. He was absolutely above anything like that sort
of mucky office hanky-panky! We are talking about
Gilbert Kessler, here! Good heavens, as I recall, I was
even the one who suggested he send Lina the flowers!
I thought she was charming and I was sorry to see
her go back to Mexico."

Tilda hunched forward, pushed her muffin plate
away. The music went right out of her. "I'm glad we
got it out in the open, Julie. We agree one hundred
percent. Gilbert was above human vices. And let me
tell you, I squelched those rumors. I gave those
women what for! 'You're talking about a man of
honor!' I told them."

That's enough, you birdbrained gossip!

"Let me tell you, Julie, I made a few enemies on
the Kessco premises, but Gilbert was honorable as
the Pope himself and I have no regrets!"

Much later, in her bedroom, after the late news,
during Ted Koppel, as Julie was tearing a piece of
dental floss across the sawteeth of its dispenser, a sort
of midnight memory kicked in on a streak of black
lightning.

She remembered Gilbert calling Lina a "smartass
from South of the Border" and complaining she
always came in late. *Gil and Lina, the Mexican computer
programmer?* It was a big laugh. *Not Gil and anybody,*
she thought, sank back against the pillows, turned
off the light and tried unsuccessfully to go to sleep.

Hours later, wide awake, she went downstairs, put

Lo Que Vendra on the CD player and sat on the taupe
couch in the den with a cup of mocha, her feet automatically moving, working on their own, tapping out
the dance steps on the rug under her feet as if they
were as programmed as the electrical timing devices
in poor Gilbert's factory.

CHAPTER SEVENTEEN

Julie, standing next to Heather's desk in her silver shoes, thought of her emotions as a leash pulling her in all directions. *Three hours of sleep, crazy Tilda, the headlines I keep reading to Gilbert—Wall Street, subway rape, Gotti, Earthquakes in Colombia, Three Children Die in Fire, Cop Killed at Routine Traffic Stop—bad news, bad days.*

When she'd arrived at the studio a bit early tonight, Taras was on the dance floor with an instructor from one of the other Fred Astaire Dance Studios. Damaria. She was tall, with a pale face, red enamel lipstick, an expression that was both tense and detached. Her elbows, knees, hips, everything was wrapped in what looked like white Lycra, and like figures of computerized animation, she and Taras moved in perfect synchronicity. With the slicked-espresso hair typical of Latin dancers, the woman had the absolute fluidity of a professional performer, and a smoky, beyond-the-horizon sexiness.

Julie could not take her eyes off the Lucite shoes, the woman's prominent iliac crests, tight, little girl's buttocks. She watched Taras maneuver her into kicks, bends and twists to music that was unfamiliar, loud and aggressive. Intimidated by the woman's primal agility, nimbleness and artistry she'd never be capable of, her leash pulled her to turn, walk out and never come back. Instead, Julie stood as fixed in place as the pots of artificial trees gathering dust in the studio corners.

Why hadn't she followed her inclination to call off this lesson and all future relations with the Fred Astaire Dance Studios and dance instructors present and future? The guilt about Gilbert had leaped out again, all fangs sharpened, after last week's kiss. It wasn't so much the kiss, but the fact that she'd day-dreamed through her cups of mocha, Lehrer's evening news, the weekly manicure appointment she'd recently reinstated and the headlines. She'd never for a moment put it behind her. Now, instead of feeling distant and businesslike watching Taras dance with someone else, she'd been mesmerized, her reason shut down. It was jealousy, pure and simple.

"Aren't they, like, *potent?*" Heather sighed, as the lesson came to an end and Taras led his partner off the floor.

I hate him, hate her, let me back up, come in again, what's wrong with me, I'm about to turn fifty-four years old!

"Yes, aren't they?" Julie smiled, and complimented Heather's new earrings.

"Ready, Harry?" He was all business again, greeting her with a headwaiter's impersonal smile, looking crisp as ever. Yellow-on-white or white-on-yellow stripes, gray pants, shoes with a shoeshine shine. He led her to the floor, hand on her elbow, then left her to turn on the stereo. Julie reminded herself that kiss or no kiss, she was the paying customer, no change there.

She watched him come toward her, his limitless self-assurance in every step. How lackluster she must seem now! A gifted beginner, yes, but in contrast to the preceding limber, elastic, and exotic whiz, how clunky and matronly she must seem, a Madam Middle Years Trying Her Best. She hated him.

It wasn't going to go well tonight. Julie turned even more aloof than she'd planned to be, which made her limbs and movements stiff and unyielding, and even the music—he'd slipped something new into the CD player—seemed remote, unfamiliar, having nothing to do with her whatsoever.

She became all elbows and knees, missed steps, lost the rhythm. At one point, when he turned her into the open position, she felt a twinge in the back of her leg, a pull that shot up through her thigh and into her buttock.

"What's wrong, Harry?"

"I should have been prepared," she said, feeling like a marionette, strings tangled. "Sorry."

"Let's try it again."

She was better this time, but again a tingle shot up and down in a circuit from her toes to her hip.

"You okay?"

She was not okay. She felt crowded with emotional potpourri—hers and everyone's. It wasn't just her leg, or Taras, the kiss or Gilbert, who this morning, had opened his eyes, really opened them wide, and then, seeing nothing, had stroked the bedclothes between fingers that looked like mummified remains as she folded away the *New York Times*. It wasn't the wedding either, to which she wasn't paying enough attention, couldn't seem to focus on whether the cake should be chocolate on the inside, whether the table flower arrangements should be monochromatic, and who should sit with whom. No wonder Gaby was a bundle of gloom, with a mother who'd practically murdered her father, and was now on some mystifying tether—and never quite *there*. Julie felt prodded, pinched and helpless, and as it turned out, her escape into tango had proved to be no escape at all; the striped shirtsleeves of her instructor, circling her unsteady self, were yet another zone of cosmic peril.

"I can't stay tonight, Taras," she said as she fled to the door. She'd call Heather tomorrow and cancel the rest of the month of August lessons. There were only three or four more paid-up ones anyway. It would be easier on the phone, would mean not having to speak to Taras or see him face to face again. It would mean she wouldn't have to see him dance—really move, in the most provocative, exciting way—with a woman in white Lycra, ever again.

With some feeling of relief, Julie made her way down the stairs and to her car, and noted with small satisfaction that she'd parked very well, wheels close and parallel to the curb, and that there was no ticket on her windshield.

The next morning, Julie could not get out of bed. The last time her back went out, it was a pain that began at the waist and radiated vertically, up to the shoulder blade, down to one buttock. This time, Julie bit her lip, felt her eyes tear, the pain little knives, proceeding in her toes and maneuvering, stabbing, piercing, jabbing her upward in a snake of torture along its own path on the right side of her body.

Her first thought was that now she wouldn't be able to visit Gilbert in the hospital.

To get to the bathroom, Julie crawled along the floor, inching her body like a human caterpillar, the tears running down her cheeks, her elbows digging holes in the carpet. *Oh, God, stop.* Who had invented pain? Had thought up muscle spasm as a *tour de force* of torture? It was hideous. Julie barely managed the toilet, her teeth, a wet sponge across her face. The comb and brush were out of question and getting back to the edge of her bed, a twenty-minute tourniquet of torment.

She lay exhausted on the floor next to it, closed her eyes and tried to lose consciousness.

Yet somehow the pain was like a hot cup of something comforting; she felt she deserved it. It was the delayed punishment she had coming since October, since she'd walked away practically unscathed from the mangled body of the man she loved. "If you get Dr. Goetz on the phone it will be okay," she told the horror-stricken Mariadora when she appeared at the bedroom door. "I've gone through this before. And you know, Mariadora? Suffering makes me . . ." she couldn't finish. *I'm really getting mine!* She meant to say "strong," but thought instead "relieved." And finally said, "just tired."

Mariadora, with whom Julie had never actually had more than three or four consecutive-sentence conversations, lived in the here and now and also the ephemeral somewhere else, but her intentions toward Julie had always been solid and kind. She demonstrated toward her employer not only affection but a sort of proprietary protection. Julie knew Mariadora had loved Gil more, endlessly sought ways in which she could especially please The Mister, as she reverentially referred to him, but since the accident, no longer able to polish his tassel loafers to glossy luster, line up his socks in military order in his bureau drawers, or pick up his favorite, Blue Mountain Coffee, at the Mount Vernon deli near her apartment, she had switched her allegiance and warmth to Julie. There were the novice-cook's meals under foil, the roses from the garden, the nightgown placed just so across the folded-down bed. There were many surreptitious, worried glances thrown her way during the day and now she hurried to call not Dr. Goetz but Karen. She was her favorite—so it always seemed—of Julie's daughters, the one she said had "most of The Mister in the face and here." She pointed to the left breast pocket of her seersucker uniform, under which she thought her heart rested.

"You're such a good girl, Mariadora," Julie managed to say, although the smile of gratitude she tried for turned into a wince and then a whimper. "Do you think you can help me climb back into bed?"

CHAPTER EIGHTEEN

Ordinarily he would have prescribed a painkiller on the telephone, but Joe Goetz told Julie that she and Gilbert had a special place in his heart and she'd suffered enough for one year. So, even though his wife was having new neighbors at a barbecue tonight and needed him to flame the coals, he was here. More as a friend than a doctor, he whispered, stroking Julie's fingers.

He discussed the traction alternative for her spasm, wrote out a prescription for Flexiril 10 milligrams three times a day and placed it neatly on the night table next to her. Then, saying that he'd stopped in this morning to look in on Gilbert and—shaking his head like a very palsied patient himself—reminded her that even rich people could not afford $100,000 a month indefinitely, insurance coverage notwithstanding, to maintain a fantasy that there was life.

Julie bit her lip and tried to concentrate on what he was saying. She momentarily imagined she saw around Joe Goetz an aura, a delusion coming from pain, last year's Naprosyn found in the medicine cabinet and hot tea, but she almost felt she could reach out her fingertips and touch the gleam around his hair. Then it faded, and she noticed the mole next to his eyebrow she'd seen a hundred times, and his eyeglass frames, too small for his large face. He was after all, not a celestial being, but quite an ordinary person.

As he stood to leave and began moving toward the door, she called him back.

"Joe, tell me something."

He turned and stood at the foot of Julie's bed.

"I never thought I'd ask anyone this, but, was Gilbert faithful? I mean, as a husband? As far as you know?"

Joe's eyebrows shot up. He took his too-small glasses off and held them under his chin.

"What a question, Julie. What a question!" he said. "Why would this come up now?"

"Flat on my back. Too much thinkorama."

"Now, really, Julie." Joe Goetz rubbed the temple of his glasses against his chin for a moment. Julie felt he was choosing his words carefully. "Gilbert has a single occupancy heart, Julie, and you are its single occupant," is what he came up with.

And that was it.

As soon as he'd left, Julie berated herself for asking. Gil hadn't, had *not!* Home every night for dinner, two or three quick business trips a year and a hermetic devotion in his eyes whenever he looked at her, was proof as solid as the foundation of Number 66 Morris Lane. Julie wished she'd never brought it up.

As soon as Gaby walked in the door, bringing a bunch of jonquils and an assortment of cold soups and a chicken salad garnished with dates and grapes, Julie, her knees propped up by two pillows, told her about the doctor. "He's not a holy man," she said, catching her breath every word or two. "It's not his job to send Daddy to the Eternal Footman."

"His wife walks like a duck," Gaby said, kissing Julie's cheek. "Let's not talk about Daddy with you in such pain." She began walking around the room, straightening picture frames, fiddling with the curtains, touching the hand mirror on top of Julie's dresser. Why was the girl so fidgety? Now she stood in front of a painting of the Russian River she and Gilbert had bought on their first visit to the wine country. "We're not sure about Bermuda. September is hurricane season. We were considering Napa Valley for a honeymoon." She sounded not at all honeymoon-minded. "Of course, Wally is all for Portugal where the cork trees grow—" Gaby rolled her eyes, "and I want Patagonia, but we're trying to be realistic."

It was only when Karen and Susanna arrived, each bringing something wrapped in foil or boxed in Tupperware, and Karen said, "Why the long face, buddy?" that Julie guessed she'd been right about Gaby; this was no blissful bride-to-be. Julie watched her daughter take off the cardigan half of her old cream-colored cotton sweater set and fold it across the footboard of the bed. It seemed mannered and sluggish, like a diversionary tactic.

"What is your *problem?*" Karen continued. "Is it Daddy?"

"Of course it's Daddy! It's everything! Last night Wally and I spent an hour and a half trying to come to agreement about which song the orchestra would play for our first dance. We can't decide on where to go on our honeymoon. Wally's mother sent us a check that bounced, then Wally pulled a muscle teaching tennis, and I'm not sure if I even like my dress."

"Your dress is a Greek column of pure gorgeousness!" Susanna was looking in the mirror over Mama's dresser, pulling at her new bangs, which she said the hairdresser had cut too short and now revealed too much of her shaggy eyebrows. "And why not *Cheek to Cheek?*" She'd been to a wedding where they'd played that very number. Everyone thought it bouncy and charming. Even Dieter.

Karen didn't like that choice. And neither did Gaby, who frowned and called it retro.

"It's a standard. Standards are supposed to be retro!" Susanna stopped yanking at her bangs to give her sister a look.

"Why not *Badlands* then?"

"Talk about retro! You know how I feel about Springsteen!"

"The whole world loves Bruce except *my* sister!"

"I'm not allowed to have a dissenting opinion?"

"Girls, please!" Julie wanted only world peace, beginning right here in her bedroom, this minute.

"Okay, okay! But just make sure the bandleader includes a few tangos," Susanna said then, and gave Mama a big smile.

Julie, grimacing, moved a leg and the pain asserted itself in the middle of her buttock. *Ow.* She wanted to talk about her tango lessons. One of the girls would have to call the studio next week to cancel them permanently; she wasn't up to doing it. No, that wasn't quite correct. She was up to calling—the cordless was right here next to her—but she didn't want to explain anything, not to Heather, certainly not to Taras. The reality was that she didn't want to lie and say it was her back. It would make Taras feel guilty, and it certainly wasn't his fault.

"Listen, girls, about the tango," she began, but was interrupted by a knock on the bedroom door. It was Mariadora, holding in front of her as if she were making a presentation, a cellophane bag of something or other.

"Somebody ring the doorbell," she said.

What's that? The girls wanted to know, pulling her into the room, taking the sack of what looked like canola beans out of her hands.

Susanna and Karen exchanged looks; Julie knew they suspected the harmless, sweet Mariadora of many sins: coveting Julie's wardrobe, sticking her fingers into cake icing, sloppy floor mopping, eavesdropping. They knew Julie would overlook everything.

"Man give me this," Mariadora said.

"What man?" Julie asked, but Mariadora shrugged. "Young man, she gone in a minute." In moments of stress, she got her pronouns mixed, which led Susanna and Karen to send covert looks of mirth across the room at each other.

"There's a note here," Gaby said, and Julie, suddenly yearning for quiet, for music, maybe for a nap, asked timidly if, since it seemed intended for her, she could please be handed the package and the note.

She read it, but not aloud. It was written on the back of his professional calling card, and simply signed, T. "Harry, Please let me visit," it said.

"Coconut jellybeans," Julie announced to the girls, and she held the package tight in her hands, as if it were a pocketbook she was protecting from a purse snatcher.

"You love coconut jelly beans! Who sent them?" Karen wanted to know.

"A secret admirer!" Susanna said.

"A *thoughtful* secret admirer." Gaby had left her station in front of the painting of the Russian River and managed an agreeable expression that became nearly a smile.

"Just the *Fred Astaire Studios,*" Julie said.

"Fred himself!"

"That adorable instructor, I bet."

"Adorable? He's *adorable*?"

"I bet he has a crush on Mama."

"And maybe Mama has a crush on him!"

The girls were friends again, bustling around the bedside, dishing chicken salad on plates and pouring tea into tall glasses.

Julie's back hurt as much as it had this morning, sent sparks of electricity up and down through tissue and muscle, radiating around some joint buried below the last rib on her right. But for a moment, she was distracted. Taras's note, the candy, the thought and the effort, reached an ephemeral spot the tablets in small bottles on her night table couldn't. There was actually a moment of respite when the pain lost a round. *Taras.* Julie moved herself very slightly under the scalloped cotton summer coverlet Mariadora had carefully placed over her this morning and tried not to let a glimmer of anything show on her face.

The girls were watching her.

"I'm sort of tired," she said. It was true, actually, but in reality, she wanted them all to clear out. She wanted to be free to picture the shine of his hair and the outline of his mouth when he faced her on the dance floor. She wanted to think about his face in the rain and the way his chino pants hung on his hips. She wanted time alone now, to concentrate on reuniting herself with all these images. She was not so interested in chicken salad; her appetite was for opening the package he'd sent her, to taste the sweet coconut for which he must have made a special trip to the mall, searched its levels for the shop in which candy was piled in glass bins, looked through assortments in every color and flavor until he'd located this particular, special favorite of hers, and his. Her appetite was also for rereading the note he'd written, examining his handwriting and drifting off, in solitude, to allow herself to feel like an adolescent, drift into dreams of being firm and young again and feel as she'd felt long ago, before Gilbert and before the girls, when smoldering, yearning, and disorderly conduct were still a possibility.

CHAPTER NINETEEN

The sky was rouged to a poetic rose when Gaby left Mama's. She knew Wally was now in their apartment waiting dinner for her, but she drove slowly, wanting a few moments to herself before heading home. Ella Fitzgerald's voice filled the car, wanting someone who would watch over her. It was tears music at the wrong time, helping wring out Gaby's heart.

Two weeks ago, after the wheelchair tournament, Gaby had gently tried to nudge Stretch into seeing new possibilities for Mitzi. She'd described the matches in infinite detail, didn't mention the time she'd spent checking out Multiple Sclerosis on the Internet. "Amazing what disabled people can do," she'd said. The motorized wheelchairs, new Canadian Neuroscience Research Center, so many support groups, and had he heard about Pycnogenol, definitely a nutritional breakthrough? *Maybe, maybe!* All manner of propaganda had fallen from her lips, before and after he'd kissed them in a motel near the Cross County Center. It was the week Mitzi was off in Scottsdale visiting her mother, the week she'd told Wally she'd be working late, very late. Then, at some point during their lovemaking, someone had knocked on their door. Perhaps it was the cleaning people, or another guest at the wrong room, but Gaby felt Stretch freeze in her arms, saw his face turn to plaster. He waited for the intruder to knock again, but whoever had been outside, moved on. Stretch sat up and took a sip of the iced vanilla coffee she'd brought along in a thermos, and Gaby thought *I wouldn't be surprised if he crossed himself.* There was no maybe here at all. Motel moments, weekend trysts and a Steuben glass heart paperweight, the birthday present from him she had to hide in a drawer of her desk in the office, was all Gaby saw quite clearly she would ever have of Stretch. Just as clearly, she knew it was better than the void of no Stretch at all.

Shingo and Benita Raffle were sitting in the living room when Gaby walked in. Four cigarette butts were crushed into a porcelain Villeroy & Boch pie plate, Wally's idea of a substitute ashtray. Benita, wearing yellow pants and a white sweater with yellow tassels hanging on it here and there, was just putting out a stub, waving at the air above the ashtray with her free hand. "I gave up chocolate ice cream but for this vice"—she now waved her hand in front of her mouth, and the tassels waved along—"someone will have to call the vice squad." She was looking somewhat but not completely apologetic, dimpling, in fact, as if everyone had always forgiven her for everything, pretty blonde girl that she was. "And how is your mother feeling?" Her own mother, she explained, was idiosyncratically bipolar.

Wally, a dish of peanuts in his hand, pointed to the bedroom to change the subject. "Wait till you see what Shingo and Benita brought as a wedding present!''

Gaby had never seen Shingo wearing anything but tennis clothes before and had to adjust to him in jeans and a madras sports shirt with snaps instead of buttons. So different from Wally, with his acquired taste for Banana Republic shirts, J. Crew khakis, Coach belts, Church's shoes. Standing politely—Gaby was reminded of English boarding school manners—Shingo explained they'd finally gotten his van fixed and brought up the gift before it broke down again. "If you guys don't care for it, you can exchange it at any time." Like a man in a lineup, Shingo never looked completely at ease.

Gaby knew she wouldn't like whatever they'd picked. If Benita liked it, how would she? Then, she hated herself for being so difficult, so negative. They all got up and followed her into the bedroom, hovering behind for her reaction, where the gold-framed poster was standing upright against the foot of the bed. They had rigged a floor lamp to throw extra light on it.

No surprise, the five-foot high poster: ALFAMA, and the year in art deco print, 1938, and what looked like a Visigoth with a spear standing on a twisty, cobbled street. The whole thing was a bit hard to make out, so dark it might have been painted at night by an artist who was, like Benita's mother, idiosyncratically bipolar.

"No cork anywhere?" She kept her voice as light as she could, noticing that Benita's shoes were toeless and that her toenails were painted gold. *Gold.* What would the credentials department of the American Society of Psychologists have to say to that?

"What do you think, it grows on trees?" Shingo let out an appreciative sound, *a substitute for a laugh,* and Benita said she'd looked, really searched for something with cork trees, if only in the background.

As Gaby looked at the poster, lists of innocuous adjectives zigzagged through her head: *Interesting, exotic, unusual, impressive,* with which she might, without actually lying, redeem their choice. Instead, she looked down at the gilded toenails standing on her bedroom carpet, and said, "It was so thoughtful of you," knowing very well that she was politely saying: "I hate it" and that they all instantly knew it was what she meant.

It gave Gaby some small perverse joy to see how awkward the moment, how disappointed their faces. Everyone was looking at the floor, thinking, thinking, thinking!

"I really like it," Wally jumped into the breach, trying to make up for the cold splash with his warm towel of friendshippy approval.

"Well, where will we hang it?" Gaby challenged, and all eyes turned to Wally, who had put up his hands, palms up, in a gesture of heaven-will-provide.

"We won't be living here forever," he said mildly, tossing it off, *problem solved,* as if they could afford to move and very soon, to a place with museum wall space.

The reality was that Daddy, wanting to keep them nearby, had actually bought them this apartment. Wally insisted he'd pay the $200,000 back as soon as the business was really on its feet, and the furniture, a few pieces from the den on Morris Lane that Mama had redecorated, the wedding gift Edward Fields rug, and the blonde leather sofas, had been subsidized by her parents, one way or another. It was only recently that Stretch was paying Gaby what she deserved— nothing to do with the sex, he assured her!—only in the last six months that Wally's product lines and marketing strategies were beginning to look really promising. Continental Cork was finally inching toward the big time, with orders from Citibank for quiet flooring, Comp USA for cork mouse pads and

The Mall of America for elevator wall coverings, to name a few heavy hitters, but these were still baby steps. For the moment, and until they repaid Daddy, it looked as if she and Wally would in fact be living right here, in these three-and-a-half rooms, with a clock, some photos and a few of Mama's old bird prints taking up the wall space.

Back in the living room, the subject twisted away from the poster to tennis, the wedding, the head-lines—police brutality in Camden (which Benita ascribed to brutality in early life), illegal aliens shot in a basement in Queens, a political scandal in French Open country—and back to cork. Gaby looked a few times at her watch. Short of closing her eyes and taking a nap, no one could have been more obviously bored by guests, and while she seemed to be two people, one watching herself with horror at her rude-ness, the other continuing spoiled-rotten behavior, she continued to cross and uncross her legs, sigh and add next to nothing to the conversation. Soon, very soon, they took the hint, shifting in their chairs and looking at their watches, exclaiming in surprise how late it had amazingly become.

While Wally walked them out the door and down to the elevator, Gaby picked up the pie plate with its half-dozen cigarette butts and marched it into the kitchen, hoping her behavior would set off sparks as soon as he returned. Instead, Wally insouciantly put a frozen pizza into the microwave. He was so laid-back, he might have just wakened from a nice snooze.

She dumped the butts into the garbage pail, adding a very pointed *Ugh*, as she slammed shut the cabinet door below the sink and ran water over the dish.

"So you didn't like the poster," Wally began, sound-ing tentative and wary, ready for anything, like a dog who is sensing an earthquake. He was, however, main-taining a neutral smile, as if her taste in art was the only little problem here.

It made Gaby all the more angry. She yearned for a hard battle, a view of Wally's worst side and their real differences, wanted causes to hate him, so she could blame him in some way for the way she was deceiving him.

"You *like* it?" she asked.

"We don't have to keep it, Gab."

Gaby opened the refrigerator and spotted a cellophane bag filled with lettuce, a red onion and those fancy tomatoes with stems attached she loved. Wally must have stopped on the way home, bought them, along with enough greens for the salad he knew she'd want for dinner. He was infuriatingly thoughtful, forever thinking of her and trying to find ways to please her. So white hat, so *bland*.

"You need Prozac just to look at it," she began, while he was putting cork placemats—the latest design, white doves—on the kitchen table. Last month, when he'd brought them home, Gaby had liked them. Not now. She wished she had an arrow to shoot into them.

Wally ignored the edge in her voice. "I'll ask Shingo to pick it up, bring it back to the gallery." *Unperturbed!* Wally was not mentioning Gaby's attitude toward their guests, *his friends,* as anyone in his right mind would. Wally would stay unruffled through a massacre at the post office.

"I'm sorry you asked him to be your best man. I really think he's—not the greatest choice. Really. I mean, he's shifty. All cloak and dagger, like a mole."

"But we had this discussion months ago," Wally countered, busy now with knives and forks. "What do you want to drink, Gab? We may be out of cranberry juice."

Infuriating. Maddening. Wally was so *not there.* Once removed, like the spirit of Dionysus, just dropped in to set the table and pour the wine.

"Water is fine," Gaby bit off. She was tired, hungry,

and he refused to fight. "I want to cancel the wedding!" was on the tip of her tongue. She'd never come this close, but then she got a red-alert flash, a vision of poor Mama, lying in bed, knees up, fielding pain, a different Mama with the same face in the same body. Gaby saw her again as she looked, hands curled around the bag of candy her dance instructor had brought over, dreamy-eyed and remote, transformed into this new, unavailable, somewhat distant soul. It wasn't only the bad back; these days she was so cloudy one never knew what she was thinking. Gaby pictured herself standing at the foot of her bed, telling her the wedding was off.

"Didn't you and I discuss Shingo and you said if I chose Dieter, Elliot would be upset and if I chose Elliot, Dieter would be hurt?" Wally asked now, mild as Jesus, while she was clattering around the kitchen and thinking black thoughts.

No wonder her sex drive was nil with Wally. Who could make love to an absentee lover? Who could be engaged in sex with a man so *disengaged?*

"Shingo is so—bookie-like. And the *psychologist,* I mean, did you see the *pedicure?*"

"Gaby, should I mix up some of that mustard, red wine vinegar or do you want to use bottled dressing? Benita's not a shrink *yet* and maybe she overanalyzes, but she's basically okay. And she's usually right on target."

"I SAID, did you see the goddamn gold toenails, Wally?"

"Oh boy, weren't they something?" Wally said, shaking his head, as he took out an ice tray and started putting ice cubes methodically into Gaby's glass. "You sit down, Gab, you're tired. I'll make the salad. No garlic, right?"

Gaby sank into a chair and rubbed her palms together. She felt a breeze at the back of her neck, as if someone had put a hole through the roof and

blown cold air across her back. *The hell with everything.*
"I think we ought to call off the wedding," she said.

Wally dropped an ice cube, blinked, stooped to
pick it up, dropped it into the sink. He spun on his
heel to look at her.

"Are you serious?"

Gaby couldn't answer. Her vocal cords, her throat,
maybe every muscle in her head, was in paralysis.

Wally pulled up a chair to face her and they looked
at each other for what seemed the length of the reading of a psalm. Then he reached over and took her
hands in both of his. "Nerves," he said. "C'mon,
honey, don't be ridiculous. It's wedding jitters. A little
disagreement and you're going to call off our wedding?" When she didn't answer, he added, "You know
what Benita said when I walked them to the elevator?"

Gaby gave him a blank stare.

"She said that sometimes a tragedy like the one
that happened to your father can totally change a
person's personality. This isn't you. You're just not
you."

He was right. She was not herself. She was bitchy-
mean-hateful. For the moment, she couldn't speak
to agree with him.

Wally leaned closer. "It's like being hit with a club.
You get sort of a concussion. A concussion of the
soul. That's what she said."

She could smell the shampoo he'd used on his hair.
Prell. Same as Stretch's.

A minute later, he had reached over to wrap his
arms around her and covered her face with kisses,
while Gaby, eyes closed, pictured Stretch when he'd
told her day before yesterday that she'd brought harmony and blue skies back into his life.

CHAPTER TWENTY

Ruthie sat in the bedroom vanity chair Mariadora had pulled over to Julie's bedside, and covered Julie's hand with her own. Two rings, possibly new, sparkled on her fingers, the familiar love-and-kisses bracelet on her wrist. She'd had her hair cut short for summer and looked quite different—younger and bouncier, more the way she'd looked years ago. Before leaving for the day, Mariadora had brought up a tray for the patient, another of her culinary enigmas hidden under aluminum foil. Ruthie peeked as soon as Mariadora left the room, and her face said it all: a nutritional zero and no competition whatsoever for her green and healthy cucumber and dill soup.

Julie's back felt worse today. The Flexiril seemed not to be working well at all, and the pain was like a throttling buzz that ran a course through her right side no matter which way she turned her body and shifted her legs. She'd hitched herself into the traction device Susanna had found in the attic, the same canvas pulley and weight system she'd used last time her back went out, and now found it practically impossible to sleep. Being wakeful and immobilized meant more time trying not to think: with five weeks to go, would she make it to the wedding? If she wasn't at Gilbert's bedside every day, would the quality of his care decline? And Taras—the coconut jellybeans had knocked her for a loop. She imagined him shopping for them, trudging through the mall, checking the stock in its various candy shops, rejecting this or that one, finally finding her favorite—*their* favorite—with some sense of—what? Pleasure? Delight? To go on this errand, to be that *thoughtful*, well, no wonder despite trying to bump him out of her thoughts, she kept seeing the way the water had run down the sides of his temples that day in the rain, and randomly, in the middle of a television newscast—a crisis in Uganda, a landslide in California—a newscaster's chin or eyebrow reminded her of his chin, or his eyebrows, or the way he had of holding his head.

"So. It looks as if you've had enough of the tango for the moment, dear," Ruthie said, after telling Julie she'd only "stay a minute, just long enough to get a bit of soup into you" then putting down the spoon after Julie said as delicious as it was, she couldn't manage one more sip.

"Susanna called the studio and told them I wouldn't be back." Julie was simultaneously jabbed with a little pain dart right above her hip. She bit her lip and squeezed shut her eyes, glad to see Ruthie, but hoping she wouldn't stay long.

"It's just not *fair.*" Ruthie squeezed Julie's hand where it rested on the cotton coverlet. "You've been through so much this year, dear. On my way over I thought, well, how could I help? What can I *do* for you, dear?"

Julie demurred, saying the girls were doing her shopping, calling constantly, were the best caretakers, then stopped short, remembering that poor Ruthie's only offspring and potential caretaker had died at age 15.

"Perhaps," Ruthie continued, "you'd like us to go to the hospital and look in on Gilbert? We'd be glad to." Ruthie and Lou had wanted to visit Gilbert, had expressed that desire long ago, right after the accident. "You've never let us visit. Never let us go to the—" Ruthie's voice stopped, as if a tape had run out. Her face drooped, one eyelid in particular. Last year she'd said she was going to have her eyes done, but hadn't followed through. Come to think of it, she'd said it the year before, too.

"I just didn't want anyone to see him the way he was." This was no time to have to be on the defense, Julie thought, realizing that Ruthie had felt hurt, had been carrying this modest little indignation around like a torn photograph. She imagined Ruthie and Lou batting it back and forth over pasta and wine, or late at night, in bed. "And Gilbert our best friend," they'd say. "What is she *hiding?*"

"If it means so much to you," Julie eked out, shifting slightly, trying to find a more comfortable spot, "Go. Gilbert is . . . well, be prepared for a—shock."

"We—wanted to say—good-bye—in case, you know." Ruthie's lower lip, her one droopy eyelid, everything seemed all of a sudden in dejected sync. Her bounciness was gone; was water actually gathering in one or both of her big brown eyes? She touched the collar of her gold chevron-stripe jacket. "Is it new, Ruthie?" Julie had asked fifteen minutes ago. Like the body under it, it now also seemed to have gone completely limp.

Ruthie lowered her voice. "I wasn't going to say anything, Julie. I really wasn't. God, don't you have enough problems?"

"What—?"

"Dear, I am scared. Scared out of my wits."

"Scared? Of what?"

Ruthie's sigh sounded like a plucked guitar string. "I haven't even mentioned it to Lou. He gets, well, you know how he gets. Crazy with worry."

Was this about her eyelid? Or, *what*? "Ruthie—?"

"I've been spotting, Julie. Two weeks now."

"Spotting?" *Spotting.*

"Yes."

"You haven't been to the doctor?"

"Tomorrow, at eleven."

"Oh, Ruthie, it'll be nothing."

"My mother died of the big C. Breast, then ovaries. Twenty-one months from start to finish, remember?"

Julie remembered meeting Ruthie's mother, Before and After. A henna-headed live wire who quoted lines from movies going back fifty years, the Before. A powdered, lipsticked cadaver in pink evening dress in a coffin, the After.

Just as Julie grappled her way through trying to find a comforting response, the telephone rang. "Shall I get it for you?" Ruthie, pulling herself together, reached for the telephone.

"Please," Julie said, trying to remember if Ruthie's mother drank or smoked or had had some major trauma to account for it, the big, ghastly C.

"Who shall I say is calling?" Ruthie was asking, her face instantly changed into amanuensis efficiency as she covered the receiver and handed the telephone to Julie. "Terrance?"

"Taras," Julie told her, "my dance instructor." Taking the receiver, she could feel her cheeks and forehead begin to glow. The telltale flush, so embarrassing, but Ruthie was thinking of cancer, not Julie's red cheeks.

His voice. It was probably not extraordinary, was any man's unremarkable baritone, but for Julie it was vivid and mnemonic. It brought back not only the yellow radio in her mother's kitchen, but dreamy summers and old songs and the fluster of adolescence.

"Harry, I want to come to see you," he said.

No. You can't.

"Thank you for the jellybeans, Taras. It was very thoughtful of you."

"May I come to see you?"

No!

"Friday? I have a free day. No classes after two o'clock."

Ruthie was preoccupied with the remains of the dinner tray. Julie briefly watched her examining Mariadora's contribution without seeing her. She was in the grip of an off-the-ground feeling, a throwback, in disuse for thirty-odd years. For a moment, nothing came out of her mouth.

"Harry? Are you there?"

"Uhmm."

"Friday. Let me come to see you, just for a few minutes, Friday."

A logjam in her head. A fly had found its way into the bedroom and now made its appearance on the base of the porcelain lamp on Julie's dresser. Someone would have to zap it.

"There's a fly in my bedroom," she said.

"I won't stay long," he said.

"At what time would you like to stop by?" she said.

What did I say?

Hearing Julie's voice wobble, Ruthie turned, eyebrows up, and looked at her friend, just as the beautiful melody of Taras's voice was telling her he'd missed her, and, speaking her name again, asking if Friday at four o'clock would be all right.

CHAPTER
TWENTY-ONE

When Taras came to 66 Morris Lane the first time, he brought Julie Kessler a bouquet of cymbidium wrapped in cellophane. On that first day, he brought the lavender flowers and Mariadora found a vase, and led him up to Julie's bedroom. By then, she had almost canceled his visit five times. It was in this room that she and Gilbert had slept side by side since the night they moved in, walked naked, made love, fought and reconciled, and when Dickie died, where both had shed tears; this was her private cell, her cloister, her sanctum sanctorum. She was mad to allow her dance teacher, *this gate-crasher,* to step over this intimate threshold, like allowing him to lean over and look under her skirt. Wouldn't even her open-minded daughters say it?

But, they wouldn't. Karen knew he was coming and might have told Gaby yesterday when they were both at Gilbert's bedside. Neither one had called to warn Julie not to dare invite the upstart from Fred Astaire Dance Studios upstairs but only to tell her that inexplicably, Daddy had gained a pound. They didn't know, of course, how the back of Julie's neck would feel, how the moisture would gather over her eyebrows and under her breasts when she saw him in the bedroom doorway. He hesitated just long enough to seem framed by the doorjamb, a perfect composition to photograph, frame and hang in a photo exhibition.

"Harry." His voice had now arrived in her room, and under his glossy, freshly combed hair, his knitted, worried brow. The eyes, same color as Karen's. "So, where's the fly?" That was the pivotal moment when a flag went up, when her determination to stop what had not even started flip-flopped and was gone. People always said there existed the force of mind over body, but Julie had remained skeptical until this Friday afternoon at four o'clock. But, as his polished shoes took self-confident strides across the white-on-white squares of her carpet, and as he took the cushiony steps toward her, she couldn't feel—or just forgot—the pins and needles in her lower back. Behind him, Mariadora, vase in both hands, stood looking left and right for a spot on which to park it. "Right here, on the night table," Julie managed, *where I can smell its blossoms,* which, as it turned out, didn't have any scent whatsoever.

There were a few seconds of awkwardness when Mariadora, showing no facial expression of any sort, retreated from the room, closing the door behind her. Julie had left the pulleys and metal harness of her traction device behind and had earlier moved to the old chaise near the window in preparation for his visit. She hadn't used the settee twice in the ten years since she'd read picture books to the girls. It stood in the corner, had faded from a rich blue to a wishy-washy shade the color of old dungarees. Julie had pulled on Gilbert's robe, then changed her mind, and with Mariadora's help, saying it needed cleaning, replaced it, not without a jabbing-scissors blow to the right hip as she pulled her arms from the sleeves.

Instead, she picked a robe of her own, the azalea silk one she'd bought in the shop in the Regent Hotel the winter she and Gilbert were in Hong Kong. She remembered Gilbert helping choose the color, signing the travelers' checks. It didn't cling, was opaque and did not speak of intimacy or sex. It made her look demure.

He wore his familiar striped shirt on this first Friday visit had added a tie and linen-type-but-not-linen jacket, the necktie a splashy thing Gilbert would have donated to Second Chance on the spot. Now, jacket off, collar open, he seemed more himself, more relaxed, even a little more actively, dangerously, intrusively, a man.

That first time, he reached into his pocket and pulled out a packet of photographs. The girls would have called it sharing. The pictures were of his son, Tommy, who Taras sometimes called T.J., my son, or, Little Guy. On that first occasion, as she sat on the chaise, both legs up, a cushion placed just so behind her back to prop her into the least painful posture, he handed Julie the pictures one after another, often apologizing for the light, the pose, the camera, the composition. He seated himself on the same vanity chair that Ruthie had pulled up next to Julie a few days ago and leaned forward, his hands spread on his knees. As Julie examined the snapshots, she looked for the resemblance between father and son, scrutinized the background in every picture like an FBI agent poring over crime scene photos. His house, his car, the pattern of the dishes on his kitchen table, the clock on the kitchen wall, a teakettle shaped like a chicken. Whose sleeve was that in the corner, the person out of camera range? Who'd chosen the strange Moroccan wallpaper and ruby glass pitcher in the dining room? And whose were the photos held by magnets to the refrigerator? "We were on the Cape; see that tree in the background? An hour later a storm blew up and just uprooted it.'' Or, ''That's my landlady's ten-speed. She let the Little Guy borrow it.'' ''This is the dog I was telling you about? She sheds like crazy and growls at the Con Ed trucks, but I swear, Ridgeway turned T.J.'s life around. He's been pretty much a perfect citizen since we got her.'' Julie listened hard. What she was looking for but never finding were traces of a woman. *What happened to Thomas's mother?* Many times Julie began to formulate the query, but stopped. When Julie had asked Karen about Elliot's ex, living in Madrid, Karen had answered, ''Mama, please, don't go to Spain.'' Taras's signals were clear as water. Julie would not go to Spain now.

Instead, she began talking about her own mother. It had been years since she found anyone—aside from the girls, who never knew either of their grandmothers—interested enough to hear about Violet Frost, née Freedfeld, Julie's spoiled, ingenue matriarch, a woman who had a different hairstyle every week, knew every Hammerstein, Hart and Gershwin lyric ever written and owned 60 bottles of perfume. Violet, who had Julie's face exactly, also had a sweet singing voice and a bulldozing determination to be a big band star. Julie remembered the look of disdain on her mother's face when she herself, dousing her eight or nine or ten-year-old body with her mother's Shalimar, tried to emulate her vocalizations. *Off! You're off!* Her mother's angry soprano still rang in Julie's ears. ''Not that she was mean or abusive, just so terribly disappointed. I had no voice, couldn't carry a tune, so I was less than nothing to my mother.'' Julie's eyes, in the presence of Taras, filled and she looked away. *How embarrassing.*

Violet's talent got her as far as a nightclub somewhere in Queens, and a second husband who owned shopping arcades on Long Island. They died together a week before Christmas when a car rolled off the back of an auto transport truck in front of their Buick on the Long Island Expressway. It left Violet's children suddenly rich orphans. Julie was seventeen and Dickie twenty-four, their real father having disappeared permanently into the armed services when Julie was not yet three.

"When did your mom die?" Taras asked, possibly to fill a silence. Julie thought calling Violet "Mom" quaint and endearing, making her feel childlike and as vulnerable as she was then. It was the day after her mother's death when Dickie had walked into the house bringing his college roommate, Gilbert Kessler, who had long since been invited to spend the Christmas holidays. Gilbert's own mother was already dead and his much-older father on the verge. Sitting between them at her mother's funeral, Gilbert had his arms around their shoulders while Julie and Dickie gripped each other's hands and tried to do what distant relatives recommended—be brave and be together.

It turned out that Gilbert, the mature college graduate student, who had already gone through the funeral of his own mother, seemed then like a dashing uncle providence had plunked down onto the extra bed in Dickie's room. He pulled them through the holidays, telling stories, playing phonograph records and quoting lyrics from the bluegrass songs he loved so much. He played the trumpet and was learning the banjo. For Julie, falling in love with him was an inchmeal procedure that took years, the beginning inch that first Christmas.

Unlike the girls, who never let her get through a sentence, Taras was seemingly transfixed by Julie's every word, beaming straight into her eyes. For the first time, she talked to him about her own accident, from the time she and Gilbert left Gaby's engagement party, all of it that she could remember. It already seemed like an event passed into history, softened, distant, less hideous. Taras began stroking her fingers as she spoke. It seemed exactly right, a tender, friend-shippy I'm-here-for-you touch. There was no timidity about his half-finger, either; this take-me-as-I-am confidence Julie admired enormously, had tried to instill in each of her daughters. She herself was still trying for the self-assurance that her own mother had little by little squeezed out of her.

"My mother died in nineteen sixty, when we were living in Riverdale. I was tying a red ribbon on the dog's collar when the telephone rang."

Taras stretched his mouth into an expression that looked as if he was trying to remember where he'd left his keys. "Nineteen sixty? The year Kennedy beat Nixon. Three years before I was born. Actually, I was born the day John Kennedy was buried. Which is why we didn't get to the funeral." She gave him a half-hearted smile, thinking, *the year after I graduated from high school. He is younger, so much younger than I thought!* He caught her expression. "I may seem young, but"— he tapped his shirt pocket with his half finger—"I think old. Bad luck and circumstance and, so"—he shrugged—"so, I had to resign from being young. I don't even remember being a kid. I think I signed my own birth certificate."

He added, "And, *I* never could carry a tune, either."

Susanna drove Julie to Ruthie's chiropractor, who, ebullient and full of theories about mattress manufacturers and spinal alignments, did in fact give her a series of adjustments, three days apart. The torment of Julie's Rube Goldberg traction device and codeine gave way to a return to the comfort of her steaming bathtub, perfumed with chamomile herbal salts

Karen had brought from the Body Shop. Julie finally
was able to take a quarter mile walk, sit through a
dinner with Susanna at Lusardi's, and visit Ruthie,
who was leaving for Boston to consult with her
nephew, a big surgeon at Mass General. And, to visit
Gilbert, who had these last weeks lost not only the
pound he'd gained, but two more.

All the time she'd been recovering, during the six
or so visits Taras made, first to her bedroom, and
later, when she was well enough to greet him in the
den or the kitchen or on the patio, he had not once
tried to kiss her again. Twice he'd come after Mariadora had left for the day, once using the house key
hidden in a fake rock near the front step, and on
those two occasions—she was able to walk to the front
door to let him in; later—they were alone in the
house. As they lounged on the patio with the light
outside growing dim, the lamps flickering on in the
garden, the smell of the roses and the stars glittering
in romantic collusion, he still kept a polite distance.
A gallant, dancing knight; the girls would have a laugh
if they could read her thoughts.

When she awoke these days, her first morning
image was no longer of Gilbert lying in a living death
four miles away, but of Taras. She still knew nothing
much about him, but heard the sound of his voice,
saw the white glint of his smile with its endearing,
unique, alluring, *adorable*, overlapping front teeth,
the wet sheen of his hair, the window-mannequin
shoulders. Even with her head in her pillow, she imagined she could smell his aftershave.

She wondered how this had come to happen to
her, still a married woman who loved her husband.
Now, lying in bed or soaking in her bath, or simply
walking through the garden with the music of the
tango coming from the sound system, her body with

back pain diminished, then gone, seemed lithe and immortal. It felt the way it used to, very, very long ago, even in the years before Kennedy was president, the years before Taras was born.

CHAPTER
TWENTY-TWO

"I think she's got a thing for her dance instructor," Susanna told Karen on the telephone the day they were finalizing arrangements for Mama's birthday celebration. She didn't actually believe it; Mama had been at Daddy's bedside for hours yesterday, brought a tape recorder and played his bluegrass music, still hoping for some response even at this late date.

"You can't be serious?" Karen's voice shot up an octave.

"Well, she wouldn't let us have this family party Saturday night. He's taking her to dinner. A special birthday surprise, she told me."

"The tango guy? The one in the picture?"

Susanna had stuck the seashell-framed photograph of Mama dancing with Taras up in the spare bedroom, and now thought she ought to go upstairs, take another look at the man, in the unlikely case her kidding remark actually carried a grain of truth.

"He's taking her out on a *date*? How old is this guy?" Karen wanted to know.

Susanna giggled. "Younger than Mama. Much. Maybe he's taking her to his high school prom."

"What's his name, anybody know?"

"Taras. It's Ukrainian," Susanna said.

"Taras what?"

"Oh, you know dance instructors don't have last names!"

"Imagine Mama going out on a date, let alone with a Fred Astaire dance instructor!"

"He came to see her a few times when her back went out, but you knew that."

"Elliot thought that was just making nice, maybe to prevent a lawsuit."

"Elliot's a cynic."

"Cynicism comes with life experience," Karen said. "Or age," Susanna responded, immediately wanting to take it back. "At least he's an American citizen!" Karen shot back. Perhaps what caused Susanna to slip was envy, which sometimes leaked from the machinery of their relationship. Or it simply might have been mystification. Against all odds, this May-December marriage of her sister's seemed to be healthy and working. Unlike her own.

This morning, with no warning, and for once with no signal cramps, she'd found a spot of menstrual blood on the same white linen sheets on which she and Dieter had made love more than a dozen times this month alone. And later this morning, Dieter, silent, full of what might have been unspoken anger or just indigestion, left for Manhattan and the offices of the Kaiser-Gelb hotel chain with a cool kiss on her cheek and no clues as to how he felt, what manifestation of dissatisfaction or trip he'd spring on her next.

She'd changed the sheets, almost tearfully, before going off to her own office, tried to reach Mama. She had urgently wanted to talk to her mother, despite the possibility that Mama would still continue to be detached and out of reach. Last night, after dinner, a lobster salad because Susanna refused to eat pork products on a night when the temperature was nearly ninety degrees, Dieter had headed upstairs to his computer, and his E-mail sessions with Liesel.

"And what did Liesel have to say today?" she'd asked, keeping her query pleasant, as they were already in bed and about to turn off the lights.

"She has a rash on both hands. She was helping washing dishes in the restaurant and the soap they are using, she's allergic. Her skin is rupturing."

"Erupting," Susanna gently corrected, and made the appropriate empathic sounds. She tried getting more information; he'd been up there for what seemed like hours and really, how long could anyone discuss a skin rash? But, he snapped off the light and before she could ask whether Liesel had gone to a doctor, his head had buried itself in his two white linen feather pillows and he was, or pretended to be, fast asleep.

Now Mariadora picked up the telephone and told Susanna Mama was unavailable. "Missuz in the bath," she said, and then started to add something else, but stopped herself. Maybe someone had come to the door, or Mama had called from upstairs. In her hurry to get to the office, Susanna never gave it another thought.

Karen and Elliot's Soho apartment was not the funky loft she'd always said she wanted, but an apartment in a converted ironworks factory fitted with a marble and wood lobby, a concierge and mirrored elevator. It was originally Elliot's place, gutted and redone by Karen because Elliot had rejected a loft— on the basis of poor elevator service, draftiness and noisy pipes. So Karen settled on his six rooms, two-

and-a-half baths and two terraces in The Soho Sovereign. The hallway leading to the apartment was hung with black and white photos of the worlds' bridges in gold leaf frames, and the apartment door, one of only two on the floor, was painted glossy black, with white trim.

Inside, sitting on a rectangle of gray, white, and yellow wool carpet in the living room, sat a black-and-white Fornasetti cube coffee table surrounded by charcoal leather—a steel-footed couch with black-shaded lamps on either side, two chairs, and two ottomans. An oil painting of what might have been Adam and Eve or an apple and an orange on a yellow background took up the wall behind the couch practically to the ceiling. A black-lacquered screen stood in one corner, an electrified stone water fountain burbled in the other. Karen had put the roses Mama had brought into a black glass vase and set the vase on the window sill of one of the row of uncurtained windows.

Karen had assembled a tray of hors d'oeuvres ordered from Dean & Deluca and had personally prepared the long drinks. She called them Karen's Sea Breeze With a Twist, squeezed some lime in with the grapefruit-cranberry-juices-plus-vodka over ice, and everyone said the drinks were marvelous, even Dieter, who took a sip and said they were excellent, but preferred to stick with his vodka Gibson.

Susanna thought Mama was looking better and better. Her hairdresser was on his August vacation so she'd gone to the new Irish girl, who had cut it shorter, given it bounce and brought Mama's hair into the new century, making her look, as Gaby said, "ready to do a moisturizer infomercial." Susanna couldn't help but notice that she laughed more easily these days, had been most amused when Wally told everyone about the wedding photographer, who used a rhesus monkey named Sophia as a studio assistant. Mama talked more, too, less about Daddy, more about this and that, the neighbors' new poodle, the gardener fighting the aphids, and Ruthie DiLorenzo, who was going in for surgery next week. A little about Taras, too. Susanna listened closely when Mama said she would be going back to her dance classes after all, probably within a few weeks, as soon as she felt one hundred percent. And yes, he was taking her out to dinner tomorrow night, for her birthday. Well, why not?

Elliot, who had spent last weekend with Karen visiting friends in Bridgehampton, had gained a bit of color in his cheeks and looked healthier than he had for a long time. When Mama said she was going to sign up for more dance classes, he took a sip of his Sea Breeze and remarked that the tango instructor's special attentions had not been for nothing then, had they? Susanna saw Mama's smile wiped off just like that, as if a squeegee had run across her face.

"Oh, I don't know," Gaby said, "I think Terrance really likes Mama. Who wouldn't?" and she patted the sleeve of Mama's new white cotton piqué jacket.

Elliot whistled a few bars of *I Get Ideas* and danced a few steps as he passed a tray of stuffed cherry tomatoes from guest to guest. Mama's expression was hidden behind the paper napkin she was using to blot her mouth. She passed on the tomatoes.

"It's Taras, a Russian name," Karen corrected, and asked everyone to try the Limburger, which was a special mild type, flavored with caraway and not made in Limburg in Belgium, but definitely imported from Germany.

"We were in the cheese shop," Elliot was saying, as he spread a bit on a piece of pumpernickel, "and I said, 'Karen, Dieter is sure to appreciate the effort, so let's buy a jar, and get some poompernickel to go with it'." He held out a piece of bread spread with

cheese to Dieter on a paper napkin in his palm and
waited for Dieter to reach for it.

"No thanks," Dieter said, while Susanna's own
palms, clasped together, began to sweat.

Elliot looked staggered, as if Dieter had refused a
raise. "You don't want to try the Limburger?"

Dieter shook his head vehemently, as if he'd been
offered a cow's head, still moving. "It's smelly. I never
eat it."

"You never eat it?" Elliot looked to Karen as if to
say, 'How could we have made such a titanic mistake?'
and then looked again to Dieter, in disbelief. "I
thought all Germans thought Limburger was *Wund-
erbar.*"

To Susanna the remark resounded like the crack
of a whip.

"I am not all Germans," Dieter said, his face a
mask one could hang on one of these glossy gray
walls. "Just one of them."

Elliot let out a little ha-ha. "Well, that's lucky,
because we don't have room here in the apartment
for all of them."

Susanna waved a white flag. "Dieter isn't much for
cheese, Elliot. Neither am I." It wasn't actually true,
and in fact, not long ago they'd both eaten some
Liptauer that Susanna had concocted from a recipe
of Lotte's. Dieter had called it *Vonderful.*

"Don't worry about it," Karen said brightly. "I
don't blame him. It does smell like hell. We'll give
it to the night man. He'll love it. His name is Fritz
and he sure looks like a Nazi. Just getting on the
elevator with him gives me the creeps."

Susanna wanted to shoot up out of her chair to
protest, show Dieter her outrage on his behalf and
on behalf of all the kind, good, non-Nazi Germans,
but she had sunk deep into the charcoal leather and
at most could lift herself forward in the cushions to
throw Karen a fiery look. Was her sister insensitive

or just stupid? Was she seeing the dilating pupils, the lips stretched taut, the angry show of white teeth— her German husband's face?

No. Karen was cooing to Elliot, "Darling, see if Mama wants another drink," as if they'd all just finished a jolly sing around the piano. "And Gaby, you and Wally haven't even tried this eggplant dip. It's the greatest!"

Elliot, whose hands always seemed on or near his wife, patted her shoulder tenderly. Today it was covered in layers of variegated-green gauze that spoke of craft fairs in India. "Julie, another Karen's Sea Breeze?" he asked, in what Susanna now considered a wheezy, annoying voice. Her brother-in-law? Grandfather-in-law is how she saw him at this moment, tan or no, not just creaky, but malevolent. The question was, had he turned Karen into this downtown maharani—or had she always been so thoughtless, so lacking in sensitivity, so Soho showgirl?

If it hadn't been Mama's birthday, if they weren't going out to Balthazar after she'd opened her presents, Susanna would have simply gotten up, taken Dieter by the hand and made a short speech at the door on their way out. "If Daddy were here, you'd have heard it from him!" was what she'd say.

But, it would tear Mama apart.

Instead, she and Dieter stayed through dinner, fixing weak smiles on their faces through three courses and endless conversation about the wedding and honeymoon—Portugal and Spain; Gaby had given in— answering questions about the travel business with a yes or no, or concentrating on passing the slices of birthday cake. Mostly, they were staying very silent, a pair united by fury, Susanna thought.

Until they were in the car heading home. "I'm always the *German,*" Dieter said first, his voice a tight fist, and then, "alvays the kraut. Fuck Nietzsche and Wagner and Hans Holbein the Younger, screw

Goethe and all the good music, art, food and books. I'm alvays in the shadow of Limburger cheese and Eva Braun, and it's nearly sixty years after the war already.''

"Please, Dieter, don't you think you're overreacting a bit, dear?" Susanna protested, but he bulldozed on.

"Your family is not very Jewish, Susanna. Just Jewish *enough.*"

Panicky and wretched, Susanna could think of nothing more to say.

And later, in a tone he might use to tell his wife he was thinking of having new soles put on his shoes, he mentioned casually that he was sending his frequent flyer miles to Liesel for an airplane ticket to America. He wanted a decent doctor to look at her rash, which seemed to be spreading. She could stay right here for a while and come to the wedding; there were all those extra bedrooms.

Although an invitation to Gaby's wedding had been sent—a courtesy and nothing but!—it had been Susanna's wish, hope, burning desire, that the girl stay home in Germany where she belonged. The wedding was no time to have her underfoot, requiring special attention, having her tag along to showers and the reception, having to include her in every family prenup event! Besides, she'd cooperatively and happily, already sent regrets.

"What about her job at the restaurant?" Susanna asked, her voice sounding like a near-drowning victim just dragged out of the water.

"She's taking off the time." For the first time this evening, Dieter looked relaxed and content.

"And when—" Susanna struggled with the question, trying not to replay "Jewish enough" in her head, "will she be arriving?"

"In plenty time for the vedding," Dieter said, adding that he might also send her a check for a nice new dress.

Not five minutes later, he asked if Susanna's period was over? He was in the mood for love.

CHAPTER
TWENTY-THREE

By the time Taras rang Julie's doorbell, the late afternoon thunderstorm that had pelted all of lower Westchester had stopped, left a dark watercolor sky over Scarsdale, and a reflecting sheen on every surface up and down Morris Lane. Leaves and driveway macadam and the tops of garbage pails glowed, and so did the wine red roof of Taras's old Buick, standing at the curb in front of the Kessler house.

She'd seen it before, hardly noticed its make or color, but tonight, because it would take them to a yet unnamed restaurant—"One place you've never been, Harry. Guaranteed."—she took note of its shape and color—and its age. This ancient vehicle was what Scarsdale called a station car, fit only to leave at the commuter train parking lot, hand down to the family teenager, or use when the Lexus or Range Rover were being serviced.

Watching from the living room window, Julie saw Taras step out of the driver's side, and take self-confident strides toward the front door. The storm had cooled the air and broken the heat wave, but it was still hardly jacket weather. He was wearing one anyway, blue-gray; Julie was reminded of the boys in her daughters' dancing classes, with their jackets just this color, their white trousers, (his were dark) and their shined shoes. She could practically hear the piano playing the ancient fox-trots to which all three girls had shuffled in a church-basement dance school twenty years ago.

When Julie opened the door, the familiar smell of his aftershave filled the foyer even before he'd stepped over the threshold. This must also be his wardrobe's best—a French blue shirt with open collar, dark pants, and the jacket, everything certainly just washed, steamed, pressed.

"Harry, look at you! Whoa! You are looking boffo!" He took a little dance step back, as if she'd bowled him over.

Never mind "boffo," Julie wished she'd not chosen this white halter dress outfit she'd worn at Ruthie and Lou DiLorenzo's Fourth of July barbecue last year. It had looked so good on the model in the newspaper ad but wasn't it too revealing? Too young? Her upper arms, well, they weren't as firm as they'd been, were they? And since Traci had stopped coming to the house for those floor exercises, what about that small, after-dinner bulge below the waist? If she hadn't spotted her white piqué jacket with eggplant dip at Karen's last night, she would have tossed it over her black silk pants and really felt ready for this occasion.

Which she had been contemplating nervously all day. She had fussed with her hair at the mirror an hour ago, practically for the length of the CD playing *Adios Pampa Mia* in her bathroom. And, put on her Carolina Herrera while thinking, *Aren't you ashamed of your old self?*

Too distracted to really examine the row of greeting cards that Mariadora had arranged in a careful row

on the shelf in the front hall, she had also forgotten
to put away the rose-printed umbrella, the compact,
the somber, cabled cashmere cardigan her daughters
had presented her with yesterday. She had instead
brushed her eyelashes with her Estée Lauder lash
brush, patted her cheeks with Lancôme blush and
turned herself around in front of the floor-to-ceiling
mirror in her bedroom. She inhaled his overload of
Aramis—did he think she was hard of smelling?—as
she unwrapped his gift, another CD, another tango.
When he helped her slip her little yellow sweater over
her shoulders he said she looked elegant and didn't
ask how old she was. Certainly it was politeness and
not disinterest, although she'd told herself if he
asked, she'd tell. *Fifty-four, okay, but feeling exactly as I
did thirty years ago, even before motherhood! Half a century
plus, but so what? Tonight is my night!*

The car had been vacuumed, anyone could see that,
probably shampooed and for all she knew, waxed, the
full treatment they were always trying to talk her into
at the car wash. It looked as if it had rolled out of a
showroom, well, a previously owned Buick showroom,
except for the softball glove on the back seat. Thomas's. And a toy rubber shoe. The dog's.

"Where are we going?" she asked, not that she
cared. They were on their way and she was a reckless,
wind-in-the-hair twenty again.

"To a place where there's 'a full dinner pail'. Know
who promised a full dinner pail?"

She guessed Grover Cleveland and could tell he
got pleasure out of correcting her. "McKinley. Stood
for the gold standard. Shot by an anarchist who was
hiding a gun under a handkerchief. You never knew
that, Harry?"

The car did not cough or groan as she fully
expected, but the left signal didn't work, neither did

the A.C., which meant that the windows had to stay open, but the air, swooshing past, even on 287—the hell with the hair blower, the brush and the hair spray—seemed to her sweet as rainwashed night mists at summer camp.

Julie relaxed. Without intending to, she began to tell Taras about last night. Well, how to put it without sounding disloyal, but Elliot and Karen had offended Dieter, it was impossible to miss, and the tension! But she censored out criticism, these were her children after all, but there always seemed to be stress just when everyone should be holding together, what with their father—she stopped, glanced at Taras's profile, fixed and intent, unreadable eyes hard on the road.

She always stopped short when it came to describing Gilbert. Just yesterday, arriving on the sixth floor of the hospital, she saw a doctor and two nurses running down the corridor, heading for Gilbert's room. But, the crisis was in the next room, where a patient had fallen out of bed and as it turned out, suffered a fatal stroke. When the body was rolled past the open door of Gilbert's room, Julie had to go into the bathroom to compose herself.

Taras's car radio—it worked—was set at low volume Lite FM, the nice middle-aged background music for the road, *waitaminute,* maybe in deference to her? Somewhere around Yonkers, *Happy Together* came through the static. It was the song Gaby and Wally had just chosen as their first dance together. *"Me for you and you for me,"* Taras sang along with the lyrics. *"The sky will be blue for the rest of my life,"* Julie sang, joining in.

Taras's eyes left the road to look at her. "You're not off key to me," he said.

He parked on a side street, Seventh, near Second Avenue. "Twenty thousand Ukrainians live in this neighborhood. My mother used to take me here when I was a kid, when we lived in Kips Bay, before we moved down south. There were ninety thousand refugees here then. That's what happens. Every ethnic group. They arrive, they thrive, in six years they move on. That's it in Chinatown, and all over. Six years and it's good-bye." That was Taras, full of quotes and facts, not many about himself. Most things about him until now under lock and key in his head, like conceptual art, like Gaby.

He pointed to the huge spire of a Gothic church. St. George's Ukrainian Catholic Church. "I had my First Communion there." He took Julie's arm and led her to First Avenue. "My father had a friend who was a barber, so my mother took me down here for my haircuts. Can you imagine? A Ukrainian haircut? And all the time what I really wanted was to be just like my peers and grow up to be Thomas Jefferson." He let out a hard-edged little laugh. "I suppose my mother had all my best interests at heart; she just didn't know what my best interests were."

Julie saw a teenaged Gaby coming up from the basement, a boyfriend, flushed and wild-eyed, zipping up, behind her. A screaming fight, nasty exchanges, tears. Julie thought she was acting in the girl's best interests, making it into a big, explosive, unforgettable confrontation, when she should have had a quiet talk with the child instead, one of her many mothering errors. (Hadn't she actually lost control, slapped teenaged Susanna once for calling Gilbert a "fossilized piece of shit" when he wouldn't let her go to Times Square on New Year's Eve?" And been much too hard on Karen, just because she was the oldest?) Scarsdale's best mothers had daughters who had declared war on one or both parents, or moved as far away as jets could take them. Luckily, the girls, all three, had forgiven the lapses.

Taras kept saying, "So many changes," when they

passed a woman in a long blonde curly wig begging from a wheelchair, a black man kneeling on the sidewalk, drawing in colored chalk. The artist was barefooted, the soles of his feet the color of the cement. Julie noticed other feet, shoes she'd never seen in Westchester: multicolored or high-platformed or theatrical or falling apart. The footwear of urban denizens. *Denizens.* The word seemed to fit perfectly. Their T-shirts were emblazoned with messages and images, their hair twisted, braided, frizzed, one dyed the colors of what turned out to be the Ukrainian flag—turquoise on one half of the head, dark yellow on the other. Skin the color of Julie's was not in the majority. Julie felt the way she'd felt in Asia and South America: the foreigner.

Tompkins Square Park was busy. "This is new," Taras said, and stopped in front of a bronze statue of a man sitting on a bench. His bronze dog, with a duplicate of his master's face, sat on the ground beside him. A summer evening, a park, twilight. Air steaming, altogether different from the green and green-money fragrance of Scarsdale. "Nothing is ever the way you remember it. Have you noticed that?" He sounded wistful; Julie found that real and endearing. "Except the Statue of Liberty and a bad back," she said.

He smiled so nicely.

On all sides of them, benches were jammed with humanity. People sat with newspapers, hot dogs, bottles of water, radios; here a man with a cockatoo sitting on his shoulder like a fashion accessory. A pair of lovers, arms wrapped around each other, bodies twisted in public passion, sat kissing. As if it were a reminder, Taras inched closer to Julie, took her hand. And so what? He'd held her hand dancing a thousand times. But this was Tompkins Square Park, and this was tonight. His fingers put pressure on hers, turning Julie's hand erogenous.

They walked along St. Mark's Place, passed tattoo and body piercing establishments one after another. In between were basement shops, or stores open to the street, spilling watches, socks, sunglasses, silver and scarves, just like the bazaars in Morocco and Izmir. Music came out of a restaurant, the interior dark and throbbing. He kept holding her hand as they walked, even when he stopped to show her the little museum on Second Avenue, or the butcher shop where his mother used to buy kielbasa, or "Number 77, St. Marks. Know who lived here? Leon Trotsky. The barber always talked about giving him a haircut, telling me he should have saved a curl."

What would the girls think of the way she was spending her birthday? "Another planet," she said, when Taras put a dollar in a panhandler's hand. "Aren't we lucky?" he said. *By some definition,* she thought. "I'm having a boffo birthday. Really."

They stood at the window of another shop, this one closed, boarded up. Someone had written in black and underlined in red,

> "To my darling,
> 'We sang together and parted
> Without tears, without much talk,
> Shall we ever meet again?
> Will we sing together once more?'—Ivan."

"That's from a poem by Shevchenko," Taras remarked.

"Is it really? Are you sure?"

"I'm sure. My mother knew every poem by heart. I grew up with him, don't forget."

"But isn't that amazing?"

"Amazing?" Taras watched her with indulgent interest as she read the poem.

"I mean, a coincidence! Your namesake, right here."

"This is a Ukrainian neighborhood, Harry! He's everywhere!"

"I wonder about Ivan. Probably had his heart broken by a beautiful young woman."

"With purple hair and a nose ring," Taras said.

"Oh, you cynic!"

"Just summarizing," Taras said, meaning "surmising."

Julie did not correct him.

He took her into a shop called Surma. It was dim and small and teeming with Ukrainian souvenirs, newspapers, and what Gilbert always called throwoutventory. Taras led Julie to the back of the shop, where in a jumble of merchandise, his eye fell on a glass jewelry case. He asked the sales clerk to pull out what looked to Julie like a religious symbol or a fraternity crest. Gold, possibly even actually fourteen karat and studded with a row of small stones, maybe garnets, a chain to go with it. "I want to buy this for you. For your birthday," he said, and reached for his wallet.

"But Taras, you already bought me a CD."

"I want you to have it. It's a trident. Symbol of the Ukraine. I want to give it to you. Look, Harry, let me buy—"

The fact is, she'd never wear it. How would she explain to the girls, and to the world, the symbol of the Ukraine hanging around her neck? It wasn't even her taste; garnets always reminded her of old ladies who read tea leaves. The necklace smacked of secret societies, no doubt about it. "I can't accept it."

"You don't have to wear it. Just keep it."

"No, Taras. But the thought. I'll keep that, okay?"

* * *

He took her to a café called Veselka for dinner.
Veselka meant rainbow in Ukrainian, he told her.
The place had a cashier and a takeout counter, waiters
in T-shirts. They sat outside at a little white table and
looked at the menu and each other. He ordered a
Pilsner Urquell for himself and a glass of red wine
for her. The wine arrived in a chunky wineglass and
tasted too sweet, but she finished it and had another.

Taras ordered cold borscht and Ukrainian meatballs and stuffed cabbage and kasha. The dishes came
out looking lumpy, creamy and alien, heaped on
plates that were large and plain and white. Kasha was
the side dish and Julie was sure she'd never get a bit
of any of it down, but the borscht was tangy and the
meatballs were decent and the stuffed cabbage was
better than the stuffed cabbage she'd made from a
Joy of Cooking recipe when the girls were small.

To Julie, tonight, ambiance and food meant nothing. Taras and the candle flickering between them
in its frosted glass ball was the full screen across the
basket of bread. When Taras put his hand over hers
on the table, she stopped talking, just stopped in the
middle of a sentence to examine every one of his
features once more, as if she were preparing to take
a pencil out of her purse and draw his likeness on
the table. *My head—it's clear Daum crystal, it's trapping
light, so surreal, tonight is my birthday and I am living.
Definitely living.*

She was just mellow enough to eat every bit of her
dinner, living it without tasting much of it, her face
glowing above her white halter dress. Her appetite
pleased him. He was talking about his son, about
Thomas Jefferson, about the dance studio, about his
landlady, and when Julie's mind wasn't wandering—
what happens next?—she was absorbed by his small
stories. If the scope of his life was modest, if he had

traveled nowhere much and mispronounced a word now and then, she didn't process it. She felt roseate, actually yes, happy. She suddenly repeated, "Shall we ever meet again? Will we sing together once more?" sounding a bit high and silly. It came out of nowhere. Anyone overhearing would think, One too many. Luckily, no one had heard, just Taras, whose hand was back on the table, his thumb running back and forth on hers. Looking into his eyes, in a moment packed with Merlot, delusion and artlessness, she read everything into them she wanted to. Looking over their coffee cups at his lips, provocative, *inflammatory*, dark in the light from the candle, she got a seismic wave of courage. "I'm feeling wonderful. It's still my birthday. Would you like to come back to the house? We can turn on the music and dance," she said.

CHAPTER
TWENTY-FOUR

There was a problem with the outside speaker. When Taras put the new CD on the CD player, the switch that should have transmitted the music to the patio was frozen. "Do you have a screwdriver?" he called to Julie, who was in the kitchen, washing the purple grapes she intended to put on a plate and bring out to the terrace. It was more a question of wanting to be doing something—moving, moving, keeping her hands busy to stop from showing she was nervous, than offering refreshments. When they'd arrived back at her house fifteen minutes ago, she'd switched on the lantern lights outside, the ones she and Gilbert only used for parties, and brought out a few citronella candles. Taras had helped her move aside a few chairs to make room, create their flagstone dance floor, and now, the glitch, there was no music.

And then, there was "I got it, don't bother with the screwdriver," he called from the den. *Hey, that too; he's good with his hands!* Unlike Gilbert, who couldn't, or wouldn't fix anything that wasn't an electric timing device. It should have made no difference, and yet, it did. It was manly. It spoke of strength. You could lean on a man who got things to roll or spin or play, who understood the miracle of machinery. "It wasn't the switch; a wire was loose." With his hand on her shoulder, Julie felt taken care of, secure. Carrying the plate of grapes out to the terrace, she was serene, imagined things were in order again, that she was in control, as she'd been before the accident. It was the music, the black summer sky with its sickle moon and pinpoint stars, the familiar smell of the roses bordering the hedges, the cut grass, and faintly, what was left of his aftershave. Feeling as if she were levitating above the wrought iron lawn furniture, watching herself float across the topiaries and the flagstones, she heard the sound of the wind chimes hanging from the roof over the back door, a gift from Karen and Elliot a few birthdays ago. *Put down the plate and calm down. Naranjo En Flor,* the first selection from the tape he'd brought her, was coming through the speakers, not loud enough to bother the neighbors, just loud enough to slip in and tank up her bloodstream. That's how it felt, hearing the sob and moan of a voice singing with a heart in its throat, bringing the Argentine pampas, sheep on the road to Calafate, the Andean cordillera, and all of Julie's buried geography schoolbook images into the garden of 66 Morris Lane.

Taras held out his arms and she stepped forward. His hand on her bare back, her fingers circled by his, her sandals ready, and now, the tango. Those blue shirtsleeves—his jacket rested over the arm of a kitchen chair inside—had been waiting for her all evening, all week, and maybe since she was the age her daughters were now. Other lifetimes, mysticism, the occult, sprang from the dark corners of the garden. *Don't take any of it seriously.* She was careful at first, took her first few steps tentatively, but her back had finally healed and the dance with all its steps and

moves came back; her hips and knees obeyed nicely,
the hesitations in place. She remembered the dance
instructor, Damaria, fluid in her white Lycra dress,
and became Damaria, lithe and elastic. She became
more than she was, everything strange and improbable, ghosts and voices from the past, satyrs and
nymphs, ancestral demons, all seemed almost possible, just hovering out of sight. It was the spell of the
guitars and violins, the tenors and baritones, the wine
and her birthday, making Julie's body swim along to
the music and to Taras, like a supple spirit in the
warm air of a rococo August night.

They danced on the flagstones and on the grass.
They danced diligently, with perseverance, with determination. Their bodies whipped and turned, bent
and swiveled; their legs twisted one around another,
kicked and kneed and kicked again. In August, there
were always shooting stars, everyone saw them, "Look,
there's Perseid!" she remembered Gilbert or the girls
saying, after a barbecue, or as they were standing in
the driveway, on their way into the house after leaving
someone else's. At odd moments now, she looked up
at the sky over the garage while the music churned
around her, and saw none, not one falling star. Everything above was steady and fixed, the perfectly
designed night ceiling standing still, as if waiting for
the moment when the guitars stopped and the dance
finally ended.

The Celestial Designer provided a firefly over Taras's shoulder, just as his arms gathered Julie, age
54 tonight, to his chest. He stood holding her, just
wrapping his sleeves around her as if a sudden current
might at any minute threaten to sweep her away. For
a second, she remembered who she was, where she
was—*don't take this seriously!*—and thought of tearing
away, racing off down the driveway, running for her
dignity and her life. Then, he kissed her and Scarsdale
vanished from under her feet. Her own history, hus-

band, daughters, and the green leather desk directory that listed the names and phone numbers of everyone she knew, did a fast and unpredicted fadeout; in the light from the garden lanterns and the shadow of her grand house, Julie Kessler lost her bearings.

It was nothing sudden like the kiss in the rain, but sweet and indolent, smooth and scorching, a residue of the music, the night and the dance. Taras's hand moved to the back of her neck, and just before his lips swam down on hers, in the second before she closed her eyes, she caught sight of the firefly again, no, two now, between the chaise longue and the topiary trees, in the dark a row of ballheaded sci-fi spectators. The fireflies looked like props, sparkles, nature's tiny stars planted strategically by some little god who might just be hiding behind the hedges bordering the driveway. *It's real, I'm living this.*

He pulled away to look into her eyes, and then to kiss her again. Now, the world intruded; a cat meowed in a neighbor's yard, a car door slammed somewhere down the street. This evening, this birthday never to forget, would come to an end. She lifted her hand, touched Taras's mouth to wipe off a bit of lipstick. "I'm so happy," he said, "so goddamn happy." His eyes looked languid, that's how she read the drooping eyelids, the slight moisture between the lashes, as desire she hadn't seen in a man's eyes in thirty years. She wanted to kiss his eyelids, his eyebrows and the space between them, move her mouth to his neck, to his body. She'd all but forgotten what it was like to feel this potboiler of sexual longing. As she inhaled the scent of her roses, the humid vapors of the earlier rain and the last faint fragrance of Aramis, he whispered, "Would you like me to stay?"

What are you doing? she thought, as she took his hand, and led him through the kitchen, the front hall, and up the stairs, to her bedroom.

* * *

The room was dark and she did not turn on the light, not even the small reading lamp on her night table. The only light came from the ceiling fixture in the hall; now they were two silhouettes facing each other at the foot of the bed. She'd had too much wine but still not enough. *This is so awkward, what next?* and for the moment that they stood there facing each other, her thoughts raced to worries about her body, and why had she put all those silly little throw cushions on top of her bed? The spell of the summer night left outside, she was now nipped by reality, and wished for *Penthouse* breasts, a concave stomach. She should never have stopped her floor exercises, the ones Traci had taught her. But then, Taras said, "I'll race you," and, growing accustomed to the dim light, Julie saw the shape of his shoulders and the way his profile looked in the half light, and that turned the switch, fixed the loose wire in her own head; everything was all heat again now. Wearing a strapless bra under her dress, lucky it wasn't one of her old Lily of France numbers with the frayed straps, she unbuttoned the halter at the back of the neck and stepped out of her dress. In a moment, he was naked, had won the race, was kissing the swell of her breasts above the lace, undoing the hooks at the back of her brassiere.

He led her to the bed, sweeping the dozen little throw pillows to the floor and pulling back the coverlet in what looked like two effortless, gliding motions, the man who knew machinery, knew the machinery of sex. He pulled off her panties all the while kissing her shoulders, her breasts, and then, the tips of her fingers. He moved her hand to touch him, and now, *oh no!* for a split second, Harriet saw Gilbert's face as he looked when she saw him yesterday—the look of a man already embalmed. She'd been kissed in the pantry off the kitchen by a friend's husband once, felt the brief rush of guilty passion, but never this.

It had only ever been Gilbert. Taras's upper body was hairless and smooth, unlike Gilbert's chest and back, which was covered with fine, familiar hair, and three benign, raised moles. The smooth surfaces of Taras were all new and strange. He was beside her, his hands and mouth running slowly across her body—a blind man exploring with zealous, gentle fingers. She had never held another man's equipment, this most amazing private thing, living its own engorged, exciting life in her hand. Gilbert knew how to make her come; after all these years it went methodically, and perfectly. A bit routine perhaps, but good and dependable, pretty speedy, his body as familiar to her as her own. This was different—it was exploratory and tense, thrilling and frightening. Taras worked so hard at her pleasure, reading her with his lips and hands, stopping and starting until, trying to be quiet out of habit, as she had when the girls were asleep in their own bedrooms down the hall, she still let out stage whisper cries, not unlike the thrums of a guitar, when he kissed where only in her long life Gilbert's mouth had gone. Then she stroked his right hand, the one with the missing finger, and impulsively kissed with moist passion the half left. It was so natural, so automatic, the need in the midst of the fireworks of ardor, to show him it included whatever was a part of him, was his, imperfect or not, and with the finger at her mouth, her breathing came short, the heat rose in her, *What if I faint?* She tried to hold back, but, so sorry, *It's been so long!* the bed rocked under her as she came. Julie felt tamed and weak, grateful and overwhelmed, when he let out a roar certainly loud enough to be heard up and down Morris Lane, and shook in seismic tremors on top of her.

CHAPTER TWENTY-FIVE

Julie, who had never slept naked and thought she could never fall asleep with Taras in her bed, curled up against him and drifted off almost immediately, her nightgown still where Mariadora had folded it under her pillow. Not for the first time, she dreamt of Luffy. When she woke at four, listening to the even breathing of the man, the virtual stranger, whose back was now turned to her in peaceful sleep, she concluded that Luffy represented the omnibus of the best of her life. It was all wrapped up now, wasn't it, dead and gone, the time when the girls were small, the time when Gilbert was here next to her? The optimum time, rich with probabilities, had likely ended with the passing of her darling cat.

Julie felt emotionally split, two Julies, neither exhilarated nor experiencing the afterglow one would think she was due. She wanted Taras gone, back where he'd come from in his own life, wanted him to become simply a feature attraction of an evening she'd remember forever as psychedelic. He didn't belong here in this room packed with more memories than there was cat hair on Luffy's head. This was Gilbert's bed too, his body's impression still in the memory of the mattress. What had she done?

But then, no, she didn't want Taras to leave, wanted him here, near her, within touching and kissing distance. Even if it was unseemly and shameful, nothing more than a middle-aged woman's fling fantasy, she would forever remember the latex feel of his skin and the way he'd held and kissed and kissed her, even after sex was over. Gilbert had rarely, if ever kissed her after making love, except perfunctorily, a quick thanks, I-have-to-catch-a-bus buss. But Taras had said again, "I am so happy, it's a boffo high is what it is," and waking slowly this morning, wrapping his arms around her, looking into her eyes, a love song come to life in her own bed, added, "Honest to God. Only with you."

He called home from the kitchen, where Julie was preparing muffins, eggs scrambled with chives—one of the girls' favorites—and coffee. His landlady, Taras said, would give Thomas breakfast and take him with her to church. She'd covered the chaise with an old blanket and the dog had slept there, shedding all over it; he reported all this to Julie as she poured his coffee. He took sugar, no milk; she must try to remember, sugar, no milk.

He'd admired the salt and pepper shakers on the shelf; had she really been in Kyoto, Melbourne, Nice? He touched the hand-painted Mexican tiles, examined the dry sink and told her he'd never seen a kitchen anywhere like it. "It's one of the wonders of the world," he said. What's more, he'd never eaten better eggs, tasted muffins like this and now, this minute if she didn't believe him, he'd get a mirror so she could see for herself how much bluer her left eye was than her right. He leaned across the table to kiss her again. "And to me you're another one of the wonders of the world," he said.

She'd combed her hair, creamed her hands out of nervousness and put on lipstick. Sitting with her coffee mug across the table from him, she was feeling comfortable if not necessarily alluring in her ancient fleur de lis robe. In morning light, she'd faced his eyes on her fifty-four-year-old thighs, stomach, breasts. Which, despite the body's accumulation of time, its fight with gravity, its endurance of three bouts of childbearing was nothing to be ashamed of, and yet had walked this earth almost since the time of World War Two. This was morning, and this was reality, but he'd made love to her again in bright, unforgiving daylight.

Her shyness had diminished and her eyes moved to his hand. Maybe a woman had actually bitten off the finger during lovemaking. This morning, it seemed actually possible. Taking a sip of her coffee, Julie's eye caught a house finch at the window. It landed briefly on the sill before fluttering off into the trees. It was not as colorful as a cardinal, not as rare as a bluebird, but it flashed a bit of stunning crimson. Over the years, Julie had watched many like it dart through the trees of her garden, but today the bird seemed orchestrated. It seemed a symbol of hearts swollen by the little red arrows of Eros.

When he talked about himself, Taras had a way of looking at the top of Julie's head, directing his gaze to her hair or to the air above it. Hesitant. He looked away from her eyes the way the girls used to, when they were reluctant to come clean about something.

A night of love is what it took to open him up. *He trusts me now.*

"I was teaching dance on cruise ships and my regular partner left to get married, so the talent agency arranged for a new partner. She was from Louisiana, another Ukrainian believe it or not, and she and I danced really well together. So see, we had all that in common?" To Julie this sounded like an apologetic preface, the sort of things people say to justify some subsequent mess. "She was eleven years older than me, I was young, I thought it was love, and you can guess the rest."

Julie interrupted. "Eleven years older? She was?"

He shrugged, nodded a nod that meant So What?

He likes older women. Not just gay men do; a piece of cosmic luck.

"Well. Oleksa got pregnant, we got married, and for two or three years, things chugged along. We moved down to New Orleans to be near her mother who was sick, did some performing in the local hotels, but times were tough. Then, her mother got complications of a heart bypass and diabetes and went into a nursing home. Like my own parents' house up in Detroit, Oleksa's mother's apartment was filled with icons. It turned out that two were worth a little something. A nice surprise. When she sold them, Oleksa and I had enough to leverage a loan to open a small dance studio."

Julie tried to imagine his life as a married man with a baby. But, Taras as a family man, a changer of diapers, a taker-out-of-garbage and a doing-laundry Taras, now *that* was miscasting.

"And, so we did open a small studio and I began to give exhibitions with a very talented instructor, Inez. Pretty soon she and I were invited here and there, once to Atlanta, once to Memphis, like that. We won money prizes and got publicity for our little business. Oleksa and I thought we might expand or franchise the studio. She couldn't leave home, she was still nursing; Thomas was less than six months old and I admit, I was on the road with Inez a lot."

Taras's eyes took on an I'm-gone look. He kept stopping, starting, stopping.

"I think at some point, after her mother died, Oleksa snapped."

Home with the baby while her hunky husband was dancing his way across the South with Inez? Julie pictured Oleksa, smoky eyes and olive skin, fire in her heart. She imagined Oleksa reaching into a kitchen drawer, taking out a knife. She looked at his finger.

"Not quite. It's not what she would have liked to have cut off, believe me." He got up and walked to the sink, turned around to face Julie. Sunlight falling from the window threw streaks across his bare chest turning him into a charcoal study of light and shadow.

"She began praying to what was left of her mother's icons. She thought I'd fallen for Inez, that we were sleeping together."

"Were you?"

Taras was looking so hard at the top of Julie's head that she imagined he'd spotted insect life in her hair.

"Almost."

Oh, sure.

"We were in Jacksonville, there was the water, there was the moon, her motel room was right next to mine. To be honest, it was a big temptation, a magic moment, but it never happened. Inez was married, too. She loved her husband, and there was Thomas. We came close and that was that." Taras sighed. "At the time, I still did love my wife."

Taras turned his back to Julie, ran some water into a glass and took a sip. He set the water glass down and turned back to her with a deliberation that looked like it had been written into a shooting script.

"A self-proclaimed voodoo queen lived down the street from us in the *Vieux Carré* and she became interested in Oleksa's Ukrainian statues. They became friends, next thing you know, Oleksa goes from praying to her mother's icons to buying crazy stuff from the voodoo queen—herbs, roots, snake fangs, potions, like that. *Gris-gris.*"

"What's that?"

"It's like a charm that can do magic things, good or bad. It had ingredients, like alligator teeth and grave dirt, who knows what else. All I know is, it made the house smell like shit."

"Grave dirt!"

"Yes." A small smile. "Tip of the voodoo iceberg. There were oils and incense, Tarot cards, toad's feet, as I remember, then came guinea hen eggs—"

"Where do you get those? Not at *my* A&P." A bit of wit, but he was not smiling.

"She called herself Lala and went into deep trances. I mean, her eyes rolled up in her head, it was like— I can't describe it— here one minute and gone the next, into her own idea of religion."

Julie thought of Mariadora's herbs and the ribbons she tied on the bedposts. Goofy, but hadn't a small part of her wanted to believe anyway?

"Not funny when Oleksa was really into it, seriously into witchcraft, let me tell you. When she started with black candles, that's when I said, 'I'm out'."

Black candles! The narrative was losing its credibility. Was this true or truth embellished?

"I told her to cut it out. I didn't want Thomas growing up in that atmosphere, not to speak of the fire hazard. I told Oleksa to get rid of all the stuff; she'd actually built a little altar in our dining room. It was hocus-pocus-mumbo-jumbo every night. And there were new friends—people you wouldn't want to meet on a dark street, or in sunlight, for that matter—like, like guys with turkey bones tied around their necks and snakes carried over their shoulders like backpacks.

"Anyway, Oleksa demanded I fire Inez. Which I just flat out wouldn't. Next thing I know, Oleksa takes Thomas and goes to the cemetery at midnight—I'm dead serious—to communicate with the spirit that's going to zap Inez.

"I blew my stack. A few nights later, when I'm in the studio, Oleksa squeezes two black candles into people-shapes. After I'd gone out, she lit them. She fell asleep, they burned down, burned a hole right through a table in the living room. When I came home and smelled the smoke, I figured if I'd been a half hour later the place could have been ashes. I lost it. Next morning, I asked for a divorce.

"Oleksa's response was that if I try to take Thomas away from her, she's gonna get me. She's gonna put an evil, Lala curse on me."

Julie smiled. "It sounds like a two-thumbs-down movie."

"I laughed in her face. I got myself a lawyer, we went to court and by this time, Oleksa had really gone over the top. She came to court wearing all black, nose rings, chains on her wrists and tattoos on the backs of her hands. She rattled on about spirit guides and the dead, whatever. The judge takes one look at her and big surprise. She looked uncompetent. I got custody."

"Uncompetent" was not lost on Julie. "But, your finger—still there?"

Taras didn't answer, took another look at the top of Julie's hair, then at the clock on the wall over the refrigerator. There was a long moment of silence.

"Now don't tell me, Taras, that your wife put a curse on you and it had something to do with your losing a finger?"

Taras stopped looking at the clock. He swallowed as if he'd just downed a stiff shot, and shook his head vehemently.

"I got two years of college, I got two years of night school, three more semesters if I ever find the time, and I'll have a degree. A Bachelor of Science. I never thought I'd wind up a dance teacher. That's life. Born in New York, raised part there, part in Michigan, part in Louisiana. I just sort of fell into it when a friend took me to a dance studio that was hiring. I needed money, had some talent, thought of doing it part time, signed up, and here I am. Went from wanting to be a president of the United States, to doing the mambo and cha-cha-cha. Well, there you go, there's destiny doing a U-turn, but Harry, believe me, I've never been a believer in voodoo."

"Me too not."

"I'm a believer in—" He looked at the floor, at the ceiling, searching, Julie assumed, for the correct vocabulary assortment. "Crosscurrents. Life's crosscurrents. Circumstances, luck, good and bad, coincidence, and," with his half-finger, he tapped his chest, "that propeller inside.

"I took Thomas to Detroit because my mother and father still lived in this little Ukrainian community there, and the week after I arrived, Pops, who'd worked for Chrysler for twenty-five peaceful years, was now retired and operating a small Seven Eleven two miles out of the city. A week and a day after I arrive, he's shot in a holdup. Two teenagers, one with a 9-millimeter handgun stolen from an uncle, two-thirty in the morning. They stole sixty-six dollars, his wedding ring and his Timex watch. It took Pops three weeks to die. Four months later my mother has a stroke crossing Annabelle Street. I guess she never recovered from the shock of what happened to my father. I moved away after her funeral."

Julie folded her hands on the table in front of her. She saw the "propeller inside" out of spin, saw a preview of how Taras would look when he was an old man.

"I had some awful dreams, Harry. Stephen King shoulda been there taking notes."

She got up to get the coffeepot to pour Taras another cup of coffee. Sugar and no milk or milk and no sugar? She didn't want to get it wrong now. Taras had paced to the window, looked out, then came back to the table, pulled out his chair and sat staring again at the top of her hair. Sugar, no milk.

When she put the coffee in front of him, he took her hand in both of his and shook his head. "Okay. This is the good part." He looked as if she'd pulled out a hypodermic and told him it would only hurt for a moment.

"One day, I'm visiting my father in the hospital, my finger begins to hurt. When I look at it, I see what looks like a red blister, and at first I pay no attention. A blister, big deal. But not three hours later, the pain is like I'm holding the finger on the barbecue grill, it's hot and swollen double size, and I'm getting the chills, shaking in my chair, so when the doc comes into the room to see my father, I ask her to look at it. I'm embarrassed, my father about to check out and I'm asking the doc to look at my *finger*. But you should've seen the expression on that lady's face. I swear, I should've brought my point-and-shoot.

"She asks me to step out into the hall, and before I know it, she's called in another doctor, the two of them are eyeballing the finger, the longest damn five minutes of my life. They right away take blood tests, get me a bed and all of a sudden, presto-changeo, I'm in a backless dress and I'm a patient. Necro-something, they say. Fash-something. Fasciitis, I wrote it down. Ever hear of it? I never could pronounce it to tell the truth."

"What? What is that?"

"It's something called the flesh-eating disease. That's what it is. It's a staph infection, almost like gangrene. And I'd never been sick a day either, never in a hospital except to get a few stitches in the ER when I slipped playing ice hockey in grade school."

Julie had read something about outbreaks a few years ago, seen something on the evening news and remembered a conversation she'd had with someone who knew someone who lived next door to someone in Connecticut who had contracted it—another ghastly calamity that seemed safely far away, not to have touched anyone she had ever in her life met.

"The next morning, not twelve hours later, I find myself in the recovery room with nine-and-a-half fingers. A speed-of-light amputation courtesy of First Michigan Health Care. I was staggering, woozy and still running a fever at my father's funeral."

"Taras. This story is unimaginable."

"Not a particularly heroic way to lose a finger. Not very sexy, is it? And no one knows exactly what causes the damn disease. To this day. A little cut on the finger or no cut on the finger, a little bout of the flu or no bout of the flu. Lots of question marks"—Taras gave a sardonic smile and pulled his hand away from Julie's—"and no answers. I was lucky that it wasn't my hand, my arm and then, my life. Twenty-four more hours and I would have been sharing the spotlight with my old man at Duzak Funeral Home. So the docs said. "Harry, you're one of the only people in the world I've told about this."

"But why, Taras? It's not shameful."

"I don't know. The whole thing is, so, so, I don't know. Unbelievable. A soap."

The telephone rang. Julie didn't move.

"A streak of lousy luck, and then, this job in New Rochelle. And now, I've met you. I think you're my rabbit's foot. And more than that. The whole fucking bunny, in fact. Aren't you going to answer that?"

"Mama," Susanna said when Julie picked up the phone. "I've been crying all morning."

"What's wrong?" Julie asked. "What is it?"

"It's Dieter. He's being absolutely impossible."

CHAPTER
TWENTY-SIX

It started as a peaceful Sunday morning, Dieter mellow, Susanna preparing an egg for herself and for him, his beloved *Pfannkuchen* with lingonberries on top. The sex last night had been short but sweet, the weather this Sunday morning cooler than yesterday; there was actually a light breeze, unusual for August. They ate breakfast on the deck that overlooked the yard. Although Susanna didn't have her mother's love for gardening, day lilies managed to thrive along a small rock wall and a carpet of white and pink impatiens bordered the twin pear trees that shaded the garden.

Susanna felt she deserved this perfect weekend morning, after a stress-filled workweek.

Sitting at her desk at work on Friday, a paper cup of cold cappuccino in her hand, she'd tried not to show agitation. It was unseemly, unprofessional. A major corporate client, one of her top three accounts, had called from San Francisco, his voice rabid. Why had she arranged to put his staff in the San Francisco Majestic, when she might have put everyone in the

Nikko for less? Did she not know that there was con-
struction being done, the noise and dust were deplorable, the bathroom fixtures were so loud they kept
everyone awake? Hadn't she checked these things
out?

He'd given her the impossible charge of finding
eighteen hotel rooms at absurdly short notice, expected all the rooms to have views, and to make certain that he and his wife had the presidential suite.
"Bravo Bravissimo," Daddy would have said, if he'd
known Susanna had aced the order with only ten days
to go. And here was the upshot, her reward: Mr.
Ingratitude about to call her a terrible name, gearing
up to pull out of Travelstar and take his business
elsewhere. In the middle of this crisis, Mama called
to tell her Ruthie was going for surgery and it looked
serious and Gaby called to ask if it was too late to
change honeymoon plans? She hated, loathed,
abhorred the idea of Lisbon. For sure it would mean
visiting twenty-five of Wally's Portuguese relatives.

But Dieter had calmed Susanna down, told her to
take it easy, sat her in a chair as soon as she came
home and poured out her heart, massaged her neck
and told her she took everything too hard. "What
cannot be cured, must be endured," he said, and she
was sure she'd heard that from him before and that
it was one of his translated proverbs. Never mind. He
meant well; he was *trying*.

Now, after breakfast, Dieter oblivious but continuing to be thoughtful and courteous, told her to sit,
please, Schatz, and he cleaned up the kitchen, made
even the faucets shine while she sat outside and read
the newspaper. She said nothing when he went
upstairs to check his computer for E-mail. Hadn't he
done that last night just before turning off the light?
Yes, he had. Wasn't this becoming an obsession? Yes,

it was. Liesel's rash was no better. "She vill be arriving
on the fifth," he announced a few minutes later, so
buoyant, so chirrupy, but Susanna managed a con-
vincing smile when he said, "Lufthansa." Big surprise.

Neither Dieter nor she had ever again made reference to the evening at Karen's. Along with all their
assorted marital skirmishes, unpleasantness between
them lay buried somewhere deep under the mattress
of their king-size bed, pulverized bit by bit by their
lovemaking. That's how Susanna saw it.

She had surreptitiously made a visit to her gynecolo-
gist, who assured her that she was in perfect venereal
health and urged her to be calm and patient, to
picture water lilies and serene meadows during sex.
"The only women who get pregnant immediately are
those who don't want to be," he'd said, hiding what
might have been a smile under his white mustache,
and offered her a mint from a dish in his consulting
room. She liked him, but began to wonder if he wasn't
a bit too old, and perhaps not on the cutting edge
of the latest in fertility developments if he was talking
water lilies and meadows. He seemed humane
enough to ask for advice, judging by his manner and
the pictures of his children and grandchildren on his
desk. How should she break the news of a pregnancy
if there was one, to a husband who all this time
thought she was still swallowing an Ortho-Cept every
day?

What was she thinking? The doctor's eyebrows,
white tufts over small glasses, raised. He urged her
to tell him about her decision immediately. "Afraid
to," Susanna responded.

"At some point, darling—" the doctor began, folding both hands on the desk between them and
stopped, chewing and swallowing his own mint, then
added, "you'll have to. Why not now?"

She looked down at her own hands squeezing

together in her lap, the large stone of the engagement ring Dieter had given her when the love between them was unblemished and unconditional. She said nothing. To admit it, put it into words, was out of the question. He'd head out the door with his suitcase one last time. And she'd die without him.

After she'd finished the Sunday paper, put on a pair of Bermudas and a T-shirt, grabbed the hose and washed down the deck littered with a bit of garden debris from Saturday's thunderstorm, Susanna went into the den, where Dieter sat watching a replay of a soccer match. She was feeling benign, happy and loving. She'd daydreamed about a little Dieter, who'd be multilingual. Dieter would teach him German and she could speak her bit of Russian to him when they weren't speaking English. She would make certain he learned everything, picked up things from every culture and more: piano, chess, sailing. She saw herself teaching him to tell time with the very same cat clock Daddy had used to teach her. And she would give him all the self confidence she lacked. "Bravo!" she'd say, at every opportunity.

"I thought I'd look in on Daddy and then we'd go over to Gaby and Wally's," she suggested after she sat in a chair and watched the incomprehensible action on the TV screen for what seemed like a semester but was actually five minutes. The silver tray she'd bought her sister had arrived from Tiffany and Susanna was eager to see the engraving, not to speak of the other gifts, which were beginning to pile up at Gaby's apartment as well as at Mama's house. Dieter was otherwise engaged. Men in uniforms chasing balls were stereotypical male icons and so what? Even Daddy had been mesmerized by field sports, even had those box seats at Shea one year.

"Maybe after the match, Schatz," Dieter said. His

concentration was intense. "It's Stuttgart versus Werder Bremen. It's close." He strained to catch every kick, leaning forward when someone or other finessed a play that made the crowd on the TV screen jump up and roar.

But during a commercial, Dieter disappeared. A few minutes later, Susanna found him upstairs, in the guest room. He had certainly not crossed that threshold in a year but now, here he was, big as life and horizontal. He had unfolded the convertible couch and was lying on its open mattress, his arms folded across his chest.

"What are you doing?" Susanna asked, knowing full well exactly what he was doing.

"I'm trying it out, Su. Just trying out the mattress."

"So, how is it?"

"In the middle, here, is a bump. I tell you, it's very uncomfortable." He got up, making a face. "You try it."

Susanna hesitated. She had an idea what was coming. She would, nevertheless, humor him. She kicked off her sandals and stretched out on the mattress.

"Well?" he asked.

"I didn't feel any bump," Susanna said.

"It's not a good mattress," Dieter said. His face looked more than worried. It looked deeply concerned. "It's thin, and there's a"—he used his hand to illustrate—"like a bas relief, right here, in the middle. You can't feel it?"

"What are you saying, Dieter?"

"For one night, two nights it's okay, but for more, I don't know."

"I find it quite comfortable. I could sleep here for more than one or two nights."

"I vould hate to see Liesel sleeping on a bump for more than two nights. Don't forget Susanna, she's gonna be here a long time! And she has a rash. Very uncomfortable!"

Susanna hadn't forgotten for how long Liesel was going to be here, not for a nanosecond. "I could sleep on this mattress for a week or ten days. I could sleep on this mattress for a year. I could sleep on this mattress forever!"

"Now, Su," Dieter looked down at Susanna, who was still stretched out flat, arms spread-eagled, on the mattress, and shook his head. His expression was sad. "I think you should get up, we could talk it over."

Susanna shot up. "What are you suggesting, Dieter?"

"I suggest we buy a nice new bed for this room."

"What!"

"Just a mattress and box spring. There's room if we take out this sofa."

The couch was actually a hand-me-down from Mama, who had redecorated the family room and bequeathed this convertible to Susanna and Dieter. To Susanna it was still perfectly good; she had a mild sentimental attachment to its nicely upholstered navy blue stripes, around which she had decorated the room. Deep blue walls, a dark red and blue oriental rug and a large still life had turned it into a cozy guest room/study. Last year she'd added navy tassel window shade pulls and scarlet throw cushions, which were now lying on the floor where Dieter must have thrown them. Susanna picked one up and hugged it to her chest.

The problem was not the sofa. This was the sunny, spacious, warm bedroom she had covertly earmarked as a nursery, and for the last few months, Susanna had made surreptitious, detailed decorating plans. No bunny wallpaper or hokey Humpty-Dumpties, just a sparkling white room with an antique crib and some framed illustrations from old children's books. A growth chart between the windows, the obligatory rocker already biding its time up in Mama's attic, and on the floor, a woven wool rug, custom made for The Baby. Susanna had rehearsed her announcement to

Dieter, should she get pregnant. "I am expecting, Liebling."

"And what are we going to do with this sofa?" she asked now, keeping her voice steady, anxious to stay out of anything that could escalate into a war mode.

"We could move it into the basement," Dieter said, looking both anxious and eager to please. Susanna had come to hate that look, which always managed to defuse her anger. At this moment, bristling, seeing red, she wanted to throw her arms around him.

Or slap him. He was going to turn this room upside down, and most likely their lives, to accommodate Liesel. Nothing was too good or too much trouble for the princess of Potsdam. He was waving a red flag right in front of Susanna's eyes; it was his baby, not hers, who would be established in the nursery.

"I'm not budging on this one," Susanna said. "Liesel can check into a motel if she can't stand the bump. Mama's convertible stays!"

There was a static moment of cold silence between them. Susanna glared and Dieter looked as if he'd been sentenced to death for stealing a loaf of bread. "I don't understand you," he finally said, clanging shut some new door between them. His eyes looked as if at any moment they would drip with tears.

"But I understand *you*," Susanna said. The day, with all its bluebird promise was spiraling quickly into a grim pile of verbal lava. "Your heart only beats in Germany. Your lungs only function well when they inhale the pure air of Berlin. You only feel comfortable when you're with those, those—"

Dieter's hands flew to his hips. "Nazis?"

"You said that. I didn't say it!" Susanna protested. She was in fact, hesitating before saying "Krauts." Krauts and Nazis were a whole different ball of Teutonic wax! "Waitaminute—!"

"It's there, Schatz, it's always there!"

"No it's not! I'm an American woman who wants

a husband who isn't hung up on Schnitzel and his fat daughter!" Susanna wished she could take back the word, "fat," which had gone amok out of her mouth. "I didn't mean fat," she said, subdued, but it was too late.

She could practically see rays of fury coming from Dieter's eyes, beaming across the room at her. She felt as if she'd fallen down a flight of stairs and he was standing at the head, refusing to pick her up. "Liesel is a beautiful woman," he said, his face and voice granite. "One more vord about my daughter, one more vord—!"

Susanna panicked. "I only meant . . . well, she could cut down, couldn't she?"

His arms dropped to his sides and for a moment Susanna thought he might really take a swing at her. She almost wished he would; it would show him as the brute he was. He was, however, not a brute at all, but an amalgam of human qualities that included chauvinism, paternal love for a hefty daughter, stubbornness and a heart that was almost, but not quite, pure gold.

"It's not about Liesel, Susanna."

"I never called you a Nazi."

"You're a Jewish girl from Scarsdale and all of you, including your father—"

"My father?"

"Even him, too, the poor guy."

"How did Daddy get into this?"

"A nice man. Doesn't trust Germans. Never forgets for a minute where I'm born. Not who I am, see, it's where I'm *from!* Every conversation, he asks me if it could happen again. Every time!"

Susanna pointed a finger at Dieter as if it had a trigger she was about to pull. "Bullshit!" He wouldn't have dared attack Daddy if Daddy were alive enough to defend himself. "Anti-Semitic kaka!"

"It's in the blood, Schatz. Every last one of you—

think I'm responsible for Adolf and the whole fucking holocaust!''

"And what about *your* father? He was in the war, no? He sure as hell wasn't fighting on *our* side!" Susanna's heart was full of mayhem. She felt as if she better sit down, right now, or she might tip over, fall into a heap on the red and blue rug. Dieter, silent, a face and body surrounding a volcanic storm, stamped out of the room, pushing past her, and slamming the door behind him.

"Dieter is being impossible," Susanna told her mother on the telephone a few minutes later. She could barely get the words out.

"Oh, Susanna dear, I can't talk now. I'll get back to you as soon as I can."

"Why? Mama, why can't you?" Susanna said.

"In a while, dear."

"I'm going to run over to the hospital and visit Daddy," Susanna said, keeping her voice steady with great strain and difficulty. "When are you going to be there, Mama?"

"I'm not going today, dear, I don't think so."

"Not *today*? You've never missed a Sunday!"

"I'm tired. Really tired," Mama said. "I think I'm just going to stay home."

"Are you all right, Mama? I've never heard you say you were too tired to visit Daddy."

"I'm all right. Perfectly all right, dear. You go ahead. Give your father a kiss for me, will you?"

CHAPTER
TWENTY-SEVEN

The photographer's studio was in Port Chester in a loft building, once a cigar factory, on Rectory Street. Wally and Gaby sat together under floodlights in front of a white screen, smiled and leaned against each other, were caught by the camera head-to-head and cheek-to-cheek, sitting on adjacent stools or standing one behind the other. The photographer had, for real, a Rhesus monkey that brought them coffee in Styrofoam cups. "Helps to get the smile on my subjects' faces," he said, when the monkey resumed its perch on his shoulder.

When the session was over, the photographer told them they looked as if they'd just drunk a love potion so help him God, and was looking forward to photographing the wedding. "All you Kessler girls are piperoos," he said, and then he mentioned he would be leaving his studio on the first of September. His new landlord disapproved of monkeys and he would be opening a place up in Nyack right after Labor Day.

Nyack. Two syllables, five letters: It was like walking

across a rug and touching a wall switch, a tiny electrical jolt, a little *ssss,* an equatorial spark. Nyack. It's where he lived. With his wife, in a house on Merland Road, number 476.

"A nice town," Wally said. "I took my mother to lunch up there once." Wally was one of those people who could be counted on to fill in a gap in any conversation, like a perfect dinner guest. "All jaw," Daddy once affectionately remarked about him. *God, if Daddy knew.*

"It's a town with a heart," the photographer said, shutting off lights, rearranging the stools. The monkey hopped off the photographer's shoulder and threw the empty Styrofoam cups into a garbage pail.

"Bit of a commute for you?" Wally was taking off his necktie, folding it into his pocket.

"It's ten minutes over the bridge, that's all," the photographer said, scribbling his new address on the back of a card and handing it to Wally. "See you in Nyack, Sophia." Wally waved to the monkey as they left the studio. To Gaby he said, "I guess now I've seen it all."

Gaby hadn't been in Nyack since Karen dragged her to a craft fair there, and that must have been when she was still in college. The place was funky, as she remembered it. *A town with a heart.* Gaby imagined a village with affection tying everyone together like a common language. Hugs on Main Street, church suppers, roof railings. She had once asked if Stretch was still making love to his wife. It took him quite a while to answer. "I'm not making love to Mitzi. Once in a blue moon, we have sex." "Isn't that the same thing?" Gaby had asked, picturing him lifting his wife into bed from her wheelchair, then cautiously body-to-body on top of it. "You know better than to ask me that." *There's no such thing as a blue moon.* As for sex without love, well, she thought of Wally, who just this morning had enveloped her in his arms before breakfast, and yes, she'd responded, and yes, they'd done it. It was good enough too, but it was different from sex with Stretch, a body thing, a warm ritual, a paint-by-numbers kind of sex, more than a crazy, sky-is-falling thing. And, she certainly did love Wally, so much about him, the good-boy goodness; her feeling for him coming in waves, surging at odd moments, but then fading again, replaced with red-handed remorse.

Stretch had a habit of putting her palm to his mouth and kissing it and he'd done that when she'd asked about having sex with Mitzi, distracting her by switching her on, and simultaneously closing the subject. She had hoped to hear that he never touched Mitzi, the poor, sick soul, never went near her. So much for self-delusion. In the town with a heart, he was living a full-perk married life.

Ten minutes from the bridge. A few minutes after Wally had kissed her good-bye as she dropped him off at the station, Gaby stopped at a light on the Boston Post Road and called her office. She didn't speak to Stretch, just told the temp at the switchboard to leave him a message: she wouldn't be in until tomorrow. Then she turned the car around and headed for Route 287 and the Tappan Zee. It was not a question, she decided, of having a grand passion, but of a grand synergy. There were no twelve-step programs for sobriety in love, no friends of Bill W to help her quit wanting to see his street and his house, the view from his windows, the trees in his yard. It's where Stretch lived and ate and had sex—"once in a blue moon"— not with her.

"Limerance" was what Benita had called her passion for Shingo, "A fever of the soul." That was it,

it was the soul fever that propelled Gaby's car over
the bridge, off at Exit 11 and down Route 59. It had
her turning left and right and left again, along the
unfamiliar cement roads in this golden oldie of a
town, searching for Merland Road.

She stopped three, maybe four pedestrians on Main
Street who had never heard of it. The town had an
earthy, lived-in look, more colorful than she'd
remembered it. Porches, rockers, three-story frame
houses that looked inhabited by white-haired gran-
nies sitting on horsehair sofas in dim living rooms.
Huge old trees with massive trunks, rubber tire swings,
a clothesline! When had she last seen towels and
sheets hanging in a yard? Adirondack chairs on wide
lawns, here and there a pickup truck in a driveway.
Nothing like Scarsdale.

Driving toward the river, oblivious to its gloss and
art-photo shimmer, she spotted a mail carrier. He
gave her detailed directions, and still, she managed
to get lost. Finally, when she decided to head back
toward the bridge—she had to pee, shouldn't have
had the coffee at the photographer's—she found
herself at the corner of Merland Road and River
Street, back near the center of town. Her hands perspiring and squeezing the steering wheel, she turned
into Merland. House numbers, too often obscured
by foliage or ambushed placement, were hard to read.
His, number 476, was in brass numerals next to the
dark green front door, and again, on the mailbox at
the curb. It was not what she'd pictured, but what
had she actually expected? She'd imagined him in
a house with distinction and personality, saw him
stepping out of a front door onto a veranda with
pillars or a grand Tudor surrounded by a weed-free
lawn carpet, a domicile that suited a man she saw as
Homeric.

Stretch's house was one of a series, a three-story
Victorian, narrow and tall, like most others on this

street, with a small front porch not twenty feet from the sidewalk, just wide enough for its one (dark green) wicker rocker. And, taking a closer look, there, on the side, a ramp, painted the same evergreen, almost invisible from the street. Gaby pictured the wheelchair that would roll up and down, its occupant maneuvering its wheels. Had Stretch himself built it for her? Or negotiated with a carpenter, discussed size, width, slope, to make it safe, make it convenient for Mitzi?

Then, that chair. Did he sit there alone? Did Mitzi? One chair, not two; no side-by-side-by-candlelight on summer evenings. And the windows, lace curtained on the second floor, uncurtained on the third, and the main floor—were those Roman or balloon shades? It was hard to tell through the dark screens. The windows were open; someone was home. Mitzi could at this moment be looking out of a window right into her car. But there was no sign of life at 476. Down the street, a mother was pushing a stroller, coming this way, accompanied by a Boston terrier on a leash. Two teenagers whizzed by on bicycles. Gaby couldn't stay here more than a minute; someone might notice her just sitting behind the wheel casing a house in the middle of the afternoon, call the police.

Gaby had to pee more urgently. The young mother was approaching with her stroller, looking right at her. Gaby felt as if she'd already committed a crime against the neighborhood and one close look at her through the windshield would give it all away. The dog pulled ahead and the woman passed; Gaby took a tissue out of her glove compartment and wiped perspiration from her upper lip. What in God's name would Mama, would her sisters, say to her behavior? They would call it twisted. That's the word they'd use, she could hear them saying it. *Twisted*. Sign her up for five shrink years with medication accouterments.

Now, at any minute, she could actually lose bladder

control. As she released the brake, put the car into gear and was about to step on the gas, the door of number 476 opened.

Out stepped a boy. His child. Nine or ten, a dark T-shirt with a faded picture on the front, over a Speedo. A towel in his hand, a pair of rubber goggles dangling from his fingers. Sneakered feet. She knew his name, knew everything: strong in math, weak in every other academic subject, athletic, lacking in social skills but interested in going on nature walks with his father, fascinated by slugs and snakes, fishing pole his latest birthday present, no longer bedwetting. Named Marco, after Mitzi's father.

What Gaby hadn't expected was the hair. Stretch's hair, the same red, more of it, the same slight wave across the forehead. And the forehead, freckled, like Stretch's. And the same chin, nose, mouth, the same everything. Or, that's what she saw. A miniature of his father, more than a family resemblance, a replication.

Now, a car was coming up in her rearview mirror, coming to pick him up it looked like, slowing down in front of the house across the street. Just as Gaby was about to pull away from the curb, the front door opened and the daughter stepped out. Smaller, younger than the boy. Eyeglasses. Striped bathing suit, towel over her shoulder, a green frog water tube around her waist, flip-flops with plastic daisies between her toes. This must be Beeps, Stretch's pet name for Bernadette, who was named for the saint. Gaby knew about her eye operation, her collection of Pez candy dispensers, her passion for the two family cats, Fred and Ethel. Beeps was a bad eater and looked it—skin over bones. Beeps was afraid of things too, dark corners and summer moths, and especially spiders. Was starting flute lessons after Labor Day.

Beeps looked nothing like her father, could have been anyone's child. Could have been her own self, at six or seven. Gaby was reminded of her own baby

fears—men in dark uniforms, large dogs and especially, spiders. She had looked like Beeps too, emaci-
ated, until she reached her teens, and like this child
just getting into the blue VW at the curb, loved and
adored the family feline.

Gaby remembered the day Luffy left for the vet's,
never to return, a summer day like this one. Hours
later, before the sun had set, Mama had called her
in from the yard. There was still a playhouse in the
garden then, although they'd all just about outgrown
it by that time. She'd come out of the garden to get
the news, an orange popsicle melting and dripping
down her wrist, been told Luffy had died a peaceful
death at the vet's a few minutes ago. Gaby had thrown
the popsicle into the garbage pail at the end of the
driveway and run upstairs into her room to cry it out
alone. Sat hugging her stuffed wallaby until Daddy
came home from work.

He'd sat on the edge of her bed to comfort her
but had to pull out his own handkerchief to blow his
nose. Daddy crying! And saying Death cured Luffy of
his disease, don't you see, Gaby. Luffy just went to
heavenly sleep, Sweetheart.

She must have been the same age then as Stretch's
Beeps today. Beeps, a name she'd always thought too
cutesy, now here in the flesh, a vulnerable child with
a mother in a wheelchair and a father *cheating. Cheating,* a screeching word that connected Gaby to this
family in a poisoning-the-water way. Gaby wanted to
call Mama on the car phone this minute, just to hear
her voice.

Recently her mother seemed to be her own good
and solid self again. Even when you had soul fever,
the sort that didn't show on a thermometer, Mama's
voice in crisis was like having a cool hand put on your
forehead. Gaby tried to put the call through, pushed
the buttons of her cell phone furiously, with no idea
what she would say, but Mama's answering machine

picked up and Gaby put the phone back into its
cradle. Then, taking one last look at Stretch's house,
she stepped on the gas and sped off.

On the way home, she found a diner. Bought a
Coke and used the toilet. She'd never thought about
his children in three dimensions. Until now, they
were photographs, a pair of bloodless images. She
thought about paths not taken, another two jobs she'd
been offered after college, one right here in Westchester with Spinoza Research. If only she'd taken
either of those market research jobs, Stretch's children's faces would not be burning a match under
her heart.

Gaby imagined the landscapes of Stretch's life with
this girl and this boy, his family days and nights, a
home behind curtains and shades, closed to her. Had
she ever in her life felt this *demoralized*, this hellishly
jealous?

Gaby addressed her reflection in the restroom mirror as if it would give her an argument, hardly aware
her lips were actually moving. "Daddy. What's happened to me? I used to be a decent person, wasn't
I?" She realized a woman with a gray frizzy perm had
come out of a toilet stall and was standing at a distance, bug-eyed, watching her.

"You okay?"

"I'm all right."

"You sure, dear?"

"Yes, okay."

"I sure hope it's not about money," the woman
said, stepping forward to wash her hands.

Gaby shook her head.

"About a man, then?" Gaby didn't answer, but the
woman caught whatever small light signaled yes in
Gaby's eyes.

"Isn't it always? I could have guessed that one first,"

she said, as she soaped up. "I'd get a nice little Siamese cat if I was you. They're very smart, and they'll never let you down," the woman said.

Gaby, managing a polite smiling nod, looked hard at herself in the mirror; her face had been transformed. She'd lost her looks completely since she'd seen herself this morning in her own bathroom. Her cheeks looked hollow, her face too thin, those little lines at her mouth and now, the beginning of musical bars across her forehead. Maybe it was just the fluorescent light, but maybe not. She saw the face of a thirty-year-old Jezebel, a woman who was sinking, sinking fast.

CHAPTER
TWENTY-EIGHT

Ruthie DiLorenzo, her face looking as if she'd just come back from a spa vacation, answered the door herself. She was wearing a long, flowered robe and bright makeup and Julie noted a new ankle chain peeping out above her bronze bedroom slippers. "One would never believe you just came back from the hospital," Julie said, kissing her cheek and following her to the screened porch at the back of the house. It was only as she walked behind Ruthie that she noted her bent posture and slow steps—"It's the stitches"—maneuvering around the dark mahogany furniture in the living room.

"I've been taking extra vitamin B12 and folic acid supplements," Ruthie said, "and I'm feeling wonderful. A little weak, of course, but generally, considering how they cut me up, pretty good. I hope Lou told you how much I appreciated the basket of fruit. The peaches were the size of volleyballs; you should have seen them!"

Julie assured Ruthie that Lou had called to thank her. She didn't mention what else he'd said. "She's a fighter, my wife." "I'm optimistic," he'd added, and his voice had stopped cold. Julie thought they'd been disconnected. Finally, clearing his throat, "I'm praying to God and I'm holding on to her with both hands, Julie. Both hands!"

Now Julie helped her into a wicker settee, despite Ruthie's protests. Julie had brought her a bouquet of Elizabeth Taylors from the garden and a shopping bag filled with assorted Crabtree & Evelyn goods and together they set upon digging out the hemp soap and the wheat germ oil, the sisal washcloth, the Calistoga cologne and the colored sponges, the fish-shaped fingernail brush. "A treasure hunt," Ruthie said, her voice a bit weaker than usual, but packed full to the bursting with cheer. Perhaps it was part of the therapy, this stainless steel optimism, part and parcel of the mind-body approach. Ruthie apologized for not being able to provide decent refreshments. She held out a plate of oatmeal cookies and told Julie there was cranberry juice or iced green tea in the refrigerator, ice in the ice bucket. ". . . you know where everything is."

Julie did know where everything was, here in Ruthie's old, familiar house with its scatter rugs over wall-to-wall, green velvet draperies inspired by Scarlett O'Hara, and on the walls, English animal print tag sale treasures. She found a glass vase, filled it with water and the roses, placed it on a desk near the window in the living room where Ruthie could admire it. "They're your real children," Karen had said once, pouting when Julie delayed their walk to kindergarten to spread Epsom salts in the flower beds and take out the hose to water them. It was true Julie took great pride in the health and chubbiness of the blooms and here, with the light streaming directly onto the flowers, they glowed neon red. Julie had for years tried to grow roses without the thin white stripe that Rosarians felt should be hybridized out of the petals,

but now she acknowledged that in her garden, in her
daughters, in herself, in life, streaks of imperfection
would always triumph.

Ruthie called them prizewinners and said that the
only time she'd tried growing roses she'd been bitten
by a bee, and Julie should be very careful in the
garden; bees are to roses as pooches are to hydrants.
Ruthie had said this many times over the years, and
that was the good and bad thing about old friends,
Julie thought as she brought out two glasses of
cranberry-mixed-with-green tea on ice, the same things
got said so many times. In friendship, as in marriage,
there had to be a certain redundancy. "I can't tell
you how terribly sorry I am about the party," Ruthie
said again, while her hand, with rings intact, trembled
slightly as she carried the glass to her Revlon-red
mouth. And Julie repeated the words of consolation
she'd spoken yesterday, or was it the day before? "It's
all right, Ruthie, of course Gaby understands, and
Karen said she'd be just as happy to have it at her
place. Nobody expects you to get out of a sickbed
and throw a wedding shower."

"I'll try to get down there though, you know I will,
I can't miss it," Ruthie said. "I've already ordered a
set of embroidered linen hand towels for her, wait
till you see them. Your girls, why, they're like my own
daughters." Julie, not wanting Ruthie to see worry in
her face, jumped up from her chair and said she'd
forgotten the paper napkins, and did Ruthie still keep
them in the second drawer below the silverware next
to the refrigerator? In the kitchen, she spotted the
dried palms now faded and curling that Ruthie had
pinned to the bulletin board next to the back door
and probably forgotten since Palm Sunday. Gilbert
always called Ruthie's faith ingenuous. Julie envied
it.

"So what's been going on? What have I missed in
town?" Ruthie asked, all bright eyes and upbeat

smiles, and Julie said she'd have to hear about the operation first, every moment of her experiences at Mass General.

"A four star hospital, a one star experience," Ruthie said, brushing off the subject, and she took another sip of her juice and asked Julie if Gaby was excited about the wedding, and where had the kids finally decided to go on their honeymoon?

As Julie rattled on to Ruthie about Gaby's endlessly changing travel plans and the caterer's idea of serving baby lamb chops as appetizers, as she chattered about Gaby's disinterest in her honeymoon wardrobe, the seating arrangements, even the gifts that were piling up faster than Gaby could send thank-yous, her mind spun around a single axis—Taras. The Mrs. Julie Kessler known for paying credit card bills in full on the first of every month, recycling glass and paper, using good pricing judgment in Second Chance, reading newspaper editorials word for word, and conservatism in the choices of haircuts, friends and charitable contributions, *that* Julie stood a distance away and watched the fixated, besotted Julie she hadn't known existed, carry on.

Carrying on was what she was up to, in bed with him, one whole afternoon last Monday, *who would believe it,* or at the stationery store looking for sappy greeting cards to send him, listening to Julio Iglesias hour after hour in the bathtub, keeping her adolescent, moonstruck self the darkest shameful secret since she first slept with Gilbert the month before they became engaged. All the while the current Gilbert—she'd missed visiting two days in a row last week—rasped oxygen through tubes and machines, still very much a living and sentient husband.

Today, sitting in Ruthie's painted wicker chair, oblivious to the butterfly garden of bee balm, evening primrose, artemesia (Lou's pride and joy) on the other side of the screen, oblivious to the drink she was sipping, the oatmeal cookie she was nibbling, Julie noted that Ruthie was fidgeting, the glass in her hand shaking precariously. She got up, put her own glass down and went to sit next to her friend. "Are you all right?" She was full to the bursting with wanting to tell her about Taras; if not her best friend, who then? She put her arm around Ruthie's shoulder, remembered now the last time she'd done that. At the George T. Davis Funeral Home. And later, when they'd put little Guy's ivory white coffin into the ground up in that Valhalla cemetery under a blistering, inhumane sun. Judging from Ruthie's face, suddenly drooping, every feature letting go of its cheer, even her perky nose seeming to give in to the reality; she remembered it too. Or, perhaps, thought that now it was her turn, and no amount of fish oils or folic acid supplements would save her.

"I'm not going to face St. Peter yet," Ruthie, the brave soldier, was trying unsuccessfully to pull up the corners of her mouth.

"You'll be fine," Julie assured her. "Chemo's no fun, but I'll be here, and so will Lou."

"Oh, God, Lou." Ruthie threw her hands together, squeezed them as if she were squashing a bug between her palms. "You know what he did? He filled every vase in the house with flowers and put them up in the bedroom. It was like coming home to a—"

"Garden of Eden," Harriet said helpfully. She noticed a new network of lines peeping out from Ruthie's bangs, which perspiration was sticking here and there to her forehead.

Ruthie lifted her chin and a smile almost appeared, "Or, the George Davis Funeral Parlor."

"Oh, come on, Ruthie."

Ruthie's hands suddenly flew up to her face. All Julie saw were the rings flashing, diamonds, a sapphire or two, winking, catching the light. She tightened her grip on Ruthie's shaking shoulders.

"Sorry, Julie. I didn't intend to turn on the faucet," Ruthie sobbed.

"It's all right. I mean, it's ding ho," Julie said. "The kids always say—" She looked around the room for a box of Kleenex.

"It's not ding ho! No. Not ding ho at all! I can't die with a mortal sin on my soul. I can't!"

"Mortal *what*?"

"Mortal sin. I committed a mortal sin."

"You know, Ruthie, that is very incriminating terminology."

"It's not just terminology."

"Well—who hasn't?" The face of Taras came and went. Last night, he'd found a park in New Rochelle, a grassy knoll that sloped down to the Long Island Sound, the security guard at the gate no longer on duty, and they'd rolled out a blanket and drunk some Australian wine his landlady had recommended, eaten takeout chicken sandwiches and made love under a starless night sky that had actually cleared the park of people and misted them with rain. "Who's perfect, Ruthie?"

"Twelve years ago, September."

"What did you do?" Julie jumped in with a real, heartfelt smile of her own. "Steal a bath mat from a Marriott?" She spotted a square, painted china box on a table near the door, out of which a tissue stood at floppy attention.

Ruthie's hands fell away from her face to her lap and her eyes moved to the glass on the table. The newly lined forehead, the smeared mascara, a brush-stroke of shadow under each eye morphed her from a pretty middle-aged woman into someone Julie's daughters would say was an uglified distant relative.

"Telling Father Molloy wasn't enough. Six Hail

Marys and two Acts of Contrition won't do it. I'm hardly sleeping."

"Neither am I—"

"You're my best friend," Ruthie's words suddenly took on a voice-dubbed quality. "You've always been pure gold. Julie, please understand. I can't die with this on my conscience."

Julie's hand dropped from Ruthie's shoulder. Acting instinctively, she got up and moved across the wooden, painted floor of the porch, which she had long ago helped Ruthie stencil with vines and leaves. The color was fading and the floorboards looked worn in spots. How long ago was it they'd kneeled side by side with those Tommy Dorsey standards coming from the stereo and paintbrushes in their hands? She couldn't remember.

"Remember, I was out of my mind. And it was only once or twice, maybe three times, Julie, I swear. On my life," Ruthie said, wiping her eyes with the backs of her hands just as Julie, having pulled a tissue out of the china box painted with stars, the sun and a smiling moon, stood frozen across the room.

CHAPTER
TWENTY-NINE

As soon as Julie was back in the car, she began rummaging in her pocketbook for a prescription Joe Goetz had given her months ago. Julie had filled his first Xanax one in October, right after the accident, but after taking only one or two pills, discovered they were making her woozy. She'd fallen asleep in the bathtub once and stopped taking anything stronger than Tylenol. Joe had given her a lower dose prescription, and she'd folded it into her wallet, "just in case."

Just in case was now, but her first stop was the hospital. When she stepped off the elevator on Gilbert's floor, she practically ran into her favorite nurse, the fifth floor standard-bearer, Dolly, whose eyebrows went up when Julie appeared. Julie had been at Gilbert's bedside not three hours ago.

"Air-conditioning's been turned up, Mrs. Kessler," Dolly said, assuming Julie was coming back to check on the temperature in Gilbert's room. She'd remarked it seemed too warm this morning.

Without answering, Julie swept past the nurse and raced down the hall. An orderly was standing in the doorway, chatting with a nurse's aide; Julie brushed past them too, ignoring their greeting as they moved aside to let her pass.

Taking the chair that ordinarily stood at the foot of Gilbert's bed, she dragged it across the floor next to its head. A succession of roommates had come and mostly gone, and since Gilbert was encumbered by the buzz and the hiss of conspicuous electronic maintenance, he was more often then not the solo occupant of his double room. Now, the other bed, the white and waiting rectangle half obscured by its half-drawn privacy curtain stood flat and empty a few feet away. Julie imagined herself stretching out on that inviting space, taking her shoes off, falling asleep here to blot out Ruthie and Gilbert, if only for a few hours.

Instead, she sank into the chair, threw her purse to the floor, and stared at her husband's face, scrutinizing it as if she'd never laid eyes on him before. The room had cooled too much and she began to shiver, thought of calling Dolly back to have them turn the air down again, but then again, perhaps it wasn't the room temperature at all. Memories besieged her as if a photo album of her life had been opened on her lap; scenes from the earliest hours she and Gilbert had spent together, beginning with the first honeymoon breakfast in San Francisco, to moments in a room not unlike this when Gilbert took a photo of her holding a day-old Karen in her arms, to the time he'd almost died of food poisoning on the Côte d'Azur.

He lay fetally curled and unmoving next to her now, his living, skeletal remains like coat hangers piled under the sheet, the skin bluish, a bit of saliva frothing in the corners of his lips, a thin, purplish mouth Julie no longer recognized.

"I loved you so desperately," she whispered, not knowing for sure if it was true. She loved him yes, but sometimes not, wasn't that the case? There were lapses in her affection, not unlike road work detours along otherwise smooth highways. He could be so long-winded, for one thing. "Get to the point," she'd wanted to say sometimes. And then, he could brag now and then, couldn't he, drop the names of all the wonderful places they'd been? "When we visited Beaulieu," or, "The best hamburger I ever ate was in Sydney, wasn't it, Julie?" He made her his accessory, which got her back up every time. "Guess who we sat next to at Du Cap? Frankie himself!" She'd sit there trying to smile, squirming. And no one could talk to Gilbert before ten. His morning self was silent, sometimes surly, a person better to be avoided. He could be impatient, too, if room service or a waiter was slow, on a bad day had practically bitten the head off the nice old man at the garage for making him wait too long to put air in his tires. And all those "Bravos!" Truth be told, she was tired of hearing them. Thirty-five years of "Bravos!" could wear one down. Funny how all those personality puddles came up muddy now. Yet, his were the smallest of faults; Gilbert was her loving, attentive, thoughtful, desperately conscientious man, so reliable, and so loyal.

Or so she'd thought, all these years. Hers and hers alone, despite all around her, her friends' husbands, and the girls in Second Chance being felled into spasms of despair by perfidious mates. And all the while Julie was so secure, so sure, almost smug. Gilbert had never, would never, and she felt so above it all when she listened to these women's stories of strange phone calls coming in the middle of the night, motel receipts found in pockets, their men's mysterious absences or jazzy new underwear. These episodes in other people's lives seemed as alien to Julie, with her loving, darling faithful Gilbert at her side, as Katmandu. *Not Gil.*

It was like a trash fire now, right here in this room. She leaned toward him, picturing it, just as Ruthie had described it, Gilbert putting those old Tommy Dorsey records on the phonograph when there were still 33 RPM records that would turn on a turntable, and those few times, the only times she swore, all started when they'd begun to dance, very ironic since Gilbert wouldn't ever dance with Julie except at weddings, under duress. Then, Ruthie, tissue to her nose, her eyes, her mouth, went on, describing how they held each other, Ruthie so needy with Guy dead and Lou in the hospital. There was the kiss, and before she knew it, "It went completely out of control." The first time only partial penetration. *Partial penetration!* It became so graphic, Julie could see it all, and it was like a double dose, so much more than she needed to know. "Partial penetration," just an almost-accident, like a brick coming loose and falling off a wall to create total havoc, throwing everything out of control. Practically the same thing.

Out of control is how Julie felt now, as if she could open the window five feet away and just scream her head off until someone led her away and slapped her face to calm her down. Or simply jump out, hit the concrete below and it would be over in five seconds— if she were lucky enough to land on her head.

Oh, ridiculous. Here she was, in the middle of an affair with her tango teacher, where did she have the right to feel as if a roaring wind had blown away the integrity of her married life? Yet, a tremor had developed in Julie's hands. Ruthie and Gilbert. Gilbert and Ruthie. Her best, closest friend. "Lou knows nothing," Ruthie had said, giving Julie a dog's look of pleading. *At any moment, she might reach over and lick my hand,* Julie thought, and promised not to tell. Ruthie was possibly going to die, but Julie might tell

Lou anyway, the hell with her. And the hell with Gilbert, the partial penetrator!

She leaned forward again, putting her face close to his. "Can you hear me?" she asked, and got no response. She put her finger under the ventilator tube coming out of his mouth. His skin felt like a raw chicken wing just pulled out of the refrigerator. He didn't move or react. Julie took the lobe of his ear and pinched it, hard as she could. Then, gave it a mean twist. Anyone alive would scream with pain; Gilbert's mouth bubbled saliva, the *ssss* of the machinery went uninterrupted. Julie, her fingers still holding his earlobe, bent closer. "I'm in love with Taras Goodman, my tango teacher," she said, speaking clearly, slowly, loud enough for her husband, if there were any auditory functions left, to hear. "We make love all the time. He's the best, the very best lover. I've never had such sex."

A noise at the door; Julie did not immediately turn to look. "Mrs. Kessler," Dolly's voice was cheerful and oblivious. "I think we finally got the right temp in here, don't you?"

As if she'd slid on a pat of butter Julie suddenly went down, grabbing the metal foot of Gilbert's bed, barely breaking her descent to the floor. She would think later that it felt as if the floor had shifted, actually rocked, trying to send her flying, trying to punish her.

"My goodness!" Dolly said, rushing to her side. "Are you all right Mrs. Kessler?"

The deck of a ship in a storm is how the tiled floor felt. Julie held tight to Gilbert's bed. She certainly deserved to be thrown down, to crack a tibula or fracture her knees. What had she done? Never in her life had she felt so wicked, so black-hearted. *Callous! I'm sorry, Gilbert!*

"I'm okay. I just lost my balance," she told Dolly

when she was able to catch her breath. That was it:
Lost my balance! This isn't me, Gilbert!

Dolly took Julie's elbow to steady her. "I told them
not to wax the floors. Told them a hundred times!"
she said.

CHAPTER THIRTY

It was Sunday night, they sat opposite each other in a booth at a half-empty diner on Route 9. Taras had wanted Julie to join him this afternoon when he took his son to buy school clothes, but she'd declined. She'd been in no frame of mind to make friends with Tommy, was barely holding herself in check now.

Her reaction to Ruthie's ritual confession had made her feel like a car veering full speed ahead, steering wheel missing. "Am I a priest? Why did you have to tell me?" she'd cried into the car phone an hour after leaving the DiLorenzos, after it all really sank in, in one of three follow-up calls after her visit. She'd stopped for gas, wanting to turn right around to confront Ruthie again, ask her questions to which she was afraid to hear the answers. She wanted to scream curses about friendship and betrayal, but kept her voice down because the garage man was handing her back her credit card. She continued the conversation from the privacy of her bedroom as soon as she got home, called Ruthie unstable, treacherous, deceitful and false-hearted, threatened to tell Lou, but then, called back, and apologized for everything she'd said. The woman, her best friend so long, did have cancer after all. They both cried, Ruthie told Julie she'd given a gift of a thousand dollars to her old parish in the Bronx as penance, was planning to tell Lou herself after all. "I can't live with it, I can't die with it!" Julie told Ruthie she could understand how a man could come along, take you in his arms, make you forget honor, the weather, the history of the world, obliterate everything . . . Taras.

What was she looking for when she tore into Gilbert's dresser drawers, pulled out amenity shoehorns and hotel shampoo and old menus he'd saved? What was she hoping to find in the midst of meaningless scraps of paper covered with Gilbert's unintelligible scribble-notes to himself? What in fact, did she find? A change of address notice from his barber, an old birthday card signed by all his employees: "To the best boss in the electric world, you give us all a charge!" frequent flyer miles documents and free coupons to a car wash. Love letters? Gilbert wasn't the epistolary type. Receipts from Tiffany? Documents proving other deceits? Not likely.

It was Julie's foray into madness, with attendant flurries of paper, bank deposit slips, stock purchase confirmations, gallery opening notices, a postcard from Alaska. She tossed them, missing the wastebasket, hardly aware what she must look like to Mariadora, who stood by, looking traumatized, offering a cup of mocha, a pair of aspirin? Mariadora hated change, and this was big change. Mrs. Kessler had gone *muy loco.*

I'm justified! Plain vanilla infidelity was one thing; Ruthie DiLorenzo was another. Gilbert doing her best friend was not like getting it on once or twice with a waitress he'd met on a business trip to Des Moines;

no. Sex with Ruthie was the unthinkable nadir, the bedrock of treachery. Gilbert was no longer poor Gilbert now. In Julie's eyes he had all these years been Mr. Deceit, helping Ruthie on with her coat, pulling out her chair, asking her nicely, politely, if she'd prefer California white or perhaps a bit of Dubonnet, as if she were an ordinary guest at their table. Ruthie, with her hoity-toity fake society accent. All the while, pretending they were just good old friends, the two had shared the decadent secret, that they'd touched and kissed and done who-knows-what-all else to each other. He'd actually gone and done the deed, as the girls used to call sex, slid himself into her best friend, while Julie was doing what? Watching *Charlie Rose*? All these years, Julie's own children were calling Ruth Auntie and kissing her cheek whenever she came to the house. And, thinking their father was perfection incarnate.

A few hours after the paper storm, calmed down after a good soak, Julie had called Joe Goetz.

While she waited for him to return her call, she visualized Gilbert, the man who couldn't/wouldn't ever dance, leading Ruthie across the floor of her living room to the tempo of old Tommy Dorsey records.

If Gilbert had danced with and made love to Ruthie, how many others were there? The Mexican computer woman, a bank employee on her lunch hour? How far-fetched that had seemed a few weeks ago. Now no swinish thing at all seemed impossible. Old signposts materialized: What about that woman who kept calling, trying to get him to invest in Broadway shows? Did he not finally invest money in *Cats* after he said it was a sure way to lose your shirt? Was that *Cats* woman another Someone he was partially penetrating? What about the little French au pair their neigh-

bors had back in the seventies? She always seemed
to be coming by to borrow *TV Guide*. She was only
eighteen, but one never knew . . . had Gilbert, home
almost every night at six, lived a sedulous secret life?
All this time, she'd been spending hours, sometimes
days, sitting at his bedside; just the day before yesterday she'd bought some Keri lotion and rubbed his
cardboard arms with it when Dolly wasn't looking.
Massaged his fingers. Whispered in his ear. "Gilbert,
I'm here," as she always did. *You bastard.*

At the diner tonight, Taras drank tea, not coffee.
"My mother had a samovar," he explained. "My
mother had a coffee pot," Julie said, lifting her cup
of terrible diner espresso. He laughed. She relaxed.
She wanted to reach over to kiss him, put her hand
on his cheek, straighten the collar of his very new
striped shirt. She'd bought it for him last week when
they'd walked through the Westchester mall. Now she
wanted to buy everything she saw for him: lisle socks
and silk pajamas and crocodile belts with gold buckles. She wanted to fill his closet with the most beautiful
cashmere sweaters, stuff his dresser drawers with linen
handkerchiefs and designer scarves. He'd never had
much; now she could pull out her American Express
card and see to it that he'd get the best of everything.
Still, she knew enough to hold back. Taras would
not want to feel kept; no good man would. When
she offered to buy him a new pair of dancing shoes,
Florsheim's best, he demurred. He allowed her to
buy this shirt because she directed him to wear it only
on nights that she'd scheduled a lesson with him,
saying that it would give her the greatest pleasure to
see him in a shirt she'd picked out herself. The stripes
of this shirt were light and dark gray. She remembered
Gilbert having one something like it once, wearing
it with his gray suede jacket, spilling tomato sauce on

the front at Pinocchio. She'd offered to try to clean it with club soda, but Gilbert waved her off. "You'll never get the stain out. It's easier to buy another one." Knowing you could replace anything, you didn't much appreciate what you had. Taras was not so spoiled; having seen his pleasure when she bought it, seeing him wear the shirt tonight made her unabashedly happy.

Taras said he'd already told his son all about her. He'd been thinking about his future and wanted her to know that she'd be in it, and that one day, when he opened his own dance studio, one way or another she'd be a part of it. He looked serious, even fervent. Julie tried to picture herself as a Heather taking appointments at the desk—very unlikely—or a Damaria guiding clients across the dance floor—even more unlikely. That's what she thought, but said instead she was considering having a piece of apple pie if he'd share it with her.

He talked and talked, not so much about his past as about the future. The dance studio he'd staff to free his days. He might also get a job teaching American History, maybe at Iona College, where he intended to finish his degree. Julie's mind wandered as he described a teak dance floor under crystal chandeliers and a ceiling painted in many deep colors, like the colors of Ukrainian Easter eggs. She remembered one of Gilbert's country music song lyrics: *Lord willing if the creek don't rise,* could have even hummed sixteen bars on the spot. Instead she said she thought a scoop of vanilla ice cream would be good on the pie, no?

After lunch at the mall last week, he'd also allowed her to buy a pindotted cummerbund that he would wear with his tuxedo when he took her to Gaby's wedding.

"What will your daughters say when we walk in

together?'' he'd asked, not once, but several times,
each time framing the questions differently: ''Will it
upset you if your daughters—?'' ''Are you sure it's
all right if I'm there with you—?'' ''You won't be
embarrassed—?'' How sweet, she thought, it worries
him.

''Oh, Taras, if my children see me happy, they'll
be happy,'' Julie said, and Taras told her they sounded
like lovely women, but she deserved to be so cher-
ished, and he loved her probably as much as they
did. ''Thomas Jefferson spoke six languages and I
only speak one. I wish I had five more to tell you how
I feel about you.''

He reached across the table and put his hand over
hers, and Mrs. Julie Kessler had no thought, for once,
about the diners left and right, who might look their
way and think she was his aunt, or a friend of his
mother's, or perhaps, his boss, buying him dinner.

Joe Goetz apologized for returning her call so late.
A four vehicle crash on the Hutch, one dead, one
almost; had she heard the sirens? She hadn't. He
hoped he hadn't waked her.

No, he hadn't. Julie was wide awake, looking
through Gilbert's closet to see which things would
go to Second Chance. The shop would open again
for fall consignment the day after Labor Day. The
pile of plastic shoehorns would go into the recycling
bin.

''What's up, Julie? Are you all right?'' Joe asked.
He himself sounded exhausted.

Julie was at the moment holding one of Gilbert's
cashmere sweaters in her hand. ''I think it's just about
time,'' she said. ''The day after the wedding. That
would be the thirteenth, Joe, all right?''

There was a silence.

''Are you there, Joe?''

"One hundred per cent. And you, Julie. One hundred per cent?"

"Yes."

"I'm so glad, dear."

"I'm holding his sweater in my hand, Joe. He's never going to wear it again, you know."

"Oh, I know. And now you do, too. We've all been waiting, dear."

I've reached the last page.

It wasn't only about the betrayal. It was about the probability that for many years all their evenings together, their vacations, the exchange of anecdotes and birthday presents, the kisses, even the sex, had all slid along on the well-maintained steel track of habit. Stuck together on the parallel rails of marriage, Gilbert had hopped off long before. And hadn't she?

When had they last had a really good laugh together? When had he whispered a secret, told her he loved her, held her hand in a movie? When was the last time she saw herself as beautiful in his eyes? And when was the last time she'd eagerly anticipated, really *looked forward* to an evening alone, just the two of them without the children, at home together?

Finally, the simmer of heat in her had cooled; she was able to stop loving Gilbert, and hating him.

"I'm ready, Joe," she said.

CHAPTER
THIRTY-ONE

Susanna stood at the drugstore counter, the CLEAR
BLUE EASY in her hand. She had already tried EPT
and ANSWER, each time astonished and frustrated
to read the negative results. There was always the
possibility, she told herself, that she had some urinary
abnormality that caused a failure to reveal what could
only be early pregnancy; she was definitely feeling a
bit queasy mornings and wasn't her period already
six days late? Then too, she'd read an article in some
women's magazine, a first person essay it was, written
by a young someone whose home testing kit kept
giving her positive results after a rape. It turned out
she wasn't pregnant at all, and was suing the pharma-
ceutical company for millions. If it could give false
positives, couldn't it in fact, produce false negatives?
Yes, it could!

Passing the Hair Care aisle, Susanna's eye caught
a new Clairol product promising highlights, silky
smooth waves and thicker, healthier hair. She read
the package instructions and put the box in her shopping cart. After the fight in the guest room, the chill

between Dieter and her had continued for two days
and two nights. They'd slept back to back with no
more than a "Good-night" spoken in hard-edge tones
as she turned off the light, and their meals—a few
salads Susanna had thrown together after work—were
eaten in the kitchen at different times. "We have to
work this out," she'd pleaded, hours after the fight.
"We have to fucking discuss it!"

It wasn't until Dieter had to go to a party in Manhattan celebrating the hiring of a new PR firm for the
Kaiser-Gelb chain that anything more than a polite
sentence had passed between them.

Dieter wanted her to go with him. A new hotel was
scheduled to open next month in St. Petersburg and
there would very likely be Russians at the party. Susanna's ability to speak the language, talk about Russian
poets and playwrights and the role of the Soviets in
the world war, gave her, and therefore Dieter, an
edge. The ice broke when he asked if they should
drive or take the train, and Susanna, so refreshed
with happiness that the cold war was over, forgave
him everything. She told herself that words spoken
in anger did not carry real weight and convinced
herself that all marriages—except perhaps Mama and
Daddy's—had their minor fractures.

She ran out and bought fresh sheets for the guest
room couch, resisting the impulse to buy the elegant
fern-patterned ones she really liked, and kept to Dieter's white-sheets-only edict, but found some with hand
embroidery and scalloped hems that Karen would
call *"beau monde."* More important, she bought thick
foam rubber padding for the convertible sofa mattress, and showed it to Dieter, who, well, reluctantly,
it was obvious, agreed it would help Liesel spend her
nights in America sleeping in comfort.

That night they made love and as it usually happened after a bout of hostilities, the sex was hotter
than fire, and after sex, he told her he loved her

despite any differences they might have; she came this close to confessing about the birth control pills and then, because he let out a happy yawn just as she was about to begin with, "What would you think if I told you—," she let the moment slip, closed her eyes, snuggled up to him, and went to sleep.

Tonight, they would go to the party at the Grand Hyatt, united warmly once again, in the role of the successful, attractive couple from Westchester. She'd left work right after lunch, and failing to get a last-minute appointment at the hairdresser's, would shampoo in the latest potion and let it do its promised Clairol work. She plucked her eyebrows assiduously, squinting at herself through her contacts. In the deepest corner of her heart she hoped that she was, like the rape victim, a chemical anomaly, and that she might very well still be eight months away from becoming a mother. What Mama kept saying was absolutely true: Susanna had always insisted she was not interested in motherhood, but she was the new Susanna now. She dreamed of a golden-haired darling in Baby Gap who would replace Liesel on Dieter's love map, change forever his center of gravity and keep him, body and soul, at home in America with her.

As she prepared to shampoo glints and gleams into her hair and steam the wrinkles out of her gold silk dress, Susanna thought about the forthcoming trips she and Dieter had planned: St. Petersburg for the hotel opening, right after Gaby's wedding. This coming Christmas (so the debacle of the last Yuletide would not be repeated) she'd hoped they'd finally get to Tahiti. Although, if she were well along by then, how would she feel in her elastic-waist maternity pants and tent blouses in a place reputed to be the most romantic spot in the world? No matter, she'd deal with that then. Tonight was here, tonight she would shine. Hopefully.

In the car, driving into the city, with the East River glittering along beside the FDR Drive, Mozart on tape, the evening ahead of them, she took a covert look at her husband. Dieter, who did not believe in working out, indulged in a diet rich in animal fats and skipped anything green that wasn't cucumber salad, had added a few pounds, yet, the extra weight flattered him. In his tuxedo, he looked healthy and fit. No, the word was *breathtaking*. A bona fide *head-turner*. No amount of Clairol, no gold silk (threaded with metallic gold thread) dress could transform her into the latter-day Aphrodite he deserved. She leaned closer to him thinking, *I'm so lucky to have him*.

Walking into a party at which Susanna knew no one made her nervous, but Dieter stayed at his wife's side and began introducing her as "My last wife," which made people smile and broke a bit of ice. Pretty soon, with a glass of champagne in her hand, Susanna felt more comfortable, and did what she knew would please Dieter: she moved off to circulate. She spoke Russian not well, but had pulled out her old textbooks last night, rehearsed a bit, and was able to chat about post-Soviet Irkutsk, the old KVD, Murmansk and the Kamchatka Peninsula. Once or twice she caught Dieter looking in her direction; each time she read it as uxorious pride written into raised eyebrows and a small, spy-movie smile.

The buffet was twelve feet of assorted delicacies from sea and land and Susanna watched Dieter pile his plate with beef instead of salmon, cheese instead of baby asparagus or broccoli, and as usual, she held back and said nothing. They sat at a tiny table to eat and Dieter leaned across his heaped plate to whisper, "Three different people told me I had a charming vife." Susanna's heart filled, her cheeks glowed and even the chandeliers above her head seemed to have a holiday luster. She took another swig of champagne and thought, *we're okay, we're more than okay, everything will turn out fine.*

Waiting for their car at the garage together an hour later, Susanna had what she'd later think of as a premonition. She wanted to stay at the party, keep the evening frozen in time, the way she'd put a piece of her wedding cake in the freezer, imagining it keeping its sweetness intact forever.

"You know, Dieter, this has been a perfect evening," she said, and he leaned over, and in front of two other couples waiting for cars and the garage attendant, put his arm around her shoulder and planted a warm kiss just where her cheek met her ear. "You were vonderful," he told her, just as the car pulled up and the attendant opened the door for her.

Just as the first, subtle menstrual cramps began radiating under her gold, threaded with gold, party dress.

She might almost have missed Liesel in the flow of people coming off Lufthansa Flight 400 from Frankfurt. The girl had changed considerably since that last time in Potsdam, and if it weren't for her cuckoo hairstyle, one would have called it a successful makeover. She'd lost weight, enough to make a difference, was wearing a white shirt, dark gray pants and a black cardigan tied loosely around her shoulders, become a natural gold-brunette, and, if one forgave the hair and theatrical sunglasses, looked ready for the better streets of America.

She and Dieter hugged and kissed and kissed and hugged for what seemed to Susanna the length of an overture, but then, Liesel, wearing long sleeves to cover her rash, put her arms around Susanna, gave her a warm hello kiss, and said, "I brought you a nice present, it's in my baggitch." Susanna was pleased to glimpse the gold Statue of Liberty on a gold chain around her neck, but secretly nervous about the red blotchy spots, which had extended to her hands and might after all be contagious.

It seemed like a fortuitous beginning. At the luggage carousel, Liesel chatted about the flight, about the man who sat next to her from Berlin to Frankfurt and talked the whole time only about his dog's asthma, addressing Susanna more than her father, because Dieter was preoccupied with finding her luggage, distinguished by colored pom-poms as per his E-mailed instructions. Susanna responded to Liesel's tales with enthusiasm and interest. "You are looking very pretty," she told the girl, imagining how she would like to take those little rooster fasteners out of her hair and do away with the bouquets of tufts that stuck up here and there like little brooms. Maybe she'd treat Liesel to a cut and style with Harold.

"I brought a dress for the vedding, is long, is okay?" Liesel wanted to know, and Susanna told her she was sure it would be fine. "I didn't buy yet anything for the bride," she continued, and Susanna assured her there would be plenty of time. She was beginning to feel comfortable with the girl, who seemed to have matured dramatically in a year's time. "And your English is so good," Susanna complimented. Liesel blushed becomingly. "Oh, not so good," she said. "I am studying some little in the mornings."

Dieter finally jerked Liesel's suitcases off the carousel and then, being very careful not to lapse into German—Susanna had reminded him this very morning that it was rude—he and Liesel preceded Susanna out of the airport and to the car.

As he loaded the trunk, Susanna and Liesel stood together, amiably comparing German weather with that of New York humidity, keeping the conversation flowing nicely.

"Papi told me your fahder is very sick," Liesel commented, shifting her huge leather purse from one shoulder to the other.

"Sad to say, he's already ringing death's doorbell," Susanna responded, and Liesel's eyebrows moved empathically together, just as Dieter slammed down the trunk and said, "Everybody, ready? *Wir gehen jetzt*—I mean, let's go, my little chickens!"

"I'm your little chicken?" Liesel said merrily, and without asking, opened the front passenger door and hopped in. Without hesitation, the girl had stepped into the car and taken Susanna's seat, leaving Susanna standing alone alongside the car door. Then, Liesel, without interrupting her conversation with her father, who had started the engine, reached back as an afterthought to pull up the button that locked the car's back door for Susanna. Susanna blinked, disbelieving. The seat next to Dieter was not his daughter's; it was *her* seat, it's where *she* always sat, right next to her husband, where *she* belonged. What kind of manners did the girl have? Why had Dieter allowed this? Didn't he see she was standing there, still outside the car, like some loser in a game of musical chairs? Couldn't he interrupt his chatting long enough to see what Liesel had done?

Susanna, fuming, thought of speaking up, then changed her mind. She would not be the one to start the visit on the wrong foot. And yet, it was rude, it was outrageously insensitive of them both to force her to open the back door of the car to take the seat she always considered a guest's, a passenger's, a handy spot for cargo. Her displacement to Siberia, she felt, already boded ill for the rest of Liesel's stay.

She sat there stewing, while father and daughter chatted it up in the front seat with some definite lapses into the language she had come to hate, and listened to their dialogue, to the laughter at little private jokes she didn't get, feeling as if she'd been precipitously demoted.

"You're so quiet, Schatz," Dieter said at one red light, checking on her in the rearview mirror. "You okay?"

"She's maybe thinking of her fahder," Liesel offered, "aren't you, Su?"

"Among other things," Susanna said, testily.

By the time they reached Bedford and Dieter pulled the car into the garage, Susanna had talked herself into a tempest. While he opened the trunk, hauled out Liesel's pom-pommed cases, while Liesel walked around the garage, examining the garden tools hanging from its walls and remarking on the twelve-speed bicycles neither she nor Dieter ever used, Susanna was preparing her diatribe. As they all stepped into the kitchen, Dieter caught the look in her eyes and became instantly anxious. "Did you see what Susanna prepared for you?" he asked Liesel, opening the refrigerator to show his daughter the assortment of delicacies, German and American, baked, fried, steamed and pickled, that Susanna had bought or made in preparation for Liesel's visit. "My vife is the most vonderful cook. You vant to try some *apfelkuchen*? She made it from a recipe from the *New German Cookbook*. It's better than sin!"

He had put down the suitcases to open the refrigerator, and now, picked them up again. "I show you the guest room," he said. "Susanna made it beautiful for you!"

Not another word had been said about the convertible sofa mattress. It was an issue that had come to hang between them like a rope gone slack, with no one picking up his end. Susanna had made up the bed with the extra layer of foam rubber, 200-thread-count white embroidered sheets and an Amish quilt patterned with stars. On the pillow she had placed a piece of chocolate wrapped in foil. Next to the bed,

on a low chest at its side, she'd arranged a small
bouquet of field flowers and a few magazines.

Now she trudged up the stairs behind the guest,
wanting to see the girl's reaction.

Liesel stood in the doorway a moment, taking it all
in. Then she broke out in exclamations. It was Oh
and Ah and Beautiful! "Vonderful! You made it so
nice here for me," she said, turning to Susanna and
giving her an enthusiastic, spontaneous hug.

"You like it?" Susanna cooled down a bit, telling
herself to decompress; maybe the mores in their
native country were different; maybe sitting in the
back of an automobile was a position of honor and
respect in Germany.

Liesel loved it: the bed, the pictures on the wall,
the view of the garden, the chocolate, although, "No
sveets for me, no more," and even remarked on the
charm of the little reading lamp that used to be Susanna's when she was in college. Susanna, composed,
flattered, opened the closet to show Liesel the space
she'd put aside for her clothes, the new padded hangers, the empty shoe rack for her shoes.

So it was all "vonderful" here, and she wasn't a bit
tired, despite the long trip, and now she would
unpack, and present her gifts: one for Papi and one
for Susanna. But first, she had a surprise, a very big
surprise, some important news.

She sat on the edge of the bed, looking at her father,
her expression going from conspiratorial-smug, to
little-girl embarrassed to coy. She blushed, laughed
nervously, the laugh sounding exactly like her
father's. "Sit down," she commanded Dieter, and he,
very obediently, stopped fiddling with the locks of
her suitcases and sat in the chair that attended the
desk. Hands on knees, he looked ready to get the
news, unlike Susanna, who tensed without knowing
why. She'd pulled up the leather ottoman that had
once served Daddy's feet in the old den in the house

on Morris Lane before Mama had it redone and tried to prepare herself.

"Vell," Liesel said, fiddling with the little tufts of hair above her ears. She looked at the ceiling, then at the window.

"Vell! I too vill soon be married. I am engaitched." She held out her hand to show the ring, a nice ruby(?) in a bezel setting—very modern—neither Susanna nor Dieter had spotted until now.

"But who?" Dieter seemed stunned. A little muscle worked in his cheek; apparently no hint of this news had come by E-mail.

"You remember Mr. Klammerer? You met him at Christmas, you had a nice talk with him at the party."

"Mr. Klammerer? Your boss?"

"Yes."

"He had a mustache? He's originally from Bonn?"

"Exactly. But he has shaved off the mustache. No more mustache. I didn't like it." Liesel beamed at her father, then at Susanna, possibly proud of her power over her fiancé and his facial hair.

"I thought—didn't I meet also his vife?" Dieter was up from his chair and rubbing his forehead with two fingers. "Her arm was in a sling, I remember, a skiing accident, no?"

"*Ja*. She fell in Zermatt. Anyvay, he is getting a divorce." Liesel looked thoughtful, then her face morphed into delight. "And he has made me assistant manager. I no longer have to vork Sundays."

Dieter, raising an eyebrow, looked at Susanna for a reaction. She responded with a shaky smile. "So, we should get out the champagne, Liesel? We should celebrate, no?" he asked, a bit uncertain. Susanna could see her husband's wheels spinning: a married man, an ex-wife, alimony. No wonder the news hadn't sped through the Internet.

"We should, we should," Susanna said, trying to remember if there was a bottle of anything good in the house. She was thinking that even though Liesel had broken up a marriage, Mr. Klammerer might take the spotlight off Dieter. Daddy's girl would now become Mr. Klammerer's girl; this could be good news. "So when is the wedding?" she asked, her mood bright. The sun would shine again!

"As soon as the divorce is over. Maybe four veeks, six the most," Liesel had taken the chocolate off the pillow and was unwrapping it. "Maybe chust one, to celebrate," she said. "Yes?"

CHAPTER
THIRTY-TWO

Gaby, about to be a married woman, felt as if she might at any minute fly apart. The last-minute details of the wedding: gifts for the bridesmaids, table favors and menus, the final meeting with the minister, gifts piling up in her apartment and at Mama's house, the manicure and hair appointments, purchase of going-away outfit, arrangements with the limousine service, thank-you notes, were the blood on her hands. Since her trip to Nyack not a day had gone by that she had not considered canceling her wedding. At work, she'd hardly looked at Stretch. Two new accounts, a cell phone company and a nutritional food spray product kept them busy and somewhat separate. With Stretch's children's faces swimming before her eyes Gaby was breaking in a new employee and scheduling focus groups; oblivious, Stretch was busy with client meetings and the accountant. When there was time to think, Gaby's indecision was like a knotted rope around her neck. She could neither slip it off nor tighten it; the wedding was ten days away.

When the telephone woke her at seven-thirty this

morning, she was shivering; Wally liked the air conditioner turned on high. Or maybe it was the dream she was having about an execution in Texas she was about to witness, the lethal injection decision an item on last night's television news report. These days Gaby was dreaming often of death and mayhem.

Wally was already up and showered. He stood next to the bed, a towel around his middle. He handed her the phone, giving her a questioning look. It was early for sibling chats. "It's Susanna."

"Did you hear the news?" Susanna began.

Gaby shot up in bed. "What news?"

"Mama's letting Daddy go. Hold on. I'm already in the office. I'm going to conference in Karen."

When Karen got on the telephone, she was weeping. Like a power button pushed, it also instantly turned on Gaby's tears. "But it's what you wanted," Wally protested, sitting on the edge of the bed next to her. He took her free hand and stroked it.

"Yes, it's what we wanted," Susanna said, overhearing him. She too, sounded ready to cry. "Mama called me last night late and asked if I'd call you both. She was so distraught I would have gone right over there, but she wouldn't let me and what with Liesel here—"

"How come *now* all of a sudden?" Gaby interrupted. "What changed her *mind?*" Her father's face, as he'd looked when he'd tucked her into bed when she was five years old appeared in front of her, his image as clear as if he'd materialized in the room.

"Maybe reality finally sank in," Karen offered. Gaby could hear Elliot muttering something in the background. "Elliot says it will be a relief for everyone," Karen added. "He would have offered to sit with Mama a while last night, but he's having real perio problems. Those painkillers make him very drowsy."

Gaby did not want to hear about Elliot or his dental difficulties now. She wanted to get back into bed and pull the covers over her head. Maybe this was all a dream, maybe if she was lucky, she was still sleeping. How could she face work today?

"And she's going to wait until after the wedding," Susanna continued. She stopped to sniffle. "Considerate as always. That's Mama."

"Well, of course," Karen said. "She wouldn't want to mess up your big day, Gaby."

Big Day. Gaby hated the term, Big Day, which she'd heard a thousand times in the last few months. "When's the Big Day?" "Ready for the Big Day?" "Good luck on your Big Day!" "I just have to, to, to"—Wally handed Gaby a tissue—"get used to the idea." This was no dream. This was life—Daddy dead, Mama a widow, their youngest daughter blackhearted and wanton.

"It's good that Mama's finally accepted the inevitable. It will give us all closure," Karen said.

"Closure!" Susanna's voice sounded sharp and weepy at the same time. Wally's eyebrows went up; even he heard it. "You know I hate that word! If Daddy dies, it's not going to give me *closure*. Closure is buttoning your coat, not losing your father!"

"Well, *excuse me!*" Karen shot back.

Gaby let the phone slip away from her ear. "I can't bear it. They're fighting," she said to Wally. *"Fighting!"*

He sat down next to her on the edge of the bed and put his arm around her shoulders. She leaned on him for a moment, then put the phone to her ear again. "Stop the bickering!" she said into the mouthpiece, which her own tears had wet.

"I'm sorry, I'm sorry," Susanna backed down. "You know me when I have the curse. You know how I get."

"You *always* have the curse," Karen snapped back.

Gaby blew her nose. "Wally, could you please turn down the air? It's cold in here. So cold!" Gaby cried.

* * *

The figure lying on the bed near the window of Room 816 had so little similarity to that Daddy, that if Gaby had walked into this room accidentally, she might not have recognized him. His complexion had taken on a mummy cast, his fingers, twitching periodically, looked like ghoulish replicas of hands, and altogether, the skin of his face, stretched over its skull, reminded her of the rubber Halloween masks that frightened her when she was a child. She sat in the chair in the corner nearest his bed, a chair with plastic upholstery and wooden arms, an uncomfortable chair, designed perhaps, to discourage long stays, and thought of all the hours Mama had put in here. Maybe it had just worn her out. *Poor Mama.*

Gaby now thought of her father the night of the accident, at her engagement party. With the champagne in his hand as he raised his glass in one of many toasts, this real daddy, not the one who lay waiting for a coffin between the two metal restraining bars of his hospital bed, had wished happiness, a good life, had thrown in a few of his customary "Bravo Bravissimos" and kept telling her she'd found a man who would forever take good care of her. He'd talked about marriage being like a pair of scissors that despite moving in separate directions would be joined forever, would cut whatever tried to come between them. Wally had leaned over to give her a kiss and echo, "Bravo" into her ear. Daddy, wiping moisture from his eyes with Mama's handkerchief, had looked so extravagantly happy.

Gaby watched the drizzled morning light brighten through the picture window that overlooked the roofs of White Plains, trying unsuccessfully to remember even one psalm, one prayer. Instead, she decided to make promises: to always be there for Mama, to make a greater effort at friendship with her sisters, to be charitable and thoughtful of others. "And I'll make it up to Wally. We'll become like a pair of scissors," she said softly, imagining that on some level open to spirit and intention, the message might—against all odds—get through to her father.

Then, another image of her father interrupted; was it the same summer of the high dive? She remembered sitting on his lap while he examined a bee sting on her knee. She was always getting bee stings in Mama's garden, one every summer it seemed, and this one was particularly bad, a golf ball swelling, which is why Daddy was allowing her, when Mama stepped out of the room, her first sample of the terrible-tasting Scotch he was sipping. Daddy had a smile warmer than a wool blanket, Susanna always said. "This awful stuff has drowned more people than all the swimming pools in America," he smiled. "Make two your limit all your life." She'd thought of that admonishment many times, often when she thought about Stretch.

Stretch.

"I'll be a good and faithful wife," Gaby whispered to the lifeless form of her father, soon to be put to rest in the upholstered isolation of a casket. Then, oblivious to the hum and buzz of the machines, the sickroom reek of disinfectant, she said, "Thank you for everything, Daddy dear." And finally, leaning over to give the cavity that used to be her father's cheek a final kiss, she whispered, "I'm going to stop seeing Stretch. I promise."

CHAPTER
THIRTY-THREE

"You know we love you," Susanna was saying.

Julie was seated in the middle of Karen and Elliot's charcoal leather couch, an empty coffee cup in her hand, the remainder of what she'd left of her piece of lemon coconut cake on a plate on her lap. She was admiring again the row of framed paperback book jackets, her daughter's amazing handiwork on the wall opposite. The guests were gone, the caterers finishing up in the kitchen, the opened shower gifts in a mammoth heap in a corner.

Julie felt that this event, compared to the bridal showers given Susanna and especially the very festive one Karen's college friends had given her, seemed subdued. There were some women from Gaby's office, two old friends from Scarsdale High School, two from college, and Tilda Novak, who came with her daughters and brought a most generous gift, a Cuisinart, no doubt a big-gun peace offering. The atmosphere had been decidedly muffled. Gaby, a too-calm recipient of a bonanza of household items from Crate & Barrel and Williams-Sonoma, dispensed with the usual explosions of Oooohs and a clapping of hands in favor of muffled Thank-Yous and Just What I Neededs.

A small party is what it turned out to be, with Ruthie DiLorenzo mercifully calling in sick after all, and Wally's mother, in no shape to come down from Norwalk. Gaby had vetoed Julie's friends from Second Chance on the basis of weak acquaintance, but extended an invitation to Liesel, Dieter's daughter, who chose not to come. "She has a rash, it seems to have spread to her hands and fingers, and don't forget, her English is weak." Liesel just felt too shy, Susanna went on to explain. "She would have felt very uncomfortable." She threw Gaby a meaningfully wicked wink nobody could miss.

Susanna had plucked her eyebrows and added a rinse, giving her hair a new bit of life. Best of all, she looked particularly buoyant, a good sign. Maybe Dieter had agreed to a bout of fatherhood. "Will you have another cup of coffee, Mama?" she asked Julie now.

Julie, impatient to leave, declined. She would not see Taras tonight, but would call as soon as she got home. He told her this morning he'd be waiting to hear her voice before he went to bed tonight. They often spoke three times a day. Julie had told him about her decision to end life support for Gilbert. Had said nothing about Ruthie's confession.

"We'll leave in a few minutes," Gaby, Julie's chauffeur tonight, said, distracted. She was looking over the list of presents and their donors that Karen had recorded as each present was opened. The tradition of threading ribbons through a paper plate to make a bonnet for the bride-to-be was observed, but posing under a ribbon-adorned paper hat for Susanna, the photographer, made Gaby, her new short hair all but disappeared under it, look out of character and definitely uncomfortable. She'd gone the extra style

mile by wearing a brand new sleeveless black dress,
gold button earrings and a gold bangle on her wrist,
but that was about as gala as her daughter would
go. "A bit of blush couldn't hurt," Julie had timidly
suggested before the guests arrived, but Gaby's eyes
rolled up with a "Mama, it's not showbiz!"

Julie put her disappointment aside, assuming that
if this party had fallen slightly flat, if her bride-to-be
daughter seemed pale and less than ecstatic tonight,
it was her way, and hopefully not because of Gilbert.
Hadn't they all been after her all this time to let him
go? To Julie's relief, not one word had been spoken
of their father tonight.

Disheartening, however, was the obligatory sibling
skirmish. Before the guests arrived, the girls had
clashed in the bedroom on the subject of the order
in which the salad would be served. Susanna had
insisted it be presented after the main course as the
caterer suggested, but Karen felt that doing it the
French way was pretentious. Gaby entered the fray,
suggesting that a dinner shower was in itself pretentious; why couldn't they have had a nice, simple lun-
cheon like everyone else? Karen exploded then. "You
are actually making me nauseous!" she said, and took
a dramatic deep breath. She'd chosen a dinner party
so Elliot's weekend would not be disturbed; this was
the evening he taught his book binding course as
Gaby well knew and anyway, weeks of planning, a
beautiful *risotto ai porcini*, a *pollo scarpariello*, a lemon
and coconut cake; what the hell sort of gratitude was
this?

The fight ended when Gaby apologized, explaining
she'd been under terrible prenup stress, Susanna
backed down, allowing Karen, the hostess, to direct
the caterers, and the doorbell rang as the first guest
arrived. As soon as the door opened, the girls meta-

morphosed into a welcoming committee of hostess bonhomie. Julie relaxed, proud of their manners and graciousness. The shower was a success.

The guests gone, now the girls were in harmony, laughing about Tilda's eye makeup and gold-and-black spectator shoes, reading again the amusing messages on the pile of bridal shower greeting cards stacked on the coffee table, and discussing which gifts were ding ho and which would have to go right back to Crate & Barrel and "should never have come out of either a crate or a barrel in the first place."

Then, out of left field had come this surprising "You know we love you," a preface to something that made Julie's back stiffen against the gray couch cushions, a dangerous residual twinge that made her toes move together on the carpet under her feet.

Followed by, "We know how much you love Daddy," Karen's lowering her voice forebodingly. "We certainly do." She was in stunning cobalt silk today, and on what looked like a rope, a hunk of some bluish semiprecious stone hung, sitting on her breast bone. She'd also had her hair cut, and now it framed her face, a curl or two hanging over her forehead. She kept blowing it out of her eyes.

"Listen, Mama, we want to talk to you about your bringing this tango teacher of yours to the wedding," Susanna began.

Julie, taken aback, blinked a few times, looking from one to the other. "Taras?" she asked. Karen, legs crossed, was seated in one of the charcoal chairs facing the couch; Gaby had pulled up an ottoman and was sitting next to her, and Susanna stood behind them both, a fresh cup of coffee in her hand. To Julie, it was now obvious that this was not a friendly cluster.

"This is hard to express." Gaby looked at Karen.

Karen's hand moved supportively to her sister's shoulder. Julie was nonplused by this extraordinary show of sisterly solidarity.

"We feel, I mean, we're very happy you've enjoyed the dance lessons, but Mama, little did we know that you'd want to bring this tango man—well, we think it's a bit—reckless."

Julie smiled, relaxed. Mariadora had been talking. What did they know? And what if they did know? They were worried about her, each one looking so concerned and serious. She imagined what Taras would say if he heard himself called 'tango man.' "He's a very nice person," she said, with an indulgent smile. She wanted to comfort them. "Not a fire-eating dragon, girls!"

"He may be a very nice man, but we don't think he's a very nice man for *you*," Susanna responded.

Julie wanted to jump up and put her arms around them. They had turned into lovely young women, one and all, and more than that, they were showing what she already knew: they loved her, cared so very much about her welfare. They must have already discussed Taras among themselves, churned up anxiety in private sessions or on the telephone.

"For one thing," Karen said, picking up where her sister left off, "he's not much older than I am, is he?"

"Well, look at the age difference between you and Elliot," Julie pointed out, not sure she should have brought that touchy subject into it. Sure enough, Karen's face fell, but, only for a moment. "Not the same thing," she countered.

"Not the same thing," Susanna echoed. "You know it's entirely different, Mama." They both had become so defensive that Julie wished she could take it back.

"It's more than that. He's a—he's a dance instructor! Well, I mean, Mama, he's from another world entirely." Karen uncrossed her legs, leaned forward. Her face went into iron and steel.

"That's true, very true," Julie said, and added, "And, Dieter isn't?"

"You can't compare Dieter to a tango teacher!" Susanna shot back.

Perhaps it was wrong to throw that up to her daughters, but they were painting Julie into a corner, weren't they?

Gaby was nervously pulling on one of her gold earrings. "Mariadora said you're spending a lot of time with this fellow!" It was a remark Julie pictured as followed with not just one, but a row of exclamation points. "What do you talk about? I mean, what kind of conversations could the two of you possibly have?"

Gilbert had always wondered the same thing about all three of her daughters and the men they'd chosen, but that was unfair; Julie knew that happy couples found their own subjects. Like most married people, she and Gilbert had generally talked about who would put gas in the car and which toothpaste to buy, in addition to who would make the best secretary of state. She held back the fact that she and Taras never seemed to run out of things to say to each other, *between bouts of sex,* either.

"We talk about you, for one thing. And his son."

"He has a *son?*"

"Oh, my God, he's not married?" Karen asked and Julie was surprised to see a look cross Gaby's face that she would have called startled. Her cheeks, without blush, turned very pink.

"Oh, no, not married. But, he's quite a devoted father."

"That's very nice. How old is his son?" Susanna wanted to know.

"About twelve."

"Twelve. Well, there you go. He could be your

surrogate grandson!" Susanna's mouth twisted into an upside-down C. Harriet hadn't seen such a bitter expression on her daughter's face since *she* was twelve and discovered she'd been left off the guest list of a friend's birthday party.

"Well, so be it," Julie said gently, trying not to sound displeased. The girls were in a league and a union, and that was good, but they were in a bloc united against Taras—*awful*.

"Don't you see what Susanna's saying? You're old enough to be a grandmother and here you are, going around with that tango man, who is probably after something, we don't know *what*, for all we know, I don't like to say it, but your *money*, yours and Daddy's, and sure as anything you are going to be hurt down the line, maybe even taken for all you've got—!"

Julie felt her back go very rigid. She tried to relax, did not want a reprise of her killer back injury. All those muscles and tendons geared for war; isn't that what all the mind-body people said? *Stay calm!* "Did it occur to you that the thing Taras is after, the thing he really wants, is not money, but my company, *me*?"

Gaby shrugged her small, childlike shoulders. "Mama, you are so *ingenuous*," she sighed.

"Give me a bit of credit for having both feet on the ground, girls! I was not born yesterday!" Julie's plate of cake remains trembled on her knees.

"That's it exactly, Mama! You've been through so much and don't forget, you're getting older. Perhaps your judgment isn't exactly what it was," Karen said.

"Older! Good heavens, what are you saying? Yes, I'm older, but not old. Are you planning to push me into assisted living quarters?" Julie's back now really began to hurt.

"Mama, don't get upset." Karen smoothed down the cobalt fabric that covered her knees. "Don't go off the deep end! We don't think you're *old!* We just think you're old enough not to go around with some—some—two-stepping tomcat!"

Two-stepping tomcat made Julie taste fire. *Ganging up*, she thought, that's what they're doing.

Susanna came to sit next to her. She put her arm around her shoulders and said, "Don't be upset, dear, you know we don't want to see you hurt. We all love you."

Julie nodded half-heartedly. She kept thinking *Two-stepping tomcat*. She wished she was at home this minute, sitting in the den, holding the phone to her ear and hearing his voice. Better still, in bed, his head next to hers on a pillow.

"If you knew him—" she began, finding her voice, "you'd never say—" but they cut her off.

"Oh, Mama," they burst out, almost in unison, "get *real!*"

"He is a wonderful man," Julie insisted.

"Be that as it may," Karen continued without missing a beat, "we really think it would be wiser if you didn't—I mean until last week we didn't realize you had any such intention—but we really think you shouldn't even *think* of bringing him to the wedding."

At that, with her back twinge-ing on her dangerous, vulnerable, right side, Julie shot up, pulling away from Susanna's encircling arm. The cake plate slid to the floor without breaking, scattering remaining cake and crumbs on the small rug under the coffee table. "Wait a minute!" she cried. "I'll bring whomever I please!"

"Mama." Gaby's eyes grew round and moist. "It's *my* wedding. Don't I get a say in this?"

"Your wedding? Who paid for it, Gaby? Who?"

"I think you should think it over, Mama!" Karen said. "How is he going to fit in? He's going to make you look so—"

"So *what?*" Julie wanted to pick the cake plate off

the floor and hurl it at the wall, see it smash into pieces.

"So fatuous!" Susanna said.

"Undignified," Karen added. "Ridiculous!"

"Like you brought a gigolo, or something." Gaby looked beseeching. "Please, think it over, Mama."

Julie looked from one daughter to another. She saw them as they once were, tiny darlings in footed sleepers, sitting on either side of her on the blue chaise while she read them *Are You My Mother?* Where had these little flowers gone? How had they been transformed into these thoughtless, insensitive and stubborn lionesses?

"I've already invited him," Julie said, shoulders square, her back ramrod straight. "I have no intention of rescinding my invitation. And now, girls, if one of you will please bring me a couple of Tylenol and a glass of water, I'll be ready to go home."

CHAPTER THIRTY-FOUR

"Dieter! I'm back!" Susanna called out as soon as she got home from Gaby's shower. She'd put in a full day at the office, booked fourteen members of a Bedford family into the Camelback Inn for a family reunion, managed to upgrade a corporate VIP although Delta had told her twice that First was sold out and found a last minute flight to Vegas for six members of a Buick dealership who'd had another flight canceled. Directly from the office, she'd rushed into the city to Gaby's shower. Now she was home, wanting to put up her feet, drink a cup of tea and talk to Dieter about Mama and what looked like an actual affair of the heart with a *tango teacher*. Karen had last week been at Mama's and had had a surreal conversation with Mariadora, who, with a winking and rolling of her eyes, insinuated, intimated and implied a relationship Susanna did not believe, until now.

"Dieter!" she called again but there was no answer. Putting down her purse and taking off her shoes, she began to climb the stairs. Could he and Liesel both be asleep? By the time she reached the first landing, she heard what sounded like creaking doors in a horror movie. Somewhat anxious, she stopped to listen. Not creaking doors, not the meowing of hungry kittens, this muffled sound was coming from the guest room. Having read one too many autobiographies, seen one too many television documentaries about father-daughter incest, Susanna had a flash of icy fear: *what if?* But, no, ridiculous; it sounded in fact as if Liesel were crying. Then, creeping quietly up another step or two, Susanna heard Dieter's voice muttering in German, sentences and paragraphs she couldn't understand, punctuated by alternating silence and little cries, then Dieter's voice, louder, angry? Liesel hiccoughing.

Susanna stood at the top of the stairs, uncertain about whether to knock on the guest room door or simply wait, eavesdropping, until the door opened. "I'm home!" she called tentatively, not wanting to be discovered spying out in the hall.

The guest room door opened; Dieter stepped out, closed the door behind him. He looked uncharacteristically mussed, although disheveled would have been too strong a word. He was still in his business clothes, his shoes were laced, his tie was simply slightly loosened.

"She's impossible," he whispered, shaking his head, stretching "impossible" to make it sound like two words. He was perspiring. "She vants to go home!"

"Go *home*? Why?"

Dieter took Susanna's hand and pulled her away from the door so they wouldn't be overheard. He lowered his voice.

"The doctor, the very best, I took her right down to New York Presbyterian, to the dermatologist there, and you know vat?" He resumed shaking his head, more speedily now, as if he were ridding himself of a sparrow that had landed in his hair.

"The rash?" Susanna asked, momentarily befuddled. Now she remembered what she'd forgotten: the medical appointment he'd made for Liesel three weeks ago.

"It's not what ve thought, not from the vashing of the dishes in the restaurant, the rash, no, nothing to do with it."

"Really! What then?"

"This Dr. Belsky, a young woman, a very nice person seems to be, she says 'psoriasis.' Where that comes from I don't know. I called immediately Lotte but she says too, nobody in the family, nobody got it before."

"Is that why Liesel is crying?" Susanna thought she might go downstairs, make the girl a cup of tea, give her a bit of woman-to-woman comfort. Psoriasis. Not a pleasant diagnosis, but not a life-threatening disease, after all. There must be medication, cortisone ointments perhaps, probably new therapies; tired as she was, Susanna would offer up some words of hope and solace. The girl was in a strange country far away from home, and the thought crossed Susanna's mind, that if Liesel turned around and went back now, Dieter would go running right after her. "I can go talk to her," she offered. "I'm surprised she's that upset."

"She vasn't upset right away," Dieter said, "She thought a cream would take care of it, but no. Dr. Belsky said not. In Potsdam she tried already steroid ointments, coal tar treatments, sunshine, now she has to take something by the mouth."

"Like what?"

"A medicine." Dieter reached into his inside breast pocket and pulled out the prescription bottle of pills. He held it at arm's length and moved to the light to read the label. "Looks like Soriatane. Something new, you've heard of it?"

"No."

"I never either."

"So? It's not hopeless?" Susanna knew nothing
about the prognosis but seemed to remember a counselor at summer camp putting ointment on her knees
and telling her it was psoriasis and it would never go
away. Science, however, had moved along. "All Liesel
has to do is swallow a pill, right?"

"Yes." Dieter took a breath and made an angry
mouth, shaking his head yet again. "But she von't!"

"What do you mean, 'she won't?' "

"Just as I said, she von't. She just—*vill not.*"

"She refuses to take the medication?"

"Exactly."

"I'll go have a talk with her, should I?"

Dieter nodded yes, looking grateful.

Susanna, getting a second wind, did not hesitate.
She'd skip making tea, or the girl might fall asleep
before she got back. Formulating some words of compassion and support, she knocked softly on Liesel's
door. First thing tomorrow she'd look for a psoriasis
support group on the Internet, find alternative treatments, specialists. She'd be Liesel's kind American
mother while she was here. She knocked again. Liesel's voice, muffled and distant, finally responded
with a watery "Yes?"

"It's Susanna." She pushed open the door a wary
inch at a time and stepped into the room. Liesel was
sitting cross-legged on the couch, which Susanna had
made up as a bed with those expensive embroidered
sheets, that pretty Amish quilt. She was wearing a
white, short-sleeved nightshirt patterned with what
looked like acrobatic cats, an open box of tissues at
her knee. Her hair was wet—just shampooed and
even at this distance smelling of lemon—but the first
thing Susanna noted was the rash. Liesel, with a pen
in her hand and a bunch of postcards in her lap,

caught Susanna's reactive flinch; the girl's arms were a scaly, red, peeling mess.

At first Susanna thought of pretending she hadn't noticed, but then thought better of it. "Does it hurt?" she asked.

"Ven I scratch," Liesel said.

Susanna sat at the foot of the bed, nodding, trying to figure a kind and sensitive way to continue. "Your father is very upset," she said.

"I know," Liesel looked as if she'd burst into tears again. The postcards were scattered between her knees, most of the Statue of Liberty at night.

"So. It's fortunate that over here, we have wonderful doctors," Susanna said brightly.

"Ve have vonderful doctors in Germany too," Liesel quickly countered.

Wrong tack; she'd gotten Liesel's back up. Susanna tried not to stare at the patchwork of flaky red skin not three feet away from her. The rash was encroaching on the back of the girl's left hand, and at least one thumb. "This specialist your father took you to is one of the best."

"*Ja.* He said so."

"And she thinks you ought to take this new oral medication."

A petulant nod. No answer.

"So." Susanna waited a moment while Liesel picked up one of the postcards, turned it over in her hand. "So, your father tells me you don't like to swallow pills."

"I'm not going to take anything I don't know in the mouth."

"Is that reasonable?" Susanna tried to find some nugget of understanding, some explanation for this obdurate, infantile behavior. Was this a cultural thing? A far-away-from-home thing? A superstition? Or just flat-out stupid distrust of America and its doctors?

"Excuse me, Liesel," Susanna continued. She tried not to be aggressive, tried to keep her voice motherly. "It seems to me you'd want to take the pills. They may help you! They may clear up the rash! Don't you want to get rid of it?"

Liesel's red-rimmed eyes went into slits. A tear rolled out of one; she plucked a tissue out of the box at her knee and wiped it away. Another one took its place.

"My business," she said.

"Really, Liesel—"

"Not yours!"

Susanna swallowed a sharp retort: *Wake up, you little German idiot,* but she didn't say it. "I don't understand you, dear," she said instead. "I just don't."

"Vell, I don't vant to talk about it, OKAY?" Liesel's voice became assertive and loud, loud enough, Susanna thought, to wake the dead.

"OKAY!" Susanna yelled back. The *brat.*

"So a good night then!" Liesel picked up the tissue box and looked for a moment as if she might hurl it, but just slapped it back down on the quilt next to her hip, instead.

Dieter, who had himself probably been eavesdropping and heard every word exchanged between them, rushed into the room.

"Du bist aber ein undankbares Kind!" His face was red, his eyes shimmering anger, and a stream of angry words Susanna didn't understand poured out of him. Susanna wanted to applaud Dieter, pat him on the back, give him a big kiss for whatever he might be saying to the girl. A good talking-to in any language was clearly what she needed.

Liesel's response was to cower against the pillows, close her eyes and begin to scratch her upper arms. He was going on and on; a few familiar German curses were interspersed in a high-pitched monologue. *"Ich habe aber nicht mehr Geduld!"* Susanna understood.

He'd run out of patience. He was really letting her have it. Maybe, Susanna thought, watching her, it was time to let up. Maybe enough was enough; Liesel would surely give in now, make an effort, swallow a pill. She looked terrified. Susanna thought of running downstairs to get a glass of orange juice from the kitchen, remembering *Just a teaspoon of sugar makes the medicine go down*, an apropos song lyric, from *Mary Poppins*, wasn't it?

But suddenly, Liesel held out her arms and cried out, and a switch was turned on. With one hand on the doorknob, one flying to her heart, Susanna hoped she'd heard wrong. She knew so little German, just a word here and there, a phrase, a greeting. "Schwanger!" is what Liesel cried out to her father. "Ich bin *schwanger!*"

But, Susanna knew *Schwanger* well enough. Liesel, that lucky little priss, unmarried, a baby herself, was pregnant.

CHAPTER
THIRTY-FIVE

It was late afternoon on a day the city was steaming; she put ice in Stretch's vanilla coffee and held an ice cube on the inside of her wrists, hoping it would calm her down.

He was at his desk, wearing the glasses she'd helped him pick out at the optometrist. Gaby had told him they made him look professorial, dignified, playfully added he looked "almost like one of us." When she stepped into his office now, he took them off, but didn't get up. She handed him the cup and stood facing him, ready to bolt. She started quietly, a bit pedantically, then her voice barreled along, gathering momentum and passion, never her style. She could not admit she'd spied on him, but wanted him to know it wasn't all selfishness.

Since her trip to Nyack his children had appeared like specters over the screen of her television set, across the windshield of her car and as faces on billboards at the railroad station. Symbols of handicap access—suddenly ubiquitous—evoked the ramp at the side of his little porch. "I think of your children.

Your wife. I think of Wally. You know we're not religious, but Jewish guilt? It casts long shadows." Daddy's face, too, bubbled up somberly, now invited itself into every nook and cranny. "I can't sleep. You know I've been working up to it, well, you and I are running down the wrong road! I went to say goodbye to Daddy—" here she stopped to pull herself together, "Oh, God, it's hard, but Stretch," her eye went to the suede couch, the Spot, "my wedding. It's Sunday."

"I know," he said. "I've marked it carefully on my calendar." A sardonic half-smile came and went.

It was of course, not the first time she'd talked of ending it. But before this, Stretch always veered into another subject or sealed her lips with a whisper of dissent, or a kiss.

Now, calm, totally in control, eyes on her eyes, he said, "Well, it's not a surprise. With your Big Day coming up of course, I sort of expected it."

Big Day again! Big Day! Big Day!

He got up from the desk, surprising her by offering no resistance. He kept saying he understood, no arguments, no bent knees, just kisses and heat, his hands, his lips and breath, an office dream sequence, the whispered I-love-you's, the almost-sex behind the locked door of the whiskey-colored room while the staff buzzed normal business—high-top running shoes today—on the other side of the one-way mirror. Despite being discreet and covert, some people in the office must by this time suspect what was happening under their noses. That fact had dawned on Gaby long ago, but she'd been too swept off, too dazzled to notice or care. Now she backed away from Stretch. This was no dream sequence.

"It's over," she told him. A vanload of guilt lifted from her shoulders. She'd ended it. She felt she could fly. *It's over.*

After her honeymoon, she would come back to clean out her desk; there was no possibility of continu-

ing to work at Global Enterprises. She explained that
now, haltingly, kindly, suggesting that if he cared for
her at all, Stretch could make her departure easier
by writing her a blue-chip letter of recommendation
"longer than the Twelve Step Bible." "You have such
a persuasive way about you," he responded, acting
the cool boss, smiling dispassionately, as if they'd just
met an hour ago. He agreed, almost too quickly, to
write the letter, never to call her again, to send regrets
in response to the wedding invitation he'd already
accepted. Gaby congratulated herself. She'd been
strong, behaved with honor, okay, belatedly, but nevertheless. She imagined Daddy's eyes looking at her,
all approval and light.

Gaby left the office, went down the street and found
a dark bar, sat on a barstool under a huge television
screen and tried to finish a double shot of bourbon.
Watched a TV report of an investigation of corruption
in the Mexican government without seeing it. The
place was all stale cigar smoke and blue ozone and
she could get only half a shot down. The times she'd
actually tried to get high, she remembered Daddy's
two-drink caveat. Stretch had laughed when she
related this: "My Dad said two *bottles*. Hey, maybe I
heard it wrong?"

The relief she'd felt an hour ago had dissipated.
She imagined her sisters, hands on hips, asking her
to explain her obsession. Who could explain reckless-
ness and idiocy? When she was with Stretch, she was
The Baby again, pampered and protected. He listened to each word she spoke with interest so intense
one might have thought he would be required to
quote her verbatim. He seemed consumed with wanting to know the minutiae of her life; best of all, he was
wildly jealous, and his jealousy was lurid and delicious.

Wally had no idea what the word Jealousy meant.
Remembering suddenly that he had asked her to
pick up the best man's gift, a monogrammed pocket

watch he was giving Shingo, she got up to leave. It gave her an errand, something helpful to do for her fiancé, who was working late these nights so he'd be able to take off for two weeks to go on their honeymoon. She left the bar and stood at the corner, waiting for a taxi. All of a sudden, Stretch was next to her, appearing from nowhere, or more likely from his meeting at the Brotherhood Synagogue around the corner, pointing a thumb at the bar she'd just left. "For me it's always saloon allergy season." His hair, in fading sunlight, itself glowed like a sunset. His office cool had vanished and he hardly seemed like the same man she'd left there an hour ago.

"If you just ask me to leave Mitzi, I will."

She held tight to her Coach satchel, suddenly too large, too heavy. "What?"

"You heard what I said."

Gaby stood frozen for a moment. Perspiration trickled down her back.

"You're a Catholic. You don't mean it."

Her arm still raised to hail a cab, she watched Stretch pull out his billfold. He flipped it open to show her something in one of its plastic window compartments, a memento he'd been carrying in his wallet the whole time, next to the family pictures. No photo, no *billet doux*, no perfumed handkerchief. Just the small black button that had popped off her sweater the first time they'd made love. He smiled a sad smile. A cab pulled up. "I can live without the Scotch, but not without you."

She pulled open the taxi door.

"Ask me just once, Gaby!" She stepped into the cab.

Stretch leaned into the taxi with his signature look of guilt and melancholy. A drop of wetness trickled from his temple to his chin. His voice was pleading. "Gaby—wait. You want to hear the second step? 'Came to believe that a Power greater than ourselves could restore us to sanity.' Okay. It turns out you're it. My Power."

The few sips of bourbon Gaby had had were making her fizzy. He loved her enough to walk away from Mitzi; he was decent, he was Catholic and yet, here he was, sacrificing religion, principle and family for her. It was an unimaginable triumph. He kept swallowing hard. She watched the knot move in his neck, the dear, familiar Adam's apple, looked at his eyes under his sunbleached eyebrows, and was wild to kiss him. Instead, as she reached into her ridiculously deep purse, scrambling to find a tissue, a car horn sounded, an impatient driver behind the cab, leaning on his horn, and the cab driver looked up at his rearview mirror. "We gotta move," he warned.

Gaby pulled closed the taxi door, and as she saw Stretch's shoulders sag, his face tailspin into disappointment, she imagined herself an old woman sitting at some country window, looking at a late twenty-first century sunset, and still remembering this tableau, forever seeing Stretch as he looked right now.

But, as the cab pulled away from the curb and made its way into Manhattan traffic, she thought of her father, and then Mama; whatever happened before they found each other had ceased to exist for them. Their bond, pure, permanent and indestructible, was Gaby's shining ideal. Wally was kind and good. He loved her. Babies would come and their lives together would fall into place. Their union would work, the way marriage had worked, with the mortar of loyalty and love, for Mama and Daddy. Wouldn't it?

CHAPTER
THIRTY-SIX

The forecast was rain, the caterer came prepared with huge black umbrellas, but the day of the wedding turned out to be cloudless, rain-free and balmy. A white tent in the garden covered rows of gold folding chairs decorated with white ribbons and white rose garlands and a white-carpeted aisle ready for the ceremony, an adjacent tent covered the dance floor, the bar, the dinner and buffet tables, and the platform that waited for the five-piece dance band.

Julie, dressed and ready, her hair combed, fluffed, re-combed, sprayed, combed again, a drop or two of Carolina Herrera behind each ear, sat at the edge of her bed, fighting off a great sense of foreboding. The girls' attitude toward Taras was one thing, and there had been tension galore at the rehearsal dinner last night as well. Gaby had whispered, "She shouldn't even be here," into Julie's ear just as Wally was helping his mother off with her jacket. The purported hostess had arrived wearing a lovely dark blue suit but mismatched shoes, poor soul, which were not noticed until she got up to toast the bride and called

her "a most beautiful sping." Gaby's eyes rolled and
Karen covered her mouth to hide a titter; Susanna,
in total gloom and hardly speaking from the beginning of the dinner to its end, didn't even seem to
notice. Dieter sat between his wife and daughter looking as if he had been tied to his chair and would
bounce up like a spring as soon as someone cut him
free. The girl, Liesel, in long sleeves and lace gloves,
seemed to be having a difficult time following American conversations, although Karen and Elliot tried
all evening to include her. She excused herself many
times to go to the ladies' room, perhaps to get away
from everyone or maybe just to scratch her itching
skin in private. Julie followed her once, hoping to say
a few kind words, make her feel at home, but the girl
stayed in the cubicle so long that Julie gave up and
left.

When Julie got up to say a few words about Gaby
and Wally the room grew very quiet, and when she
mentioned Gilbert, saying that she knew how much
he would have loved being here with her tonight,
she, despite everything, had to hold back tears. Then,
the best man, Shingo, wearing a jacket missing a button and accompanied by his girlfriend (who had put
glitter in her hair), toasted the bride and groom quoting Shakespeare: "Whoso findeth a wife findeth a
good thing," which Julie recognized as not being
Shakespeare at all, but from Proverbs.

And although the beef in this small out-of-the-way
steak place was tasty, it was served almost cold, the
lettuce was iceberg and at least one of the waitresses
was chewing gum. Everything except the weather por-
tended a debacle for today.

Now, in half an hour, the wedding would begin.

Julie checked herself in the full-length mirror on
the back of the closet door and wondered what Taras
would say to the mother of the bride dress Karen had
helped her choose. Julie had overruled Karen's first

choice, a hand-embroidered brocade shift with a matching coat, thinking, but not saying, *I can't dance in this*. The final choice, this pale periwinkle silk with its layered, flowing skirt and deep U neck was ready to make an appearance downstairs, to "wow them all" as Karen had assured her. Julie had gone to four different shoe stores to look for the sort of Lucite shoes she'd seen on Damaria, but couldn't find anything remotely like them. She settled on a bronzey pair of sandals with sky-high heels. "So Joan and David," Karen had said. Julie wanted only to wow Taras.

His radio voice woke her at eight-fifteen.

"I finally get to meet the family. Should I be nervous?"

Yes. "Of course not."

"You'd think I was the one getting married." He did in fact sound subdued.

"Taras, don't wear buckles on your shoes." Taras had once told her Thomas Jefferson refused to wear buckles because he felt it was undemocratic. His laugh was analgesic.

"Laces, Harry, and I paid Tommy a dollar to polish my best dancing shoes last night. You'll be blinded by the shine."

I might be blinded by the shine, but the girls won't be.

The moment Gaby stepped out of the limousine in her bridal dress, an off-the-shoulder Greek column of white silk with delicate pleats to the floor and a seed pearl crown holding her veil, Julie, watching from the living room window, felt a rush. *The Baby, getting married.* As her youngest daughter stepped carefully out of the car, holding her veil, setting her white satin slippers gingerly over the curb, Julie was overcome with the memory of Gaby's terrified five-year-old self, holding her hand on the way to kindergarten. She was the one who kept close to her, to home and to Daddy. She was the neediest, most clinging and most vulnerable. And then, as an adult, a different person altogether.

Julie threw open the front door and helped her daughter over the threshold, told her she looked ravishing, followed her up the stairs to her old bedroom, where Karen and Susanna, her matrons of honor, just arrived and breathless, waited with a blue garter, Gilbert's mother's string of pearls and the photographer. He took a few shots of the bride sitting at her old vanity table, being kissed by her two older sisters, posing with her mother.

Wearing identical deep apricot dresses, matching shoes, amber and pearl chokers and button pearl earrings, Susanna looked tired, Karen breathtaking. Gaby, the boyish haircut softened by her wedding veil, had an aura, if not exactly of joy, at least of grace. Julie had a wistful moment: *So little time between formula and flight; if I could only walk them to kindergarten just one more time!*

The girls were looking at an old, framed photo of Luffy that had been sitting on Gaby's painted dresser for all these years, reminiscing about the cat's life and death. Julie wondered what had happened to the shell-framed photographs of her and Taras; had all her daughters gotten together and decided that they'd throw them right into the trash? A moment later, when the photographer told Gaby she was lucky the sun was shining on her Big Day, the bride asked for a tranquilizer. "Mama, do you have any in the house?"

"Really, Gaby? Now?" A tranquilizer for Gaby, when for all the world she seemed a walking Miss Serenity?

"I'm really on edge. My very first wedding." A nervous smile.

"In that case, I'll get us both one, dear." In response, Julie got a puzzled look. "You? Why would you need one, Mama?"

Because of all of you! But she was not going to begin a dustup now. "I'm fluttery . . . my last daughter's first wedding, after all."

By the time Julie returned with the pills and glass of water, Mariadora, head to toe in a buttercup yellow butterfly print, was at the bedroom door telling them it looked as if one traffic policeman might not be enough, a car was blocking the caterer's truck in the driveway, the minister's wife would not be staying for the reception after all, and the groom had arrived with his mother, "with her looking like she needed a bit of a sit-down."

"And you wonder why I need a Xanax?" Julie asked brightly, until she saw Gaby's face, which looked as if she had just been summoned from a holding cell to walk her last mile.

She took the pill, gulped down half a glass of water, and then, flopping down on the edge of her old bed, grabbing the Steiff wallaby that had been sitting on the blue-and-white dotted bedspread almost her whole life, held it close and looked ready for a good cry.

"What?" Susanna said, "What is it?"

The photographer, sensing crisis, said he'd be waiting downstairs and made a quick exit.

Julie went to sit next to her daughter, put an arm around her shoulders.

"Oh, I can't, I don't think I can, how can I?"

"Can you what?" Karen asked. She'd been running her fingers through her hair at the mirror, but stopped cold, spinning around to face her sister.

"Marry Wally."

"Oh, no," Karen said, resuming attention to her

hair, "you're not going to do a cabaret of wedding jitters at this late hour, Gab?"

"Honey, pull yourself together," Susanna said. "One-hundred-fifty-six people are gathered together—"

"You love Wally," Julie felt as if a pebble had lodged in her chest, "don't you, dear?"

Gaby, her latter-day ice princess, was reverting to the old, dependent child she knew so well. "I don't know. I just don't know how much is enough to love someone to marry them. That's the problem. The marriage test, we took it together, measured our compatibility, answered a hundred and sixty questions, but not one about true love. True love was omitted from the Prepare-Enrich Inventory. There's no scale there for that, see? No market research whatsoever. Does anyone know?"

"Get over it," Karen said, "will you, please? Wally's great. We all like him. He's cute, hair loss or no." She stopped to emphasize she was kidding, and waved her hand as if her sister's qualms were house flies she was shooing off.

Susanna, morose until now, rubbed her palms together and paced the room. "You're supposed to have doubts. I had doubts. I mean, Dieter was so— German. Let's face it, a problem. I bet Karen had doubts, didn't you, Karen?"

"I guess. I don't remember. Maybe. Elliot doesn't like modern. To this day."

Susanna stopped pacing, stared at Karen. "Modern? Are you serious? You can't be serious?"

"We worked it out," Karen said. "You just work things out."

"Well, I did have some reservations, on my wedding day. I certainly did," Julie cut in. *Please, for God's sake, no crisis now!* She remembered the double Scotch she had to drink to get the courage to face married life so early, when all she really wanted was to be a sorority co-ed, go to football games, be a cheerleader, dance at proms. Not until later did she regret the academic lapses. Not until later did she assess the damage of being Mrs. Gilbert Kessler before she had a chance to sponge up life as Miss Julie Victoria Steinhart. Not that she was so brainy, nowhere near as intellectual as her brother, but she could have been—what? A landscape architect, if that wasn't reaching too high, or maybe, at the very least, a credentialed social worker; she would have certainly been a very caring one. She would have done well, done good. Or a teacher of languages. She'd had to drop her Italian language classes, French literature classes, Spanish conversation group, whenever they interfered with Gilbert's travel schedule. She'd always been good at languages, knew more Italian than, "Bravo Bravissimo," for sure.

"And look how well Mama and Daddy turned out!" Susanna, cheerleading herself now, declared.

Julie felt the pebble in her chest growing into a stone. It was more than the lost sociology, philosophy and language classes, midnight dormitory kaffee-klatsches, more than his betrayal with Ruthie, who must already be downstairs waiting, well enough to put on jewels galore for this occasion, well enough to remember her night with Gilbert even as his daughter walked down the aisle, but there were so many other realities she'd buried deep under the floor of all those married years.

She thought of them as small offenses, one piling on top of another like pellets, that, added together, began to accumulate into a veritable Vesuvius. He wouldn't let her carry her own passport, would he? All those years, two passports stuck into his breast pocket because she was someone who, like an irresponsible child, couldn't be trusted not to lose hers. A defining symbol of his view of her, wasn't it? He filled out forms, wrote the checks, all of them, generous to a fault, but, she had no checkbook of her own—until she'd put her foot down two years ago. Their finances were the mystery of life, known only to Gilbert and his accountant, and maybe to Milt Gladstone. The places they went, from dinner on Saturday night to the trips they took around the world, were never her choices. Everything was always *his* program, *his* preference. Then, she remembered the showing off, the name and place dropping, the bragging at parties, and just a minute, *what about sex?*

The times he couldn't sleep and would wake her— knowing she'd be the one to have to be up at five or six to feed a baby or prepare a child for school or administer eardrops—he'd have a need and that was enough. He'd wake her to make love, and sulked for the rest of the day if she turned him down. So, of course, she'd learned her lesson. She never said no.

And the damned bluegrass? She'd kept still about it, accommodated to disparate tastes in music, that was marriage, after all, but after thirty-five years of hillbilly guitar and down-home schmaltz, she was all twanged out.

Downstairs, in the first tent, the musicians were tuning up.

Gaby got up, stood frozen with her wallaby in the middle of the floor of her old bedroom and said, "God, I wish Daddy were here. How I wish! He'd tell me what to do."

Susanna let out a sigh that sounded like a musical note. "He'd say it was your decision, that's what he'd say. Guaranteed."

"Oh, Gab, come on! You made your decision long ago. Is this a time to waver? To drive us all crazy? Daddy would tell you to grow up, go downstairs and say, 'I do', and get on with it," Karen said sharply, and then, more kindly, "It'll be fine. It'll be ding ho, Gab."

"Would he, Mama?" Gaby asked. "Would Daddy just say, Go, no matter what?"

Would he? All the weight of decision would now and forever rest on her, and at this moment, Julie felt shortchanged on wisdom. There were no absolutes here, only guesses. She could not read this daughter's mind, feel her heart's pulse, or flip her coin. She could only throw out clues and hope for a fireproof resolution. "Daddy always said love isn't a question of looking into each other's eyes so much as a question of looking in the same direction," she said, scrutinizing her daughter's face, thinking she hadn't put forth a strong enough, definitive enough precept, but downstairs, guests, the minister, the groom were waiting. What would Gilbert say? She would keep Gilbert out of this. Her time of carrying her own passport and calling all the shots was here. "Love is a seesaw and perfection, darling, is only a figure of speech," she said. "Is there something we don't know about?"

Karen was adjusting Gaby's veil, in a gesture that was now warm and big-sisterly. "You don't want to lose Wally, do you, Gab? That would be terrible, wouldn't it, Su?"

Susanna nodded. "I'm crazy about Wally. So is Dieter."

"I love him too," Julie said. *More like a son than the other two,* she didn't add.

Gaby hesitated for a long moment, looking from one sister to another, then to Julie.

"You actually had doubts on your wedding day, Mama?"

"It took two Scotches and deep breathing to get me to the altar."

"Really?"

"Really." Julie was sure she hadn't said enough.

There was a knock on the door. Mariadora was back. "The minister, she is asking, is everything okay?"

"Yes. Okay," Gaby said. "I'm ready. Let's go."

CHAPTER THIRTY-SEVEN

Standing in the receiving line next to Wally, Gaby felt as if the wedding guests were on a conveyor belt, handshake-ready, a blur of outstretched arms, pastel dresses and perfume. The minister's words, his pink and round-ball bartender's face, with the exception of a few lines of Blake's, "And throughout all eternity, I forgive you, you forgive me," and with a smile and a quote toward Susanna and Karen, "For there is no friend like a sister, in calm or stormy weather," slid by like music from a passing car. The walk to the altar, the slipping on of the two matching gold rings, the *Lohengrin* and Mendelssohn, the throwing of the bouquet, caught by Tilda Novak's older daughter, had pleasantly come and gone, and thanks to Xanax, had passed into history as a nicely choreographed hour without pain or punch.

The photographer bobbed here and there, a few white balloons were let fly into the air and now, while guests sipped champagne in the second tent, the photographer maneuvered the wedding party into the garden, to take photographs in the verdant setting of dappled, end-of-summer light and Mama's remaining roses.

Last night, it was decided that Wally would stay in Norwalk with his mother. Gaby, superstitious enough to prevent any glimpse of the bride by the groom on their wedding day, had stayed in their apartment and slept alone. Not slept, exactly, but stared at the ceiling, gotten up to make a cup of tea, returned to punch the pillows under her head, turn on the light to stare at her engagement ring, turn off the light, walk to the window to look at the empty street, and mostly, to think.

Following in the family tradition, Gaby was not a religious person, but until recently, relatively honorable, with some adolescent slips in high school. One sexual misfire—it was an experiment in sex, it was feeling hot, not love, not even the puppy kind, just an afternoon of Russian Roulette intercourse following a sex education class. He had no rubbers; it led to a pregnancy. Only Susanna knew. It was Susanna to whom Gaby went, short of breath and mad with panic and guilt, and it was Susanna who took her to Planned Parenthood in faraway Mount Vernon. The boy was on vacation from Exeter, a druggie that year, but still, a sixteen-year-old with a conscience. He got some money together, said it was because he sold a watch, but Gaby thought he'd stolen it from his father. Then, through some benevolent accident, some miracle beyond miracles, Gaby was saved from the horror of the doctor's office, the hardball procedure; on the morning of her scheduled appointment, she awoke with cramps and expelled, with blood, the gelatinous tiny mass—the baby, ten weeks—in the upstairs toilet of 66 Morris Lane. She flushed twice, that was it. And in her recollection, it was the happiest moment of her life. The fifteen-year-old Gaby thanked God then, promising she'd reward him by being good for the rest of her life.

But being good was open to interpretation: sleeping with Stretch was being good to him, who needed her so badly. And being good was marrying Wally—for him. And being good was marrying; without ever saying it, she knew Mama wanted to see her "settled" with "a nice boy", a boy just like Wally.

It went back and forth. She couldn't go through with it, no. Then again . . . she'd looked at the suitcases packed and ready for the honeymoon at the foot of her bed. Apart from the cork trees and the relatives, it would be a wonderful trip, but then again, *married.* To Wally. Forever.

They stood in a row in front of Mama's roses. The bride, the groom, the two matrons of honor, Elliot, Dieter, Mama, Wally's mother, in subdued sage green today, and with shoes that matched the dress and each other, and Shingo, who looked unrecognizably natty in his gray morning coat, his hair embalmed to his head. The photographer raised his hand at the exact moment he wanted everyone to say, *"Fromage!"* and just as his hand went up, Gaby moved hers to brush away a bee. It was a late bee, a survivor not expected in Scarsdale this second week in September, a centenarian yellowjacket, sent, Gaby thought, as a token, a warning, some sort of sign. But it didn't bite her. It bit Mama, twice, once next to the neck of her dress at her collarbone, once, more critically, on her right ear, above her diamond earring.

She let out a cry and there followed the commotion, the ice brought, the restorative glass of Scotch (she refused to touch), the swelling, the bee squashed by Shingo with a linen napkin, and suddenly, there was Taras. He'd come out of nowhere, might have dropped from the sky, Susanna later commented;

"He must have been hiding behind some bushes, watching," Karen said to Gaby under her breath.

He jumped in. There was no other word for it: his leap to Mama's side, his fast-as-whiplash maneuver to be next to her, to hold her hand, ask her if she wanted to lie down, forget the reception, she should put her feet up a few minutes, rest, if she wanted to. It could only be called a *jump*, or a *leap*, as over a hurdle. The hurdle, as Gaby saw it, was Karen, Susanna and her own self, the soon-to-be ghost of Daddy, the tight knot of family, an age and class difference, and the occasion. This Fred Astaire dance instructor, having come out of nowhere, was out of place, out of time, an interloper. And he was squeezing Mama's hand as if—as if she were *his*.

Gaby watched this as if from a tree branch. She remembered her own bout with a bee in this very garden, if not on this spot, well, no more than six feet to the left or the right. She thought back to Daddy, his ministrations, his love pouring out of him from his endless father's supply. If she hadn't taken the Xanax, she would have let out a scream of protest over the rooftops of Morris Lane. She would have made a scene, reminded Mr. Tango Feet where he was, who he was, that this was her goddamn wedding day, and if anybody was going to take care of her mother, it would definitely not be him.

But all the while Taras continued to be there, helping Mama into a garden chair, holding her as if she were Camille about to cough her way into heaven, whispering something or other into her ear, dabbing her cheeks with a handkerchief. And the rest of the wedding party, her sisters, their husbands, Wally and his mother, stood back, allowing it to go on.

Perhaps it was because Mama's expression, when Taras was holding her hand, was beatified. Susanna and Karen's faces were blank, maybe in shock and disbelief? Mama was flushed, holding his hand—

kerchief to her chest while he now held ice in a linen napkin to her ear, looked at him as if he had stepped down from Mt. Sinai or from the balcony of the Vatican. He let her hand go for a moment, pulled down a random white balloon that must have lost its helium and its way to heaven, and tied it to her wrist. Didn't Mama see how *smooth*, how *slick* he was? Gaby wanted to run over and shake her mother, whose eyelashes fluttered, like those old-fashioned dolls with up-and-down eyelids over glass bead eyes.

"Mama!" Tranquilizer or no, Gaby took a step toward them, murder in her heart. She'd promised Daddy to protect Mama, hadn't she?

Mama looked up. "I'm so sorry for causing such a commotion, Gaby, dear. I should have had the garden sprayed. My own fault. I'm only glad it wasn't you the bee decided to sting. It was really stupid of me. I'm fine now. Just fine." She let out a sunbeam of a smile. "Girls, say hello to Taras," she said. "He's been dying to meet you."

CHAPTER
THIRTY-EIGHT

Susanna sat next to Dieter, a glass of champagne in her hand, desolation, frustration, and green jealousy eating at her heart. Sitting on his other side was Liesel, who should have known better than to wear a backless black evening dress and white lace gloves to an afternoon wedding. More to the point, she should have known better than to get herself in trouble with a married man who would now have to leave his wife to marry her. Breaking up a family is what Liesel was doing, and being rewarded for it with a baby in the bargain—by the same bumbling higher power that was sending Susanna menstrual blood and cramps every twenty-eight to thirty-three days. Susanna hoped the girl would see psoriasis as a punishment from the gods, but today the rash seemed to be bothering her not at all. The little homewrecker was now tapping her foot to the music, smiling. Had enjoyed the black caviar on the little tiny potatoes, the pâté on toast, the smoked trout, the Cajun shrimp, the spring rolls and every other hors d'oeuvre she could get her gloves on. Eating for two, she'd said in German, with a coy smile at her father.

Now Dieter was leaning over to say something to her and she was nodding, raising her eyebrows, all ears. This small intimate exchange, one of many that Susanna had had to witness in the last few days, was chipping away at her decorum and restraint. Was Liesel whispering something to her about the bride and groom? The way they'd danced to *Happy Together,* the first dance together, well, Wally was a fine tennis player, but on the dance floor he looked as if in fact, he'd rather be playing tennis. And Gaby looked ready to lie down and fall asleep. It was the Xanax, Susanna knew, but the bride looked absolutely wasted.

More likely they were discussing Mama, who was behaving like an infatuated member of Generation X, the way she'd let this dance instructor fawn all over her, the way she'd looked at him when he "came to the rescue," Mama's words, the very instant she'd been stung by the bee in the garden, the way she was looking at him right now. They were standing together at the buffet table, the balloon tied to Mama's wrist, next to Ruthie and Lou, all self-conscious smiles; one would have thought they, not Gaby and Wally, were the bride and groom.

Nevertheless, she was ready to defend Mama, if only Mama wouldn't allow this Taras person to be constantly touching her. It looked as if he had seventeen hands, moving to her shoulder, her waist, her elbow, her hair, tenderly examining her swollen earlobe; what was she thinking of, letting this ballet of his fingers continue—wait, was he actually missing one?—in front of one-hundred-fifty-six wedding guests?

It was the tango that finally did it. Mama had made the request of this little band, and of course they'd come prepared with a few salsa, mambo, cha-cha-cha pieces for Latin fans. Now they struck up *La Paloma* and the dance floor cleared of all the couples who were finishing the fox-trot and intimidated by the tango, and that left only three or four pairs, including Joe Goetz and his wife, Shingo and his girlfriend in a you-wouldn't-believe-it-unless-you-saw it white lace dress with a hem that went up here and down there, and now, Taras and Mama.

Joe Goetz's wife, who as Karen said, walked like a duck, also danced like a duck. Soon, Mama and Taras were going at it like a pair of professionals who had rehearsed these steps and kicks, these dips and swirls, these swings and lurches, for a lifetime, in order to perform here today. Joe Goetz and his wife, aware they were being upstaged and outclassed, stepped to the sidelines to watch. So did Shingo and Benita and the two other couples on the floor, allowing Mama and Taras to really let loose, to rotate, revolve around each other, spinning apart and moving together, bending, twisting, the sun and moon of the parquet dance floor, the sun and moon of this wedding reception.

She was right up against his body, or was it the other way around? He was plastered, *plastered* against her, *crushing* her, it was so goddam intimate, like he was holding her hostage on the dance floor, pressing his sternum against her breasts, flattening them, then it was pelvis to pelvis, like a conversation between their two bodies—*Mama, what the hell are you doing!* Then they were cheek to cheek, and it looked organic, as if blood was rushing between them.

And the worst thing, the *worst!* It was the zombie look of ecstasy on his face. And *hers!*

Mama did have talent, a total surprise. Other guests, leaving dishes of filet or salmon en croute or stuffed lobster, gathered at the edge of the floor to watch. They included Tilda Novak, in royal purple to the floor. Susanna watched her eyebrows in flight to her flaming hairline. It was more than the dance. It was the interaction of the knees, the bodies, the looks, the touches. It was the sexual innuendo, the subtext. Taras and Mama looked hooked on each other and headed for bed.

Karen, her face red meat, appeared at Susanna's side out of nowhere. "These lessons were your idea," she hissed. "She's a married woman. The man she's married to is Daddy. He is not officially dead until tomorrow! And she's too old! Why the hell is she acting like a hot chiquita just imported from South of the Border? Did you see him when the bee bit her? Have you been watching him—all over her? Did you notice, he has a finger missing? Do you suppose he's served time, something happened to him in prison? Why are we allowing this?"

"She is a vonderful dancer, your mother," Dieter said to Susanna, having not heard a word Karen said. Next to him, Liesel, before popping a piece of buttered roll into her mouth, nodded enthusiastically in agreement. Susanna imagined Liesel was thinking of her own mother, probably contentedly crocheting booties in Potsdam instead of practically having sex on a dance floor in Scarsdale. Susanna, who didn't much care for champagne, sipped away a glassful, and another, and when the second glass was empty, allowed a waiter to bring her a third.

Wally and Gaby cut the cake while the bandleader played, *The Bride Cuts the Cake* and then Shingo got up to toast the bride and groom, saying although men were from Mars and women from Venus, these two were both born on the planet of www-dot compatibility, and then he raised his glass again and said, "And if Gaby is anything like her mother, Wally is in for one swinging life!"

People laughed. There was applause, someone let out a whistle, but Susanna and Karen exchanged desperate looks. Susanna polished off what was left of her third champagne, and felt it go right to her knees.

This was a mistake; hadn't Daddy always said to stop at two? Karen raised her glass of Coke and put it against her forehead; she was not drinking, although the occasion called for it, demanded it. People would be talking about this forever. Susanna mouthed the words, "This is hell" to Dieter, but he didn't hear or understand. Liesel was leaning her head against her father's shoulder, had wrapped an arm around his elbow. Susanna wanted to pull her glove off his sleeve, tell her he was OFF LIMITS, but more than anything, she wanted to confront Mama, who was now arm in arm with Taras, talking to her Second Chance ladies, who were all seated together beaming approval at her from their table. One could only guess what they'd say as soon as she turned her back.

A piece of wedding cake was put in front of Susanna, and she was about to push it away, when Elliot got up, and tapping the microphone someone had put in front of him, began to speak. This was unexpected. Susanna looked at Karen, whose attention was now diverted to her husband, her chin up, eyes reverential. His tuxedo shirt stood away from his neck, revealing skin that reminded Susanna of a Shar-pei. She thought of what was ahead for her sister in this marriage: bypass surgery, wheelchairs, Pampers. Poor, gorgeous Karen.

A look across the room at Gaby, standing near the wedding cake with Wally, confirmed that her little sister, off in her own groggy world, had also been taken by surprise by Elliot at the microphone.

He cleared his throat. He'd put on his steel rims and peered over them, giving him a paternal, Ben Franklin look. He raised his hand and smiled left and right, as if this were a fund-raiser and he were about to announce a gift of two million. "Hello, everybody!" he said in his laryngitic voice, and the place slowly quieted down. He'd had a few too, that was clear. For reasonably subdued Elliot, this was a major enterprise.

"Go, Elliot!" somebody yelled. Someone tapped a fork against a glass. "I just wanted to add my two cents," he continued, and when there was total silence, "Thank you one and all. Since the father of the bride is unable to be with us I decided to say a few words. I know if he were standing here in front of you, Gil would be bursting, just busting out with happiness and pride. 'Marriage is a great institution and no family should be without it!' " Elliot waited for the laugh, which came and went very quickly. "Gaby is a special young lady, the cream of the cream, and she's chosen one helluva fabulous fella. I am really thrilled to welcome him into the fold as my new brother-in-law. Let's hear it for the youngest Kessler woman and the reigning king of cork!" There was a burst of applause, a few whistles, fork-against-glass-clinkings, table thumpings, and cheers. Then both of Elliot's hands went into the air again. "Hold it everybody! Hold it—!" He turned to the band leader. "Can we have a drum roll please?" The band leader signaled for a drum roll; the place went dead quiet and Susanna leaned forward, both hands around the stem of her fourth glass of champagne.

"I have one more thing to say. It's a little announcement. My beautiful wife allowed me to make it public here tonight. We are going to add our own little member to this wonderful family. Karen, get up and show the world what a happy pregnant woman looks like! And Julie, darling, you get up and show yourself to everyone! Did anyone ever see a more glamorous grandmother-to-be? *Mazel tov*, Mama! Take a bow, darling!"

CHAPTER
THIRTY-NINE

They'd sailed across the floor, his arms dear and familiar, the moves and steps by this time second nature. As Julie became aware that the floor had cleared for them, that there was a circle applauding, admiring, maybe even envying her this balletic drama, she felt disembodied, light as the white helium balloon he'd tied to her wrist. Even after the dance ended.

Until Elliot's announcement. It was not pure bliss to be told Karen would be sent a little package from heaven in this public address sort of way. The jolly surprise should have been announced in private; a hundred-and-fifty-six people did not simultaneously have to be in on Karen's new status. And her own. Becoming a grandmother had until now been seen by Julie as a future possibility, a promised bonanza, and according to friends who'd been so blessed, The Big Payoff. But now, she vacillated between joy and distress; Karen and *Elliot*? Hadn't there once been talk of adopting a pair of older siblings from an orphanage in Romania? Instead, someday soon, Karen would have the care of two babies, one new, one grown old. Then too, the poor child, why hadn't they given any thought to a baby born to a Daddy old enough by a mile to be a grandfather?

And finally, to her great shame, Julie also thought, What will Taras think of making love to a grandmother? But Taras had been the first to embrace her, whisper, "Congratulations, Grandma Harry," and tell her the Ukrainian word for grandmother was Babcha. Should he call her Babcha from now on?

With Taras at her side, Julie had been in the middle of a conversation with Lou and Ruthie DiLorenzo. Lou had lost weight—it was the worry, without a doubt—and looked paradoxically like the athletic quarterback he'd once been. Ruthie, too, was pink-cheeked and looking robust in deep rose chiffon, the new brunette wig a great improvement over her own hair. Congratulations poured out of her as if she were reciting lines. Julie's dress, she thought, was "downright sublime" and brought out the "shine of blue" in her eyes. When Lou stepped away to get a fresh drink, her own eyes were pleading for amnesty.

Julie was inching toward forgiveness but her heart hung back. She wanted to be relieved to see Ruthie bouncy and smiling, but she'd never look at her friend with wholehearted affection again. On the other hand, she did know that seeing Lou his old party-mood self again made her happy. Impulsively, Julie took his hand and gave it a squeeze she meant as *Look at me, I'm smiling and one day so will you.* "Hey Julie, we were afraid your dancing was gonna set the tent on fire," he said.

Even before Elliot finished speaking and the applause and cheers died down, Julie, sinking into a chair, surrounded by well-wishers, air-kisses, and raised champagne glasses, heard what sounded like an outcry and a commotion at Susanna's table.

A moment later, Susanna streaked across the dance

floor, now sprinting, then stumbling across a chair someone had pulled out near the entrance of the tent, finally disappearing outside. Julie, alarmed, quickly jumped up to follow her, nearly knocking over an empty champagne glass. Taras was very tactful. "I'll have another piece of cake and wait for you."

As she ran into the house, calling Susanna's name, she passed Milt Gladstone, who was coming out of the powder room and who stopped her to offer *"felicitations"* and *"Susanna est en haut";* Julie excused herself and rushed off, guessing that if Susanna was upstairs, she'd have gone up to her old room. It had been redone years ago, turned into a combination office and storage place but sure enough, on an old daybed, heaped with linens Julie was sorting to give to Second Chance, Susanna sat, her eyes rabbit red and swimming in tears.

Grasping an old linen napkin from the pile on the daybed, she raised her eyes to challenge Julie. "You knew about it," she accused. Her voice sounded like the words were being strummed on an old guitar.

Julie, dumbfounded, asked, "Knew about *what?*"

"About Karen. Didn't you?"

Julie should have guessed immediately. Karen expecting, Susanna not. The sibling theater of operations. The Rivalry Olympics. She thought again that she should never have had her children born so close together. Gilbert's idea, not hers. "No, of course not. I had no idea."

She tried to take Susanna's hand, but her daughter pulled it away. She used a crumpled napkin to wipe her eyes and Julie noted that more than one piece of crisp linen, ironed carefully by Mariadora last week, was now stained with mascara. And so were Susanna's cheeks, and the bodice of the cheerful, sunset-colored dress.

For a few moments, Julie sat without speaking. She watched Susanna try to pull herself together, waited while her daughter's eyes roamed the room, took in the dresser that used to be filled with her sweaters, nighties, ballet tights, moved to the fabric-covered walls where once her Fleetwood Mac posters hung. The tears continued to flow.

Like God's page turned to a new insight, Julie thought to say, "You didn't even cry this hard about Daddy." She intended only for Susanna to put things in perspective, but it turned out to be exactly the wrong thing to say. Susanna had certainly had more than two glasses of champagne, for one thing. Susanna's eyes filled with cold fire, her mouth twisted in a way Julie hadn't seen since the girl was a defiant fourteen caught cutting school.

"Well *you* did, did cry about Daddy, Mama, did you not? You cried some, yes you did. But not for long, Mama, not for very long! Your t-tears, your tears dried up pretty fast, Mama, didn't, didn't they? Now it's Goodnight Sweetheart to Gilbert Kessler, Hello Sweetheart to Mr. Dancing Shoes. My darling father is history, and all it took, all it took for you to dry those tears in a hurry, was some little stud with gel in his hair!"

Julie shot up. She, who had slapped this daughter just once, when Susanna was six and threw a tantrum in Saks Fifth Avenue, now leaned forward, her hand raised, to land a second smack, this one across her grown daughter's face. For a moment she glared at her daughter, the child she'd always thought her most sensible, whose eyes were now dry, half-closed and hard as a bookie's. She let her hand fall to her side.

"You're upset because of Karen." Julie tried to keep the tremolo out of her voice, with no success. "It's human, Susanna. It's understandable and I forgive you for shooting at the wrong target, but now

pull yourself together, get off your ass and go back
there and congratulate your sister!''

Susanna's bookie eyes narrowed. ''You're telling
me what to do?''

''I'm telling you what to do. I'm still your mother!''

Susanna's face flushed and crumpled, so much like
the six-year-old face that had screamed its way down
the cosmetics aisle at Saks so many years ago. ''Still
my mother? Not the mother I used to know! The
mother I knew and respected would not make a fool
of herself, carrying on, canoodling with that ridiculous Lothario!''

''*Canoodling*?''

''That *gigolo!*''

''GIGOLO!''

''Mama dear, please think about it. You are fifty-
four years old! What the hell do you think you're
doing? And what the hell do you think *he's* doing?''

Julie spun on her heel, sped out of the room and
into the hall bathroom where she leaned against the
door to compose herself. After a few minutes, when
her breathing was back to normal, she caught a look
at herself in the mirror over the sink. The light was
harsh in this room; the gloss of the white-on-white
wallpaper reflected a glare from the window. In the
mirror Julie noticed that the lines that ran from the
corner of her nose to the edges of her lips had deep-
ened since she'd last really looked. Ruthie called them
smile lines, and always said, ''And they're nothing
to smile about.'' Julie traced those creases with her
fingers while the faint sound of music from the tent
outside, and the word, *Gigolo,* echoed and re-echoed
in her ear.

CHAPTER FORTY

Gaby threw her arms around Karen. "Incredible news! So, when exactly do I become an aunt?" Wally was at her side, shaking Elliot's hand. "Hey, this really is ding ho! You beat us to the punch, Papa," he was saying, when Gaby spotted Susanna lurching out of the reception tent, and Mama untangling herself from Taras, set to follow. Gaby also caught sight of Dieter, half out of his chair, looking like someone who'd just discovered he was on the wrong train.

"What's going on with Susanna?" she asked Karen, who was by this time engulfed by congratulations and the purple sleeves of Tilda Novak. The band had started playing *Baby Face* and Gaby, a bit unsteady on her feet and trying to clear her head, stood momentarily undecided about whether to follow Mama.

Right after the cake had been cut, after *Happy Together* played and while Gaby was having a dance with Shingo, Wally's mother began taking off her green shoes and trying to polish them with a linen napkin. Gaby signaled Wally, who was in the midst of a dance with Benita Raffle. Perhaps one day Gaby would sit with a grandchild and describe the way her new husband's expression instantly changed; a smile dying a quick death, all color leaving his forehead and cheeks. He quickly led Benita off the floor and rushed to his mother's side. He took her shoes off the table and put them back on her feet, gingerly, tenderly, calming her with nonstop conversation, all the while oblivious to whoever happened to be watching. He was stroking her hands, and without so much as a smidgen of embarrassment. A few moments later, he led her to the dance floor, did a few steps with her, then kissed her cheek, and finally walked her out to the waiting limousine that would take her back to Norwalk.

The tears in Wally's eyes, his arms around the solid green package that was his mother, made goose-pimples rise on Gaby's arms. She'd wavered and faltered, yes, but made the right decision, cut her losses and married the noble, selfless prince of cork. And, she vouched to be as good, as caring a daughter to her own mother as he was to his. Well, at least she would try, and now was as good a time as any to begin.

The sun was in fact lower, the sky was getting dusky, the house was shadowy when she walked into it, and at first, Gaby didn't see Mama sitting at the top of the stairs. "Here, Gaby," she said, all that was Mama gone out of her voice.

Her mother's dress was pulled over her legs, elbows on her knees, her chin on her folded hands, eyes downcast. Tranquilized into calm, Gaby stood at the bottom of the steps, her hand on the newel post, trying to make sense of it. The band's beat sixty feet away seemed distant, the wedding reception, on another planet. Someone was laughing—or shouting out there, enjoying her party, while Mama stroked the fabric stretched across her knees, looking shot down and hopeless.

"Susanna," Mama began. *Chilling,* like last October, when her face looked just like this.

"Taras," Mama continued, her voice an echo from a mountain; oh, so that was it. Susanna must have said something about her King of Dance. Mama was insulted, not sick; a different matter entirely. Gaby ran up the steps, sat next to her mother, putting an arm around her shoulders. "We want you to wake up, Mama." She spoke gently, hoping she was communicating understanding and objective wisdom. "We all do. Because we can see what he is, and you can't. You're under a spell. Right now, you're like a different, new, unfamiliar person. We don't even recognize you."

Her mother straightened her shoulders, getting back in control. "Not an excuse," she said, "for Susanna to call Taras names. I mean, Taras is a—" she needed a minute, she said, to get her thoughts together, to say it right, "Taras has been a wonderful . . . friend."

Friend? Who was she kidding? "Listen, Mama, it's hard, sometimes, to give up someone who is bad, really bad for you." *Bad for you.* Gaby allowed herself a flash of Stretch, that look on his face when she closed the door of the taxicab, the Steuben heart she'd left in the drawer of her desk.

"Bad for me? What a thing to say! He's saved my life! Don't you understand, thanks to Taras, I've been—well, maybe not reborn, exactly, but, okay, *reconstituted!* Wait, *restored.* Can't you see all my life I've always been someone's someone, and then, what happened with Daddy, anyway, after that, I was just two-dimensional, bleeding guilt, desiccated, like, well, like those prom corsages you girls used to hang upside down to dry. Couldn't you see, was your vision so cloudy, that you didn't know that after the accident, without Daddy, without a Someone to comfort me, I was hardly breathing?"

"What about us? Aren't we enough?" Gaby asked. "Aren't your daughters *enough?*"

"You children held me to life, don't misunderstand, and to me you're everything, all I have, and yes, you're everything, but no, you're not enough."

Gaby wondered if what Karen suspected could be true: what Mariadora had insinuated the day Karen came up to take a look at Gaby's accumulating wedding gifts. Could Mama actually be *sleeping* with this man? Having *sex with him* in her own—and *Daddy's*—*bed?*

"And then, thanks to you, thanks to my wonderful, caring daughters, the tango, I mean, not only the dance, but what came as a result, a whole new experience, well, all right, it did, it changed everything, and as for Taras, why, you don't even know him. You just met today and after all, one pleased-to-meet-you-I've-heard-so-much-about-you conversation is hardly enough to give you the slightest idea of what a person is really like."

"But, Mama! He's like three years older than Karen! And, with all due respect, one look at him, I mean, that back number tuxedo, and the hair gel, well, can you see yourself with a man—a boy, I should say—like that? Everybody laughing behind your back, thinking these terrible thoughts and gossiping all over Scarsdale—"

"It's not Scarsdale's business, Gaby, it's not yours, either. It's *my* business!" Mama clapped her hands on her knees so hard, it reminded Gaby of elementary school, getting chalk out of board erasers.

"No, it's *our* business, because we love you, we care what happens to you, and, and we'll still be here for you long after Taras has left you. For someone *my* age!"

Mama put up her hands, as if she could ward off the falling debris of words, but Gaby couldn't stop.

"Look, Mama, frankly, the way you carried on— the way you and that *cement mixer* behaved, like a pair, a pair of—"

"Overheated teenagers!" Karen had arrived. ". . . and you, don't forget, you're going to be a— grandmother. A granny, for God's sake!" She'd come in quietly, was holding a half-full glass of orange juice, taking little sips and now, not so quietly, was rattling ice cubes. "Why did you all run out of the reception? Why didn't you come to congratulate me, Mama? What's happening here?" She had taken off her shoes to rub her feet and now sank onto one of the bottom steps of the staircase. She said she shouldn't have eaten the salmon en croute. The croute was making her nauseous.

"Couldn't you have told us first? Before you announced it to the world?" Mama was sounding level now, a bit stern, like she had when they were small and wouldn't take even one bite of cauliflower.

Karen looked chastened. "Elliot thought it would add a little punch to the wedding reception," she said in a smallish, defensive voice.

Gaby thought the reception did not need added punch. She wanted in fact to get back there right now, to her party, where she'd left Wally sitting with Shingo and Benita, who was already pretty tanked up and still miffed over the return of that turkey of a poster. (Karen said her monstro white dress with lace inserts was meant to compete with the bride and must be her idea of a payback.)

Mama, softer, more serene, was now offering Karen congratulations and wanted to know how far along was she and was it a girl or a boy and was Karen feeling well and did she have a good doctor? Mama's questions siphoned off some stress, but only until Karen said that if it turned out it was a boy (and she would wait full term to find out) she and Elliot intended to name him Gilbert.

"Well, that's wonderful," Mama said, "and of course, it breaks my heart he won't be here—"

Karen and Gaby exchanged looks.

Susanna now appeared behind Mama, her swollen eyes a pair of pink biscuits. "Congratulations, Karen," she said dully. Then, "Mama, I'm sorry. I didn't mean to tear into you. I didn't mean to upset you, you know I didn't."

"But you did," Mama said. "So much!" She stood up. It was as if the lights had suddenly gone up and given her new strength.

"You're all so young, and already so cynical. Why? Has life so disappointed you? I wonder, what have I done that I shouldn't have done, or forgot to say when I should have said it? When you were growing up, what books didn't I read to you? What life's lessons did I skip? It's not the harsh world, it can't be. You've never even been to a third world country except to stay at a nice resort and sit under a palm tree. The only time you skipped meals was when you wanted to fit into a dress. You got lessons in diving, dancing, skating, tennis, and didn't you, Gaby, even take a year of fencing? Tutors for math, Karen. Braces, Susanna. Skiing. I almost forgot! Karen broke her thumb. Best doctors, of course. You wouldn't want a crooked thumb, any more than you'd want crooked teeth. Medical checkups, shots, charcoal and pastel classes for Karen, and did Daddy and I ever miss a recital, exhibition or Open School Night? I never forgot to buy the candles for any of your birthday cakes, not once, did I? I guess you each got maybe one slap you deserved and one slap you maybe almost did. And now? Where are we now?

"I mean, Gaby, you've been looking as if you were heading for an upstate penitentiary instead of a honeymoon. Of course I ask myself why. And

Susanna, you're in a perpetual hot and cold war with Dieter. When will there be a truce? As for Karen, I don't know. Are you really happy, dear?''

"Mama, what a question. Of course I'm happy! Don't I have it all? Elliot is wonderful. Do you know that he promised to buy me a nanny apartment on the floor below ours? We'll have a nanny day and night! I will never have to go through all that you had to go through. I mean, all the grunt work. I'm talking diapers and two A.M. feedings, I'm talking day in, day out baby care . . .''

"Stop talking," Mama said, looking totally disheartened. Ten years older than she'd looked dancing the tango an hour ago. "Could it be, could it possibly be, that the three of you, my wonderful, beautiful daughters," she paused to sigh, and to look back at some spot near the ceiling, "are just a bit *spoiled*? Thinking Daddy and I would never stop being Mama and Daddy? That the magic power of our parenthood would always make life right for you?

"Is it true spoiled children turn into adults who are spoiled children?''

Karen pointed her shoe at Mama, was about to speak, but Mama cut her off. "Taras is waiting for me, girls," she said, and, without meeting anyone's eyes, she smoothed her skirt and walked down the steps and through the hall, heading for the front door. There she turned and looked at her daughters, who were clustered together on the stairs. "And girls, could you possibly be a bit worried that I might live a life that doesn't revolve only around you? And is it conceivable, could you possibly be, just a tiny bit *jealous* of your mother?''

Just as Mama had presumably concluded her speech and had her hand on the front doorknob, Mariadora appeared from nowhere. She'd been invited to the wedding but preferred to be sidelined in the kitchen during the reception, possibly to guard her territory, where caterers were swarming. Now here she was, in her buttercup butterfly dress, the corsage Gaby's florist had thoughtfully provided pinned to the apron she was wearing over it. She also looked distraught, holding one of Mama's broken salt shakers, a crystal one, a piece in each hand, as if it were a shattered museum piece. Knowing it was a souvenir of Murano, where the Missuz had been photographed with the dear Mister and a gondolier, she had still dropped it in shock at the sight.

"I look out the window, I see a man, a man—what she was doing, doing with his pants open, excuse me, Missuz, but peeing, peeing with his man thing, on the Missuz's roses!"

Gaby had a feeling. Not a premonition, just a tweak, back there under her freshly shampooed thick dark hair, beneath her clean scalp, somewhere under her pearl encrusted headpiece and veil. She was at the window in a flash. She saw the car first, the Chevy Blazer, the license number she'd committed to memory.

Stretch.

CHAPTER
FORTY-ONE

By the time Julie looked out the window, the man was zipping up his pants and looking up at the house. He was tall, with reddish hair, dressed in a dark polo shirt, khakis, running shoes. She'd expected to see a vagrant, or one of her neighbor's gardeners—she'd seen one relieving himself behind the garage once—and was confused by this figure on her lawn, who looked in fact, very much more like one of her neighbors than someone who'd just stepped off a landscaper's truck.

On the other hand, for sure he was on drugs, maybe alcohol, the dazed way he was looking up at the second floor windows, his feet planted far apart, as if to steady himself. "I better call the police," she said.

Unexpectedly, Gaby jumped. That was what you would have to call what happened—a jump. Her eyebrows, her shoulders, her entire body gave a lurch in the direction of the telephone in the hall. "No, don't call the police," she said, her hand reaching out, as if to protect the telephone from Julie, who was not yet anywhere near it.

Julie pulled back, startled. This was so unlike her daughter, her sangfroid gone, a little tremor appearing at the corner of her lip. "No, don't," she repeated. "Please."

"You *know* him?" Karen accused, blared, "He's someone you *know?*"

Gaby was heading for the door before anyone could extract an answer, rushing out, holding up her wedding dress as she raced down the front walk, kicking off her white satin shoes and picking them up as an afterthought as she headed out.

Karen, skirt pulled up, was putting her own shoes back on, wanting to take off after her sister, but by some instinct, Julie held her back. Susanna and Mariadora stood behind her at the open front door and together they watched the barefoot bride, the hem of her silk dress dragging in the grass, in what looked to Julie like a very animated exchange. The man reached out for Gaby, taking her by the shoulder once, and Julie noticed what turned on a switch of foreboding: Gaby did not pull away. She let the hand rest there, let the man's big fingers stay on the bare shoulder where it had landed. Gaby continued to let him go on saying whatever it was he was saying, although he looked as if he were at any minute about to fall, as if he were keeping his balance leaning on little Gaby's shoulder. When, an instant later, his hand came up to brush her cheek, she moved her head, tilted it as if she were about to bolt, but, she didn't. She let him do that, as well.

As Gaby and the man walked to the end of the street, then disappeared around the corner, Julie turned away from the open door, then leaned against its frame to wait until she felt steady enough to move.

"Who is he?" she heard Susanna and Karen ask each other. Not knowing what to do, or where to go (shouldn't she call the police after all?), she proceeded blindly to the kitchen, to get a glass of water, or just to find a hard-back chair in which to sit and gather her wits for a moment. She was following Mari-adora, who still had the pieces of broken glass in her hand and looked nothing like the gentle soul who'd ironed a crease out of Julie's dress this morning. Her face looked as if she'd just parachuted into a war zone.

She swiveled to face Julie as they stepped over the kitchen threshold, away from Susanna and Karen. "Everything so different now," she said, the accusation resonating with sadness and thick with disappointment. The Missuz no longer the same, all hell breaking loose since the Mister was gone and the boyfriend was in his place. A stranger peeing into her beautiful flowers, a broken crystal salt shaker that would have caused some emotion, some response or feeling before, meant nothing now. Wasn't it old, valuable, beautiful, a part of a set with its matching crystal pepper shaker? An important part of her and the Mister's personal history? She spoke under her breath, not wanting to telegraph her dissatisfaction; a member of the catering crew was at the sink, rinsing dishes, another was stacking the dishwasher. The broken salt shaker was to Mariadora obviously a symbol: the last Kessler straw.

"I will pray for you, Missuz. And also the family." Julie moved forward, wanting to embrace her to both comfort and lean on, and saw not the hourly-wage person, not the servant who made the mirrors shine and the house smell of floor wax, but a woman like herself and all these years her ministering and nurturing co-pilot. And it suddenly poured out of the co-pilot: She was distraught because after seventeen blue-sky years, unexpected clouds of depravity were pulling down their ship. It was hers too! Hers through tenure and affection, through loyalty and a fidelity greater and purer than *anyone's*. She meant Julie's, that was clear. No lover except a lover's devotion to the Mister, no children except these! There was, yes, a faraway house in Honduras, a place to stay three weeks out of fifty-two, and her walkup day-off room in Mt. Vernon, but these were not 66 Morris Lane, her true and sterling home.

Mariadora backed away from Julie, not, Julie thought, because she was unused to the Missuz hugging her, but because somehow it was Julie's fault, Missuz Kessler who had led the way to this last scene of debauchery. If Mariadora had managed fidelity to her own husband, long dead but never for a moment forgotten, why couldn't Julie be faithful to hers?

She began again to assure Julie that she would pray, go to her church and kneel at the altar, but stopped in the middle of a sentence, her eyes narrowed, having caught sight of Taras, who had just at this moment appeared in the doorway behind Julie. He looked both flushed and flustered, apologized for breaking in, but he needed to call home immediately. His beeper had sounded, his landlady's telephone number followed by the 911 code, signaling an emergency. Which telephone should he use?

An *emergency?* This moment, in which the world seemed to be splintering, now seemed to Julie a test. All her adult life, her husband, her daughters, even Mariadora, had relied on her ability to stay composed. Through tantrums, household crises, blowups and blowouts, she was the sturdy evergreen. Still, now for the first time, she felt really alone. The kitchen floor beneath her feet seemed ready to sway, but she would stay upright, not allow herself to slip and totter as she had in Gilbert's hospital room.

There was no time to try to imagine what came next. She pointed to the wall phone and thought, *Taras, please, whatever the emergency, I need you; don't let me down now.*

CHAPTER
FORTY-TWO

Gaby stood on the lawn, facing Stretch, aware that within sight two white tents, like thin skins covering the past, present and future of her entire life, stood waiting for her return. Her own skin felt cold and wet, as if she'd just taken a dip in a swimming pool.

A bender of two days' duration, Stretch reported, his eyes red-rimmed, phrases and sentences spoken twice, then spoken again—and again. He'd been invited to the wedding, hadn't he? He'd been invited to the wedding, had accepted, then, she'd asked him not to come, but was that fair, was that fair, was that fair? He had not had a drink in six years come this January first. Six years, six, Scotch-free, beer-free, wine-free, not even a rum cake at Christmas, did she realize the import of what had happened to him now? He said, "inport" instead of import, and sneezed twice, reaching into his pocket, sometimes the gentleman, to get his linen handkerchief, monogrammed, possibly a gift from Mitzi. He blew his nose. He said he didn't believe she'd go through with "the deal" and wanted to see for himself. Six years come January first. He'd been invited, then disinvited, uninvited. Was that fair?

Gaby told him she'd walk him to the car.

"You've been thinking of me, haven't you?" he asked as she tried to get him off the lawn, away from the party, away from what must definitely be the line of sight from the windows of 66 Morris Lane. She did not turn back to the house to see who was watching, but imagined the eyes of her sisters and mother a burning laser following her.

"Thinking of me," he repeated, his hand brushing her cheek.

Gaby wanted to hold him, touch him, kiss him. God, how she hated Stretch at this very minute. She imagined herself lying on a gurney, just like her father, a sheet covering her naked body. She saw herself with electrodes attached to her head, a Popsicle stick holding down her tongue, a nurse gripping both feet while electric currents ran through her head to toe. She'd seen a documentary filmed at the Menninger Clinic; shock was perceived to be safe and effective these days. If it helped cure depression disorders, why not a sexual obsession that was just as surely going to ruin her life?

"How could you do this? Pee on Mama's roses? My mother's *roses?*"

He was concentrating on finding the car, which he'd parked in someone's driveway, obviously no spaces being available on Morris Lane. The traffic control man waved, assuming he lived here or was a guest leaving a bit early. Surprisingly, Stretch walked without assistance, staggering only once, perhaps just a stumble over a small branch lying on the street, but Gaby held his elbow, walked half a step behind him, just in case. Two members of the band, taking a cigarette break in the driveway, watched her guiding Stretch down the street, the guest who'd had one too many.

The familiar Chevy Blazer, license number FV783, looked as if it had just gone through the car wash. Stretch had always been fastidious about the exterior of his car, while the inside—she could see a blanket, a toy keyboard, a school notebook as she moved closer—laissez-faire. Stretch reached into his pocket, pulled out the electronic key, beep-unlocked the door and turned to Gaby. He said again he didn't believe she'd go through with the wedding and wanted to see for himself. Dry six years come January first and that's what this wedding had done to him, pushing him into Billy B's place on Franklin Street. He apologized for peeing on her mother's roses. In this life, this whole life, he'd never done anything like it. His own mother would die on Staten Island if she knew.

He seemed to sober up now, turning to Gaby but not looking directly into her face. Avoiding her eyes. He spotted something on the ground in the driveway next to his car, a piece of glitter that held his attention, a maneuver of evasion. He reached over to pick it up, perfectly steady now, and examined what turned out to be an ordinary stone specked with mica. He examined it as if it were a meteorite fallen from another planet; all this, Gaby presumed, out of the jitter of nervousness, completely unlike him.

"Did I tell you you look ravishing? God, ravishing."

"I have to go back—" Gaby said, her stomach in a twisting knot. She was looking over her shoulder, getting desperate.

"I have to tell you something. I have to tell you—"

"No, don't tell me anything." *Go,* she thought. *Don't do this to me, I can't live through this.*

"Something's happened."

"What?"

"At home."

Gaby moved back a step. The band had started up again; she could hear faintly some BeeGees thing she'd danced to back in college.

"Mitzi is going to Arizona. Her mother is taking her to Scottsdale. She's taking the kids." He looked up, eyes on Gaby's now, rubbing the stone between his fingers.

"For how long?" Every time he mentioned his wife, Gaby now pictured the ramp at the side of the porch.

"It's more than a vacation. 'I may stay', she told me. 'For the winter'. She's already called for school transfer forms. What does that, does that tell you?"

Gaby squeezed the palms of her hands together and pushed her hands against her lips. "When did all this happen?"

"Oh, it's been—she's been talking, you know. Then her mother called, it was ten days ago, the townhouse two doors down, it's all one floor, it's available for rent, option to buy, I guess it was maybe Wednesday last week, lots of back and forth, forty phone, phone calls—hey, I'm hungry. I'm feeling hungry. Did you save me a piece of cake? Goddamn it!" He had started to shiver. "I missed the whole thing. How did the I do's go?"

"She's really leaving?" Gaby watched a car go by, then two boys on a bike; she saw nothing except Stretch's face. His forehead was all perspiration, his mouth like a strand of pasta across his face.

"Get in the car," he said. "You drive. Anywhere. Please. Just get in the car, Gab. I love you. Life without you—it's a bloody fucking abyss."

Gaby stood next to the Chevy Blazer, her *what if* thoughts flaming, circular, heading nowhere. How long had she been standing here? At any moment, Wally might come running, looking for her. Dear, good Wally, a wonderful son, now and forever her husband, unless—

He was holding out the car keys to her, and now, as a squirrel hopped across this neighbor's lawn in her line of vision, as Stretch took the stone in his hand and tossed it aside, an athletic, he-man, sexy

football hero gesture, Gaby took the keys and opened
the driver's-side door.

She was not familiar with driving an SUV, kept her
hands tight on the steering wheel and drove slowly.
She reminded herself that the tranquilizer she'd
taken earlier was probably still in her bloodstream,
that it could lead to trouble. It made her think of her
parents' accident, of which she'd thought a thousand
times. Without immediately realizing it, she headed
for the street on which her mother's car had left the
road, killing her father.

"Where we going?" Stretch asked as she stopped
at a light, then made a turn onto Grand Boulevard,
forgetting how she could look to a casual observer,
a bride, still in her veil, driving a red-haired passenger
in a dark polo shirt, not a groom!—through the
streets of Scarsdale.

Soon the leaves would begin to turn, the trees would
be all gold and red, as they were when her father lost
his life here. Stretch may have sobered up slightly,
but not nearly enough to take the wheel. His breath
was boozy, he'd leaned against the car door and
looked asleep but was staring at her through his red
eyelashes.

There was no reason for wanting to visit *that* street,
to see *that* curb, *that* tree—an unidentifiable species,
maybe larch—which Karen had told her was still
scarred from the impact of Daddy's car, except to see
for herself the stage on which her father had died
his virtual death and the blue ruin of her mother's
life had begun. With the kiss of real death scheduled
for tomorrow, she felt she owed him this much.

Making a left onto the street, Gaby slowed down,
looking for the spot, the house numbers, finally passing the rock with its engraved digits: 688, and the
tree, a piece gouged out of the trunk. Karen had

described the site elaborately once in the waiting room at the hospital, down to the orange paper pumpkin in the window of the house. No pumpkin now, just the mailbox with its painted geese-in-flight at the curb and a fire hydrant next to the driveway. Gaby slowed, but didn't stop. One day, perhaps she'd come back, take a photo of these premises. Her sisters would call her morbid, but it seemed important to have some memento mori, something to put away in a box and to save. To show the children she would some day have.

"Where we *going*?" Stretch repeated. He sat up, moved his arm to the back of the seat behind her, relaxed, as if they were in the movies and the feature was about to begin.

Gaby maneuvered his car easily now, slowed to a crawl and let the house and street on which her father had ended his life sink into her consciousness. She was waiting for illumination. She imagined how it would feel if she drove the car into the rock or up on the lawn, how it would feel to kill the man beside her. She tried to imagine mourning Stretch, and understood she would do so in the same way she loved him, as a figure she had created out of the whole cloth of her imagination, allowing him a stature and color that had little to do with the somewhat sad, weak and needy man he was; she had embellished him, turned him into a concept, a safe haven from grief, an adolescent illusion, a bit of Daddy.

"Where we headed? An adventure?" Stretch asked.

He reached out and let his hand slide across the front of her dress, let his fingers slip along the fabric, trace the slope of her breast. She remembered the day at Kleinfeld's when her sisters helped her with what she thought would be the most important sartorial decision she'd ever make. Her sisters had saved their own bridal dresses, paid local cleaners small fortunes to preserve the silks in cellophane, embalm the pleats and buttons and hemstitches in fluids and chemicals to have and to hold from their wedding day forward, for daughters or sentiment or simply for posterity.

But while Susanna and Karen could not bear to part with the items of clothing in which they'd said their vows, it was as if her own gown had grown sizes too small even as she was wearing it. It was chafing under her arms, pulling across the hips, constricting movement like a boned corset, and Gaby wanted nothing better than to slip out of the dress right now. As she gripped the steering wheel to turn a corner, she imagined running back to her old room, taking a shower, putting on her old khaki shorts and never having to look at this bridal dress again.

CHAPTER
FORTY-THREE

"I've looked all over for her. Where did my wife suddenly disappear to?" Wally asked Julie, a wrapped wedding gift a guest had handed him in both hands. The sheepish look that went with "my wife" registered with her, but only for an instant; she took the box and put it on the coffee table in the living room. She'd told her daughters on one occasion—they might have been eleven or twelve—that she intended never to lie for them, and should never be expected to cover up for their transgressions, but out of her mouth now came, "I think Gaby just walked Tilda and her daughters to their car." Then she heard herself change the subject, chatter on about the possible contents of the box, a gift from a college friend of Gaby's, which had been wrapped in white and tied with a white ribbon on which the friend had painted a row of pink hearts.

Wally followed her into the living room, looking at his watch: "It's getting late and we still have packing to do!" Julie moved her hands to her cheeks, knowing they flamed pink, her cheeks a lie detector from the time she was in kindergarten, and then moved one hand to her ear, still red and swollen from the bee sting. "Would you do me a big favor, Wally?" She asked him to go upstairs and see if he could find in one of the bathrooms a prescription for codeine she knew didn't exist. It would keep him busy for five minutes, possibly a bit more.

He ran up the stairs and Julie sank into the chair nearest the fireplace, staring at the pink hearts ribbon without seeing it and twisting her fingers around each other in her lap, wanting back around her wrist the rubber band she'd let Taras throw away all those months ago.

She wished she were with him now, had run out the door after him, followed him to whatever crisis he faced at home. Edgy and white-lipped, Taras had stood in the doorway of the kitchen looking like a distant cousin of the man who had not half an hour ago on the dance floor seemed like the very symbol of self-confidence and strength. With Susanna staring him down and Karen suddenly sinking to the bottom step of the staircase saying she might just throw up, he made the announcement, rather formally, that he was sorry, but would have to leave immediately. Looking perspired and ready to sprint, he said he hoped Julie, and the bride and groom, would understand. An emergency, at home. He would call later, when he had a chance.

With hardly a look at Julie, let alone her daughters, he fled—that was the word, *fled*—out the door through which he'd come.

No ideas came to Julie for the next delaying tactic; as soon as Wally returned from a fruitless search upstairs, she would not be able to manage a lie again. It was a sickening thought, that Gaby had actually gone off somewhere with the man with the red hair, suffered some sort of short-circuit of reason that allowed her to leave her husband of three hours and give in to, to—*what*?

At Gaby's age, she was safe and happy at home with three babies. It's when she began growing roses, her greatest problems aphids and black spots or a late frost. She was dazzled at the products—the pink Belinda's Dreams, pale Mark Nelsons, the favorite Elizabeth Taylors, flourishing outside the back door of Gilbert's and her small Cape Cod. Julie saw herself, her hair in a ponytail, her skin perfect, a husband who put his hand over her navel to feel the first kicks of every new life, looking out of the windows together at her roses. Before Karen, before, before Susanna, before Gaby, she'd indulged herself in airy dreams of what her life as a mother would be. Like flowers, her children. Maintenance and pampering or parenting laissez-faire, it was all the same. Streaks on her rose petals, thorns and black spots, and imperfections in her children, no matter how hard she tried. Julie had never foreseen the powerlessness of the gardener, and of motherhood.

And here came Wally, back from his search, her darling new son-in-law, oblivious, concerned for her, walking down the stairs, asking her if perhaps her prescription bottle of codeine might be in the *downstairs* bathroom or in one of the bedrooms? He couldn't find anything that fit the description, so was she absolutely sure she'd put it in one of the medicine cabinets? His expression was all concern, so like him. Solicitously, he asked if her bee bite was still causing her that much pain?

Before Julie could answer, Gaby seemed to float into the hall behind him. It was as if she'd been lowered from above, not come in through the front door at all, she'd moved so silently. She stood hesitat-

ing for a moment behind Wally, catching Julie's eye,
waiting, as if for an actor's cue, before speaking. She
looked so very young and small in the dusky hall, the
apparition of a bride more than a real one. Julie was
overcome, practically stunned speechless with relief.
"Gosh, look at the time," Wally said, pointing to
his watch, "I've been looking all over for you, Gab.
Practically everyone's gone!" And Gaby, hesitating
just for a moment, moved forward, touched Wally's
sleeve as she ran past him toward the wing chair from
which Julie had just pulled herself. She threw her
arms around her mother's neck, taking Julie by complete surprise and nearly knocking her back into her
chair.

"I just wanted to thank you for everything. For the
wedding—and everything." Gaby spoke in a voice so
injured, so small, no one but Julie could have heard.
"It's all going to be ding ho, Mama. Whatever
comes." And then she whispered, "I dropped him
off at Mary Immaculate Church and drove back here.
His car is in the garage. He'll pick it up later, okay?"

Julie held her close. Through thunderstorms and
bad dreams, broken dolls and broken hearts, it all
came back to her at this moment, a reprise of the
times, numerous as the sands, she'd circled her
daughter in her arms just like this. The room got
smaller, just big enough for the two of them, the
distance between now and then vanished. In her arms,
Gaby was defenseless, a little girl again, a sitting duck
for life.

It hardly seemed possible that this baby and her
sisters were women now, with husbands, off on their
own, out in their own lifeboats in storm and sun,
as Gil had once said. Then again, it hardly seemed
possible that she herself was fifty-four, about to be a
grandmother. How had all those years compressed
themselves into no time at all?

Julie, sitting in her vacated living room, looked around at the empty chairs, the silent piano, the stretch of well-worn carpet. *Whatever comes,* Gaby's voice echoed as she waited for the telephone to ring, waited for word from Taras.

CHAPTER
FORTY-FOUR

Susanna sat, waiting for Liesel, next to Dieter in the front seat of the car, her place reclaimed, the seat of proprietary ownership, the seat of power. Since Liesel's maneuver to sit next to her father at the airport, Susanna had learned to be quick as a gazelle reaching the car, whenever they were taking Liesel anywhere. She knew it was downright puerile and now seemed unnecessary, since the girl had taken the hint pretty quickly, and was actually working hard to learn American ways and stay on her good side. Her English had even picked up a bit of slang. ''The vedding vas really cool,'' she said, when she'd climbed back into the car after the reception.

But the wedding of her sister had left Susanna feeling locked out and dismal. First it was Mama and Taras, then Elliot's announcement, then Liesel, constantly the focus of Dieter's attention. As a postscript, Gaby's bizarre behavior with what could be a vagrant or section eight schizo, what was that all about?

It was absentee management; without Daddy, the family was sliding into ruin. Somehow even her own situation with Dieter would not be at this low tide if Daddy had been around to intervene. And Mama would not have been this lovesick dancing doll who'd looked like any minute she'd stick a rose between her teeth and unzip her partner's fly.

Liesel was now in a chatty mood, and went on and on about how fortunate Susanna was to have two wonderful sisters, that she herself had always wanted a sister. Although she spoke to them both, she seemed to be directing these comments to Dieter, throwing out little verbal darts; why hadn't he provided her with a sibling, anyway? He had told her many, many times about the marriage problems after the little brother died, but just today, as a witness to what she saw as so much lovely family solidarity, well, she told her Papa, it made her think.

As they drove up Route 684, Liesel said that she herself would surely go on to have more than this one baby. She was thinking in terms of five, or even six. That's where she and Karen were different; Karen wanted just this child, or maybe one more. And the funny thing was, she and Karen were both expecting at about the same time. In March. Karen on the 30th, she on the 22nd. Both Aries! Although she herself hadn't been sick to her stomach, not once. It was only the psoriasis that was driving her "off the vall."

Dieter turned to Susanna with a little smile to see if she was as amused as he was by the American slang. "And Liesel, are you also going to name your child after his grandfahder?" he asked merrily.

Liesel's voice came to attention. "Vitch grandfahder?"

"Your choice, Schatz," Dieter continued upbeat. It occurred to Susanna that while she'd suffered like a person chained to a dungeon wall throughout her sister's wedding celebration, he had had a pretty good eating-drinking-socializing time.

"Vat's the choice?" Liesel asked.

"My father or your mother's father is the choice."
There was hardly any traffic and Dieter had speeded
up somewhat. He was going over sixty, although he
had had vodka, then champagne, then wine and
plenty of it.

"That's a *choice?*" Liesel's voice crackled.

"My fahder vas a very talented man. He played the
accordion, you remember?" To Susanna Dieter said,
"Taught himself everyt'ing. Not a lesson. Could play
anything, you could name a Strauss valtz, he could
play from beginning to the end."

"So may I remind you, your fahder, the accordion
player who could play a valtz from beginning to end,
he flew for the Luftwaffe. He dropped bombs for
Hitler. You forget this?"

From Dieter there was a silence that came into the
air of the car like a poisonous fume.

"And my other grandfahder, Papa Friedrich, he
had just vun leg and couldn't go in the army, so he
had a bakery in his village, and vun day, the store to
the left side, a pharmacy, was closed, and the shop-
keeper vas a Jew and he vas not seen again. So the
vife came and asked could Papa Friedrich hide vun
child, just the youngest. She vanted to put the children here and there into Christian houses. My
mahder vas there, she vas there when the voman, she
came to the door. And guess vat is funny? The boy's
name vas Dieter, like your name. How is that called
in English—*Zusammentreffen?*"

"Coincidence?" Susanna offered.

"Yes, yes, coincidence. So Mami's fahder didn't say
yes or no, just pushed the door to close vith his both
hands, then locked. Didn't say a vord. Not even
'sorry'. Pushed the door to close on little Dieter's
mother. Vat happened to the boy and the whole family, is in the books of history. And all Papa Friedrich's
cakes in the bakery Mami said to me, they all had

swastikas on them, in chocolate or raspberry or schlag. How do you say in English, *'schlag'*?"

"Whipped cream," Susanna enthusiastically offered.

"Yes. Vipped cream. And so, Papa, I should name a baby for a grandfahder, you still think?" When Liesel said, "Jews" it came out "Chews"; the way she spoke sounded like a caricature, like *Saturday Night Live* doing Germans, but to Susanna, who could not, because of her seatbelt, turn to look at Liesel as she spoke, it wasn't funny. It was music.

"You don't think ve learned in school," Liesel continued, "vat your fahder and Papa Friedrich did? You think ve vere so stupid, so yo-yo's—"

Susanna caught herself smiling to hear one of America's favorite phrases misused so charmingly, so endearingly. Her heart lifted and so did her hands. Susanna, risking Dieter's wrath, risking another hour or night or week of strain and tension, lifted her hands and gave Liesel a round of applause. "Bravo Bravissimo!" she said.

"Thank you, Susanna." Liesel leaned forward and patted Susanna's shoulder. Dieter said nothing, did not flinch or turn even an inch to acknowledge Susanna or his daughter. He just speeded up; he was now going nearly seventy.

Liesel didn't stop there. She let Dieter have it, about the sins of his father and his generation, her father's own *family*, the ruin of her own country, which had lost its national pride, the tainted national anthem, the moral mistake of the government for not redesigning the flag, for not tearing down the Nazi bunkers, for not being able to agree on the scope and exhibits of the Holocaust Museum. Some of it came forth in German, some in English, all of it fervent, some of it furious. It may have been building in Liesel for a night, a week or all her twenty years.

Dieter, astonishingly, unpredictably, did not defend himself, his father, his homeland; he just stared straight ahead and pushed down the gas pedal until Susanna told him he was going too damn fast and Liesel joined in, told him he was going to kill them all. And, what the hell did he think he was doing going so fast with a pregnant person in the car, his own unborn grandchild at risk? Not to speak of his beautiful, kind and cool wife. Did he think he was on the Autobahn, or had he gone "yo-yo"? *"Verrückt,"* is the word she also used, a word Susanna understood. *Crazy.* And "Beautiful, kind, cool wife" also registered very nicely.

Dieter slowed down, without saying another word.

CHAPTER
FORTY-FIVE

As Wally was putting the wedding gift, yet another
Cuisinart, into the trunk, Shingo, who had decorated
the car not only with ribbons, old tennis shoes and
a balloon tied to the antenna, but also shaving cream
announcing that they were JUST MARRIED across
the back windshield, appeared with Benita. They
came to throw a bit of birdseed as the happy couple
made their departure. Gaby had hoped to slip away
without attracting attention; she and Wally had
parked the car in a neighbor's driveway where they
assumed no one would follow, but a few other guests
had spotted them leaving and now gathered to say
farewell, among them Milt Gladstone, who wished
the married couple *bonheur* on their *lune de miel,* and
Karen, who took Gaby aside to say that whatever the
hell had gone down with the "lawn urinator" looked
pretty deplorable and she wouldn't ask any questions,
but she trusted her baby sister to play it square from
now on. She was a married woman for Christ sake!

Gaby nodded and hugged her sister, held her an
extra minute in a moment of overflow gratitude and

whispered, "Keep an eye on Mama while I'm away, will you? Deep six that dancer!"

Benita suddenly stepped up to replace Karen in an unpredictable swoop, encircling Gaby in a farewell hug that was more a vise than affection. "Good luck, Gaby. I know you'll pull it off," she piped into her ear. How was it that champagne tasted so good and yet wound up smelling like this on someone's breath?

"What do you mean, 'pull it off'?" Gaby asked, still smiling but extricating herself and stepping back and looking Benita in the eye.

"A hard row of stumps ahead," Benita said. "I can see it. It's my business, don't forget."

Wally, already behind the wheel, was waiting for his wife to climb into the car. They would be driving to their apartment to finish packing. Tomorrow afternoon Shingo would drive them to the airport and tomorrow night they'd leave for Spain, the honeymoon her sisters' gift to the bride and groom.

"In a minute, Wall," Gaby called over her shoulder. "What are you saying?" she asked Benita, trying to stay noncommittal.

Benita held her hands up near her shoulders palms up, as if heaven was going to cooperate, maybe send down a printout. "You don't even need my training to see you two are heading into a no-win." She sounded absolutely sober on one hand, but looked pruned on the other. It was her eyes, rolling under gold eyeshadow, and her shoulders, which she kept moving back and forth, as if she were tossing off a shawl. "Though, I'll tell you, you looked like an oil painting walking down the aisle!"

"C'mon, honey!" Wally called, starting the engine. Shingo, dark eyebrows up, his mouth in a clownish pucker, was standing by with the aerosol container of the shaving cream, which had appeared in his hand out of nowhere. He was looking at the body of the car to find a place empty enough on the fender to write another message.

"C'mon Gab, it's getting late!" Wally persisted.

With bullet speed, like a sleight-of-hand demo, Benita whipped forward, snatched the can out of Shingo's hand—"My turn to be Pablo Whatsizname!"—moved back and began spraying something on the rear passenger door.

"What is she *doing?*" someone in the small crowd asked.

Someone else yelled, "Oh, let them get going, the bed's getting cold," and Karen began to move off, saying Elliot was waiting. "Don't think about anything. Just live. It's your honeymoon!" She waved at Wally and blew a kiss, practically bumping into Benita, who had backed away to admire her finished graffiti.

It covered almost the entire passenger-side door and looked like sort of a logo for America On Line. Gaby was relieved Benita had not written a four-letter word or drawn a swastika.

Wally was beginning to look irritated, so Gaby slid in beside him, allowed Benita to help tuck her dress into the car and push closed the passenger side door. Gaby rolled down the window so she could better hear what Benita was saying. She'd missed her answer the first time.

"What did you say it was?"

"It's a triangle," Benita said again, as Wally began to back out of the driveway.

"A *what?*"

"An equilateral triangle," her voice trailed off as the car rolled past, "All sides equal—"

"I think she's into geometry," Wally said, maneuvering past hedges and the neighbor's curbside Victorian street lamp.

"Does she often belt the grape like this, do you suppose?" Gaby tried to imagine Benita ushering people into a diploma-lined office and dispensing sage advice at a hundred-fifty an hour.

"I think we better get to a car wash or all that stuff will be impossible to get off." Wally, who hated criticism of his friends, offered a reply that was no reply, and Gaby, in a flash that seemed to come with the suddeness of a siren in a firehouse, thought, *triangle*. My God, a *triangle! Benita somehow knows about Stretch!*

As the newlyweds maneuvered their car through the streets of Scarsdale, Gaby could feel her whole body go stiff as lumber. As they drove by pedestrians in town, or waited for lights, some stopped to wave, or simply smile at the spectacle of their festooned vehicle, Wally, full of cheer, said, "Look! All of Scarsdale is wishing us well!" but Gaby could not even manage a smile, let alone find the words to answer.

After they had the car cleaned, drove to their apartment building and parked the car, the groom offered to carry his **bride** over the threshold of their apartment in the time-honored tradition of American newlyweds. Gaby declined. The pleated silk of her wedding dress had pasted itself to her wooden-puppet back and the backs of her thighs. Also, the moment Wally had opened the front door, she could see into the living room, where the red light of the answering machine was blinking. Who would be calling now? It seemed improbable, with just about everyone they knew just home, or on their way home, from their wedding. To Gaby it seemed at this moment a flashing hot spot of urgency, danger, risk and jeopardy.

"We're starting our honeymoon. Who do you suppose'd be calling us at a time like this?" Wally said.

CHAPTER
FORTY-SIX

Julie had just stepped into the bathtub when the telephone rang. Two hours ago, Mariadora, the corsage the florist had supplied awry and limp on the apron she wore over her yellow dress, had asked Julie if there was anything else, she was leaving. Her long-postponed vacation would begin tomorrow; she would send a postcard from Honduras. Her voice was distant and ominous despite the fact she'd caught Julie with her head in her hands at the kitchen table, tears streaming down her face. The guests were long gone, the tents would be removed tomorrow, the house was quiet and now even faithful Mariadora seemed to be giving her a cold shoulder. It was not exactly new; with her dark looks and heavy silences she'd made it clear all along what she thought of Taras's presence here.

Never since the night of the accident had Julie felt so alone. Loneliness had a bite worse than a thousand stings from a thousand bees—until the telephone rang; it must be Taras! She'd been waiting through it all—the girls' emotional fireworks, Karen's spell of afternoon morning sickness, the sour and silent departure of Mariadora.

She leaped out of the tub; the cordless carefully left—where? Her feet leaving wet footprints on the bedroom carpet, a bath sheet wrapped around her body and dragging behind her on the floor, Julie found the telephone not on the night table next to her bed where it belonged, not on the carpet next to it where it might have fallen, but unaccountably, in Gaby's old room, where one of the girls must have taken it. It took four-and-a-half rings to reach it, by which time the answering machine had picked up and the caller had hung up. *It had to have been Taras.*

At midnight, when she couldn't sleep, couldn't watch another minute of television, couldn't bear to listen to *Adios Pampa Mia* or even one other note sung by Julio Iglesias, Julie put one of Gilbert's CDs on the player and heard without really hearing, *Goin' Down the Road Feelin' Sad, The City Put the Country Back in Me,* and *Lead With Your Heart, Not Your Mind,* while she pulled out of his bureau drawers the remaining shirts, ties, socks and underwear, leftovers of his shoe-horn collection and his daily existence. Here and there she felt the bite of nostalgia, her eyes watered once or twice at a sweet memory and once in remembered anger, but mostly, she felt as disconnected as a friend cleaning out the life's stockpile of someone she'd known in some dormitory very long ago.

And in the morning, when light began to seep through the skylights, under the blinds and between drawn curtains, Julie turned off the telephone, and slept through most of the day on which Gilbert Kessler was at last allowed to reach what his beloved Wynona Judd called, *The Place I'm Goin'.*

Until the telephone rang again, waking her late in

the afternoon, at four—or was it five? She couldn't read the clock this minute, still so fuzzy with sleep, disoriented, and waking from a dream in which Taras seemed to be throwing coconut jellybeans at a bride and groom, while her own mother, Violet, so rarely appearing in Julie's dreams, stood by, silent and disapproving.

Julie could hardly believe this was Gaby, calling from where? and sounding as if her voice was coming from the bottom of a well. "Mama! Oh, thank God you're home!"

"Gaby? Aren't you supposed to be on your way to Portugal?"

"Spain, Mama, Spain! I'm at JFK!" There was no mistaking that tone, the swallowing of tears, the small voice that Julie recognized as the sound of her baby in extremis. Julie shot up in bed. It was always this way: the body's alarms, maternal hormones that surged, dating back to the time of colic, teething and ear infections, whenever one of the girls sent up flares.

"What's happened, darling?" Julie pictured the man with the red hair; there was a moment, too long, in which her daughter was trying to compose herself. Ice flowed through the hand that was holding the receiver. "Gaby, what is it?"

"It's the triangle. The triangle!" she finally said, breaking up the word triangle into two syllables, to catch her breath, to weep.

Julie looked at the pillow her head had just left, thinking, *Yes, I'm awake,* as Gaby cried, "We're not going to Spain. We're not leaving."

"Good God, Gaby, why not?"

"When we came home last night, there was a call from a neighbor of Wally's mother. She came home from the wedding, took one of those bottles of Florida sand she's collected and emptied it into the gas tank of their car."

"Dementia. The poor woman. But you—?"

"I shouldn't have laid this on you Mama, today, of all days. Of all days! Is Daddy—gone?"

"I assume. I haven't wanted to call the hospital, dear."

"Shall I come and sit with you? Do you want me to come and be with you?"

"I've told your sisters the same thing. I want to be by myself today. I finished cleaning out all Daddy's drawers last night and I'm doing all right. I'm going to fix myself a sandwich and just be myself. But Gaby, this business with Wally's mother—"

A lengthy silence, then, Julie heard Gaby blowing her nose.

"Wally drove up there last night and spent the night with her. Our wedding night!" Gaby could not get this out immediately, but spoke in fits and starts, breaking down now and again as if it was the phone that was disconnecting, "And when he came back, you should have seen him, Mama. Totally flattened. Like you've never seen him!" Gaby stopped and Julie pictured her daughter in an airport phone booth, trying to pull herself together. "And then, Shingo came to pick us up and he had his girlfriend with him. Did you meet Benita?"

"Was she the one in the white dress, the one studying to be a psychotherapist?"

"Yes, that one."

"I did meet her, but briefly. I thought she'd had a lot to drink, to tell the truth."

"Yes, Benita."

There was the operator's voice interjecting, the click of more coins while Gaby threw money into the telephone, and then, in a calmer voice, "Mama. Are you still there?"

"I'm here. Where's Wally, dear?"

"He's trying to get our luggage back. We're coming home."

"You're coming *home?* What about your honeymoon? Spain, Portu—"

"Oh, Mama, she was right. The triangle. Benita painted a triangle on the, on the door of our car."

"Why? Why would she do that?"

"She was blotto! And blotto or not, I thought she knew, I mean, I thought she meant—well, never mind what I thought, anyway, she was right on target!"

"On what target? That woman, Benita?"

"She was a little pissed because I didn't like the poster she'd picked out for us, that's true, so I think she was trying to sort of stick it to me, but even so, she was right on the money, Mama. It's a goddamn triangle, all right."

"What are you saying, Gaby?"

"He's in love with another woman. That's what I'm saying!"

"What?"

"Didn't you see it, Mama? I don't know how I could have missed it!"

"What?"

"His mother, for Christ's sake, his Mommy!"

While Julie was trying to gather her wits enough to respond, Gaby burst forth in a new gulping torrent, cut short by the return of the operator. "Look here, Gaby, are you not overreacting, dear?" Julie was rushing, hoping not to be cut off, in case Gaby had run out of change. "Being thoughtful of his mother is an admirable thing, after all."

"You just don't know the half of it, Mama. He told me he thinks it would be a good idea if his mother moved in with us. And when I protested, he said she was around long before me and she'd always come first."

"Wally said that?"

"I want to come home. Maybe tomorrow, okay? Mama, I've made a humongous mistake."

"Wait, dear. Just a minute—did you, are you sure you heard him right?"

"I have twenty-twenty hearing, Mama! What I don't understand is how I didn't get it long before this! All those nights he ran up there the minute she called. The roof leaking, the floors creaking, a shadow on the wall—any excuse. What was I thinking not to see it coming? I never even thought to check the cell phone bill. I think he called her at least twice a day from his car, too. You know, Mama, we don't see what we don't want to see, do we?"

"No, we don't, darling," Julie said. "No, we don't," she repeated, after she'd put down the receiver and let her head fall back into the comfort of the down pillows she'd splurged on just a year and a half ago, when having pillows stuffed with down actually seemed important.

CHAPTER
FORTY-SEVEN

In the end, Lou and Ruthie would absolutely not allow Julie to spend this evening alone. "We called last night and got no answer," Lou said, as he escorted Julie to his car. So, it wasn't Taras who had summoned Julie out of her bath last night, not Taras calling after all! By this time, he might have found five minutes, just *five minutes* to let her know where he was and what emergency had sent him dashing out of the house like some fugitive in a slash-and-burn movie! He couldn't guess there was a crisis with Wally and Gaby, but by this time, he must know she'd seen *his home in flames, his child in the hospital, his ex-wife on his doorstep with a summons.* By this time—

Ruthie was in the front seat, looking perky in another new wig, this one longer, wavier, darker. She said she was feeling healthier than ever, and convinced that the green tea she was drinking every day by the gallon had killed off every last C cell in her body. Then she waxed poetic about Gaby's wedding, how beautiful it had turned out to be, how lucky Julie was to have three daughters who were all jewels, well-married, such caring, good girls, so successful and happy and lovely.

Julie wanted to tell Ruthie and Lou about Gaby— what were friends for?—but thought to wait until things with Wally were resolved. It was not possible that her daughter would decide she'd made a mistake on her way to her honeymoon. Preposterous. A misunderstanding, the tension of the wedding, a spat. *They'll work it out!*

All the way to the new waterfront restaurant in Hastings-on-Hudson, not a word was spoken about Gilbert. Nor was any reference made to Taras. It was Julie who brought up the subject, but not until she had finished a glass and a half of the Royal Kir Lou recommended as "the epic best anywhere," not until she'd admired the water view and Ruthie's new guardian angel brooch.

"I've decided on October the third for the memorial service. It's a Sunday. Maybe you can come with me to help pick out a dark suit of some sort, Ruthie."

Lou and Ruthie exchanged what they thought were covert glances. It was obvious they'd presumed all talk of funeral services and other moribund or controversial subjects (like the tango) would not be touched.

"I'm okay," Julie said, and quickly looked at the menu. "What do you recommend, Lou? Is the Dover sole any good?"

"Although Dover sole means it's never fresh, always frozen, it's very healthy," Ruthie said automatically and when Julie said, "I'll go with that then," and folded closed her menu, she caught Lou's eye over Ruthie's bent head. It was almost imperceptible, the slightest shake of his head, the dark look, the shadow that meant bad news. Julie had to pretend to eat her Dover sole.

* * *

There were telephone messages waiting when she got home. All the girls had called, each assuming she was there, in the bathtub, asleep or simply not picking up the telephone. Gaby's message: "Hope you're okay. Daddy's in a better place. Don't worry about me, Mama." There were two hang-ups, and a message from Heather at the Fred Astaire Dance Studio wondering if she would like to continue her lessons with Edoardo while Taras was away?

It hit her suddenly, and it was like the falling dreams she'd had as a child. A loose step, a stair that gave way, or a tumble from the balcony of a penthouse; she'd hurtle through the air but never land: Gilbert was really gone. She was now a *widow*, a word with the sudden power to thrust her into a freefall without a parachute. *Widow*. She was struck with terror, then with guilt. Thinking of herself when she should be thinking of Gilbert. Thinking of herself, when in fact he'd still be here if it wasn't for her. She pictured his face, saw him as he was the day they were married, tried to re-create him in her imagination as he was the night he died.

But she couldn't. He was gone, completely and absolutely gone. God had turned the page.

When Julie returned from Second Chance at five o'clock the next evening, Gaby greeted her at the door. She had brought her bridal gown, which she would donate for resale and a small suitcase, which she'd unpacked in her old room. "It's just for a few days, Mama, so I can think." Somehow, Julie felt she should resist. If she allowed Gaby to hide out here, it might prevent a truce between her and Wally. If her old room was unavailable, she'd have to face whatever music was playing in their married life. On the other hand, here was Gaby, the baby, and here was her Mayday. Julie put her arms around her youngest and told her she'd make her a cup of mocha.

And then, Gaby told Julie that Joe Goetz had called, left no message, and Taras had called from somewhere in, where was it, Louisiana? East Baton Rouge, she thought he'd said, and would call back. "What is going on with you and this guy? Look Mama, blow him off, cut loose, chop out! Think of what poor Daddy would say!" Julie instead thought of what her daughters would say if they knew their sweet Aunt Ruth had seduced or been seduced by the father they'd admired before the accident and beatified after. Already Julie regretted offering her daughter, who was thirty years old for heaven's sake, asylum in her old room, and in the past.

When Taras called again, it was almost midnight and Julie was so happy to hear his voice that she held the receiver to her ear with both hands, as if it could slide out of her hands and she might lose it, and him. He did not sound far away; it was as if he were right across the street and might be at her front door in just one moment.

"Baton Rouge?" It was one of the few places on this continent that she and Gil had never seen. She imagined heat and magnolia trees, mosquitoes and pizza parlors. "What are you doing *there,* Taras?" *And why didn't you call me before this?*

He was murmuring then. He had been thinking of her every moment. *But then, why didn't you call until today?* "What's happened?" She was a wire spring, a Jill-in-the-Box, ready to fly out and spin across the room.

He hesitated, and then said, "I have to tell you something."

Julie was sitting in her bedroom in the dark; the phone had wakened her. Now she switched on the lamp next to her bed as if the light would help her absorb what he was saying.

The police had appeared at his door. "I lost it. I guess I just lost it; grabbed the kid and hit the road." The dog, Ridgeway, had been stolen from someone's yard. The owners of the dog were going to press charges and so was the woman who lived in the basement apartment, who had discovered not only another twenty missing, but had also reported the theft of a ring Taras was pretty sure had never existed. The landlady had hidden Tommy until Taras returned from the wedding. She was sending to Louisiana his clothes, American history books, photographs, everything, as soon as he had a mailing address. "A horrible crisis, Harry. We've been on the run. Sleeping in the car. I can't let Tommy begin life with a police record. I don't want his fingerprints on file."

"Of course not."

"I'm not coming back."

"Not—coming back?" The walls had moved toward her, all corners and edges. *Not coming back.*

"How can I? God, you're a mother. You understand that, don't you?"

But why Louisiana?

"I'm going to find a place somewhere near New Orleans. I've got a friend in Mandeville, it's across the lake, right near the causeway, just close enough, far enough—"

"Close enough? Far enough? From?"

"I suppose it took a meltdown like this to figure that out. A boy needs his mother."

Mandeville. Julie pictured blue skies, a lake, a bridge, some strip malls, everyone saying "Yes ma'am, y'all come back real soon, y' hear?"

"I love you, Harry." Taras was in a gas station, feeding coins into the telephone. He'd be driving to Mandeville tomorrow to see about a place to live.

He'd call again as soon as he could. With Tommy there, it was hard; he couldn't easily leave him alone in the car, kept looking over his shoulder to see if police were following. "For a while there I was coming unglued, or I would have called earlier. Are you still there, Harry?"

"I'm still here."

"I was afraid you'd hang up on me. The way I ran out. Without a word, I mean. The wedding was beautiful, by the way."

"It's all right, Taras. I knew it had to be an emergency."

A long pause.

"I don't want to be without you, Harry. It's no good. You don't know what you mean to me."

You don't know what you mean to me, a sentence of ordinary spoken words no one in her life ever thought to say to her before.

"But Harry, I can't come back."

Julie began to say she understood, yes, she did, but no words came.

"So, come be with me. Please. Maybe down the road, we can open a studio. It's a thought. Just an idea."

She looked around her bedroom, the blue chaise, the draperies she'd thought needed redoing, the picture of the Russian River on the wall, how could she leave it all? And for Mandeville: a lake, a bridge, no place to buy shoes or a good suit. And yet, she saw as Taras spoke, that whatever the future held for her could not take place on these premises. She would have to leave this house, which was no more than a museum to the past, that she had no more right seeking asylum here, looking at old photos, holding on to old salt and pepper shakers, hanging on to memories in every corner, than Gaby did.

"Don't say no, please. Think it over, Harry. A new life. Together."

A new life. Somewhere far away, an island. Hadn't she had that dream once? Joe Goetz had called, left no message. The no message meant Gilbert was gone. She and Taras, could it work? Again, she pictured Mandeville, Louisiana: Neat clapboard houses and a blue southern sky. A new rose garden. Casablancas would grow in a southern climate, and so would tea roses. She closed her eyes and saw Taras, the striped shirt, the slightly overlapping front teeth, the way she'd first seen him.

She heard Gaby climbing the stairs, heading for the shower after a night of television and tears. It was always something; it would always be *something.*

"Taras, I can't think of this now," she said, looking around the room in which she had spent so much of her life. Home.

"Gilbert's memorial service is set for October third, and after that—"

"Harry, you remember what Thomas Jefferson said? 'The earth is for the living.' "

"After the memorial service—"

"You'll decide?"

"I'll decide."

CHAPTER
FORTY-EIGHT

Dieter waited downstairs as Susanna stood putting on her lipstick in front of the bathroom mirror. The midnight blue suit could pass for black and looked right, she'd had her eyebrows professionally plucked and she liked the new hair color. It had a darker, more defined chestnut base with glossy highlights that gave her whole head a burnished glow in sunlight, and seemed bright even in dim artificial light. Dieter said it reminded him of the women who always looked sad in French movies because the men they loved had died for them. It was a little joke of course, and lately, Dieter had been full of affectionate and upbeat humor. The Kaiser-Gelb chain was doing very well with an eighty-nine percent occupancy rate, a new record, the corporation had just bought two properties on which new hotels would be built, and Dieter was riding the crest of the wave. That was one reason.

The other was Liesel and Susanna. After the fight that Dieter had with his daughter, after the hot words about the naming of her baby to-be, Susanna took a

shine to her pregnant stepdaughter. It was actually
more than a shine; Susanna felt for this girl the sort
of maternal affection of which she did not know she
was capable. The girl hated Nazis *and* stood up to Dieter! And it wasn't only the shame of Dieter's father, her
grandfather, but his brother as well, the "Obersturm-
bannführer, SS." She called the whole family *"ekelhaft."*
Susanna recognized the word, which was a delight to
hear from this unlikely source: Disgusting.

The day after the wedding, although she was still
smarting from what she saw as Karen's thoughtless, ill-
timed announcement (but was really an envy attack),
Susanna and Liesel took two bikes off the wall of the
garage, and leaving Dieter in front of some television
soccer match, went off to take a leisurely ride
together. It was a perfect September day; here and
there the first glimmer of gold appeared in trees, and
they rode through the shimmering back roads of
Bedford like a pair of good old friends. When Liesel
began feeling tired, Susanna insisted they stop and
then, sitting together on a little stone wall drinking
from the bottles of Gerolsteiner water Susanna had
thought to bring along, Liesel began to talk.

Her English was improving, good enough now to
make it clear that she was enthralled that her father
had found a woman who was worldly and sophisti-
cated, an American, so unlike her (dear) but com-
placent mother, who did nothing much except
embroider tablecloths with colored thread, cook fat-
tening old-time dishes and watch German talk shows.
In other words, Liesel had chosen Susanna as her
role model. She hoped also that Susanna would
become her baby's honorary grandmother, maybe
his godmother as well. And she hoped Susanna would
come to her wedding and sit right in the front pew
along with her father and mother and all her dear
relatives.

Susanna surprised herself by revealing that she had

wanted a child of their own but that Dieter had flatly refused. Liesel immediately took Susanna's side. No, forty-nine was not too old to become a Dad, and if Susanna wanted a baby, she should be allowed to have one! She would certainly have a little talk with her father as soon as they got back to the house. "Let's wait a few days," Susanna advised. She did not mention that she'd discarded her birth control pills months ago, and that with the appearance of menstrual blood every month, her frustration was ever so slightly tinged with relief. Maybe she was destined to be childless. The idea of her own travel agency, a partnership with Dieter, travel to every corner of the world, seemed out of sync with motherhood. Maybe, it was just a thought, she'd settle for the niece or nephew already gestating in her sister's uterus. With Elliot hardly likely to be a robust Dad, Karen might need extra help and support. Susanna would have to give motherhood further thought.

When Susanna offered to stay home when Dieter drove his daughter to the airport so father and daughter could spend her last few hours in America alone together, Liesel insisted that Susanna come along. "I'll sit in the back seat," Susanna heard herself say when Dieter was loading the trunk, and saw her husband's head shake in disbelief.

And when they dropped Liesel off at the Lufthansa terminal at JFK, Susanna was actually a bit sorry to see her go.

Now, Dieter blew the horn; he was impatient, it was getting late. As Susanna slipped into the car next to him, she felt a calm she hadn't felt in months.

"Are you all right, Schatz?" he asked.

"I'm fine," Susanna said.

Dieter looked at the sky through the windshield. "Let's hope it won't rain," he said.

"No, it should. It's in keeping for the occasion. It feels appropriate when it looks like the sky is weeping. Anyway, we need rain."

"You spoke to your mother this morning?"

"She sounds all right," Susanna said. "She's got Gaby with her, don't forget." She made a face to indicate what she thought of her sister's loco behavior, but his eyes were on the road and Dieter missed it.

"How long is this going to last? Not very long?"

"Maybe an hour. The rabbi is long-winded, and Elliot wants to speak, then Milt Gladstone, and Joe Goetz said he'd say a few words."

"I thought I should say a few vords too, should I?"

"You didn't prepare anything, did you?"

"I did. You know, Schiller said, *'Auch das Schöne muss sterben.'* Even the beautiful must die. Then I vould say how beautiful a person your father vas. You know, he treated me good though in his heart, deep in the Jewish soul, he didn't like me. A gentleman, he vas."

Her father, a gentleman. Susanna smiled to herself. The Germans had a saying for every goddamn occasion, and one day she'd cure her husband of his endless proverbs, maxims and platitudes. "Even the beautiful must die." Sometimes, though, the German proverbs were right on the mark.

CHAPTER
FORTY-NINE

The Park-Lloyd Funeral Home had provided its largest room and even this was filled to overflowing; a few men, some familiar faces and some not, had to stand at the rear, despite the extra folding chairs provided. The atmosphere was subdued in the windowless space, where even the air seemed beige, and a wall behind the lectern draped in colorless dark velvet reminded Gaby of doom.

With Mama on her left and Wally on her right, Gaby sat looking up at Joe Goetz, who mopped his eyes describing how her father had slipped into his hand twenty dollars for a pair of shoes, money he'd been saving for a trip to Niagara Falls before either of them had more than a hundred in the bank. He said he'd thought he'd prepared himself for Gil's passing for almost a year, but obviously he had not prepared enough. There was a long pause while he pulled himself together and then he ended by saying he hoped Gil could continue listening to some of his bluegrass tapes in heaven, although "God might want him to keep the volume down."

Milt Gladstone, one of the only men who had chosen to wear a yarmulke, followed. He said, "Real men don't cry—until someone like Gilbert Kessler dies," and went on to express in many words that no one had ever had a fairer boss and a finer friend. Gaby caught what she thought was the barest glimmer of a smile on Mama's lips when he wrapped up with, *"Au revoir, cher ami."* There was only the slightest shimmer of a tear in Mama's eyes. Obviously she had cried herself out.

As soon as Milt stepped down, Elliot moved to the podium. He turned to point to the gray stone urn that held Gilbert's ashes behind him, called his father-in-law a four-letter man, the letters spelling FINE, and hoped that his wonderful widow, Julie, and his beautiful daughters took courage from all the love that was being poured out here today. Karen followed, surprising Gaby; she must have made a last-minute decision to say a few words about Daddy. She held high her head and didn't break down, looking stunning even in her black maternity dress and her unusually understated double string of gray pearls. She said, "Daddy died before he could check out every nook and cranny in every country of the world and before he could experience the joys of grandfatherhood. He probably would have been the out-and-out best grandpa in the world." She kept her poise, stepped down from the platform, walked over to Mama, and gave her a long, crushing hug.

It made Gaby, already on edge, begin trembling. Wally had to put an arm around her shoulders through Dieter's small and charming tribute, through the music—a Tommy Dorsey tape Lou had brought instead of the bluegrass Daddy would have preferred—and finally, through the closing words of Rabbi Waller, who rambled on and on about the man he'd met just twice. The rabbi was suffering from seasonal allergies and although there were few flowers, sneezed at least three times—kerchooed loudly, apologizing profusely—as he said that life must come to an end but love is invincible and the Kessler family invites everyone to Julie's house immediately after the service for light refreshments.

Gaby squeezed her hands to her knees as if she were on a roller coaster hurtling through space. She had gone to the apartment last week to clean out her belongings. The leather couches and most of the other furniture would go into storage and the wedding gifts were stacked high in the bedroom. She would have to create some sort of note to go with each and every one, and what could she possibly say in these messages? Wally had already moved half his clothing to his mother's. He had called Gaby every night for a week. "We'll work it out," he'd said, fifty, no, one hundred times, but each time with less conviction, and then he stopped calling altogether, until yesterday, when he offered to drive her to the memorial service. "I'm going in the limousine with Mama. You're planning on coming?" Gaby asked, with some surprise. "He was my father too," Wally answered with a catch in his throat, which Gaby thought was both sweet and ridiculous.

"How's your mother?" she had asked politely.

Wally told her his mother had invited some church friends to dinner and tried to serve them bleach in wineglasses, fortunately pouring from a Clorox container in full view. He could not leave her alone; couldn't Gaby see that? He wouldn't "stick her," those were his words, into some home where they'd strap her into wheelchairs and shovel baby food into her mouth. Couldn't she understand his position on this? Gaby, knowing it was useless, suggested hiring a nice Portuguese lady to stay with her.

Wally said he'd do that, certainly, but he'd have to be there too, to make sure there was no "funny business," and his voice said it all: he trusted no one with the precious, the extraordinary, the quintessential symbol of perfection in a human being.

Gaby, too distracted with Stretch, had missed the red flags that were flying and flapping right in front of her face. She remembered things she'd forgotten. No, suppressed. The trophies he'd won in tournaments were sitting on the mantel in *her* house. All those visits he'd made up to Norwalk; how often could his mother's sink have been backed up, anyway? And the telephone calls, one from home every night, God knew how many from the office—this was not just concern for his mother. And the wishy-washy sex! This was no passing fancy, but a full blown, vehement love attachment. Benita had talked about Oedipus as if she knew him personally and hinted that Wally had confided to Shingo that he'd been sexually abused. By a YMCA camp counselor. Benita reminded Gaby that the triangle was also a homosexual symbol, so *who knew?*

If the shrink-to-be could paint her toenails gold and dress in white lace to go to a wedding at which she drank enough to act like a ditz, who could believe her?

Gaby could. Benita had painted a triangle on Wally's car and lifted the veil right up from Gaby's eyes. If she had any doubts, she'd heard it direct from Wally's mouth: his mother came first. No wonder Gaby had fallen into someone else's arms! She was not altogether the dirty trick she'd thought herself, not a discredit to the Kessler family or to the memory of her father. Under the circumstances, she could be forgiven, and most important, could forgive herself. At some future time.

Now, sitting next to her, his arm around her, her husband—yes, still—squeezed her shoulder, warmly, protectively and with affection, while she pressed her knees together, imagining what her life would have been like with him, and now what it would be without him, without Stretch, with no job, and without her rock of strength, Daddy.

As she stood outside on the steps of the Park-Lloyd Funeral Home waiting for her mother to free herself from the knot of Daddy's employees waiting to say good-bye, including Tilda Novak, whose face was streaked with tears and mascara, Susanna and Karen came to join her. Wally had tactfully walked her out the door, then disappeared.

"I think Mama's back to being her old self," Karen said when Elliot had gone to fetch the car. "She handled the service so well, didn't she? I was afraid she'd break down completely."

"Without Fred Astaire to lean on?"

"What about him?" Susanna asked. "We were so worried, and now look. Nowhere in sight, right?"

"The dancing man seems to be out of the picture," Gaby said. "Vanished. Gone. I think it's over. She probably finally heard us and told him to go take his tango and dance it up his pampas."

"Thank God! I was actually thinking of asking Lou DiLorenzo to have a little talk with her." Susanna was waiting for Dieter, who was still inside, using the bathroom.

"Did you see the amount of jewelry his wife was wearing? I mean, did Ruthie leave anything *at home?*" Karen had discovered a hair on the shoulder of her dress and was pulling it off.

"How could you possibly notice jewelry?" Gaby asked. "At your father's memorial service, you're counting bracelets?" Her legs were wobbly, she felt a hundred years old, and she wanted to strike out, at anybody, for anything.

"Wait a minute. How could you miss all the rings?

And the size of the diamond earrings?'' Karen's voice rose in a defensive vibrato.

Gaby, still feeling unsteady, said, ''With Daddy's ashes sitting there, I think it's a bit superficial. Frankly, slightly *shallow.*''

''The jewelry? I should say so!''

''Not the jewelry, the *noticing* of the jewelry!''

Susanna jumped in. ''Shh! Someone is going to overhear this!''

''As if I care,'' Gaby said.

''Well, *I* care,'' Karen said.

''You *always* worry about what people think!''

''The hell I do!'' Karen, her mouth pursed just like Daddy's when he got mad, said. ''You're the one—''

Susanna hissed, ''Will you both shut up please? Just cool down, both of you!'' She looked at her watch. ''It's getting late. Now where is Dieter all this time?''

Karen, now in a war mode, pulled her fingers through her hair. ''Can you, Susanna, for just one minute, let go of Dieter?''

Susanna blinked hard. ''And can you go just two minutes without playing with your hair?''

''Oh my God,'' Mama said in a stage whisper. She'd come up behind them without their noticing. Gaby got a whiff of Carolina Herrera and a look at her mother's face. ''Are you girls actually arguing? Now? *Now? At a time like this?*''

Gaby felt remorseful, then relieved when some of the Second Chance ladies interrupted to offer their condolences, saying that they were sure Gilbert would have loved all the speeches, would have been pleased with the turnout.

As soon as they'd left, Mama went on without missing a beat, ''Lucky they didn't hear you! Lucky they didn't hear Mariadora, either. Do you know that right after the service, she just came up and told me she's been having bad dreams and that she thinks Daddy is speaking to her from the grave?''

"Mariadora? She's back? Where? I didn't see her!" Gaby said.

"She sat way in back. She was wearing a dark green hat. Now she's disappeared. I told her she could come with us in the limousine, but she said she preferred a taxi. What do you suppose that means?" Mama wanted to know.

As she reached for the handrail to steady herself, Gaby thought, Nothing good.

Arriving at the curb in his car, Elliot beeped the horn. Karen held up one finger indicating she wanted one more minute with her sisters. They stood on the steps of the funeral home in a cluster while Milt Gladstone took Mama's arm and began leading her to the limousine that waited behind Elliot's car. Gaby, momentarily omniscient, saw it all: Susanna, Karen and her own self, eyes red, sore hearts stuffed with bits of anger, envy, old grudges and new ones, resentments and competition, linked arms and stood on the steps of the Park-Lloyd Funeral Home, watching Mama leave.

A calm descended. She and her sisters turned and looked at each other, smiled uneasily. Susanna suddenly reached over and put her arms around Gaby, then Karen embraced them both. They stood in this détente of a huddle for a moment, while Gaby thought: *I'm okay now.*

They'd all feel free to say whatever came into their hearts even if it cut and bruised and made each other crazy, but it was comfortable and safe, random luck to be a part of this perfectly imperfect trio—to have two older sisters to stand by or stand against, to love and to hate, to trust, to lean on if necessary, even to die defending if it came to it. She was without a husband, a lover, a job, but she had not lost everything. She was not without a future and was not alone; she had Susanna and Karen. And, she had her mother.

"Everything will be ding ho," Gaby said. "I'm getting a pair of Siamese cats, girls. Did I tell you?"

CHAPTER
FIFTY

Taras called at midnight. He'd found a house to rent, not very grand, but with a screened porch which he was patching. He'd enrolled Tommy into the junior high and was having no luck finding a job teaching dancing—yet. If she didn't think the house was elegant enough, he could book her a room at the Queen and Crescent Hotel. He had a connection there and could get her a deal. "I miss you with a capital M. Tommy's pissed at me, can you believe it, he's pissed at *me*? He says he'd rather be in jail than down here. The meeting with his mother did not go well, but we're working on it. I think she's trying. She's looking pretty normal these days, except for her hair. She's wearing it right down to her ass; you should see her. And of course, that religion. But she swore, no black candles and not a word about the gris-gris, or whatever. No taking the kid to any ceremonies, nothing like that, either. She's temping at a car rental place and teaching dancing weekends so she knows people and she's going to help find me a job. When are you coming, Harry?"

* * *

According to Julie's car radio the weather report
for tomorrow was cold and rainy. Scarsdale would be
catching the tail of a hurricane that had already pretty
much blown itself out to sea in the Carolinas, but
today was one of those shirtsleeve—sandal days in
October that melted ice cream in children's cones
and brought out convertibles that whizzed past her
on Weaver Street with tops down and radios blaring.
The girls at Second Chance had taken their sandwiches out on the back steps of the shop and eaten
lunch in the sunshine. "I'll be back in an hour,"
Julie had said, without telling them where she was
headed.

This morning, Heather had called to say that the
New Rochelle branch of the Fred Astaire Studios
would be moving to Mamaroneck. Would Mrs. Kessler
like to come up at her leisure and pick up the silver
shoes she'd left, and a Channel Thirteen umbrella
someone had left behind; was it hers?

The umbrella was not Julie's, but she'd left the
shoes at the studio the week after Taras had carried
her through the rain. Until Heather's call, Julie, with
a great deal on her mind, had forgotten all about
them. Now, walking up the familiar creaking steps to
the second floor space in which she'd first laid eyes
on him, she thought she could hear and could almost
hum along the first bars of *Yo Soy El Tango*. It was an
aural illusion, since the studio had already closed
for business. It was why, Heather explained, she was
working these hours, getting ready for the move, and
definitely feeling nostalgic. "It won't be the same,"
she said. "No it won't," Julie responded, hoping she
was keeping her expression exactly as noncommittal
as Heather's.

The girl's hair was shoulder length now and she
looked altogether like a different person, a little softer

and prettier, as Julie had predicted. She showed Julie her engagement ring, a diamond not much larger than a grapeseed, reminding Julie of her own. "How are you doing, Mrs. Kessler?" she asked politely. "Everything's fine," Julie answered just as politely.

"And how are your daughters?" Heather tossed over her shoulder, making conversation as she went for the shoes.

Her stock reply reminded Julie of the dolls the girls once had, the ones that spoke a phrase when a cord was pulled from their backs. "All doing very well, I'm happy to say."

Just last night, Susanna had called as Mariadora, who had hardly spoken two words to Julie since the memorial service, was leaving for the day. "You will never believe it," Susanna had said, and Julie steeled herself. Susanna's high pitch was unreadable. Rainbows or rain?

"After dinner, Dieter disappeared into his computer for an hour, and then, he reappeared, handed me a letter, and asked me to mail it tomorrow. You'll never guess to whom it was addressed!"

Julie, looking out the window and watching Mariadora head for the bus stop, said she couldn't guess. Mariadora stopped to pick up some street litter that had landed at the side of the house in what was left of the autumn Casablancas. *Dour and moody, but ever dependably tidy and loyal.* Once she'd thought of Mariadora as a fourth daughter. Now it made Julie sad, as if she'd somehow betrayed her.

"The Naturalization Service! Dieter is going to become an American citizen, would you believe it!"

The call from Susanna had come an hour after Gaby had walked in with the news of a possible offer of a job. "Lower pay, more responsibility." She rubbed her hands together as if she'd just washed them. Stamford, Connecticut meant she'd find a cheaper place to live than New York City, where she'd just turned down a job at Lever Brothers in Marketing. The Connecticut job was Market Research and she could drive to work. "The boss and I hit it off. Very good chemistry."

"Eligible?" Julie had dared to ask.

Gaby did not seem to take offense. "I'll ask her." A little grin. Her mood was bright, and for once, so was her sweater. Julie had picked it out and it was blue-ribbon blue, almost a statement: a long shot, but a winner. After the memorial service, when Wally had come to the house with his mother on his arm, it seemed as if God had turned another page. Gaby had sent back the wedding gifts, no longer locked herself in her old room to cry and refused Wally's phone calls. Recently, she'd started putting drops of Julie's Carolina Herrera behind her ears and getting in touch with old friends. A week ago she'd told her mother that when the apartment on Garth Road sold, she'd reimburse her for the wedding.

Like Heather, Gaby had let her hair grow. Like Heather, she looked sweeter and softer. Unlike Heather, she was not a baby anymore. If one looked closely, Julie thought, one could see shadows under her eyes.

Out of her big Coach bag she'd pulled a surprise. Skeins of wool. White, yellow, Delft blue. "I'm going to knit a blanket for Gilbert the Second," she'd said. "Karen is sure it's a boy. She's carrying high."

"Low," Julie said. "If it's a boy, it's carrying low. And I didn't even know you knew how to knit." Julie was pleased.

The old-fashioned, homespun skills symbolized the positive and solid values Julie might have called her true religion. A thoughtful production, a gift for her sister, something that required effort and work, an offering of love, meant so much and said it all. "Deeds, not creeds," Gilbert had said.

Gaby had reached into the refrigerator and pulled out a bottle of water, raised it, as in a toast. "I don't. You'll teach me," she said and she was smiling. *Smiling.*

"A shame about Taras moving away," Heather was saying, as she pulled the shoes out from a shelf half hidden by the shoji screen, which now looked seedy and more than ever ready for retirement.

"It is," Julie said, and Heather, presenting Julie her shoes, said she hoped Mrs. Kessler would come to the Mamaroneck Studio and continue dancing. "You have so much talent, and surely you wouldn't want to give up now."

She had offered her a deal, if only she stayed, continued her lessons with Edoardo. "He's brilliant. And he's from Buenos Aires—well, not too far from there, Mar Del Plata, actually. He's the real thing, Mrs. Kessler. He's won so many contests, you wouldn't believe."

Not the real-thing! "I think I'll just take the refund check, Heather. No offense, but I got very used to Taras."

"Oh, I know you did! He's wonderful. Smooth, very smooth, too." Heather gave a little shake of the head and an ooh-la-la roll of the eyes that Julie couldn't miss and didn't like. What did the girl mean by that?

"I suppose," she said, demurely, and waited for some elucidation, which didn't come. "You mean, the way he moved," she finally added.

"Oh, in every way. I mean, he was a chick magnet, wasn't he?"

Julie watched Heather open a drawer of the desk that would presumably contain her refund check and thought, *chick magnet.* She became conscious of the air, which seemed to have turned cold. They'd turned the heat off, hadn't they? "Good for business, you mean?" she asked.

"Absolutely," Heather said, and she pulled out of the drawer a ledger-size checkbook, closed the drawer and began figuring on a desk calculator the amount owed Julie by the Fred Astaire Dance Studios for dance lessons not taken. Julie stood in place, watching the girl write a check to the order of Julie Kessler, watched her omit an S from Kessler, then write her name, misspelled again, on a certificate entitling her to the opening party of the Mamaroneck Studio in November. It was as if November had already crept into this room, chilled it and sucked all the fresh air out. Dust seemed to have settled over everything here, including Julie. She wanted to take the check and run, but why she wasn't sure. Taras couldn't be blamed for being a chick magnet any more than she could be blamed for being one of the chicks. It's not as if he was seducing his students one and all, *was it?* With Julie and Taras it was love, not commerce. The real, *real* thing.

Heather handed Julie the check with a smile. "It's been a pleasure knowing you, Mrs. K," she said, and as she opened the desk drawer to put back the check ledger, Julie's eye caught something at the bottom of the drawer, a glossy picture she was sure she'd never seen before.

"Is that a photo?"

"Oh, we have a pile of them here. Would you like to take a look?" Heather pushed aside the nail polish bottles and emery boards next to them, handed them over, and excused herself to answer the telephone, which had started to ring.

It was Taras in the top photograph, as she'd thought, in a white tuxedo jacket, the one he'd worn to the wedding, dancing with Damaria. The rest were of other instructors in similar attitudes. Taras and

Damaria were striking a pose, smiling for the camera, shoulders up and out, looking rather blank, like a typical billboard advertisement for dance lessons. Predictably, he photographed well, and looked even younger here than he did in person. Damaria was in black, this dress basically strapless, with just one ribbon-like strip of material looking glued from the cleavage diagonally across one shoulder, the bodice sparkled with little beads. The rest of the dress looked pasted to her body until the hem, where it flared out in feathery layers of red. She was wearing sparkling red earrings shaped like bows and a delicate necklace a bit longer than a choker. Something about the necklace struck Julie as familiar and she reached into her purse for her glasses. But even before she'd slipped them on, Julie knew exactly what Damaria was wearing around her neck. On the thread of a chain hung the same gold and garnet trident Taras had wanted to buy for her on her birthday.

Julie put up her hand, wanting to ask Heather the question, not sure she could get any words out without giving it all away. The girl was deep in conversation and Julie waited. Finally Heather covered the receiver, looked up, a what-can-I-do-for-you? written into her eyebrows.

"When were these taken?" Julie was leaning on the desk with one hand, holding the photos with the other.

Heather swayed forward to glance at the snapshots. She shrugged. "Last year some time, I guess," she said.

"Hope you come back some time soon, Mrs. Kessler," Heather continued as a farewell, and she pushed the photos back into the drawer, went back to her conversation and waved a friendly good-bye with her free hand. How could the girl work in a room this cold? "They had a—thing?" she managed to ask, throwing off a smile that she hoped would read as passing interest, polite chitchat, or How Sweet a Dancing Couple They Make.

Heather covered the mouthpiece with her hand. Not sensitive to nuance, involved with her telephone call, her bookkeeping, perhaps her manicure, she shrugged, and with a little smile, said, "Taras? Well, who knows? My mother says that every heart has hidden paths. Don't you think that's true?" as Julie, working hard to maintain even a slight grimace that could be called a wan smile and would weigh in as the mildest of passing interest, nodded and handed back the pictures.

CHAPTER FIFTY-ONE

"It's not possible. How could you think of doing this *now?*" Susanna's telephone voice veered from angry to woebegone. "Elliot's just gotten his PSA numbers. He's high, Mama. I mean, this prostate thing is scary!"

Julie was standing in the kitchen, the note from Mariadora still in her hand. The spelling was perfect, the punctuation correct although Mariadora had dropped out of school after fifth grade. To Julie the Honduran system of education had always seemed superior to that of the United States and here was more evidence:

Dear Mrs. Kessler,

I am going back to be with my mother, very sick now. I am not able to be back to this house, with the Mister never coming back. I will pray for him. I am not taking the last salary owed, just borrowing some kitchen things.

Mariadora

The shock was what Mariadora had chosen to take in lieu of the salary owed. There were the empty shelves, looking so vacant, so bereft and *stripped*, it reminded her of a house that had been through some disaster, like a twister or a hurricane. And, wasn't it a harbinger of what would soon come, when movers began carrying out the tables, the chairs, the beds that were not just pieces of furniture, but pieces of her life?

Mariadora, never a thief, had cleaned out the collection of salt and peppershakers from around the world, all gone by the time Julie, at first thinking she'd been burglarized, arrived at home from the memorial service. Mariadora, admitting nothing, was taking for safekeeping what she saw as treasure. Was she protecting her sanctified memories of Julie and Gilbert's married life? It struck Julie that Mariadora was simply unable to part with some key memento of her service, the seventeen devoted years to this family. The Kesslers had gone awry, had been swept off in every direction, sweeping her off with it. Tonight Julie would sit down to write a reply, to send Mariadora a check and to assure her that she was welcome to the Kessler souvenirs, to keep as her own forever.

The real estate agents had already swarmed; their telephone calls interrupted meals, sleep and baths, the ringing never seemed to stop. Julie began screening calls.

Upstairs, her suitcase lay open. Next to it was a book of the poetry of Taras Shevchenko, borrowed from Susanna, marked to page 46. There she had read and reread a poem without a name:

> We sang together and parted
> Without tears, without much talk,

Shall we ever meet again,
Will we sing together once more?

Two weeks ago, because the job in Stamford had
gone to someone else and Gaby, looking as serene,
as contained and self-assured as ever, had gone to
bed and stopped eating for twenty-four hours, two
Siamese kittens waiting on hold at the animal shelter.
And yesterday—it only *seemed* like a week ago—
Susanna had called in a panic. She was seven days
late and now too terrified to buy another EPT kit.
What if it turned out that she was pregnant after all?
What would she do? She wasn't sure she wanted a
baby now and what could she tell Dieter?

Julie picked up the book of poetry. She had marked
another page and turned to it now. Who was she
today? Mother? Lonely widow? Lover? She read:

> I'll build myself a one-room house,
> And plant a garden-paradise around.
> I'll sit and wander
> In this tiny heaven
> And will rest alone
> In the garden.
> I'll dream of little children
> And their happy mother,
> A bright dream of long ago
> Will come to me . . . and you!
> No, I shall not rest,
> For you will enter in my dream,
> Stealing softly into my little Eden,
> Will create havoc . . .
> And set aflame my little paradise.

She'd wanted to read this to Taras, but the namesake of an immortal poet dismissed Ukrainian poetry
as minor, not relevant. "He was just a serf," he'd said
once, joking, or maybe not joking at all. It was not

that Taras wanted to shed his ethnicity, but he had other, greater heroes, his personal American gods. Taras quoted Jefferson and Lincoln and Roosevelt, and it was irony. Julie wanted nothing more than to hear the music of the words of the Ukrainian serf, Taras Shevchenko.

Lou DiLorenzo had offered to drive Julie to the airport. Gaby had another job interview, Susanna and Dieter were at work and in a way, it was good for Lou to get out of the house. He was now imprisoned with morphine rescue, the conversation of visiting nurses and the sounds of Ruthie's dry cough, weeping or retching. When he came to the door of 66 Morris Lane, helped Julie downstairs with her suitcase and tried to make a joke—"You smuggling elephants?"— she saw the new gray in his hair and the deeper line between his eyebrows.

"How long do you intend to be gone?" he asked Julie as he pulled out of the driveway.

It was an answer Julie couldn't give, any more than she could explain why she'd chosen to go. Was she sure he meant it when Taras said he loved her? The knotty look on Heather's face, the trident around Damaria's neck, well, any mature woman of fifty-four would have summed Taras up pretty quickly as a very iffy risk. And yet, when he'd called the very night after she'd been to the Fred Astaire Studio, after she'd told herself she'd bite off her tongue before asking him about Damaria, Julie blurted it out: she'd seen the damn pictures with her own eyes! "How many besides Damaria? Was I simply part of a Terpsichorean series?"

"What is past is past," he'd said. Julie answered with a silence packed so with hurt, fear and doubt, that he might have actually heard "The heart has hidden paths" transmitted through the AT&T wires.

All her daughters' frantic and furious warnings echoed. What if it was really about money? He'd need startup cash for a new studio, wouldn't he? Why indeed was she heading to Baton Rouge, Louisiana, as foreign to her as Lapland? Was it really the island to which she'd dreamed of escaping?

"Wait—" he'd said, and said it eloquently, as in a song lyric spanning an octave, "Wait, a minute, Harry—"

She'd fiddled with the telephone wire, stared at the ceiling.

"The trident was a gift of affection and thanks—" here his voice took a short time-out, as if he were waiting for a breath, or inspiration, "Well, she was so good with Thomas. She used to take him to her sister's. She taught him to swim there. Her sister had an in-ground swimming pool, see."

She'd pulled the wire tighter around her fingers.

"Not part of a series, Julie."

When did that little blister of paint appear in the corner of the bedroom ceiling, Julie wondered. She'd neglected everything, had stopped noticing household wear and tear, overlooked replacing burned-out light bulbs and a bent venetian blind, stopped hearing the creaks of door hinges that needed oiling. She was not herself! Had she also neglected her usual judiciousness and prudence?

"I mean, she helped me a lot in so many ways. It was a month, two months, that's all," Taras said. "It was more friendship than—"

"Than?"

"Than what we've got."

Julie remembered *chick magnet* and knew she should not have asked about Damaria. It was a jealousy trip to fantasize about Taras's other women. If there were some like her, women who might have danced and whirled in his arms, licked their lips, twisted their hips, dipped their thighs into tempting him, what had that to do with her? This was today, their day, another page.

Julie looked at her watch, thinking it was an hour earlier there, where he was. She might do that this minute, set back the hands an hour, to his time, to feel closer to him. As it was, she pictured him now, even without closing her eyes, saw their reunion like a video production in bright focus. Taras meeting the plane, the pump of blood when they ran into each other's arms, the trip to the place they'd live. She saw the roses she'd plant in their garden. As if already happening, she could smell the perfume of the place she'd never been, the sweet Louisiana air, see the clouds above the roof of the small house she'd furnish with spanking new rugs and polished tables and fresh curtains. The clouds would be the same color as the ceiling of her Scarsdale bedroom—linen white—that paint-can standard of white purity. She could see herself making pancakes at breakfast and chili for dinner. Chili! She hadn't made a pot of chili for years—not since the girls were all at home, seated around the dining room table. Taras would pour the wine and kiss her and tell her he'd never had better and then they'd make love, killing, runaway love upstairs in the sleigh bed she'd buy; she'd always wanted a sleigh bed covered with one of those Amish quilts, hadn't she? And in her own heart's hidden paths, even when Gilbert was asleep next to her, hadn't there been a longing for just such a sweet-hot, riptide flow as this?

Taras had told her again that he loved her, and that's all she needed; without putting it into writing his voice had, for her, put it in writing. "I wish I could speak more languages so I could say it in Italian, Chinese and Swahili. Only you, Harry."

She was older, she had tax-frees and munis, blue chips and zero coupons, a nice portfolio, but she remembered the lyrics of a bluegrass song that Gilbert had loved. Forget sense and danger and sobriety, eliminate coolheadedness. Dismiss everything she'd learned as Mama. She would not be Mama now. She would not be Julie; for now she would he *Harry*. It was her time, her choice, and she was free to plunge into the glorious and perilous adventure of possibility. Into *bliss*.

She wasn't too old to be in love, to risk everything, to survive disappointment. "Honest to God. Only you," Taras had said. No, she would not lead with her mind. She would, as the song advised, jump in with her heart.

It wouldn't be for all time, not until the seas went dry or the moon fell from the sky. Her girls were here, her history, her life's life, her very underpinning was rooted wherever they were and they would be waiting, impatient for her return.

But even now, Taras was probably taking a shower or putting gas in his car, or stopping to buy a good bottle of wine with which to welcome her to their "little paradise" in Louisiana. We'll drink a toast, she thought: *To kingdom come. If not forever, for now.*

"Ruthie wanted you to have this bracelet," Lou said, when they arrived at the airport. Out of his breast pocket from a plastic Baggie, he pulled out the diamond X's and O's that made up the glittering row that had marched around Ruthie's wrist, that Julie had seen so many times. She wanted to decline to take it, to flatly refuse to accept anything this personal, meaningful, valuable, but in Lou's face she read a mountain of need. He held the bracelet out to her with one hand, and reached for a handkerchief with the other.

"Please come back, Julie," he said in a voice so diminished it sounded like a poor recording.

"Tell Ruthie I love her and that I forgive her."

Julie took it from his hand, wiped her eyes and kissed his cheek, which was wet, and rough, and perhaps in Julie's imagination, smelled not of his usual aftershave, but also of the disinfectant of a sickroom.

When she handed the handkerchief back, Lou wished her a safe trip. Then suddenly he leaned over and scrutinized her face. "You know something Julie? I never noticed it before, but I think your left eye is bluer than your right. Did you know that?"

ABOUT THE AUTHOR

SECOND CHANCES is Marlene Fanta Shyer's fourth novel. She has also written ten books for children, a play and a memoir, co-authored with her son, Christopher Shyer. In addition, over one hundred of her short stories and articles have been published in women's magazines. Most recently she has been writing about her travels here and abroad.

Ms. Shyer is the mother of three grown children and divides her time between her homes in New York City and Westchester County. You can visit her Web site at *www.marleneshyer.com*